WHIRLWIND

S Whitten Snider

authorHOUSE®

AuthorHouse™
1663 Liberty Drive
Bloomington, IN 47403
www.authorhouse.com
Phone: 1 (800) 839-8640

Published by AuthorHouse 05/18/2016

ISBN: 978-1-5246-0950-4 (sc)
ISBN: 978-1-5246-0949-8 (e)

Library of Congress Control Number: 2016908227

CONTENTS

PROLOGUE

Ben tried to ignore the buzzing sound, knowing full well he hadn't gotten near enough sleep after everything that had gone down. The smack on the side of his head made him realize it wasn't just the alarm clock.

"Answer your damn phone." The voice from beneath the pillow croaked.

Ben struggled to find the braying phone, while trying not to stare at her bare ass hanging out from the sheet.

"Quit looking at my butt and answer that phone or I'm going to kill whoever is on the other end."

Ben picked the phone up off the floor where it had fallen, "Hello?"

"Hey Ben, it's me. Sorry if I woke you up, but we need to talk."

Ben wondered what she was calling about since they had just talked yesterday, albeit briefly. "Okay, I'm mostly awake. What did you need?"

There was no answer and Ben wondered if he'd inadvertently hit the disconnect button.

"Um, I wanted to wait until I was actually sure, but the doctor confirmed it – I'm pregnant."

Ben sat numbly as tests and doctors' visits were explained. He tried not to focus on the woman sleeping in his bed that he was falling in love with. Ben gave a few quick answers and promised to meet up to figure out what the next seven months were going to look like.

After hanging up, Ben sat and wondered what to do next. The past few months had been a whirlwind, and Ben thought it had finally ended last night, but clearly it wasn't over yet.

1

Eighty Four Days Earlier

Spring storms were nothing new to central Ohio, residents had ridden out the various storms each incoming season brought with it, but this was something special. The forecasters had predicted the warmer temperatures and the potential for thunderstorms, failing to mention this could morph into something much bigger.

The storm began brewing on the west side of Indiana as the warm southern winds collided with the cooler northern winds coming out of Canada. By the time the storm system reached central Indiana, hail and damaging winds were wreaking havoc. As the storm passed into Ohio, reports began to filter in of funnel clouds being spotted. Nothing had been confirmed as touching down yet, but the tornado warnings went out for all of the surrounding counties lying in the path of the storm.

Fleming County had been through severe storms in the past, but the county wasn't prepared for the tornado when it touched down outside of Blandale. Witnesses later estimated the tornado touched down for only three to four minutes, but the path of destruction told a different story. Thankfully there were no casualties, but the growing industrial park was leveled and spread around the surrounding countryside nearly five miles away.

Blanche Rollins had spent the first twenty years of her life in Kansas, so she was prepared when the first reports of funnels clouds came over the television. She grabbed Wesley, her beloved dachshund, and situated herself in the closet under her staircase. Forty minutes later, all ninety year old Blanche had in her possession was her dog, her medications, and the scattered remnants of her life throughout the county.

Stories such as Blanche's became the lead stories for most of the local newscasts, and headlines for the area newspapers. Pictures and videos were played and replayed by all of the various news agencies around the state as viral photos bounced around the internet. Fleming County quickly became a national event as everyone tried to find a source to get the latest information while crews were dispatched.

The emergency vehicles and law enforcement agencies went into high gear when the tornado reports began coming in and had stayed busy for the forty eight hours afterwards. Keeping roads open, directing traffic around closed areas and checking on injured people kept the small forces from the county busy until the federal disaster agency people arrived to take over the process.

As the sun rose the next morning, the world got a much better view of the destruction the tornado had done as it tore through the industrial park. Debris was scattered up to ten miles away, giving the television helicopters plenty of footage for the noon and evening reports.

Disasters have always brought out the best in people and its worst. Reports trickled in about Good Samaritans who opened their homes to their neighbors who lost everything in the storm. These reports were overshadowed on the newscasts by the numerous video images of people looting businesses that had been ripped open by the winds.

The local Red Cross combined with some of the local churches to set up temporary shelters to help those who needed it the most. They also organized the cleanup brigades that went out into the nearby fields to start gathering the debris. One of the biggest organizations to help with this cleaning was the YouthQuest program, a juvenile treatment facility. This program had nearly ninety young men from around the state, who were placed there as an alternative to being locked up. Part of the program consisted of community service, which at this time meant providing the man power for the cleanup crew.

* *

Dre' Watkins kicked the Pepsi can as he walked the fields. He was from inner city Cleveland and he'd seen more fields in the past six months he'd been at YouthQuest, than the rest of his life combined. He also hoped he'd never see them again, he couldn't understand how anyone would actually want to live out here.

He felt bad for the people who lost their houses, but he was only happy because he was getting out of school. His happiness about being out of school only lasted about an hour after he started walking through the muddy fields and picking up what seemed like a never ending amount of trash out of the field.

Dre' gave the can a good kick and looked over his shoulder to see where Gooden was. Gooden seemed to be watching the rowdy bunch of kids in his vicinity. Dre' bent down to look at the metal box his can had bounced off of, it was dented and covered with grime and he intended to walk on by until he saw the lock.

Locks had always been his fascination. They were a perfect test for his intellect and his ever nimble fingers. The locks had gotten him placed at YouthQuest, after the principal caught him popping the combination locks in the locker room.

The lock was an old Mastercraft that used a short version of a skeleton key. It took Dre' almost three minutes to get the lock open with the tab from the Pepsi can. When Dre' opened the box, his thrill at having beaten the lock quickly switched into a familiar feeling of dread at what he'd just gotten himself into.

"Mr. Gooden, I found something I think you should see," Dre' yelled from his section of the field.

3

2

Ben eased off his headphones when he realized he wasn't alone in his bed. Carefully turning his head, he saw a white satin night gown exposing a healthy amount of mocha colored thigh propped up next to him typing on her laptop.

"Good morning love," Zoe purred without breaking visual contact with the screen, the British accent gliding off her tongue.

Ben shifted himself around, "Why are you in my bed with me?"

Zoe arched one perfectly sculpted eyebrow, "I've never gotten that response before, maybe I'm losing my mojo."

"You know what I mean, why are you working down here, where I'm trying to sleep?"

Zoe sighed and turned from the laptop, "Well you weren't answering your phone last night, so I came down here to make sure you were alright. And now we've overslept and you are thirty minutes behind for your workout."

Ben glanced at his cell phone on the nightstand, flashing to indicate missed calls. "Sorry I put on the headphones to help me go to sleep." He knew there was no need to explain more about the storm.

"Yes, I know. You never even noticed when I crawled in with you."

"Sorry, hope I didn't snore."

Zoe smiled, "I didn't come down here for comfort, and it's nothing that I haven't dealt with before."

Ben blushed, thinking of the numerous times she had shared his room since they first met. Zoe knew him almost as intimately as his wife had. Being his handler had forced the two of them to spend more time together than either expected.

"Well it's been a long time since we've shared a room, what was the special occasion last night?"

Zoe clicked the icon on the laptop and handed it over. "You missed quite the storm last night, it tore your little town up. Look at this poor dear and her dog."

Ben stared at the screen showing the local website which had numerous photos and personal stories from first responders to the devastating tornado. He quickly read the article explaining the timeline of the tornado which touched down on the outskirts of Blandale.

After finishing the article, Ben handed the laptop back. "Are you okay? Is that why you came down?"

Zoe smiled, "Not that you provided much protection, but yes I came down when the power went out and the radio suggested heading to the basement. I brought Winston with me."

Upon hearing his name, the big golden retriever jumped on the bed.

Ben's cell started vibrating, and he glanced at the name which popped up.

"What's going on Trevor?"

"I hate that caller id shit, nobody ever just answers. They check the name first before deciding to answer. Whoever created that for phones is an asshole."

Ben rolled his eyes towards Zoe, "So did you just call to rant about caller id or is there a reason?"

"Yeah, I saw on the news about the tornado and thought it was near your little shithole town and wanted to make sure you were okay."

"We're fine, but I haven't been outside yet to check any damage."

"Well I've been calling for the past hour and got no answer, so I was getting anxious."

Ben smiled thinking about Trevor pacing throughout the house making phone calls. "No I'm fine, just had the phone on vibrate and Zoe woke me up."

"You tell that little minx she can come down here and wake me up anytime. Wait a minute is she there right now with you?"

Ben chuckled at Trevor's description of Zoe being a "little" minx. At nearly six feet, she towered over Trevor by at least four inches and that was if she didn't wear her heels.

"Yes Trevor she's laying right here beside me, working on the laptop."

"You gotta be kidding me. She's in your bed and you are letting her work on the laptop. I always wondered if you swung the other way and now I have proof."

Zoe clearly knew she was the topic of conversation, "Tell Mr. Blaine that I am completely naked and waiting patiently for him to end your conversation so we can get to shagging."

Trevor heard all of this, "Sweet Jesus, tell me she's bullshitting me. I swear to God if she is naked and you don't tap that I'll drive up there and kick your ass."

"Bye Trevor, I'll call you later to go over some stuff."

Ben hung up from Trevor describing various sexual positions he would like to see Zoe involved with.

"That was, what's the word ... uh yuck," Zoe said with her best teen impression.

Ben laughed, "Alright get out of here so I can get dressed."

Zoe again arched her eyebrow, "You sleep naked and I saw you naked most of the first month we knew each other. It's not like I haven't seen your twig and berries multiple times."

"I know you have, but when I'm sober I am actually quite shy. And could you find other terms than twig and berries, maybe tree branch and coconuts?"

Zoe shrugged, "Sorry it doesn't have the same ring to it, and I'll close my eyes."

Ben dressed in the bathroom, leaving his urine sample on the edge of the sink. He knew his workout was likely out for this morning until he checked on his property and made sure his friends in the area were okay. He felt slightly embarrassed about going to hide in the basement bedroom last night like a little kid, but the truth was storms still bothered him. Although it was weird to wake up next to Zoe, it was nice to have someone in his bed.

Ben met Zoe in Jamaica almost five years ago, although met was probably inaccurate. Ben was in Jamaica at the beach house he shared with Alexander Dramond, a bestselling author who shared the same agent. Ben had been there for almost six months, doing nothing but smoking ganja and drinking himself into oblivion on a daily basis. Dramond happened to drop in and found his friend passed out on the entryway of the house in a pool of what he hoped was his own vomit.

Alexander did the responsible thing and called Thomas Sutton, their shared agent/publicist and explained the situation. Thomas took things from there and did what he did best; he came up with a plan. Ben Princi was clearly still suffering from the depression which paralyzed him from writing when his wife was killed by a drunk driver. He thought Ben was coming out of it when he decided to return for his high school reunion, but that ended in an even bigger disaster. Ben convinced Thomas he needed to disappear for a while and get his head straight, and Thomas reluctantly agreed, thinking the time away would get him back on track.

Based on Alexander's report, Ben was much worse than when he arrived on the island. Thomas set out to find a counselor who would stay with Ben and get him through the depression and sobered up. Zoe Meloncourt, the daughter of the British ambassador to Jamaica was the obvious choice for the job. She had dual degrees in psychology and economics, and had done an internship with a residential substance abuse program in London, while earning her MBA.

Zoe moved into the estate and shadowed Ben, proving to be as stubborn about sticking around as Ben was at trying to push her out. He initially walked around the property completely nude, hoping to shock her into leaving. When this failed, he refused to speak to Zoe, acting as if she did not exist. When he finally gave in and spoke to her about the drinking, Ben expected her to pack her bags and leave. Zoe finally convinced Thomas to get Ben back stateside to get the intensive substance treatment he needed, and to get away from the carefree Jamaican lifestyle. She had tired of kicking out the numerous ganja dealers who stopped by and left "gifts". Then there were the locals who found out the rich guy on the beach was always ready for a party. Zoe had taken to sleeping in Ben's room to prevent the local party girls from sneaking into his room for afterhours fun. She had since been his handler, with her job description growing the longer Ben stayed sober.

Ben strolled down to the barn with Winston to check on the potential damage. He was a large man, easily carrying the 270 pounds on his six foot five frame, and he covered the main living areas with long strides. Despite expecting the worst, he found only some downed tree branches and his hot tub cover was on the roof of the converted barn. Sliding back the door, Ben realized all of his vehicles were fine and the storm had failed to create any holes.

When Ben bought the foreclosure property ten years ago, he never envisioned actually living here. He bought it mainly for the 550 acres the house sat on, but the barn became the draw for him. It originally had housed cattle and horses and Ben smelled them even after the last one left over twenty years ago. Ben kept the small workshop, and revamped the barn to work as a non-farming building. He then had a state of the art pole barn constructed nearby to house his toys. Fourteen vehicles were kept inside in various stages of repair or disrepair depending on your vantage point. Ben was supposed to have the 1969 Superbird sanded down and ready to deliver to Chet this morning, but he'd have to call and postpone.

Ben made a number of changes to the old farmhouse, starting with eliminating a few walls for the open concept. He had the house rewired for the upgraded appliances and high tech gadgets. He also expanded the main floor bedroom, built a deck and installed his oversized hot tub. The old wooden floors and old country style reminded him of his grandparents' home and Ben couldn't bear to tear the whole house down and build again. Zoe occupied most of the second floor, using one bedroom as her office while sleeping in the other. She also had her own private deck that wrapped around the second floor.

Ben returned to the kitchen as Zoe was finishing her grapefruit. Winston looked hopefully at the table to gauge if any scraps might be coming his way.

"Do you want any coffee? I'm going to make a pot, but I'll soften the blow if you want some."

Zoe shook her head, "No, go ahead and fix your petro. I'll just make do with some orange juice."

Ben felt his phone vibrating in his pocket as he measured out the grounds. "Hello?"

"Hey there Ben, just calling to check in on your status after the storm," Susan Maris inquired. Susan was introduced to Ben at Northwestern by her older brother, Ben's roommate Thomas Sutton. They took her under their wing during her freshman year and Ben had remained close with her since.

"We're okay Susan, how did it go for your facility?" Ben remembered the juvenile treatment facility she ran was near the path of the tornado.

"Oh the facility was fine and we've had the boys out helping with the debris."

Ben smiled thinking about the amount of complaining which was probably occurring right now. He'd volunteered a number of times with the boys on their community service projects, and usually it was a bitch fest. The funny thing was that the majority of the boys felt good about the praise they received from the people they were assisting.

"Well, let me know if there is anything I can do to help," Ben offered.

Susan hesitated, "Since you mentioned it, I do have a favor if you are available. One of our boys, Andre found some particularly disturbing items while cleaning up today and I thought maybe you could come and speak with him."

Dre's face popped into Ben's mind from the last time he spoke with the group about following their dreams. Dre had nothing but questions and attitude about how a kid like him could possibly be a success.

"Are you sure I'm the best choice?"

Susan chuckled, "Don't let his mouth fool you. Andre hasn't shut up about the things you talked with them about; he just can't show you how much it meant."

Ben glanced at Zoe and covered the phone, "Do I have a couple of hours free this morning?"

"I don't believe you have the auto ready for Chet, so you are free until 3pm."

"Hey Susan, Zoe said I'm free for a couple of hours so I'll head over."

"Thanks Ben. Speaking of your lovely manager, have things changed in your relationship yet?"

Ben felt his face redden, "Let me guess, Thomas is having his little sister do his digging for him?"

Susan laughed, "Yes he is inquiring, but this is just me wondering. I've seen you two at numerous events and it's clear you make a great couple."

"Remember she goes with me as my "date" to ensure that I don't fall off the wagon. She is my manager."

Zoe listened carefully as she tried to put the conversation together based on Ben's answers. It sounded like Susan was asking questions about their relationship, and she'd have a field day if she knew they shared a bed last night.

"Let's just call it womanly intuition when I say she might have more than just your business interests in mind. Oh and it might be best if you didn't bring her along for your visit today. The boy's attention span is short at best and having a six foot beautiful woman stopping by will cause a complete shutdown."

Ben laughed as he ended the call. "You are not permitted to accompany me today because you distract the boys."

"Being ogled by a bunch of teenage boys is not nearly as bad as being accosted by Trevor."

"You have a point, but hopefully you know Trevor is mostly talk."

Zoe looked up from the laptop, "I have no doubt Trevor would fail miserably if I returned his not so subtle advances, but I have no desire to subject myself to that form of self-degradation."

"I should be back within a few hours at the most," Ben said as he grabbed his cell and car keys.

Zoe continued tapping at the laptop, "Remind me to have a conversation with you."

"Is it something we need to talk about now?"

"No, it will wait, but I've been debating when to have the conversation and figured it should be sooner rather than later."

Ben jumped in his Chevelle and tore out of the barn, barely waiting for the door to rise far enough to get out. He wondered what the conversation tonight would be about. His thinking was interrupted by his phone vibrating again in his pocket.

"What's up Chet?" Ben asked, hoping he sounded sincere since he already knew what this phone call was pertaining to.

"What's up is I cleared a spot in my schedule for some work on your damn Superbird, and guess what there's no car here. Thought maybe the twister sucked it up or something."

Ben smiled, "I know Chet, and I'm not quite finished with the sanding."

"I figured that much out, maybe if you'd let a professional work on the car it might get finished before I collect social security."

Ben had met Chet years ago when he was in high school and had always taken his vehicles to his shop when he lived in the area. When Ben moved back to the area, he ran into Chet at the local AA meetings. Chet had been court ordered to attend the meetings or risk jail time. He'd unwillingly started going and found it had done a lot to help him get his life back on track. Ben was a part owner in the business now after loaning Chet the money to double the size of his garage. Although they were technically partners, Chet seemed to believe he still ran the show and Ben never brought up the subject because he respected the work Chet did.

"I'll tell you what Chet, if I don't have the Bird down there by Friday, I'll just drive it over and you can finish it off."

Chet was silent as he decided if this was acceptable, "Okay, but you know you aren't my only customer."

"Got it Chet."

"One more thing, stop red lining that damn Chevelle. You don't have to wind it and dump the clutch at every shift."

Ben laughed, "You've got a great set of ears Chet." He dumped it from second to third and the tires squealed as they struggled to grip the asphalt.

3

"Milnero, Chief wants to see you in his office in ten minutes."

Alex continued typing. Paperwork was the worst thing about being a detective. If it wasn't hard enough to find clues, piece them together and make an airtight case, then you were expected to have the report typed and turned in within a few hours after the case was solved. If there was a slip up or something was filed incorrectly, a slick talking lawyer was itching to get their scumbag client off on a technicality.

Alex knocked on Chief Kirkpatrick's door fifteen minutes later.

"You're late," Kirkpatrick said, motioning to the chair.

"So fucking sue me," Alex replied as she flopped into the chair.

"Why do you insist on talking like a sailor – No scratch that, sailors might be offended at your abuse of the English language."

Alex shrugged, "Too much time with scumbags and not enough money for those etiquette classes."

Kirkpatrick didn't try to contain his smile. He'd fought hard with the commissioners to bring in the young detective from Texas three years ago, and she'd done little to make him regret that decision. She was the youngest female detective for the CBI unit, but there was no question she would not be overlooked.

"So is this a social call or have I done something to warrant your undivided attention?"

The folder landed in front of her. Kirkpatrick didn't want to cloud her intuition with his observations, he wanted her doing what she did best which was trust her instincts.

Alex opened the folder and flipped through the pictures, turning each face down after looking. She made a neat stack with the pictures, doing her best to not think about the content or the abuse these girls had endured, only to focus on the perp. Somebody was sexually abusing young girls and then taking souvenir photos.

"A kid at YouthQuest found these in a locked box while he was cleaning up debris from the tornado," Kirkpatrick explained when she finished with the photos.

"Where's the box?"

"Evidence room in Blandale, but it doesn't give us much to work with. It's about a thirty minute drive over there so get going, they're expecting you and Gerald"

Alex looked at Kirkpatrick, "Why me?"

He'd expected this question, but not from her. Kirkpatrick was preparing himself for the internal turmoil Jeff Schultz was going to cause when he found out the case was going to Milnero. Schultz had the most experience on the force, but he lacked the savvy to handle a sensitive case like this. Milnero was smart, had great instincts, and could handle the media better than anyone on the force.

"You're best suited for this one."

Alex ran her fingers through her hair. "Schultz is going to blow a ventricle when he hears about this."

"Let me worry about him, I need you to get started on this as soon as possible," Kirkpatrick said, signaling the meeting was over.

"Does Gerald know about you giving this to me?"

Kirkpatrick smiled again, another of her traits showing through, a complete loyalty to her partner. "Yes I let the old goat know this was your case. Try to not let him take it over."

Alex got up to leave.

"One last thing, I don't need to tell you we need this kept as quiet as possible, the vultures will come out of the woodwork if they hear about it."

Alex knew of Kirkpatrick's dislike for the media, and she'd always done her best to not become involved in any media circus regarding her cases. She knew most of the female reporters thought she was a bitch and the males who asked her out were sure she was a lesbian.

"I'll do my best, but there are more than usual from outside networks because of the damn tornado. It's going to be hard for me to prowl around without attracting any attention."

"Do your best to blend in."

Alex shook her head. Blending in had never been her forte, and she wasn't about to start now. She was supposed to find a person who liked torturing little girls and was brazen enough to photograph it, and not draw any undue attention.

4

Susan watched in awe as Ben showed off his car. He rarely tried to draw attention to himself, but put Ben in front of a group of young boys talking about his cars and he was in his element. He had come to help clean up the field by Peterson's Filling Station, but the boys were more interested in hearing about the car first. Susan knew it was futile to keep the boys working, so she gave them a fifteen minute break.

"How much did it cost?"

Ben squinted down at the freckle-faced boy in the dirty clothes." Well I bought her two years ago for five hundred dollars."

"Bullshit."

The boys all backed away from Dre'. Ben knew it had to be Dre' who was talking, because he always had some sort of comment. Ben found Dre' amusing when he challenged everything the staff tried to tell him, so it didn't bother him when Dre' thought he was full of crap.

"Why do you say that Dre'?"

Dre' refused to look away from Ben's eyes. He was only a kid, but that didn't mean he didn't know anything about cars. This dude must think they were all stupid.

"Come on man, I could sell this car for at least a couple of G's."

Ben smiled, "Damn I hope so Dre', this is a 1967 Chevelle, and it's supposed to be worth about fifteen thousand dollars."

The guys moved away from the car like it was poisonous. Some of the guys started teasing Dre'.

"Seriously guys, I bought her cheap and fixed her up."

Dre' looked Ben straight on, "Why you keep calling your car a her?"

If Dre' had felt embarrassed about the cost of the car, he wasn't showing it. Ben respected his courage, if not his knowledge of muscle cars.

"That's a good question; men have named boats after women for centuries, so I guess I fell into that pattern." Ben turned and saw Susan was off talking with Mr. Peterson. "There also is the fact that these cars need to be handled delicately, and cost a lot of money for their upkeep, just like a woman," Ben added with a quick smile.

The boys hooped and returned his smile. Ben enjoyed their enthusiasm, even though he was pretty sure most of them were clueless as to what he'd really just said.

"So is your car just a she or does she have a specific name?" Dre' pressed.

"Her name is Raquel."

Susan rescued Ben shortly thereafter when the boys began to ask the real questions, can we go for a ride, how fast does she go, can I drive her? Ben didn't have the heart to answer, but Susan didn't hesitate to send them back into field to clean up siding.

"Boys are always the same, easily distracted by a flashy car or pretty girl," Susan chastised with a smile.

Ben blushed, "You know we really are simple creatures underneath all of our male posturing."

"Thanks for coming out, the boys really look forward to seeing you, especially Dre'."

Ben stopped walking and looked down at Susan. He knew the boys liked talking to him, but Dre' was the last one he expected to be excited about the visit.

"Dre' huh? Wouldn't have figured on that."

Susan scanned and quickly counted the eighteen boys, before turning her focus back to Ben.

"He doesn't let many people get close to him, but for some reason you made an impact on him."

"Well if you don't mind, I'll go help him with the siding."

Susan grabbed his forearm before he could walk off, "I have a couple of questions first."

"Shoot."

"How are things really going?"

Ben shook his head, "Tell Thomas that I am fine. I'm working every day on songs and I've been sober for three years, seven months and 14 days."

Susan held up her hands in surrender, "Hey I'm a good sister and you refuse to return his phone calls, so I said I'd ask. He said his only updates about you are from Zoe. The other question is for my benefit, have you been dating?"

Ben smiled slowly, "I don't think Craig would approve of our dating."

Susan smacked his arm, "Listen hear, Craig approves what I tell him to and I doubt you could handle a woman of my caliber, so stop stalling and answer the question. And I'm not talking about the flings you have, I'm talking about a relationship with a significant woman."

Ben hesitated, because he knew the truth. "I'm doing okay Susan, really … but the thought of seriously dating someone just freaks me out still. I'm very upfront with the women I go out with; they know what they are getting into."

"I'm sure you are quite blunt with them, but you have to risk the pain to enjoy the happiness," Susan called out to Ben as he walked toward the growing pile of aluminum siding.

Ben immersed himself in pulling the siding across the field, enjoying the feel of the sun on his back. He'd had a number of people trying to get him back into the dating social scene since Courtney died, but it wasn't the same. He couldn't feel the same spark, no matter how many blind dates he was set up on or internet singles match sites he was linked with. After his wife died, Ben decided to take the chance with Courtney and it ended badly, with Ben finding himself searching for peace at the bottom of a rum bottle, or whatever substance he could get his hands on.

"Do you have any kids?"

The question shook Ben out of his thoughts and he looked over at Dre'. "No, I don't have any kids."

"Didn't think so."

"Why do you say that?"

"You just don't act like you have no kids. You talk to us like we're adults, most people treat us like kids cause they have kids."

"Is that a good thing or not?"

Dre' shrugged his shoulders, "I guess you're okay. Now what can you tell me about my girl Ms. Zoe? Are you guys a couple or is she available?"

Ben returned his smile, "Hey Dre', let's just pick up all this crap."

5

Milnero waded through the pictures for the tenth time. They had been blown up, enhanced, and sorted at least that many times by her partner, Gerald Vilnew. Their partnership worked because they were so different and came at crime scenes from opposite perspectives.

"G, I'm not getting a damn thing from these pictures except a goddamn headache."

Vilnew looked up from his files and frowned, "If it's any consolation, you look like shit."

Alex flipped him the bird, "I know that's not true, because Davis asked me out again this morning."

"Oh yeah that's where I'd take my approval from, a guy who hasn't had a date in the last decade."

Alex smiled and closed her eyes, but the pictures were still in her mind. Little girls in various stages of undress, being forced to perform unspeakable acts with an adult male, such as oral and anal sex. Their tiny bodies cut and mutilated after enduring the sexual torture. Alex did her best to stay detached, but it was hard to not be overcome with the depravity of the situation.

"What do we know?"

"The bastard is confident, almost proud of his work. He's a white male, somewhere between twenty and forty with a thing for Hispanic girls."

Gerald pondered her assessment, "Why Hispanic girls?"

"I think he goes after the Hispanic girls because they are easy to snatch with all of the migrant workers who arrive each year. Might be linked with the human trafficking that runs through here. It would make it easier to get a girl and then cut her loose when he's finished with her."

Gerald whistled softly, "Damn that's pretty good from a bunch of pictures. Now we need to figure out where this box of pictures came from. There were only fifteen houses which were totally destroyed by the tornado and we're getting the names of those people as we speak."

"Be too simple if it was one of the homeowners. This person would be careful, plan, and cover his tracks. It wouldn't make sense to keep that damaging evidence in the house where somebody might stumble upon it."

"Good point, but it gives us a starting spot."

Alex leaned back in her chair and put her feet on the desk. "Let's get a list of registered sex offenders in the area and I want to talk to the boy who found the box. Maybe he might be able to give us an area to focus around."

"That might be kind of difficult. He's locked up at YouthQuest and they won't like you badgering him."

"And why do you assume I'd badger a young boy?"

Gerald rolled his eyes, "Really? You badger every male you come in contact with."

Alex gave a snort as she left the office. She had been partnered with Gerald for the past three years and they had become quick friends despite their twenty year age difference. Alex liked the fact that Gerald had treated her with respect and never tried to make any type of sexual advance, and she knew Gerald loved the fact that all the males in the department were jealous of him for having the hot partner. Alex was also friends with Gerald's oldest daughter, Angela, which made Alex an extended part of the Vilnew family.

"Kirkpatrick, I need to talk to the kid," Alex stated after waiting for him to hang up.

Kirkpatrick chewed on the pen in his hand. He wanted to keep this investigation as quiet as possible, but that would be over if they interviewed the boy.

"Alright, but let me call a friend of mine out there to set it up. I'd appreciate it if you'd be nice to him."

"Of course I'll be nice to your friend."

Kirkpatrick exhaled slowly, "My friend is a woman, I meant the kid you were going to talk to."

Alex shook her head, "That's twice, am I that horrible with men?"

"Not horrible, just intimidating."

"Sounds like a politically correct way of calling me a ball buster."

Kirkpatrick chuckled, "If the shoe fits."

6

The phone woke Ben. He'd planned to get up and workout before finishing the sanding project, but convinced himself the cleanup project had been enough exercise. Ben tried to take advantage of the one night per week when he actually slept soundly.

"Yeah," Ben struggled, trying his best to sound like he'd been up for hours.

"Oh my gosh Ben, I'm sorry. I didn't know you'd still be sleeping."

"It's fine Susan, I should have been up by now, I've got some sanding to finish on the car."

Susan hesitated. She'd tried to keep the police from talking to Dre' about the box, but they were ready to start pushing things. Dre' said he wasn't going to say anything to them, but Susan made a deal with him.

"Ben, I need a favor from you, but hear me out before you answer please."

Forty-five minutes later, Ben was staring in the mirror as he shaved, wondering what he was doing. Susan explained the only way Dre' was willing to talk to the police was if Ben went with him and he got to ride in Raquel. Ben wanted to say he was too busy, but Susan of all people would know what a lie that was. The deal was that Ben took Dre' to the meeting, sat with him for the interview, and then brought him back to campus. Ben estimated this would take two hours maximum and then he could get back to the car.

Ben walked into the police station, keeping a close eye on Dre', who was fidgeting and not nearly as cocky as normal. Clearly this was something which bothered the self-assured young man.

"You okay?"

Dre' squinted up at Ben, "I'm straight, why you nervous?'

"Yeah I am. I don't really like cops much, they always look at you like you've committed a crime, but haven't gotten caught yet," Ben admitted, noting the look of understanding on Dre's face.

"Sounds like you've been questioned before."

Ben ran his hand through his short hair, remembering the numerous times he was grilled by the police after the reunion. He vowed then he'd never put himself in that type of situation again, yet here he was again. "Yeah I've been on the receiving end of their questions."

They stopped talking when the secretary approached them in the waiting area.

"Come with me to Detective Milnero's office."

Ben walked down the hallway, feeling like he was headed to the principal's office for a discussion about some infraction. Dre' tried to act cool, but Ben noticed he was unusually quiet as they entered the office.

"Milnero will be here shortly."

Ben stared around the office, noting it looked like he expected it to with piles of files and papers sitting all over the desk. The other desk was occupied by a large black man who continued reading his paper, barely registering that anyone had even entered the room.

Ben squeezed himself into the chair next to desk, while Dre' sprawled in the other chair. Ben was trying to get comfortable and considered just standing when the door opened and Ben watched one of the most beautiful women he'd ever seen sit down in the chair. She was reading a file, closed it and tossed it onto the desk.

"Andre Watkins?"

"It's just Dre', you know like the rapper."

Alex stared at the young man, wondering if his bravado was just for show or if he was trying to take control of the meeting. "Glad to meet you Andre, I'm Detective Alex Milnero."

Ben saw Dre' stiffen when she used his given name, but he said nothing. Ben was more concerned with trying his best not to stare and remember this beautiful woman was the detective for the case. She had long black hair which spilled over her shoulders, framing her face with the darkest eyes Ben had ever seen. Ben had also noted she had some curves under her bland outfit. He vaguely remembered some of the cantinas he'd frequented in the Caribbean, and thought she'd be right at home there on the beach with a drink.

Ben realized she had asked him a question. "Pardon me?"

"You are?"

Ben stood and offered his hand, which was briskly handled.

"Benjamin Princi, I volunteer at YouthQuest now and then and they asked me to accompany Dre'." He didn't figure it was in Dre's interest to admit he was bribing Dre's cooperation for this meeting.

Alex took a few seconds to take a long look at the man in her office. She knew he was big, but when he stood up, Alex found herself stepping back to get a little distance. He had short, dark hair that looked good against his dark skin. Alex couldn't peg his eye color, but opted for hazel to be safe.

Alex turned her gaze back to Dre', "I need your help."

Ben watched Dre' relax and settle back into his chair. He'd been sure they were going to bring up some old charges or something from his past, but all they wanted was some information. Dre' knew he was a lot of things, but one of them wasn't being a snitch.

"I got nothing to say."

Ben watched the detective's eyes go dark and her jaw muscles tense. It was clear she wasn't used to anyone telling her no.

"So you have nothing to say without knowing what I want to know or what I can offer."

"I don't give a shit what you got to offer, I ain't no snitch," Dre' snarled.

Alex smiled, her teeth gleaming white against her tan face, "I'm glad you're not a rat, I don't trust anyone who claims to know information and is willing to tell. Just doesn't sit well with me."

Ben watched as Alex ran her tongue quickly around her lips to moisten them as she read the file. Dre' seemed to have relaxed, but he felt more and more uncomfortable being this close to Detective Milnero.

Forty-five minutes later Alex was wrapping up the interview with Dre'. He didn't have much more to add to what they already knew, which wasn't much to start with. Dre' was angry about being in the fields cleaning up trash for people he didn't even know when he stumbled on the box. The lock looked like a challenge, so Dre' picked it before he let his staff know what he'd found.

"So did you take anything out of the box before you alerted Mr. Gooden?"

"Nope."

"Did you look at the pictures before you got the staff?"

Dre' hesitated. He didn't want to tell that he'd looked at the pictures before he got Gooden. They might decide he needed sex offender treatment and Dre' knew he was close to graduating the program. Lying was easy, but this lady seemed to know when he was lying or even thinking about lying. He hated the way her eyes burned into his, forcing him to tell the truth.

"I only saw a couple on the top."

Alex continued writing down notes. She knew Dre' was lying, because she knew the overwhelming majority of teenage males weren't going to pass on the opportunity to sneak a peek at naked girls.

"Did you happen to see a picture of a girl with blonde hair?"

Dre' shook his head, "Naw, they had dark hair, like Mexican or something. Like yours."

Ben risked a quick glance at Alex as she wrote more notes. She casually tucked a few stray hairs behind her ear and licked her lips again. Ben wasn't sure if she knew what she was doing, but it was one of the sexiest things he'd ever witnessed.

"Well that's about it Dre', thanks for your help," Alex said closing her file.

Dre' smiled as she called him by his name, "What about what you're going to do for me?"

Alex looked him square in the eye, hoping to intimidate him, but realizing he wasn't going to fall apart. "How about if I contact your county and see if we can knock off some of your extensive restitution. I can't make any guarantees, but I'll see what I can do."

Dre' smiled, "That sounds fair, but I think I need twenty bucks so Mr. Princi can buy my lunch."

Alex knew she was getting hustled, but having the boy on her side was worth the twenty spot. He might remember something later and be of some use.

"Before you leave Mr. Princi, I'll need your phone number," Alex said as she stared up at him.

Ben fought to get the Caribbean beach image out of his mind, "You need my number?"

"Yes I need it for the forms about who accompanied Dre'."

"Oh yeah sure. Well here's a card, it has phone numbers, e-mail and the number of my manager who can find me when no one else can."

Ben eased the car out of the parking lot and into the stream of traffic. The further he got from the police station, Ben felt his chest loosening up and breathing more easily.

"Well that wasn't so bad."

Dre' gave Ben a quick glance, "Sure, how fast does this piece of crap go?"

Ben smiled, knowing Dre' was trying to bait him into just showing him what Raquel could do. "I don't really know for sure, but I'd guess somewhere between 120-130 miles per hour."

This answer seemed to satisfy Dre' as he concentrated on the passing scenery as they headed for the outskirts of town. Ben used the silence to focus on the car, and the familiar rumble of the dual exhaust lulling him into a state of calm.

"Miss Alex was pretty hot for a cop dontcha think?"

Ben flicked his eyes towards Dre' as he shifted from second to third, "I guess she was pretty."

Having a conversation with a fourteen year old boy about the merits of an adult woman wasn't something Ben was prepared for, so he slammed the accelerator down as he reached the city limits. The car shot along the highway as Dre' grinned with his hand out the window.

* *

Alex dropped Ben's card into her leather coat. She'd already typed up all of the meaningful information Dre' had given her.

"So did you do anything productive over there while I worked?"

Gerald folded the paper and took a swig of his coffee, "Looked like you had everything under control."

Alex glared at his smiling face, "What is so funny?"

"Nothing, just wondered what you were nervous about with the kid."

"I wasn't nervous."

Gerald just stared at her, "Really, because you were wearing your lips out – I thought that guy was going to have a coronary."

Alex spun her chair around away from Gerald and looked into her mirror. Her lips were swollen and moist. Gerald had told her before that when she got nervous she licked her lips and the consensus around the precinct was it was one of the most sexual things most of the men had ever witnessed.

"I wasn't nervous," Alex contended.

Gerald held up his hands in surrender, "I'm not going to argue with you, I just know what I saw. I do think it would do you some good to call him up, he was definitely interested."

Alex rolled her eyes. The last thing she needed right now was to get involved with some guy, just because Gerald thought there might be some chemistry. She'd been dealing with guys hitting on her since she was fourteen, so she'd developed a system of making sure every guy kept their distance.

"I don't know why you're also so interested in getting me married off; it would ruin my finely cultivated reputation."

Gerald smiled, "Some reputation, the "ice princess" – not something I'd be proud of. And for your information I'm not trying to get you married off, I just thought if you got laid you'd be easier to deal with."

****

Winston was waiting at the door when Ben got home with a shoe in his mouth. After a few rubs on his chest, the big golden retriever went back to resume his afternoon nap. Ben checked his phone messages, deleting the vast majority without listening to the entire spiel, but he listened to one message twice before deciding what to do.

Ben grabbed a bottle of water and sat down on the couch. He didn't really want to talk to her, but she would keep calling until she wore him down or she showed up at his door.

He punched the numbers from his memory, trying not to think of the hundreds of times he'd dialed this number, and praying she wouldn't answer and he could just leave a message.

"Hello Benjamin, it's so good to hear from you. I was afraid you were trying to avoid me."

"Hello Maggie – I'm not trying to avoid you, I've just been busy recently."

"Really, my sources tell me you're living like a hermit, only coming out to mess with your cars and having your assistant run interference for you. Or worse yet, cavorting with those questionable women."

Ben paused. He knew what Maggie was saying was mostly accurate, but it sounded uglier than it really was.

"I guess I haven't been a social butterfly, but I'm feeling better. Also I've told you Zoe is my manager, she'd be upset to be called an assistant."

"Are you Ben? Dr. Jackson called me because you haven't been to a session in three months. He hoped you were talking to someone else instead of isolating yourself. Also I don't think pillow talk with the ladies qualifies as therapy."

Ben took a long pull on the water, deciding what was the best course of action to proceed. His therapy sessions hadn't been doing any better than working on his cars or exercising, so Ben stopped going. Maggie was also right about the one night hook ups not working for therapy, no matter how good the sex was. Ben wanted to make sure they were gone in the morning, before there were any serious conversations.

"Honest Maggie, I'm doing okay, not great, but okay. I'm not ready to get involved with anyone and I have been busy with Trevor in our music business."

"Ah yes your music business with that awful little man. Are you sleeping through the night yet?"

"Some nights are better than others, but it's not too bad" Ben hesitated because he wasn't sure how far to take this conversation.

"Go ahead Ben, I know there's more you want to say, just get it out there," Maggie prodded.

"I can't see you Maggie, it hurts too much. Being around you makes me think about Courtney."

Maggie didn't respond, and Ben could hear her sniffling away her tears. He hadn't wanted to hurt her, but being honest was the only way she was going to understand.

"You selfish shit. Do you think you're the only one who thinks about Courtney? I think about her every day and it hurts when I see you because I think about what could have been. I refuse to lock myself away from life; Courtney wouldn't want either of us to do that."

"I'm not locking myself-"

Maggie interrupted, "Ben listen to me, I care about you too much to see you stop living. You need to move on, find a woman and have some kids. You'd make an excellent father."

Ben wiped away the tears streaming down his face. He didn't want to hear this, he just wanted to be left alone to deal with all of this.

"Ben, it's been almost five years, you've got to let it go and move on. You're like the son I never had and I'm counting on you to deliver some grandkids for me to spoil."

"Mag … Maggie, I do appreciate your concern, but I've got to do this in my own time."

Maggie chuckled, "Benjamin, you move like a glacier with women – I know a number of women who'd be happy to assist you."

"I'll handle my dating thank you, but I promise to call more often."

"You do that. I think Jackson's a twit, but he's right about you not choosing the healthiest ways to deal with your pain."

Ben had no reply. He'd tried to drink himself into oblivion for a couple of years and it never made the pain subside. His attempts with stronger drugs hadn't helped either, so he'd just withdrawn from everyone and everything. The past couple of years had been as good as any he'd remembered recently.

They ended the phone call minutes later, promising to meet for ice cream next week. Maggie was the closest person Ben had to family, so he knew he needed to maintain their relationship. He'd planned to work on the Superbird, but didn't feel the motivation. He rocked on the porch swing until he was dreaming of Caribbean beaches.

* *

The phone vibrated once in the desk drawer. The ringer had been shut off long ago, but it was the best method to send text messages to each other, staying connected without drawing any attention.

-Have some evidence, starting prelim investigation-

The message was only six words, but it carried a dangerous undercurrent. There wasn't any evidence to tie him with the photographs, but having people digging around so closely was unnerving.

"A fucking tornado of all things," he said aloud.

7

Alex flipped through her mail, sorting the bills onto the desk and the rest into the shredder. Her hair was still damp from her bath and Alex had wrapped it up in a towel to prevent her robe from getting soaked. She carefully applied the night cream to her face, noting the subtle creases along her mouth and eyes.

The previous owners hadn't done much with the three bedroom home, except upgrade the bathroom. Alex put in her offer immediately after touring the house and seeing the huge master bathroom. It had a full wall of mirrors and a four person Jacuzzi bathtub in the corner. Ninety percent of Alex's evenings ended with her soaking in the tub as she rehashed the current case.

Tonight's bath hadn't been as productive as usual. Alex tried reviewing and reorganizing the material from the new case, but it did little good. This was her first big lead case and she felt as if she were hunting for needle in a haystack. Gerald had always welcomed her input on cases and Alex knew she'd helped lead them to solve more than one, but now when it was her baby, she felt lost.

It also did not help that she kept thinking about what Gerald had said about Ben Princi being interested in her. She knew men checked her out regularly, and usually it was a hassle, but there was something about him that got her attention. Alex had never gone for the athletic types before, but the thought of seeing Ben's body did punch her buttons.

Alex glanced at the clock when her phone rang, wondering who would be calling this late. Her first thought was her mother, but after checking the caller id realized this was a call she needed to deal with.

"Hello Robert, what do you want?"

"Good evening Alessandra, I'm glad to see you still picked up even knowing it was me on the other end."

"What do you want?'

"Alessandra, why must you be so combative? I wanted to call and see how you are. Is that a crime?"

Alex slumped onto her couch, covering her legs with the afghan, "No, but you don't call without a reason. You aren't that caring of an individual."

"I see, so the fact we were married for seven years has no bearing on any of this."

Alex tightened her grip on the phone. Her first instinct was to throw it across the room so she wouldn't have to hear his annoying voice, but she hated to give Robert the satisfaction he bothered her.

"Why do you always focus on how long we were together, I prefer to look at the seven years we've been divorced."

This time Robert wasn't so quick with a comeback. Alex knew she'd gotten under his skin with the last little dig.

"Because you chose to divorce me, does not mean we aren't man and wife in the eyes of God. And why do you insist on using your maiden name? I want to come see you."

There it was, the reason for the call. He still wouldn't accept that she no longer wanted him. Robert called usually once a month, trying to disguise the calls as innocent or because he still cared for her, but Alex quickly figured out he was just playing with her emotions.

"No, you can't come see me and I changed my name back when we divorced so I felt like me again."

"If I came up there, you couldn't stop me from seeing you."

"Bobby, I suggest you go sit down and read your law books about restraining orders."

"A stupid piece of paper cannot prevent a man from seeing his wife, and stop calling me that. My name is Robert," he bellowed.

Alex knew she had him right where she wanted him, on the edge of losing control. "Ex-wife."

There was no reply and Alex knew he was calming himself before speaking. "I get it, you're seeing someone else and are afraid to say so."

"No I'm not Bobby, I just randomly choose a guy every other day and fuck his brains out."

"Stop talking like that, I want to come see you."

"Fuck you Robert, I'll talk however I want. Remember this Bobby, if you get within fifty feet of me, I'll slap the goddamn cuffs on you myself."

* *

Winston met Ben at the door, this time with a tennis ball in his mouth and tail wagging.

Zoe looked up and smiled, "Winston started whining and prancing around when he heard you coming down the lane." Ben found Zoe cutting up ingredients in the kitchen when he got home. "I don't know why he insists on bringing something to you whenever you come home."

Ben took the ball and rubbed Winston's ears, "He's a retriever Zoe, and it's in his nature to bring something. I tried to break my last dog of that habit and it only pissed me off."

Tossing the mail on the end table, Ben headed into the kitchen to see what Zoe was cooking.

"Out of my kitchen," Zoe ordered as she pointed with the large knife. "Dinner will be in one hour, so go take a shower or something."

Ben held his hands up in surrender, "Does this meal go along with our conversation? If it is then you are scaring the hell out of me."

Zoe glared at Ben, "Is it a surprise that I'm cooking or are you scared of the conversation?"

Ben knew he needed to tread carefully here, "Well it isn't the norm for you to cook for me. I think your words five years ago were to the effect that you weren't my maid or my cook. So using that as by baseline, yes the conversation has me nervous since you are using food to soften me up."

Zoe's face broke into her trademark beautiful smile, "Yes I am using food, but don't be afraid. You're a big boy and should be able to handle little old me."

Ben chuckled, "Right. You're one of the scariest women I've ever met, and I mean that with total respect. Before I go, do I get a hint what is on the menu?"

"We are having curried chicken, since goat is hard to find around here. We will also have rice and beans. You get no hint about the conversation, so go and take your begging dog with you."

Ben laughed and whistled for Winston as they headed off to the master bedroom. Winston climbed on the bed as Ben headed off for the shower. Ben let the hot water soak into his muscles as he sat in the oversized shower room. He was more concerned about the upcoming conversation with Zoe more than he wanted to admit. Things had been going very well for a long time and Ben was now afraid it was about to be upended. His biggest fear was that Zoe was going to leave for another job or go back to be with her parents, who he knew missed her greatly.

Their relationship which started as a business transaction established by Thomas Sutton to ensure his client stayed sober had now morphed into a friendship. Zoe still checked Ben's urine regularly just to make sure he was staying clean, but her job duties now centered more on being the manager over both Ben and Trevor. Ben expected once their music venture started creating the next wave of singers and song writers, then Zoe would naturally slide in to manage them as well. Money had never been an issue for Zoe as she had always been well compensated, but Ben decided he would raise her salary to whatever level he needed to in order to keep her.

Ben threw all the clothes and towels down the laundry chute before heading out to the living room. Winston trailed along, carrying of course one sock that Ben had missed.

"So is this a formal dinner or is a t-shirt and jeans acceptable?"

Zoe turned from the stove and stopped stirring the beans and rice, "Your clothes are fine, I just needed you to not smell like a gym locker. What exactly is CSNY?"

36

Ben started setting plates and silverware out and pointed down at his t-shirt, "CSNY is short for Crosby, Stills, Nash, and Young – one of the great bands to come out of California in the late 60's. Are we having biscuits with this meal?"

"No, biscuits are not on the menu since you are supposed to be watching your carbs. I figured the rice and beans were enough for you, and thank you for the ancient history lesson on music."

Ben pretended to pout, "I could have had some biscuits."

Zoe shook her head while stirring again, "No you said you needed to lose 15 pounds and instructed me to help you stay on a workout regimen and to watch what you eat. If you didn't mean that then you shouldn't have given me the assignment."

Ben knew she was right. Ben could hide extra weight pretty well because he was six foot five, but he felt sluggish carrying the extra pounds around. He had gained 25 pounds over the winter while working with Trevor down in Nashville on new songs and interviewing the first few prospects. Trevor was the one who came up with the idea to attract some of the new talent in Nashville to join their agency. The traditional route to stardom in country music was to write songs for established stars and then hope enough good publicity would warrant a one time record deal.

Trevor's idea was to snatch up these new fresh faces and use the songs they had written and teach them the ropes of the business. Ben bought an old bed and breakfast hotel and they turned it into their agency headquarters. Along with a studio, they retained numerous bedrooms so the artists could live on site.

While they toiled with interviewing over seventy applicants for the first group of potential artists, Ben allowed himself to slack off on working out and watching what he ate. Trevor ordered take-out food nearly every meal, so Ben found himself eating a bad diet all the time.

They signed the first group of eight to their management company, which basically gave them the opportunity to rehearse and record without worrying about where there next meal was coming from. Ben and Trevor offered an extensive library of songs they had written over the past couple of years. Ben had tried to persuade Trevor to record some of the songs himself, but he refused saying it wasn't the right genre for him.

"So how did your little trip to the police station go today?"

Ben thought quickly about Detective Milnero and how her dark eyes flashed whenever her temper was provoked by Dre's comments. "It was entertaining, Dre' kept giving the detective attitude."

Zoe searched her memory, "Isn't he the boy who wanted me to run off with him?"

Ben chuckled, "Yes that would be Dre'. He's quite fond of you. He seemed to be downcast that I came to get him without you."

"Sorry to have disappointed him."

Ben ate with great restraint. He really wanted to pile his plate with food, but he was still anxious about what this meal was really about.

"You aren't eating much, too much spice?"

"No it tastes great Zoe, I'm just a little more focused on why we're having this meal."

Zoe dabbed her napkin to her lips, "We've had hundreds of meals together, so what's the problem?"

"Usually our meals are not this formal, and you've been all mysterious about this conversation we need to have," Ben explained.

Zoe pushed her plate away, "Well we might as well get down to it then. I need to ask a favor of you."

Ben breathed a sigh of relief, "That's all a favor. Just let me know what you want, not a problem. I was concerned you got another job or were going back home."

"This is my home, and why would I get another job when I run the business around here?"

Ben nodded, "Good point, but I assume the worst when I have time to think."

"As far as the favor, you need to think about it before just saying it's a done deal."

Ben noted how serious Zoe had become, "Okay ask away."

"Well first off I'm getting older so I've been thinking. I don't really date anyone and I'm not interested in having a one night stand, but I'd like to have a baby."

Ben sat and didn't respond, not knowing exactly what Zoe was meaning. The last thing he wanted to do was blurt out something which made the situation more awkward.

"So you're telling me this so you can get some time off, that's not a problem at all. And you just turned thirty, and the only person who knows that is me and your parents – you're not old."

Zoe smiled slowly, "My internal clock is clanging like Big Ben and I don't want to have any time off. I want to get pregnant, not have major surgery."

Ben shook his head, "Okay I'm completely lost now. Why did you need to have this conversation with . . .?"

Ben stopped talking as things began to click in his head and why Zoe was staring at him.

"You can't mean you want to have my baby do you?"

Zoe laughed, "For somebody so smart, it takes you a long time to figure out things. And for the record your horrified look is not quite the reaction I expected."

"But we're friends, I can think of hundreds of guys who would gladly fill this role for you. You are smart and beautiful so it should be easy for you to find a suitable partner."

"Now you get it, I already found a suitable partner, but I don't want the full blown relationship."

Ben sank his head into his hands, "I don't know Zoe, it would really change our relationship, especially if there's a kid running around here that I know is mine."

Zoe came over and rubbed his shoulders, "This is why I knew we needed to have a set time to discuss this. I knew you would work yourself into a frenzy thinking out all of the possible problems."

Ben lifted his head and looked into Zoe's brown eyes, "Why me? You of all people know what issues I could pass along. Addictive personality, possible OCD tendencies, and that's just the obvious problems."

Zoe stepped back and took a sip of her wine, "Yes those things are there, but also is your intelligence and you are a nice physical specimen. I've thought about this and we would make a very beautiful baby."

Ben smiled, "Great I feel like a slab of beef at the market. What about me being shy? I don't know if I could even go to the doctor and produce a specimen, especially if I knew everyone knew what I was doing in the room."

This brought another laugh from Zoe, "Of course this would be something you'd agonize over, but that's the last part of the favor. I don't want it done in a doctor's office or hospital room with a specimen. I would like you to make love to me, that's how babies are supposed to be created."

Ben stared at Zoe as if she had just sprouted a third eye. "You can't be serious. If having my baby would mess up our relationship, then I guarantee us making love would really screw things up."

Zoe frowned, "See I knew you'd get all freaked out by that part. It's not like I'm a troglodyte. You might even enjoy yourself. I also know you have no problem with the physical act, judging by the number of women you hook up with. Consider it like friends with benefits, except it's a one-time deal and not to think it's a new wrinkle on our relationship."

Ben felt sick, "That's the problem – our relationship is one of the best I've ever had and this might ruin it. You know my track record with serious relationships, that's why I opt for the type of relationship I know isn't going to last more than a day or two."

"I do know that, that's why we are discussing this. You know I could have just jumped you when I climbed into your bed yesterday," Zoe answered calmly. "Also I don't think you have much control over your past relationship struggles."

Ben glanced up to see if she was being serious, "I can't answer you right now, this is too much for me to digest at one time."

Zoe walked over and sat across from Ben at the table, "I didn't expect an answer tonight; it wasn't like I expected you to throw me on the table and have your way with me."

Ben saw her face struggling to hold in her smile, "Sure make fun of me after dropping this on me."

"Humor tends to lessen the awkwardness," Zoe said solemnly. "Also if we could keep this between you and I would be appreciated."

Ben got up, "How would I bring this up to anyone? People would say I'm delusional for even saying the lovely Zoe would want to have my baby."

Ben started cleaning the dishes off the table, his mind racing. He had tried to prepare himself for this conversation, but this was a curveball he'd never seen coming. Zoe put the leftovers in the refrigerator and acted like the whole conversation had never occurred.

"Since you're cleaning up, do you mind if I go do some yoga?"

Ben looked up from the sink, "Sure that's fine, I'll finish up in here and then I've got some lyrics I want to tinker with."

Three hours later, Ben lay on the couch staring at the ceiling. His attempts to work on the songs had been a miserable failure, because his brain kept coming back to Zoe wanting to be pregnant. Winston lifted his head and looked at Ben expectantly, hoping it might be time for some exercise.

Zoe knocked and opened the door to the study, "Hey I'm going to use the hot tub if that's okay."

Ben noticed she was wrapped in her full length robe, "Go ahead, I'm just puttering around with things."

Zoe smiled, "You don't have to lie, and I know you've been in here fretting over my proposal. I didn't intend for you to freak out about this."

"Seriously Zoe, it doesn't seem like a big leap to you for us to have sex so you can have our baby," Ben said, hoping his voice didn't show the level of anxiety he was feeling.

"I weighed out which be more traumatic for you, talking about it like friends or me just seducing you," Zoe answered matter of factly.

Ben shook his head, "I almost feel like you don't think I have any say in this."

"Yes, you have a say in this decision, but if I really want to push things, ultimately you need to remember you are a man."

"What the hell does that mean?"

"Exactly what it sounds like, your penis can control your decision making and I can influence that decision if I decided to."

Ben was prepared to argue, but realized she was probably right. "What about your parents? What will they think?"

Zoe turned to leave, "I'll worry about my parents, who by the way have been nagging me for years to produce a grandchild. So you can sit in here and brood or you could join me in the hot tub to discuss this more."

Ben glanced towards the door and watched Zoe saunter towards the deck, knowing she was either naked or nearly so underneath her robe. "I think I'll just work in here for a while."

"Coward."

Ben took a deep breath and tried to clear his head. He knew Zoe was right about him being a coward to get into the hot tub with her. He'd avoided all romantic relationships since he got sober and knew his fears were driving his paranoia. There were a number of one night stands while Ben was in Jamaica, but most of those were alcohol induced and he'd never intended to have any sort of real relationship. He's started going out over the past couple of years with a variety of women, although he didn't actually have sex with each date.

When Zoe arrived to the island, she made it her mission to keep the negative influences away from Ben, which included the numerous females who saw Ben as their ticket off the island. Ben continued to hide his booze and ignore Zoe's attempts to address his underlying problems, which ultimately led to her convincing Thomas to have Ben committed into in-patient treatment.

Ben deeply resented Zoe for forcing him into rehab, but mostly he resented her for making him look at what he'd turned his life into to escape the pain. The flip side of that now was his gratitude for her perseverance at pressing Ben back into living again. Zoe had been right there with Ben as he started establishing relationships with people again and getting involved in the music scene in Nashville, she was the one constant he relied on daily.

* *

Alex slammed the tequila shot, reveling in the burn it created down her throat. She was still buzzing about the call. He still kept butting into her life and trying to dictate how it would proceed. Alex fumed as she thought about the failed attempts she'd had at getting promoted in Texas because of his friendly connections with the police departments. The old boys' network did exist and made sure she was never going to escape it, so Alex did the unexpected and applied for a job at a small police force in Ohio. That job led her to meet Thomas Kilpatrick, who offered to bring her onto his newly formed CBI detective force.

As she paced around the living room, Alex drained another shot. The tequila was doing little to calm her down tonight, but it tasted exceptionally good. She was furious she still allowed Robert to get under her skin and that he felt comfortable to just call whenever he felt the inkling. Alex decided a second bath might help her relax.

Alex lounged in the tub watching the shadows on the wall shift and move as the candles flickered. The bubbles and her pleasant tequila buzz were creating a soothing atmosphere. Alex laid her head back and closed her eyes. She had an ex-husband who was still bothering her, a case without any leads, and a man she hardly knew who kept entering her head.

Alex opened her eyes and grabbed her cordless phone.

Ben peered at the clock with one eye, trying to figure out why the alarm was going off at 11:48. The next ring let him know it was the phone not an alarm. The illuminated caller id said private and Ben considered ignoring the intrusion.

"Hello?"

No one answered and Ben mentally kicked himself for even answering in the first place. He heard her voice as he prepared to end the call.

"Hi Ben, this is Alex Milnero. I apologize for the lateness of this call."

Ben wasn't sure, but he thought he noticed a slight slurring of the words. Why would a cop be calling him this late at night?

"Its fine, I was just reading," Ben lied. "How can I help you Detective Milnero?"

Alex snuggled down into the water and stared at the stars glowing through her skylight. "It's Alex and I wanted to ask you a couple of questions."

"Okay Alex."

"You brought Dre' in today because you are a friend of Susan Sutton, correct?"

"Yes."

"How exactly do you know Ms. Sutton?"

"She's my publicist's sister and I've spoken at YouthQuest a couple of times."

"So no romantic involvement?"

Ben hesitated, not exactly sure where this conversation was headed, "No and I'm pretty sure her husband would be upset if there was any. Why are you asking about Susan?"

Alex smiled, sinking further into the bubbles. "I'm not asking about Susan. I'm asking about you, are you currently involved with anyone?"

Ben swallowed and felt his chest tighten. He was tempted to lie, but there was something about Alex that had caught his attention.

"No, I'm not involved with anyone."

There was a silence and Ben feared he had misread why Alex was asking.

"Would you be interested in meeting me for lunch tomorrow?"

Alex held her breath when Ben didn't answer. He was either trying to think of an excuse or her forwardness was scaring the hell out of him.

"I'm free, what time and where?"

"How about 12:30 at Casa Lupita?"

"That sounds great, I'll see you then."

As Ben hung up the phone, he realized he'd just taken another of the steps Dr. Jackson had hounded him to take. He knew he shouldn't read too much into the lunch, because it was probably just a friendly date rather than romantic, it took Ben a long time before he went back to sleep.

8

Ben woke up at 6:45, trying to remember if he had really talked to Alex last night. The caller id confirmed he'd been on the phone last night before midnight. Ben ran his fingers through his hair and started panicking, he had almost five and half hours until his first real date in nearly ten years. He also knew he couldn't run into Zoe this early in the morning.

"Come on Winston, we need to go for a run."

Ben ran for two reasons, primarily the exercise, but also to clear his head to think. He thought better when he focused on his breathing and the rhythm of his feet hitting the ground. Winston always tagged along, although the majority of his time was spent chasing squirrels or marking his territory.

The course was designed to circle around the property and allow Ben the maximum workout and also the best scenery. He had gotten his time for the five mile course under forty minutes, but this morning he wasn't near that pace. Ben was having a hard time staying focused because he kept thinking about what to wear, what they would talk about, and what would people say if they saw him out with someone. Then there was also the small problem of his manager wanting to have a baby with him.

Winston was waiting for Ben at the back door. He was picking burrs out of his tail, so Ben knew he'd been cutting through the woods to get to the house.

Zoe was eating her fruit while scanning the laptop. "You got an early start this morning."

Ben rubbed the towel over his face, "Yeah I needed to make up for slacking off yesterday."

Zoe looked up at Ben, "So I hope our conversation didn't prevent you from sleeping well."

"No I slept rather well," Ben replied, failing to mention the phone call he got last night.

"Are you okay? You seem more stressed than normal; please don't tell me you're still freaking out about my baby plan."

"Yes I am still freaked out about your ... request, but there's something else also. I think I have a date today."

Zoe stopped tapping and pushed the laptop away from her, "Are you serious? That's great. Do I know her?" "Wait a minute, what do you mean you think you have a date?"

Ben sat down and filled Zoe in about meeting Detective Milnero yesterday and the phone call last night.

* *

Alex spent the majority of the morning on the phone. She had started questioning the people whose homes had been directly hit by the tornado first. They were more than welcome to answer a few basic questions and Alex didn't get the feeling that any of them were hiding anything. This type of digging was what Alex hated most about the job, give her a clue and she was content to track down wherever it went. This case just gave a huge clue, but with no real direction to go except to flail around in the dark.

When Alex looked at her watch she realized she only had two hours until her lunch date. She'd spent a long time this morning picking out her clothes, opting for a black sleeveless turtleneck and khakis. Alex wanted to emphasis her figure, but didn't want to come on like a desperate woman who showed too much skin.

"You going somewhere today?" Gerald asked from his desk.

Alex gave him a scowl, "No, why?"

"I don't know, you don't usually have your hair and makeup done at the same time. And what's up with the fingernails?"

Alex looked down at her fire engine red nails. "I couldn't sleep so I painted my nails, big frigging deal."

Gerald didn't seem impressed, "If you say so."

"Yeah I say so – what else would it be?"

"If I didn't know you better, I'd think you had a date."

"Screw you Gerald, you know everyone is intimidated by me except you and I can't pry you away from Janice."

Gerald threw up his hands in defense, "Sorry I forgot about your sexual obsession with my body."

Alex hit him in the forehead with a paper wad.

* *

Ben backed diagonally into two of the parking spots furthest from the entrance. Walking was a small price to pay to protect his vehicle from incidental scratches and dings. After working so hard to fix a classic, Ben wasn't prepared to deal with someone opening their door into his baby.

Since he was fifteen minutes early, Ben popped in the ELO cd. The cd player was the one modern convenience Chet had allowed in the car, trying his best to keep it as close to authentic as possible. He hoped the music would calm him down, but he could feel damp circles forming in his armpits. Ben was beginning to think maybe Alex was drunk when she called last night and this morning she had come to her senses.

Ben felt a little guilty about his lack of conversation with Zoe this morning about the baby proposal, but she seemed intrigued about Ben actually going out for a date. She spent the majority of the morning helping him figure out the best outfit for a first, almost blind date. Zoe also felt it necessary to coach him on things to emphasize and subjects to avoid.

The song ended, so Ben locked up Raquel and headed to the door. He watched for signs of Alex but didn't notice any car which resembled a cop car in the lot.

"Hi my name is Dani, do you need a table for one or are you waiting for someone?"

Ben put down the menu and looked at the bleach blonde hostess. "I'm supposed to meet someone, but I'm not sure if she's here yet."

Dani gave him a knowing smile; she'd seen hundreds of these types of dates between married people. Although this guy was a nice catch, he looked like he was going to have a stroke.

"Why don't you stick your head in there and see if she's in there."

Ben scanned the room quickly, "I don't see her so I guess I'll go ahead and get a table. Her name is Alex Milnero."

Dani's eyes quickly came up from the reservation book, "I didn't know you were here with Miss Milnero, I'll take you to her table."

Ben followed Dani through the dining room and off into an adjacent sunroom. The sunlight was streaming onto the table through the numerous hanging baskets and plants. A flowering plant was growing through a hole in the center of the table.

"Would you like something to drink while you wait?"

"Sure, how about a Coke."

Dani gave Ben another smile and left him alone in the room. Ben watched her blonde ponytail bob as she maneuvered through the tables to the bar. When she was out of sight, Ben looked around the room again. He was only fifteen or twenty feet away from the other patrons, but it felt like a secluded area.

"Miss Milnero called and said she would be a little late," Dani informed Ben as she sat his drink down.

"Thank you – could you tell me why Alex has her own room?"

Dani laughed, tossing a few wayward strands of hair behind her ear. "It isn't really her room, but she eats here a lot and this is her favorite. We've taken the liberty of christening it the Milnero room."

Ben took a long drag on his soda, "So how long have you know Alex?"

Dani shook her finger at Ben, "Can't answer that. Alex told me to keep you entertained so you didn't run away, but I wasn't allowed to give up any gossip."

"How much would some information cost me?" Ben inquired with a smile.

"Money wouldn't do it."

Dani was about to issue her demands when Alex walked in with a bowl of tortilla chips and salsa.

"Don't let me interrupt, what were we discussing?"

Dani gave Ben a quick smile, "Well this gentleman was trying to bribe me for information about you."

Alex sat down, still munching on her chips, "Really, that does sound rather bad. I hope you weren't able to give him any."

Ben wanted to crawl out of the room. He wanted to give a good first impression and now Alex thought he was digging for dirt. Dani's eyes lit up as she kept talking, clearly enjoying the predicament Ben was in.

"Well we were still discussing my fee for disclosing any information, but you got here too soon so I'll be on my way."

Alex caught her attention before she left the room, "Dani, what was your fee?"

"Dinner and dancing if it didn't work out with you."

Ben was dying. He knew his face was scarlet and he couldn't think of what to say. Of all the ways he thought the date would start, this was a twist he never saw coming.

"So now that you are thoroughly embarrassed, how are you Ben" Alex asked with a grin.

Ben looked at her smiling face, "I'm fine, but I just want you to know I wasn't really digging for dirt."

"Dirt, that's easy to find about me, I was hoping Dani'd give you positive reports. Hey look at it like this, if this doesn't go anywhere, you've got your next date all set up."

Ben knew his face was still red. He didn't want Alex to think he flirted with every woman he came in contact with, but it looked suspicious. "Can we start this all over? You look great."

Alex looked at Ben while he stared at her. "Thank you, you don't look so bad yourself. I apologize for being late, my partner was badgering me and it took a few extra minutes to get him to leave me alone."

"Badgering?"

"Yeah he kept insisting I had a date and of course I had to tell him I didn't."

Ben smiled as he watched Alex deftly maneuver her chip through the salsa and into her mouth. She clearly enjoyed eating and didn't feel the need to hide it. Ben expected with her physique she was either perpetually on a diet or ate like a bird.

"It's probably best if you kept it a secret that we went out, might hurt your reputation."

Alex took a drink of her water, "It isn't you. Everyone at the precinct thinks I'm the ice princess or a lesbian – so admitting a date would dispel both rumors and I'd hate that."

Ben took a long look at Alex's flawless skin and thick black hair, wondering how anyone could think she was anything but a beautiful woman.

"So what do you recommend, sounds like you are the expert about the food here."

Alex finished chewing her chips and finished her glass of water, "I ordered for us when I came in, they are giving us a sampling of their best dishes. I hope that's okay, you aren't on any kind of bizarre diet."

Ben smiled, "No weird diets, I'm a big guy so I eat what I can get my hands on."

Alex smiled and wondered if he had big appetites in other areas as well, "That's what I'm talking about."

"So how did you end up with a name like Alex?"

"It's not my given name, but it gives me an advantage because people assume they are going to be talking with a man."

Ben had to agree, he wasn't expecting this beautiful woman to be a detective when he met her yesterday. He was going to ask more questions, but was interrupted by a stream of food being delivered.

Ben stared at the various plates and realized he was going to be doing a lot of running the next few days to burn off the calories. "So how did you get into being a detective?"

Alex finished loading her plate with rice and beans, "I was on the police force in Galveston, but couldn't get promoted, so when I got divorced I interviewed for the detective position here."

"How long were you married before getting divorced?"

Alex answered while chewing her food, "Seven years married and now seven years divorced. Okay give me the details, I know the basics about being a big shot author, but how are you single?"

Ben smiled, "Well I don't write anymore, so it's former big shot author. And how can you have been married and divorced that many years?"

Alex waved her fork at Ben, "For your information, I'll be thirty five this year. I googled you, so I know the basics. Are you involved with the gorgeous black woman I saw you photographed with at the Country Music Awards last year? You looked pretty cozy."

Ben's smile fell, "Zoe's my manager, slash handler, and general pain in my ass. She keeps track of my business options and makes sure I'm sober."

Alex stopped chewing, "I'm so sorry, I didn't know. I just wanted to make sure there wasn't another woman in the picture. It's some of my insecurities showing."

Ben took a deep breath, "It's okay – Guess it's better to get that out there now rather than later. I've been sober for over three years and Zoe is probably my best friend." Ben's mind briefly flashed to Zoe's baby conversation last night.

"Okay now that things are awkward, let's just talk about how you got involved with the young man you brought to my office this morning," Alex said softly, trying to nudge the conversation back to calmer waters.

As they left the restaurant, Ben argued with Alex and won the right to pay the bill, leaving a sizable tip for the waitresses. He was about to walk outside to wait for Alex when Dani came out of the bar.

"How was everything?"

Ben handed her a fifty dollar bill, "It was great and the food was good too."

Dani tucked the bill into her pocket, smiling at Ben, "Well it looks like I won't be collecting my fee."

Ben blushed, "What do you mean?"

"You two make a good couple, and I've never seen Alex smile that much before."

Alex returned from the restroom, interrupting the conversation. "What are you two up to? Dani, you wouldn't be hitting on my date would you?"

"Of course I'm hitting on him, do you think I'd let him settle for you?"

Both women burst out laughing and hugged. Ben walked Alex to her Crown Victoria, which she'd parked in the fifteen minute carryout parking spot.

"I assume you parked your hot rod in the boonies?"

Ben shrugged, "Yeah, I put a lot time and money into her, so I baby her."

"Maybe sometime I can have a chance to drive her."

"Sure that would be - -"

Ben was answering and imagining Alex behind the wheel, when Alex pulled his head down and kissed him hard, quickly brushing her tongue against his teeth. Ben was caught off guard, but didn't resist.

"I've wanted to do that, but I don't have time to wait for an appropriate time. I've got to run, but I'll give you a call later, maybe we can go out again soon."

Ben stood silently in the parking lot as Alex sped off. He'd just been kissed and set a tentative second date without uttering a single word. Clearly this was going to be a different type of relationship, and Ben knew he was going to need to stay on his toes.

****

Alex drove quickly through the downtown stoplights. She knew if she maintained the forty-five miles per hour speed she'd catch all of the lights, and if she didn't everyone could recognize her plain cop car. The lunch had gone too well, because now she was late and Gerald was going to continue with his relentless questioning. It wasn't that big of a deal she went on a date, people did it every day, so she'd just tell him the truth. Tomorrow.

"You're late."

Gerald was leaning against the bumper of his car, cleaning the mud off his Rockports. He'd suggested they check the industries which sustained damage, but hadn't been totally destroyed. The perp was a collector, but Gerald believed he would be too cautious to leave a box of incriminating pictures lying around the house where anyone could stumble upon them.

Alex didn't agree with all of Gerald's theories, but she was still grasping at shadows, so she agreed to check his hunches first while she stalled for time. The biggest thing Alex was focused on was the cocky way these photos were taken. There was a level of comfort about committing these horrific acts and then photographing them for posterity.

"Sorry I got hung up at lunch," Alex explained as she slipped out of her heels and into her hiking boots.

Gerald gave her a quizzical look. "Must have been some lunch, your lipstick is smudged."

Alex glanced in the side mirror. Her lipstick was a little off, but not that much. "I must have done it wiping my mouth, and how come you're such an expert on lipstick smudges?"

"Besides being a great detective, I survived raising two daughters. You can't make it through something like that without being able to recognize messed up lipstick or lame excuses."

They spent the next two hours trudging through the surrounding buildings in the industrial park and the adjacent fields. It wasn't obvious what they were hunting for, but both believed they would know the clue when they found it. Other than some building code violations, their search turned up a big goose egg.

"So much for my theory, have I given you enough time to finalize yours?" Gerald asked while pulling his shoes back on.

Alex gave him a big smile, "I was that transparent huh?"

"You never allow me to go first if you've got something in that pretty little head of yours."

"I'll take that as a compliment. I have some theories, but I don't want to tell you yet, we'll talk at the station."

Alex drove the long way back to the station to allow her some more time to get her theory straight in her own head before she opened it up to Gerald's scrutiny. She walked down the hallway and noticed the collection of people gathered outside of her office.

"What's going on?"

"Hey she's here, let her through so we can get this over with once and for all," Andersen announced.

Alex pushed through the people to see what the commotion was all about. There in the center of her desk was a vase with a dozen roses. Instantly she was furious, how could Robert try something as juvenile as sending flowers to her office.

"Come on Milnero, open the card."

Alex turned to face the growing crowd, "What the hell are all of you doing here?"

Andersen answered for the group, "We've got a pot running as to who would buy you flowers, so open the card please."

Alex opened the card and read the message. She was reading it a second time when her vision started getting blurry and she handed the card to Andersen.

Alex,

Thank you for a wonderful lunch. It's been a long time since I've had that much fun. Looking forward to hearing from you soon.

Ben

Alex heard groans coming from the people outside of her office.

"Who's Ben?" Andersen asked.

"A friend of mine."

"Was it Ben Princi? I saw him in here the other day," Cheryll Watkins, the dispatcher and office gossip asked. She was eagerly waiting for Alex's answer and erupted with a scream when Alex nodded.

'I knew it. All right time to pay Momma boys. I'll take cash or checks."

When Alex regained her composure she realized everyone was gone and now only Gerald was standing in the doorway. He was diligently chewing on his unlit cigar, acting like he wasn't paying attention to the spectacle.

"What?"

Gerald seemed to focus back in on the office, "I didn't say anything, hell I just lost five bucks."

"We are just friends."

"Sure you are, but I don't think you're trying to convince me."

Alex ran her nail along the etching in the vase, "I wasn't expecting this, I was trying to keep things quiet."

Gerald continued chomping on his cigar, "Since none of us has ever seen you date, this makes it big news and then it looks like loverboy isn't helping your discretion."

"His name is Ben," Alex replied with a tired smile. "By the way who did you put your money on?"

"I put my money on you, thought you bought them for yourself."

"Not a bad idea, but I go for chocolate or clothes if I feel the need to spoil myself."

Alex leaned back in her chair and stared at the roses, what the hell had she started by asking Ben out?

9

Ben was settling into the Jacuzzi when his cell phone started chirping. The number was blocked and he considered ignoring the call altogether, but he wasn't sure if it was Alex.

"Hello?"

"Yes, is this Benjamin Princi?"

Ben didn't recognize the voice, "Yes it is and I'm not interested in what you're selling."

The woman started talking quickly. "I'm not selling anything Mr. Princi. My name is Samantha Collins and I am doing my research thesis on modern literature. I was –"

"I'm not a writer anymore and I can't help you," Ben interrupted.

"I know you haven't published recently, but your two novels were quite successful. And there's the fact that you are the closest living author to the university."

Ben's gut was telling him to hang up, but the woman was convincing. "What do you need from me?"

"I just would like to ask some questions about the literary process and maybe compare your style with some classic authors."

Ben sighed, it seemed harmless. "Okay, when did you want to call me with the questions?"

There was a hesitation on the phone. "I was hoping we could meet for lunch tomorrow. I thought over the course of the meal you could answer my questions."

"I don't know, I usually stay away from public places."

"Yes I know you respect your privacy, and I don't want to invade upon that. Perhaps you could choose a place so you feel more comfortable."

Ben considered this for a minute. "Do you know where the Joyland restaurant is outside of Clayton?"

"It's on state route 48 isn't it?"

"Yes, be there tomorrow at 11:30, if you are late I won't be there."

Ben set the phone down and relaxed in the warm water. This day was getting stranger by the minute, first he had a date and now he had an appointment to discuss writing.

Ben had done little writing since Monica died. She had been the one to believe in his ability and pushed him to take the time to finish his novel. When she died, his confidence and motivation left as well. The numerous counselors and therapists had all stressed how writing could get him past his depression, but Ben froze up every time he opened the laptop to start writing. That's where the songwriting seemed to help. Ben seemed to hit his rhythm writing down short bursts of poetry, which didn't require him to be focused for a long period of time.

The warmth and steady pressure from the jets helped Ben relax while his mind raced until he drifted off. Sleep came at a premium for Ben so he took advantage of his naps as frequently as he could.

* *

Samantha scrambled around her office, accumulating her props to help her look like a graduate student. She'd guaranteed her boss an exclusive with Ben Princi, the reclusive writer who had witnessed his friends get massacred at his high school reunion. He countered with a promise of the morning anchor job in exchange for a long weekend at his cabin to discuss her 'qualifications'. Samantha politely declined the nauseating weekend and informed Mr. Walther that she wouldn't feel right unless she earned the job.

"What are you doing?"

Putting down her old raggedy book bag, Samantha turned to answer, "Hello Jennifer, I'm just doing some spring cleaning."

Jennifer Dobson put on her best smile. She'd been the lead anchor for almost ten years at Channel 2 and she hadn't stayed on top by not watching out for the new hires. She'd seen the way Walther had been looking at Samantha and it wouldn't be long before the petite, lithe blonde would be performing whatever sexual positions were needed to get the anchor job.

"Well this office could use a change of pace, maybe sometime we could have lunch and discuss your ideas how to improve things around here. You know we girls need to stick together."

Samantha stared at Jennifer's smile. She wondered how many people had been fooled by Jennifer Dobson's perfect fake smile. It was no coincidence that Jennifer's teeth showed whenever she smiled, because Samantha was fairly certain that Jennifer was like a big cat, lulling you into a false sense of security before the big teeth closed on your neck.

Samantha smiled back, "That's sweet Jennifer, but I'm really busy at the moment – maybe a rain check? I've got to get down to makeup so I'm ready for the evening traffic spot."

"Sure some other time," Jennifer answered, now intent on finding out what the ambitious little new girl was up to.

Samantha pulled her hair back to allow Keith to complete putting on the finishing powder before she went on for her traffic segment. She'd never imagined staying in this role this long when she signed on at the station, but Samantha had misjudged the amount of behind the scenes politics that occurred on a regular basis. Either she had been naïve when she did her internship, or the politics hadn't pertained to her.

"You're ready doll," Keith announced as he admired his work in the oversized mirror.

Samantha stared at her face, noting the delicate bone structure that had likely earned her the shot to be on screen for the traffic segment. She knew it was a fluff job, but it got her air time and she wanted to build some viewer connection for when she moved into getting some real reporting stories.

"Thanks Keith."

The job at Channel 2 was supposed to the first step in her carefully planned rise to on air reporting. She never intended to do something like traffic reports, but it was the only opening and seemed like an easy segue into what she really wanted to do. Now a year later and Samantha was no further along than before, except she knew that having sex with the production director was the quickest way to get her career jumpstarted. Samantha briefly considered tossing her morals out the window for one night, but Walther made it clear that it would need to be an ongoing relationship if she wanted to have serious air time. Samantha couldn't stomach the thought of that.

Samantha had heard the reports of Walther begging for someone to get an interview with Benjamin Princi, who remained the reigning celebrity in the vicinity. She researched Princi and found the best way to getting some face time with him might be by sneaking in the side door of ethics. Samantha had some of the same qualities as Princi's deceased girlfriend, so having that on her side might help get a break. After some internet searching she did notice that there were similarities that she had with Courtney Daniels, which was going to be her ticket to speaking with Benjamin Princi.

The research had also uncovered that Benjamin rarely spoke with any media people and almost never without Zoe Meloncourt at his side. She was listed as his manager, but every interview or YouTube clip showed her as a protective female. There was never any hint of a romantic relationship, but they had been photographed and spotted frequently at various awards shows or media events.

10

Alex lit the candles, sipping her wine as she moved around her bathroom. Ben's flowers were perched on the counter, reflecting off the mirrors creating a kaleidoscope effect.

She'd tried to focus on her notes from the case, but Alex couldn't get Ben out of her head. The lunch had been nice, especially once they relaxed and started opening up. Alex could tell from his politeness and manners that Ben was a gentleman. He also was open about his past, which showed he was comfortable with who he was. Alex's biggest concern was that he might not be the type for a casual relationship, which is what she was interested in.

Alex polished off her wine before climbing into the bathtub. If there was ever a night she needed to relax, tonight was the night.

The phone woke Alex up twenty minutes later.

"Yeah."

"Alessandra, is that any way to answer the phone?"

"No Mom, but you woke me up. I fell asleep in the bathtub."

Alex heard her mother start giggling. She was fifty-five now, but Alex always thought of her as a young girl when she started with her giggling. Bonita Milnero adored her only child and tried to call at least once a week. Leaving her mother behind in Amarillo was the hardest part of divorcing Robert, but Alex knew it had to be a complete break if she was going to have any kind of future.

"So how is my little girl doing?" It was the same question every week, even though Alex dwarfed her petite mother.

"Not too bad Mom, I've got a new case to work on, and it's a doozy. Oh and I had a date today."

Alex held the phone away from her ear as her mother shrieked, "Now that's great news, tell me all about him."

Alex gave her mother most of the vital information she had about Ben, but selectively left out some parts. Her mother would not be pleased to find out that Ben was a recovering alcoholic or that the last two women he was involved with were both killed. In her mind this would be a sign that Ben was marked for tragedy.

They ended their conversation thirty minutes later, because Alex's steamy bath had grown cold and Alex wanted to get to bed. Alex pulled her favorite t-shirt on and climbed into her bed, wondering briefly what it be like with Ben's big body in there with her. She'd sworn off men after Robert. She refused to have any type of meaningful relationship other than sexual gratification, and now she was imagining cuddling with a man she barely knew.

The phone was vibrating on the desk and Ben snatched it up quickly.

"Hello?"

"Hi Ben, I apologize for calling so late again, it seems to be becoming a pattern."

Ben squinted at the clock, "It's okay, I wasn't even sleeping this time. I was finishing up some final lyric ideas for Trevor."

"I wanted to thank you for the flowers, they were beautiful. I had a good time today, it was a nice change of pace for me."

"I hope I didn't scare you with the flowers, but I wanted you to know I had a great time at lunch. I've kind of put myself in a cocoon and it was great to have a meal with a beautiful woman."

Alex let out her breath; maybe he was just a nice guy who wanted to spend time with her. "Well I promised you another date so I thought we could set it now while I have time to think."

"One perk of my job is that I have a pretty flexible schedule, so let me know what works for your schedule."

Alex had been thinking about this question since before she dialed. The problem was making up her mind, because her brain and her heart couldn't agree on a site.

"How about my place tomorrow evening at seven?"

Ben continued staring out the window at the moon. He was being invited over to a woman's house with little chance of people interrupting them, or saving Ben from stumbling through a romantic moment.

"That would be fine, what's the address and what do you want me to bring?"

"115 South Allen, next to Peterson's Funeral Home and you just need to show up with your appetite."

"Okay I'll see you tomorrow."

Ben put the phone back in the charger and slid into bed. Winston had been sprawled across the end of the bed and he jumped down. He waited patiently while Ben got settled before jumping back up on the bed and lying across Ben's feet.

Zoe clicked off the other cordless phone after Ben hung up and wondered where exactly this new relationship was going.

11

Ben finished with his stretching and rudimentary yoga poses. He'd always scoffed at all this new age stuff, but Zoe had shown him that this actually helped him with his running and balance. Ben had not encountered any knee or foot problems since he started his runs off this way.

Winston was already gone, marking his usual spots and searching out any new scents which captured his attention. Ben started slowly, but got into his rhythm within the first half mile. These runs were where Ben still did most of his organizing and brainstorming. He'd formulated the plots of both his novels while jogging with his wife and now he threw around the latest snatches of music Trevor sent him and tried to make sense of the words bouncing around in his head. This morning he also had the distraction of thinking about meeting with a grad student who wanted to pick his brain about his former life and then he had a date tonight.

After showering, Ben left a note for Zoe next to his urine screen. Normally they spent the morning going over business matters or upcoming plans, but Ben needed to meet with Chet before his luncheon. Ben also felt Zoe was giving him some extra space since dropping her bombshell on him.

Ben pulled his Chevelle into the front parking space in front of Chet sitting in his rocking chair.

"Timing sounds a little off, you been rough housing her again," Chet complained when Ben got out.

"She's fine Chet, and how do you get anything done sitting outside in your chair?"

Chet let loose a stream of tobacco juice, "Unlike some people, I get up before the crack of dawn to start my day."

Ben smiled as they walked inside, followed closely by Chet, "What have you been working on lately?"

"Same old shit, couple of fender benders to fix and some tune ups. If you'd get off your lazy ass and get the primer job finished, maybe I could have some fun with the Bird."

"I know, I know. You forget that I'm not quite in your league."

They went into the office, still bantering about the work Ben needed to finalize the plans before he dropped his car off. Chet wanted everything to be original, but Ben wanted to have some the modern conveniences which made it easier to drive.

'Why do you have to ruin her?" Chet growled.

Ben rolled his eyes, "I'd hardly say I'm ruining the car. I just want some modifications which allow me to drive with some semblance of comfort."

Chet ran his fingers through his white hair, "I know it's your damn car, but she belongs to history too."

Ben expected this argument, because Chet always pitched a fit about putting power steering in the older cars. Chet was sixty-four and he'd witnessed the rise and demise of numerous cars. He felt it was his duty to argue in favor of the car rather than comfort. Muscle cars were works of art and weren't designed to have all the comforts of modern cars.

"Well this conversation has been productive," Ben said sarcastically.

"I'll do it, but I just want you to know I don't like it."

"Your opinion has been noted, and I of course also want a cd player installed as well."

Chet threw his tobacco into the trash, "I oughta find a damn eight track player to put in it for spite." Ben chuckled, knowing full well that Chet probably had an eight track player somewhere in the back storage areas of his shop. "Alright, I'll have the Bird here in two days tops."

Chet followed Ben back out the door, "Where are you running off to now? I thought you might actually be coming here to work."

"Sorry I can't stay, I've got an appointment for lunch."

"So that's what you call a date now."

Ben smiled, "No, I have an appointment for lunch, my date is for dinner."

Ben didn't give Chet a chance to ask any more questions as backed the car out and dropped it into first gear. Ben quickly raced through the gears, redlining the tachometer, knowing how much Chet hated it when he drove the car like this.

* *

Samantha arrived at Joyland at 11:25. She'd left plenty early, because she expected Ben to be a man of his word and use the time ultimatum as a convenient out for him. Samantha needed this interview to prove she was capable of doing more than being the cute little traffic girl.

The contrast of the bright May sunshine and the dark restaurant, caused Samantha to briefly see spots as her vision adjusted. Samantha had pulled her hair into a ponytail and only applied the briefest of makeup. She didn't think Ben would recognize her from the morning traffic spots, but she wasn't taking any chances.

Samantha scanned the room, figuring it shouldn't be hard to find the big author.

"Can I help you honey?"

Samantha turned to look at the waitress. Her nametag said Louisa and she looked like a stereotypical truck stop waitress. Bleached blond hair with dark roots, piled ridiculously high to divert the attention from her poorly applied rouge.

"I hope so, I'm supposed to meet Benjamin Princi. Do you know him?"

"Course I know Ben, he's a helluva specimen if you know what I mean," Louisa replied with an exaggerated wink.

"Is he here?" Samantha asked patiently.

Louisa smiled, allowing her dental work to show. "Yeah honey, he's around the corner in our VIP room. Said to direct you there if you were here before 11:30, and it looks like you made it with minutes to spare."

Samantha thanked Louisa and headed off in the direction she had pointed. This was just another interview, but Samantha needed to wipe the perspiration off her hands before turning on her digital recorder in her purse.

Ben looked up from the car parts magazine when the door opened. He wasn't sure what to expect, but Samantha Collins was not who he expected to see. She looked like a high school student with her blond hair, open smile, and petite body.

"Mr. Princi, I'm Samantha Collins."

Ben stood up, dwarfing Samantha and shook her hand. Her grip was strong even though her hand was half the size of Ben's. She looked straight at Ben, clearly not intimated by his mass.

"Hello Samantha, and its Ben okay?"

"Sure, I just wanted to thank you for granting me this opportunity to talk with you. I know your privacy is something you value."

Ben sat back down and found himself staring into Samantha's eyes. They were a deep blue with long lashes. "I'm sorry, I was daydreaming for minute. You reminded me of someone."

"That's fine, I hope it was someone you remember fondly," Samantha replied. She'd seen pictures of Ben's former flame online and knew she shared some similarities. This was another thing she was hoping would lead Ben to open up.

Samantha had a plan for how to lead this interview, until she walked in and saw Ben. She knew he was handsome, and it really showed when he smiled, but it faded quickly and the dark smudges under his green eyes detracted from his overall allure.

The other thing was when she shook Ben's hand. Samantha had dated big guys in college, but there was something about his gentleness, which bellied his stature. He'd touched her hand with such delicacy that Samantha wasn't certain he'd shook her hand until she glanced down to see her hand engulfed.

"Where would you like to start?"

"If I could start at the beginning that would be great. When did you know you wanted to be a writer?"

Ben leaned back in his chair. It had been a long time since he'd had to answer this question, and it hadn't gotten any easier. "You do know that I don't write anymore, I'm involved with a songwriting company."

Samantha smiled, "Yes, I figured I'd save that for closer to the end about how someone transfers from novels to four minute stories."

Ben nodded. He'd never thought about how he was still writing stories, just a shorter version. "I guess I was a junior at Northwestern. I took a creative writing class to meet a girl and found out I had an aptitude for being creative."

Samantha took notes as she noted the wistful look in Ben's eyes, "So signing up for a course to get a girl helped you find your gift."

"Yeah, something like that."

Louisa came in with iced tea, "What can I get for you young lady?"

Samantha ordered an omelet and some coffee.

Ben looked at Louisa, "Don't you want my order?"

Louisa smiled, "Don't need it, Zoe called and said you would have the chef salad and no dessert."

Samantha looked at Ben as Louisa walked off, "So is Zoe your wife?"

Ben shook his head, "No she is my handler. She manages my business and makes sure I'm sober."

Samantha flinched with the bluntness of the statement, "Sorry I didn't realize you had a problem."

Ben gave her a sad smile, "Well I'm sure you've googled me and wondered how somebody like me falls this far. The truth is I thought the booze would numb me enough to let me get back to writing."

"It never works."

Ben looked over at Samantha, "You have substance abuse issues too?"

"Not exactly, my dad was an alcoholic. I learned how to watch for the signs so I didn't upset him. It's tough to be a kid walking on pins and needles all the time."

Ben nodded, "I never thought I had a problem, until my friends forced me to see the truth. I owe them and Zoe a lot. They saved my life."

Samantha finished her drink and took some time to steer the conversation back to the topic. "So how exactly does a person go from bestselling author to forming your own record label?"

Ben stared at the beautiful young girl, wondering how to condense his past fifteen year roller coaster ride into some glib answer. There was no way to describe the joy Ben had felt when he was writing every day, stopping only to eat or to talk with Monica about potential plot issues. His wife supported and nurtured his gift, which ultimately led to the best sellers and movies. Monica didn't live long enough to see the fruits of her belief in Ben, struck down by a drunk driver as she was headed to her doctor's appointment to confirm she was pregnant.

"I'm sure you have all of the highlighted points from either Google or Wikipedia," Ben answered softly.

Samantha watched his face, noting he was slowing down and thinking his answers through before answering. "Yes I've seen the timeline, but I know things don't just happen that easily. This is not a normal progression."

Ben took a deep breath, "Let me tell you a story."

He spoke for the next thirty minutes, describing his drinking binges which resulted in him being placed in the residential placement for substance abuse. At Gladstone, he was assigned to be roommates with Trevor Blaine, the former lead guitarist for Whiptail. In spite of their age difference, they become close friends who supported each other through the withdraw symptoms. They came up with a game at night of Trevor coming up with guitar riffs and Ben would supply lyrics. They started with trying to be funny to combat the boredom, but eventually they found an easy working relationship.

Ben had no background in music other than wearing out his mother's album collection from the 60's and 70's. Trevor was a teenage guitar prodigy who was headed to Julliard, until he heard Eddie Van Halen in 1976 and then he decided he was born to play rock and roll. His ride to stardom never happened, as he and his band burned out in a white hot burst of unattained potential and increasingly heavy drug abuse.

Ben contacted his manager, Thomas Sutton, near the end of his placement and discussed with him about possibly submitting some songs to some established record companies. Thomas, sensing that his former college roommate was finally coming out of his depression, used his contacts in the entertainment field to generate some interest. He then formed the Rehab Rebel Records label, which actually did not make records, but did produce a number of songs for established acts.

Samantha scribbled notes as Ben talked, asking quick clarifying questions at certain moments. She let Ben just talk for the most part, knowing this was as therapeutic for him as beneficial as it was for her.

"It was quite a blow to Trevor when he found out the country stars were the ones who wanted our songs. His rock and roll heritage was shook, but he got over it once the royalties started coming in," Ben said with a laugh.

"So what is going on with your latest endeavor in Nashville?"

Ben shook his head, "That was all Trevor's idea. He thought we could help out some of the young musicians looking for a break by teaching them the ropes and letting them get experienced without selling out."

Samantha looked at Ben, waiting for the punch line, "Are you trying to convince me that Trevor was doing something for someone else?"

Ben had to laugh, "Clearly you've examined his background as well. He still comes across as an asshole at times, but he really is committed to this project. He lives in Nashville at the compound with the kids."

"Compound?"

"It's actually an old bed and breakfast outside of Nashville, but we call it the compound since there are barns along with the house."

They finished the rest of the meal, talking about music, writing, and cars. Ben was impressed to find that Samantha had helped her father restore a 67 Camaro while she was in high school. If all writers were like Samantha, Ben decided he would have done many more interviews.

Ben paid for the meal and walked Samantha out to her car, "I must admit you made this fairly painless."

Samantha smiled, "Glad you thought so. I hoped this wouldn't be an arduous process."

Ben gave her a brief hug before opening her door. He had enjoyed talking with Samantha, although it may have had something to do with her reminding Ben of his former flame. He enjoyed watching her eyes dance as she asked numerous questions about his life.

* *

"Alex, come here and take a look at this," Gerald said when she walked into their office. The pictures were spread out in rows on his desk.

"What do you have?"

"You look at it and tell me. Does this look like a pattern?"

Alex looked at the pictures. She tried to look beyond the obvious and look for a pattern. There had to be a connection with how the pictures were laid out in comparison.

"The eyes. He seems to focus on their eyes. Even the really explicit pictures, he has them turning their head so he can get their eyes in the picture."

Gerald grunted his approval, "Guess all my training made you a good detective after all."

Alex arranged the pictures into piles of pictures of the victims prior to being assaulted on down to the pile of pictures in death. They knew their subject was obsessed with the young Hispanic girls, but now they had another connection.

"Okay Sherlock, what does it mean?" Alex asked over her shoulder.

"I don't have a clue. I assumed since you were the lead on this case it was up to you to figure that connection out."

Alex rubbed her neck. This case was bugging her more for its lack of progress than anything else. They had struck out with the sex offender search, as no registered sex offender's homes had been damaged by the tornado. Alex had struggled with other cases, but at least she felt like it was moving along. This case seemed to be stuck in neutral.

"Gerald, can you do some computer work for me?"

"Yeah, I've got a light schedule. What am I looking for?"

Alex packed her purse inside her briefcase. "Broaden the area of registered sex offenders we're looking at and see if they have a history with only Hispanic victims. I'm going to go talk with Donna and see if she has heard any rumors in the Hispanic community."

* *

Donna Labrino was the head of Fleming County's welfare program. Being involved in the system for over thirty years, Donna knew more dirt around town than any police officer. Alex had made friends with Donna when she moved into Blandale three years earlier. They bonded because of their unusual heritage. By marrying into an Italian surname, Donna joked she was the only black Italian living in Ohio.

The nice thing about Fleming County was the county commissioners had bought land and built a number of buildings at the one site. Having all the county entities in one unified complex made access to other agencies a snap. So Alex grabbed her purse and walked across the expansive parking lot to the social services building and entered the back door for employees, which worked for anyone who possessed a county or state badge.

"What can I do for you Alex?" Donna inquired when she entered her office to find Alex perched behind her desk with her feet on the window sill.

Alex spun around and stood, "Just some question and answer."

Donna gave Alex a brief hug and started the tape recorder. The office was soon filled with Alex and Donna's voices, haggling over the names of welfare recipients and their addresses. While this droned on, Alex and Donna slipped into the adjoining conference room.

"Sorry to move us in here, but I can't get a bad reputation by consorting with the enemy."

Alex nodded. She understood that the public needed to see Donna as a Good Samaritan, not someone who worked closely with the police. "No sweat Donna, I've had conversations in worse places."

"Before we get down to business, I want to hear about the flowers you got. Rumor has it that you are actually in a serious relationship."

"I don't know how serious, it's only been one date," Alex replied with a smile. Donna had been trying to fix Alex up with every eligible man in the county. She believed it was her duty to find a good man for Alex.

"Anyone I might know?"

"Perhaps. Do you know Benjamin Princi?"

Donna gave a low whistle, "The author. Everybody in Fleming County knows who he is. My, My you do have some good taste. My sources tell me he is fine, girl!"

Alex laughed, "Yes he is quite fine. You would approve, he's also polite and a gentleman."

Donna cast a serious look, "You be careful around those quiet polite types. They act that way so you don't suspect what kind of animal they are in the bedroom."

"Well now that we're caught up on my love life, can I ask you a few questions?" Alex prodded, hoping to get the focus off of Ben and his supposed prowess in the bedroom.

"Go ahead honey."

"Have you heard any rumors about young girls being abducted from the migrant families?"

Donna fiddled with her braid. She was proud of her hair, which had started turning white after her thirtieth birthday. The nearly all white hair was always kept immaculate and usually in a perfectly braided French twist.

"I haven't heard anything, but you've got to remember only the people with papers come to see me. The ones without documentation avoid me like the plague, because they assume I'll turn them in since I work for the government."

Alex took a deep breath, wondering how much to divulge to her friend. "Can you do some covert digging? I've got a case with a number of young Hispanic victims and I think maybe it's tied in with the human trafficking operation in Ohio."

"Why haven't I heard anything about this? We've been trying to educate the families about how the human traffickers work, but I haven't heard anything about any deaths."

"It isn't public knowledge yet. I'm trying to do as much as possible before it gets out, and that is likely going to happen soon."

Donna absently stroked the braid, "All you need is info, and you're not looking to deport anyone. These families don't have any other options."

"Just info, you have my word."

"I'll ask around. Why don't you and your gentleman friend come over on Memorial Day for steaks? Angelo has been looking for a reason to fire up the grill."

Alex knew she needed this intel, so she would just have to get over her fear of being considered part of a couple with Ben. "Okay, call me and let me know what time."

Donna gave Alex a parting hug before they reentered her office and finished the charade. Alex stormed out of the office, slamming the door behind her while Donna complained loudly about the police trying to use Gestapo methods to get information.

Alex pulled out her cell phone once she hit the freeway. She'd been having a hard time concentrating most of the day, so she figured a phone call might do the trick.

He answered on the third ring.

"Hello?"

"Hello Ben, its Alex."

Ben settled back onto the porch swing. He'd been dozing in the sun, after finishing up with the sanding.

"Hi Alex, what are you up to? Catch any bad guys?"

"Not yet, but the day is still young. I wanted to see if you were free on Memorial Day for a barbeque."

Ben concentrated on the gentle swaying motion. He'd enjoyed the lunch date and he was intrigued with tonight's dinner date, but he was a little leery about locking himself into a regular routine. He'd told himself that he would take things slow this time and not jump in too fast.

Alex noticed the hesitation and knew Ben was feeling overwhelmed, "Hey my friend asked about us coming. She only knew about you because of your stunt with the flowers and everybody is spreading the gossip."

"Relax Alex, I'm not freaking out. I just don't want to rush or push you into anything too quickly."

"Right now there isn't "anything" – we're just two people going out on a couple of dates. I'm not looking for any type of commitment."

Ben could picture Alex's eyes, black with anger, "I didn't mean to imply anything, I'm just proceeding with some caution based on my track history."

Alex stuffed her anger back down, remembering she didn't know Ben well enough to know if he was trying to play mind games with her like her ex. "I'm sorry about that. I tend to get defensive rather quickly if I feel I'm being manipulated."

"That is the one thing I don't want to do, is push. I used to have issues with diving in too fast, so now I take things much slower."

"Okay then it's agreed we will just proceed cautiously and see how things play out."

Zoe gently closed the kitchen window as Ben ended the phone call. She'd never been concerned about the women Ben hooked up with, because they usually were the one night stand variety. This Alex seemed to be a different type of woman.

Ben found Zoe in the library, "Hey I'm going out for dinner tonight, that isn't a problem is it?"

Zoe looked up from her book and pushed her glasses onto her forehead, "So is this the policewoman you are going to dinner with?"

Ben smiled, "Yes, and her name is Alex. I wanted to make sure we didn't have any meetings or online presentations tonight."

Zoe shook her head, "No it's a free evening. Two dates in two days with the same woman, which is a new record for you by my records. She must be special."

Ben noted how slowly Zoe spoke and closely she was watching his reactions," I'm not sure what's going on. We talked earlier and are just going to take things as they come."

"Sounds like a good plan."

"Is there a problem that I'm not aware of?"

Zoe slid her glasses back down and peered up at Ben, "I just want to make sure you aren't getting yourself into a situation that could jeopardize your sobriety."

Ben squinted, "On that note of sobriety, do you think you could unlock the wine cellar so I could get a bottle of wine to take for dinner? It's strictly a thank you for dinner."

"I know that, because it would epically stupid for you to throw away this sobriety for one night of fun, and you know I'll be testing you tomorrow morning bright and early," Zoe replied as she rose to retrieve a bottle of Pinot.

****

Ben arrived five minutes early for dinner. He'd stopped to get a bouquet to go with the wine. Ben noted the house was small but tidy, with bare flowerbeds in the front. He assumed Alex kept things clean, but didn't allot the needed time to accessorize.

Alex answered the door with a smile. She was wearing worn jeans and an I love Mexico t-shirt. Her hair was pulled back into a ponytail, although there were numerous strands refusing to be contained.

"Hello Ben, come on in."

Ben stepped inside and handed Alex the wine and flowers, "I know you said to not bring anything, but I couldn't show up empty-handed."

Alex took the flowers and pulled Ben's head down for a quick kiss, "There that's out of the way. We got the end of the date kiss finished before I ruin our breath with onions."

Ben took a deep breath; he still tasted Alex's lips on his and wondered if she had left lipstick there. He could also smell something amazing coming from the kitchen.

"Follow me, I'll have you set the table while I finish this up and find a vase for the flowers."

Ben tagged along into the kitchen, trying to take inventory of the various pictures and notes attached to the refrigerator. "Just point me in the right direction, I can follow directions."

Alex saw Ben looking at the pictures, "The pictures at the top there are of my mother, she lives in San Antonio."

"She's a beautiful woman; I can see you're a product of some good genetics."

Alex tingled, "Flattery works every time."

The meal was like nothing Ben had ever eaten. Alex told him it was a family recipe that had been passed down for three generations. She admitted she had perfected it after numerous misadventures trying to impress her mother.

"That was fabulous Alex, I'd never have guessed you could cook like this. Dani made it sound like you ate out a lot."

Alex sipped the wine, "I don't usually cook, not because I don't know how, but more because of a lack of time or motivation."

Ben pushed back from the table, "Glad you felt motivated, because I'm definitely grateful. I'll do the dishes since you cooked if that's okay."

"You don't have to clean up, I'll take care of it later."

Ben ignored her and started gathering dishes, "Sorry you just relax and tell me about your day while I get this finished."

Alex spun her chair around so she could watch Ben as he worked. It had been an extremely long time since she'd cooked a meal for a man. "It was a typical day, following up leads on the pictures your boy found in the field."

"Sounds tedious."

"You have no idea. We have a list of registered sex offenders in the area and are cross referencing them against the area hit by the tornado. It isn't a needle in a haystack, but its close."

Ben was in a rhythm, washing, rinsing and placing things in the dishwasher. He found it easy to talk to Alex about her case and answering her questions about his meeting with Samantha this morning.

"So how do you normally relax in the evening?" Ben asked as he closed the dishwasher.

Alex eyed Ben carefully over the rim of her wineglass, "Well most evenings I end up soaking in my bathtub, listening to music, and maybe having a couple shots of tequila."

Ben hadn't expected her to be so candid, "I've got a twelve person hot tub at my house, since you enjoy soaking in a tub." As soon as he finished talking he realized he sounded like he was trying to get lucky.

Alex smiled at Ben's blush, "My mother would advise me to not trust a man inviting me over to use his hot tub, but since she's not here I guess I could accept your offer."

"That sounded like a line, but I swear I'm not trying to set anything up."

"Maybe you should try harder," Alex cooed as she went into her bedroom to pack a few items.

Ben paced in the living room, feeling more nervous than he had in a long time. He never intended to have Alex come back to his house, but it seemed like a nice way to end the date.

Alex returned a few minutes later with a packed black bag and a devilish smile, "I forgot to ask if I needed a swimsuit."

"Uh, um I'm sure we can figure something out or you could borrow something of Zoe's if necessary," Ben stammered.

"Just yanking your chain big boy. Do you want me to follow you there, or are you bringing me back later?"

"It would be easier to just take you and bring you home later."

Alex eyed Ben carefully, noting how embarrassed he seemed about this turn of events, "Okay, just don't think you can take advantage of me. I still have my gun and handcuffs."

"Oh my," Ben said with a big grin.

Ben called Zoe while they drove, making sure she was not using the hot tub tonight, indicating he would like to have some privacy.

"So will I get the chance to meet your housemate?"

Ben glanced over at Alex to see if she was teasing or serious, "I'm sure it would make things easier if I did just introduce you to Zoe. I'll warn you she's protective of me, she thinks I'm always one step from edge of falling off the wagon."

Alex replayed the information she had glanced at on her computer, noting that Zoe Meloncourt did not look anything like a manager should look like. Along with her model looks, Zoe tended to drape herself on Ben's arm when they attended the various country music events, much to the delight of the paparazzi.

"She is a very beautiful woman."

Ben nodded, "Yes she is, but mostly she's a pain in my butt. She keeps me organized and if I get off sequence it upsets her OCD and she has to pull me back on course."

Alex sat quietly, enjoying the rumble of the car. She had a hard time thinking that there was no history between Ben and Zoe. They were together all the time and they made a spectacular couple.

"You're sure this is okay, it isn't going to create any problems?"

"No, I just wanted to make sure she knew we were coming or she might invite herself to join us," Ben answered. He tried to not think about their recent conversation about Zoe having his child. "Oh there is also Winston, he'll most likely meet us at the lane."

Alex arched her eyebrow, "Is Winston a butler or something?"

Ben laughed, "I'm not rich enough to have a butler. Winston is my dog and he is extremely loving, but if dogs bother you I can have Zoe keep him upstairs."

"I'm fine with dogs. So are you going to show me what this car can do, or is it all dress up with no show."

Ben smiled, "I just wanted to make sure we were well outside of the city limits. I can't be caught speeding with one of Blandale's finest riding shotgun."

Ben dropped the accelerator and the car shot down the road. He got off the highway and used the back roads to show off a little. He knew Alex was enjoying herself as her face was flush and her eyes were sparkling like black pools.

Winston did not disappoint and was waiting at the garage with a shoe in mouth. His whining could be heard over the engine.

Alex was out of the car before Ben completely stopped, "Oh Ben he's gorgeous."

Winston dropped the shoe and rolled onto his back so Alex could rub his belly. He mocked Ben with his eyes as Alex rubbed his soft fur.

Ben led them inside, pointing out the bathroom to Alex and the living room which led to the hot tub on the balcony. Winston tagged along, following beside Alex, licking her hand.

Alex looked around the open area. The combined area of the kitchen, dining room and living room was almost as much footage as her entire house. She saw a few older pictures on the walls, which she assumed were Ben's parents or grandparents.

"Do you want anything to drink?" Ben asked while he got a bottle of water for himself.

Alex debated, she really wanted another glass of wine, but she knew Ben's sobriety issues, "I guess I'll just have water also."

Ben closed the refrigerator, "Hey, if you want something stronger it's okay. We have it downstairs and I'll just have Zoe get you something. You can change in the bathroom and I'll get the water going."

Ben headed out to the balcony while Alex used her detective instincts to examine the living room. The room was clean and organized, so either Ben was a neat freak or there was someone hired to clean. The furniture was new and coordinated, although Alex noticed the glaring omission of a television. Guys and televisions were like peanut butter and jelly, God ordained to be together.

The bathroom wasn't much different, either it was kept clean because it was the guest bathroom or Ben was obsessed about cleanliness. Alex thought about her own bathroom, which attracted dirt, hair, and foreign substances like a magnet.

Ben was sitting on the couch when Alex returned from the bathroom. She hadn't needed to change, her suit was underneath her clothes, but bathrooms revealed a lot about men.

"So how is the water coming?"

Ben stood as she returned, "It should be ready in about ten minutes." Alex sat on the couch and pulled Ben down beside her, "While we're waiting, there are a few things I need to get off my chest."

Ben took a deep breath. His experience had told him this was never a good way for a conversation to start. "Okay, I'm all ears."

"No you're not, and that's part of the problem. I've only been out with a couple of guys since my divorce and I think I do things to make sure the relationship doesn't progress."

"Alex, I'm lost. What are you trying to tell me?"

"I felt something between us and it scares me. I told myself seven years ago that I'd never allow myself to let a man have that power over me again."

Alex was looking at the floor by the time she finished talking. She gasped softly when Ben lifted her chin until she was looking directly into his green eyes. "It's okay Alex, I won't hurt you."

"I figured that out, you're a nice guy. I'm worried about hurting you because I'm afraid to commit."

Ben shook his head, "I'm not looking for a commitment. I'm just enjoying being with a beautiful woman."

"Whew, I'm glad that turned out fine. I was a little nervous about having this talk. You seemed like the total commitment type and I can't do that."

Ben pulled Alex into the crook of his arm, memorizing the smell of her hair and the feel of her body pressed against his. "Relax please. We've went out a couple of times and it was fun, I'm not looking to get married yet."

Alex turned to make sure he was joking, "Okay funny guy. My other question is where in the hell is your television?"

"I don't have one up here, but there's a big screen in the basement."

Alex leaned back against Ben's chest, "You are something else Mr. Princi."

Ben shrugged, "I'm not a big TV watcher, but I will watch movies occasionally, so it seemed a waste to have televisions everywhere."

"So you saved money on televisions and invested in a hot tub instead?"

"Something like that."

Alex shifted to look at Ben, "This hot tub isn't like your fail safe get lucky charm for the ladies I hope."

"No it isn't," Ben replied with a smile as he pulled Alex off the couch. He could have sat for hours talking to Alex and feeling her body pressed against his, but the hot tub overflowing would be a problem. It was also safer for Ben if he kept his distance so he wasn't tempted to hold and kiss her.

The water was at the correct level, so Ben turned the water off and threw in some aloe leaves. Zoe had taught him this trick while they were in Jamaica. The scent wafted around the house for hours and she swore by how soft her skin was from the leaves. Ben had learned how to grow the plants to have access whenever he wanted some.

Now that the water was perfect, Ben tried to decide on what music to play. Ben had lied about the money he saved on televisions, because it all went on his house being rewired for speakers throughout the house.

"Any musical preferences?"

"Surprise me, I like everything except heavy metal."

Ben put his iPod on shuffle and turned back towards the living room. Alex was standing there with her oversized shirt on, but she had removed her jeans. The shirt covered everything, but Ben couldn't take his eyes off her long legs.

"The, uh, water is ready whenever you are," Ben announced, purposefully staring at her eyes as he pulled off his shirt and climbed into the steaming water.

Alex slowly unbuttoned her shirt, knowing the effect it was having. When she finally discarded the shirt and climbed into the water, Alex knew her black bikini was having the desired effect.

Ben offered his hand to help Alex into the water. He couldn't help noticing the black bikini was contrasting nicely with her dark skin. Ben also caught a glimpse of a tattoo on her lower back.

Alex settled down into the water, positioning herself in front of a nozzle which sprayed directly on her lower back. She now knew her soaking tub at her house was never going to suffice after this.

"I hope the water temperature is okay."

"You have no idea how good this feels. What are the leaves floating around?"

"Pieces of aloe."

Alex leaned back enjoying the moonlight and the churning water. "I've got to ask. I would assume you learned the aloe trick from a lady?"

"You would be correct. Zoe taught me about the aloe effect."

Alex sat up quickly, "Speaking of your manager, is she here?"

Ben nodded, "Her bedroom is upstairs but since she knew I was having company, she will not be coming down."

"She knows you were bringing me here? Do you guys have a signal like a tie on the doorknob to let the other one know when the hot tub is occupied?"

Ben chuckled, "It's nothing as intricate as that. Neither of us has company over often, so I just mentioned to her that she would not be welcome in the tub tonight."

Alex laid her head back and gazed up at the star filled sky. This was exactly what she needed to get her mind off the case and her ex-husband. She could feel Ben's eyes on her.

"What are you thinking?"

Ben took a deep breath and broke his stare, "I was thinking this might have been a mistake."

Alex sat up quickly, that was not what she expected to hear. "Did I do something wrong?"

Ben realized he'd said the wrong thing, "No it's nothing like that. I just haven't been alone with a woman for a long time and I'm not sure where things will go."

Alex's face lit up, "I'll make easy for you. Come over here with me and we'll talk. I can assure you there will be no sex tonight, so no pressure."

Ben slid over next to Alex until his thigh touched hers. "You make me feel like a teenager who's never been around a woman before, that's why this is so weird."

Alex lay back again, enjoying the feel of the water and Ben's muscular thigh against her leg, "Tell me why someone with your qualifications is nervous around women."

Ben looked at Alex to make sure she was being serious, "Let me tell you a story."

12

Alex woke slowly as her phone vibrated next to her. She opened her eyes to the note on the mirror informing her coffee was ready. Alex couldn't remember the last time she slept this well.

Ben had walked her to the master bedroom last night and gently kissed her goodnight. Alex knew she could have taken his hand and pulled him into the bed, but after hearing his past she knew slow and steady would have to work.

After pulling on her jeans and a shirt, Alex wandered out into the kitchen to the gurgling coffee. She poured herself a cup and went to the window to watch Ben practice some form of yoga on the deck. He was wearing some pajama looking bottoms and his upper body was glistening with sweat.

Alex watched with awe as Ben contorted his muscular body into position after position, noting that he was a seriously sculpted man.

"The view is nice isn't it?"

Alex turned to stare at the tall, beautiful woman in the silk dressing gown, which did little to cover her obvious curves. Zoe Meloncourt in the flesh.

"Hello, I'm Zoe," she announced, shaking Alex's hand before pouring herself a cup of coffee.

"Alex."

Zoe smiled slowly, "This is some good progress for Ben if you spent the night."

Alex shook her head, "No it's not like that, I stayed in the bedroom – alone. I'm not sure where Ben slept."

Now it was Zoe's turn to shake her head, "Sounds like him. He finally invites a beautiful woman over and he still is the perfect gentleman."

They stood together watching Ben take some final cleansing breaths, sipping their coffee.

"Speaking of being a perfect gentleman. Ben tells me your relationship is purely platonic," Alex stated, trying to keep any question out of her tone.

Zoe smiled, "It's probably more than platonic, but more business oriented than emotional."

Alex noted the wistful look in Zoe's eyes as she spoke, realizing she probably had feelings for Ben, but he was clueless. "I hope I'm not interrupting anything, or rocking the boat."

Zoe finished her coffee, "Nothing of the sort. I can't tell you the last time Ben had two dates with the same woman, so good for him."

Alex could feel Zoe staring, "Is there something else?"

"Just don't hurt him. He's got a lot of baggage and is really skeptical of jumping into any type of relationship."

"Duly noted."

Ben pulled his shirt back on and wiped the sweat off his forehead, trying not to focus on Zoe and Alex talking in the kitchen. They were both smiling, but he thought it looked like two cats circling each other, feeling each other out.

"I see you two have met, sorry I wasn't in here to take care of that," Ben said.

"We're big girls," Zoe replied.

Alex nodded, "Not a problem. I hate to be a bother, but I need to get back to my house so I can get to work."

Ben took a few minutes to slip on some clean clothes and hustled back down to the kitchen. The last thing he wanted was Zoe inserting herself into any type of long standing dialogue with Alex.

Thankfully Zoe was not in the kitchen when Ben returned. "I'm ready to go now, sorry for the delay."

Alex set her coffee cup in the sink and took a quick inventory. Ben had slipped into some worn jeans and a t-shirt and clearly taken time to brush his teeth.

"You know men have it so easy to get ready. I need at least thirty minutes before I'm ready to let anyone see me," Alex said with a smile, while tucking some wayward strands behind her ears.

Ben returned her smile as he placed the coffee mug in the dishwasher, "I can't imagine how thirty minutes could possibly make you look any better."

Alex chuckled, "Okay mister writer man, you sure know how to make a girl feel good, but we've got to go. I've got an overprotective partner who will be grilling me for showing up late."

* *

Alex took the time to bring a box of donuts for the crew, hoping it would cover for being twenty minutes late to work.

Gerald eyed the donuts carefully while everyone pushed to get their favorite flavor. Alex knew she wasn't fooling him, but he had the good sense to wait until everyone was gone before he started his interrogation.

"So I didn't get any of your kind?" Alex asked innocently.

"You know if I eat one, Janice will smell it on my breath and have me doing some kind of bizarre workout to burn it out of my system. It's not worth the aggravation."

Alex studied the paperwork intently, "So any new developments?"

Gerald watched her carefully, "No new developments. Are we going to play this game?"

"What do you want me to say Gerald? I had dinner with Ben last night and I got to work late."

"I hope you were late for a good reason."

Alex flicked her eyes to see if Gerald was serious and noted the twinkle in his eyes, "I don't kiss and tell, so get to work."

Gerald started dialing, "Hell you barely kiss, I never expected you to tell."

* *

Ben headed straight to the shower after returning from dropping Alex off at her house. The ride back seemed to be more tense than last night and Ben wondered what that was about. He'd felt some of the tension when he came inside from his yoga and found Zoe and Alex talking.

Zoe stopped tapping at her laptop when Ben came into the kitchen, "So Alex seems nice."

Ben grabbed the orange juice and poured a glass, "Real subtle Zoe."

"Well I tried. So let's have it, tell me about her. Alex is nothing like the little birds you usually choose."

Ben nodded, "Fair enough. I don't know, there's something about her that intrigues me. I'm not sure if it's because she's a detective, or that she's closer to my age."

"There is something to be said for dating closer to your peer age group. Your usual birds haven't been out of prep school all that long, it's no wonder they can't hold your attention."

Ben smiled, thinking about some of the disastrous dates he'd been on the past couple of years. He questioned if he chose them on purpose to ensure he wouldn't form any kind of relationship.

"Do you remember when I took Chrissy to the CMA's last year?"

Zoe laughed, "She's exactly who I was thinking of. She poured herself into that ridiculous outfit and then passed out within thirty minutes."

Ben held up a finger, "In her defense, she told me later she hadn't eaten in two days and the champagne was too much for her."

"Whatever her reason, it was classic seeing you carry her out of the awards show. Also I really doubt that she was an engineering student."

"I do think she was in college to find a husband, but remember you set her up with me."

Zoe huffed, "I would hardly call it that. We surfed through that stupid dating site and she seemed to be a suitable match."

"She did have some good attributes."

Zoe snorted, "Those were fake, love. No way that skinny little bird had a chest like that naturally."

"If you say so," Ben said casually as he headed out to the barn. He needed to do some work on the cars to help clear his head. Zoe had already text his schedule to him earlier and this was going to be his free time for the day. She knew Ben had to have some cushion built into his day so he could tinker around, or he got irritable.

The sanding project allowed Ben to just concentrate on the rhythmic motion he developed while jamming to his iPod. He'd created a loop just for his work on the cars, and the speakers pounded away with rock and heavy metal.

Two hours later he headed back inside, covered with fine dust and grime from the car. He stripped down to his boxers on the porch and headed for his room.

Zoe was still working in the dining room when Ben walked through. She considered making a humorous comment, but decided instead to just enjoy the view. She'd set up a Skype meeting with Trevor for later this afternoon, and she needed Ben to be focused on work. She knew he used his garage time to unwind and get his thoughts straight. Zoe tried to stay out of the garage because it was dirty and full of tools she had no idea what they did.

When Ben emerged again from the shower and headed for the porch, he realized Zoe was still in the dining room, "Hey sorry if you were in here when I went through earlier."

Zoe smiled, "Remember I've seen you with a lot less than your boxers."

"Still, it was not considerate. Are we still on for the meeting with Trevor?"

Zoe pointed to the clock, "You've got about thirty minutes to eat something before the meeting."

Ben rummaged in the refrigerator, "Do you know what he wants?"

"Trevor claims he has a great idea to further market the music, but he's not giving up any specifics."

Ben spooned the yogurt onto his plate and topped it with some granola, "That's my boy."

Zoe stole a bite of the yogurt when Ben sat down at the table, "Speaking of mysterious, how did your meeting go with the college student yesterday. I forgot all about her with everything else going on."

"She is nice, but there was something off about her. I've been trying to think about it, but it just keeps dancing out of my grasp."

Alex stopped in the captain's office before leaving, "Excuse me sir, but we might have a solid lead on the case. Hopefully we'll be able to provide something for the next press conference."

Kilpatrick looked up from his tablet, "Okay Milnero, find me something. The press is going to tear us up if we can't deliver."

Alex met Gerald in the lobby and they headed for his sedan. Gerald had no problem letting her take the lead in the case, but he refused to let her drive when they rode together.

"Robert Griffin, fifty-four years old, a Tier III sex offender with lifetime registration requirements. How does somebody like that hide that he rents a storage unit?" Alex asked while skimming the detailed printout.

"Come on Alex, nobody hides stuff better than sex offenders. They are sneakiest criminal you encounter."

Gerald had gotten the paperwork from the storage facility which was obliterated by the tornado. The owner had been more than happy to turn over his records, especially once he heard that one of his renters was a person of interest in an ongoing investigation. What they found has a questionable unit that was rented by Griffin Roberts, who paid in cash each month, but had no corresponding documentation. Gerald cross referenced the name with registered sex offenders and it led them to Robert Griffin, who lived on the edge of Blandale.

"You would have thought he would do better at hiding it," Alex said as they parked around the corner from Griffin's apartment. "And come on, switching your first and last names is not terribly ingenious."

Gerald pounded on the door while Alex stood off the stoop, "Mr. Griffin, open up."

Alex edged around the corner of the building, trying to see if there was a back door. There weren't any visible windows or doors leading out the back of the apartment, but Alex wasn't taking any chances. Gerald continued to hammer on the door with no success, while Alex slipped between the hedge and the house. The rear entrance was off to the side and she crept up to peek inside.

"Hey Gerald, come back here," Alex yelled as she pulled her gun.

She could see someone's ankles inside lying on the floor, around the corner of the refrigerator. Gerald peered inside and called 911.

"Your call boss, do we break in the door?" Gerald asked while holstering his weapon.

Alex flicked her eyes at Gerald and mouthed the countdown. Gerald kicked the flimsy storm door with his size 13 shoes and it burst open.

"Police, Mr. Griffin?"

Alex stepped inside and felt the emptiness of the house. She would check each room, but she knew it was vacant. The most pressing concern was finding out if the body in the kitchen needed ambulatory assistance. The discarded shotgun and head wound told Alex she could call 911 and cancel the need for an ambulance.

Gerald bent down over the body and squinted at the remains, "Looks like Griffin's last registration photo."

Alex slipped on the latex gloves she kept in her pocket and started looking around the kitchen. A note on the counter caught her attention.

Sorry, Couldn't take it anymore.

"Got what looks like suicide note here," Alex announced.

Alex and Gerald stepped outside and waited for the crime scene unit to arrive. It was always the hardest thing for detectives to do, but they often missed evidence or compromised it if they went looking for more answers without the CSU approval. They would already be unhappy that they went inside without having booties on, but that was the nature of the beast.

"Good work kid, if we find some evidence to link Griffin to the pictures, then this case is closed and the captain is going to be very happy," Gerald announced while chewing on his cigar.

Alex smiled, "You found the connection, but it does look good. Just need that evidence."

* *

The text came in shortly thereafter.
"Police on scene, problem solved."
He read the text twice and deleted it. It seemed that their problems were over and without any damage. He was going to have to think about a long term plan because the rules had been broken. The protocol was established long ago and it was designed to be fail safe, but taking the pictures and keeping them was unthinkable. It was bad enough that some of the girls were being pulled out of pipeline, but he'd known this was happening. He'd have to devise an appropriate punishment to ensure this didn't happen again and to make sure everyone knew who was in charge.

He'd looked the other way when his son first started with his hobby in high school. There would be a group of fifteen headed to Toledo and somehow only fourteen would make it there. There were excuses and reasons why one hadn't made it, but he knew his son was indulging in his own carnal pursuits. His suppliers were alerting him that something needed to be done about the loss of product, but he turned a blind eye to his only child. Now this was blowing up and he was going to make sure everyone knew the rules applied to everyone, family or not.

* *

Ben leaned back in his chair and shook his head. Zoe was asking numerous questions about the fine details, because Trevor got hung up on the big picture. His grand plan involved opening up the ranch like a boarding house slash recording studio for four unsigned artists, and possibly filming it as a reality show.

"You know Trevor, we'll need to have Thomas look at the legalities of this venture before we proceed," Zoe said as she fired off emails on her phone.

Trevor's face broke into a huge smile on the screen, "Already done, love. I approached him about this a couple of weeks ago."

"Good job being proactive and don't ever call me love."

Trevor's laughter filled the room.

Ben sat and thought about this step. He'd started to ease back into the public spotlight a little more recently, but he wasn't sure about this big of a step. Trevor wanted him to be there for most of the filming to add the authenticity.

"I don't want to be involved with the filming," Ben announced. "I'm fine with the project, but I'm not willing to relocate just to be part of the filming."

Trevor took this in stride, "Whatever, I'm sure the public would rather see me anyways. You can come down for special guest appearances and you could bring along Zoe for the bikini episode."

Zoe looked up from her phone and gave Trevor the finger.

"Okay, so Thomas will be contacting you within the next few weeks so we can get this project rolling," Trevor announced as he signed off.

Zoe watched Ben as he rolled his shoulders and drank his water. She knew he was running this project through his head and trying to foresee what major problems could arise.

"It might help if you talked out loud."

Ben opened his eyes and smiled at Zoe, "See this is why I don't need to ever get married, I've got you to read my mind."

Zoe put her phone down, "Don't patronize me, you don't like this venture."

"Logically it makes good business sense, but the idea of being on a reality show is not something I'm cut out for."

Zoe disagreed, but thought it better to not go there now. "I agree with Trevor on this, but I'll never admit it. And there is no way I'm participating in any bikini episode."

Ben laughed, "Hey some national exposure might help you with your baby problem."

"I don't have a baby problem. I've got it all figured out, but I am stuck with a reluctant donor."

"That's not funny."

Zoe stood her ground, "It wasn't meant to be. I've been checking my ovulation charts and I'm at my peak for the next forty eight hours to get pregnant. I don't suppose you'd be interested in a quickie before you head over to Chet's."

Ben knew his facial expression was not good. "I thought we agreed to think about this before discussing it further."

"No you wanted time to think and stall, I would like to get pregnant before I am forty."

"I'm not stalling," Ben responded.

"Really, because from where I'm standing it sure looks like stalling."

Ben was going to argue, but ultimately knew Zoe was right. He was terrified she had even asked him, and now he was searching for any way to get her focused on something else. He'd hoped Trevor's idea was going to be that thing, but it had come up again.

"Hey I've got to get over to Chet's."

Zoe waved him off, "Go, but remember I'll be here when you get back. Oh and is your girlfriend coming over tonight?"

"She's not my girlfriend," Ben said over his shoulder as he sprinted out the door.

Ben got out of the barn as quickly as he could, hoping that he wouldn't have to deal with Zoe right now. She hadn't mentioned anything about her request for a couple of days, so Ben had hoped maybe she was not serious and just yanking his chain. Clearly he had misjudged her intentions if she was calculating her ovulation cycle.

Trevor's idea was actually fairly sound, Ben thought as he drove towards town. This presented a great opportunity to snare some of the new talent in Nashville before they floundered or got picked up by the existing recording labels. Trevor could give the recruits some hands on experience with the process and also some fact based stories of the potholes on the road to stardom. They'd already made some inroads with the young talent by opening the ranch, so the next step would be to ride the reality television wave.

* *

Alex walked back to the car with Gerald. She'd just finished filling Captain Kilpatrick in with the preliminary results from the CSU, which seemed to indicate they had found the perp. There were a few more printed photos that had been found tucked into a hollowed out book in the living room. Alex was certain they were identical to the ones sitting in evidence right now.

"I'm sure Kilpatrick will take that information to the press," Gerald said as he pulled away from the crime scene.

Alex nodded, "I'll feel much better after we have all of the tests back, but Griffin looks good for it."

They drove along in silence. Gerald knew Alex liked to have time to process and decompress after solving a case, so he just drove. Alex cracked her window and let the wind blow through her hair. She'd always enjoyed riding with her mother in Texas with the windows down, and that was where her mind went every time she did this.

"So do you have a date with lover boy tonight again?"

Alex glared at Gerald, "No there is not a date tonight, and his name is Ben."

Gerald parked the car in the back in his reserved spot. "Maybe you should bring him around to the house sometime, so Janice can meet him."

"I don't think so. It sounds like a good excuse for you to give him the third degree."

Gerald feigned shock and then shrugged his shoulders, "You got me. I need to make sure this guy is okay, before you start getting serious."

Alex grabbed her bag and headed for the office, not knowing how to deal with all these questions. She never expected to have to ever answer any questions about her private life again. Being with Ben was enjoyable, and she could tell he was the type of guy who wasn't just looking for a good time, but she didn't know if she could deliver more at this time.

She was typing in her notes by the time Gerald made it back to the office.

"Look I'm not trying to pry; I just want to make sure you don't get hurt."

Alex stopped and looked up, "I know, but I don't think I know what's going on with us yet, so it's hard to answer your questions."

Gerald slumped into his chair, "I don't give advice often, but here is some. I know that son of a bitch hurt you years ago, but not every man is like him."

Alex blinked back the tears. She knew Gerald knew about her marriage with Robert, but she didn't think he knew all the details. It also hurt to have someone care enough to be that blunt with her.

"Now dammit stop crying and do something."

Alex came over and hugged Gerald from behind, "You're such an asshole, thanks for the advice."

* *

Ben dropped the car off at Chet's and drove his Durango back towards the house. He'd spent over two hours with Chet, discussing paint schemes and what project to work on next. Ben enjoyed hanging out at the shop and bullshitting with Chet, but he knew he was dragging his feet so he didn't have to go back to face Zoe.

Great he thought, I am a coward.

The phone vibrated on the seat, and Ben checked the id.

"What's up Zoe? I know I'm running late."

"You need to inform me when you have your little unscheduled meetings with college students, because she's been calling here ever since you left."

Ben sighed, "Okay I'll call her."

"She sounded nice, and I must say she was asking a lot of questions. Does she know you have a girlfriend?"

"Bye Zoe and she's not my girlfriend."

Ben ended the call before Zoe could respond, knowing she was going to make another comment. He wondered what Samantha wanted now, since he was pretty sure the earlier interview was all she needed for her paper.

Ben located Samantha's number on his phone and called.

"Hello, Ben?"

"Hi Samantha, I heard you were trying to get in touch with me."

There was no response. "Yes, I need to meet with you again if that's possible."

Ben frowned as he drove, "What's this about? I thought we covered everything for your paper."

"It's about the paper, could I just please meet with you?"

"How quickly can you get to my house?"

"Ten minutes, I was already in town when you called me back."

Ben rattled off the address for Samantha to put in her GPS. He hung up and headed for the house to prepare for whatever she wanted this time.

Zoe met him at the door with some papers to sign.

"What are these?"

"It's the paperwork to renounce all your parental rights to our baby."

Ben was in mid signature when he stopped, "Are you out of your …"

Zoe threw her head back with a laugh, "That was priceless. I'm joking, it's the releases for the project in Nashville."

Ben continued signing with a frown, "It wasn't that funny."

"Sure it was and now I know how to yank your chain whenever I feel like it. So to speak."

Ben shook his head, "Anyways, Samantha is stopping by shortly to ask me some more questions or something. Could you stick around?"

Zoe hesitated as she gathered the signed documents, "Am I a chaperone?"

"Sure that's what we'll call you. I just get this vibe with her and I don't want anybody insinuating anything."

Zoe finished with her paperwork and sat down, "Interesting you didn't want a chaperone last evening with Alex. She's very beautiful by the way."

Ben checked to see how sincere Zoe was being, "I didn't think I needed a chaperone with Alex, because nothing was going to happen. I agree with you she is very pretty."

Zoe turned to the approaching car in the drive, "Well, well it looks like you have another pretty young thing interested in you."

Ben opened the door when Samantha approached, noting that she looked much different than at their previous meeting. She was wearing a grey business suit, which her blonde hair played off of nicely. She'd also done some subtle things with her makeup, bringing out her eyes.

"Samantha come on in. This Zoe Meloncourt, my manager."

Samantha shook Zoe's hand and sat in the offered chair, "This is weird, but I'm just going to throw it out there. I'm not a student and there never was a paper to write."

Ben looked from Samantha to Zoe, not understanding what this meant. "So you just wanted to talk with me?"

"Yes, but it's a little more in depth than that."

Zoe was tapping away on her laptop at the table, glancing occasionally at Samantha.

"So what do you want Samantha?" Ben continued, trying to control the edge coming into his voice.

Zoe looked up and stopped tapping, "Stop talking Ben. She's a reporter with the Channel 2."

Samantha stood up, "Wait. It's true but it's not what you think."

"You don't know what I'm thinking."

"True, but I can tell from your expression that you're really pissed. I wanted this story about you so I could get a promotion."

Ben walked into the kitchen, "Oh that's great, use my interview to further your career. I don't know why I'd be pissed."

Samantha tried to follow Ben, but he put up his hand.

"Just get out."

Tears ran down Samantha's face, "I wanted to be honest with you. After meeting you and hearing about your wife. I couldn't go through with it and I knew I needed to tell you the truth."

Ben opened the door, "So glad you got that off your chest."

Samantha ran to her car and pulled out, barely missing the car headed up the drive. She couldn't see clearly with her mascara running, but she was pretty sure it was the detective from Blandale investigating the Polaroid case.

Zoe continued scanning her laptop, giving Ben the basic aspects of Samantha Collins bio from the website.

"She fooled me good."

Zoe glanced over at Ben as he lay on the couch, "Well I'm sure she played her part very well. I know men have issues with thinking straight when a pretty little blonde bats their eyes. They don't even pay attention to the questions they are answering."

Ben looked up, "Listen she didn't look like that when we met. She looked like a college kid in jeans and a sweatshirt. I don't think she was batting her eyes at me."

"If you say so. Uh oh, you've got more company," Zoe announced as she maneuvered into the living room.

Ben got off the couch to see Alex walking up the path from her car. He opened the door and walked out to meet her.

"I didn't expect to see you today."

Alex smiled and pointed over her shoulder, "I hope I leave happier than she did. She almost ran into me, but I doubt she could see through all of the tears."

Ben looked at his feet, "Yeah I'm responsible for that. She lied to me about a project and I found out she was a reporter."

This seemed to make perfect sense to Alex as she nodded in understanding. "So she was the college student. Interesting to see you do have a hard side to you."

"I guess it's usually under wraps. Why don't you come inside?"

Alex did a quick inventory of the kitchen as she entered; noting Zoe was in the living room, pretending to work on her laptop. Ben walked in, frowning at Zoe, who seemed to show little interest in taking his hint.

"Hello Alex, I didn't know you were coming over or I would have made myself scarce."

Alex doubted this, but went with it anyway. "I didn't plan on coming over either, but we got a break in the case, so I had some extra time while we wait for forensic results."

"So you solved the case."

"It looks like it, but I won't say it until all the evidence confirms it."

Zoe glanced at Ben, "Sounds like you don't relax unless all of your I's are dotted and t's crossed."

Alex wasn't sure if she was talking about police cases or her personal life, but the statement hit closer to home than she was willing to admit.

"Could we step outside and talk?" Alex asked as she pulled Ben back towards the door.

Zoe watched Ben go outside and his shoulders tensing up expecting bad news. He always reminded her of a little boy who made his body rigid to deal with upcoming pain.

Ben slumped down in one of the chairs while Alex paced. He knew this wasn't going to be a good conversation, mainly because Alex wanted this dialogue held outside without Zoe's interference.

Alex knew her pacing was making Ben more anxious, but she always thought better when she was moving. She also didn't want Zoe inserting herself into the conversation, and she seemed unlikely to leave the living room area.

"Can you stop moving for a second? You're making me really nervous."

Alex stopped, smiled, and continued pacing, "I need to move. I've been trying to formulate this speech in my head the whole way over here."

"A prepared speech is never good," Ben said, hoping to sound nonchalant.

"Here it is. I like you. We've had fun being together and I'd like to continue doing stuff."

"I sense a but coming."

Alex frowned, "There is, but not what you expect. I'm really rusty at this relationship thing, so I might need some space at times. I know my instinct is to push when I feel someone is getting too close and I'll try not to do that with you."

Ben smiled, "Okay that wasn't so bad. So you're saying that we are both cautious about being in a relationship and that we both might need space at times."

"You make it sound simple, trust me it was much more complex during my drive over here."

"How about we agree to just let things proceed and stop blowing it up into something more than it is at this time?"

Alex blew out the breath she's been holding, "I agree this wasn't nearly as bad as it played out in my head while drove over here. So I've had a good day and I'd like to celebrate."

"I'm all ears, what did you have in mind?"

They decided to bypass going out and Ben threw on some steaks. He manned the grill while Alex and Zoe searched the refrigerator for ingredients to make a salad. Zoe offered to give them some alone time, but Alex insisted she stay and enjoy the meal with them.

Alex thought keeping Zoe near was a great way of making sure things didn't go too far too fast with Ben. She didn't trust herself to handle the raw yearnings she felt for him. It had been a long time since she wanted more than a quick roll in the hay, but it would so easy with Ben. He presented a very simple solution to her pent up sexual energy, but he came with some scary baggage. He kept himself walled in so no one could get in to hurt him, so letting her close would involve more than just a sweaty bout of sex.

Alex nearly cut her finger slicing a cucumber, as she imagined how nice that would likely be.

"Doing okay over there?" Zoe asked as she rinsed the multiple types of lettuce.

Alex nodded, "Just day dreaming a little bit and not paying attention."

"Our boy will do that to a girl."

Alex stopped cutting and focused on Zoe, "Can you give me some background? It's clear Ben's isolated himself, I'm just not sure why."

Zoe tore the lettuce into bite size pieces, watching Ben on the deck. He was leaning on the railing, waiting for the perfect time to flip the meat.

"I don't know how much he's shared, and I don't feel it's my place to give it all to you. But I will provide an over view."

Alex mover over closer to the sink so Zoe could speak more freely.

"These are observations, not facts. Just a disclaimer before I begin. Ben was extremely depressed following his wife's death, possibly suicidal. He never went to any professional or had any therapy and I think he began using substances to ease his emotional pain. Since he has gotten sober, I believe Ben has wrapped being sober up with not having any intimate relationships. He's terrified of falling back into that black hole again. Ben's been on a sexual sabbatical for the past two years or so, which indicates how much he fears opening himself back up."

Alex mixed the ingredients for the salad while she weighed Zoe's words. She knew there was a troubled past, but she wasn't aware of the other factors.

"Sorry to throw all of that out there, but the rest you need to get from him."

Alex nodded and peeked out the window at Ben as he closed the grill, "I appreciate the information, it just kind of complicates things."

"I figured as much. I think it'd be great if you'd just screw like bunnies."

"Thanks for the visual, but I have to be careful," Alex replied. "I can't just jump in bed with him for the sake of sex."

Zoe turned, "No probably not. It won't just be sex for him, although getting laid would help him relax."

Alex laughed, "Huh, my partner told me the same thing yesterday. Too bad Ben wouldn't just consent to a quick roll in the hay."

"I doubt it would be quick and his childhood guilt would eat him up for just having sex without a serious relationship."

Alex looked at Zoe carefully, "So you haven't tried to take your relationship to the next level with Ben."

Zoe grabbed Alex's hands, "I've considered pushing things with Ben at times, but he's made it clear I am just his friend. When you combine that with our business relationship, Ben isn't willing to risk losing that for a romance."

Alex wasn't sure what to think about this. Ben lived in this house with an incredibly beautiful intelligent woman and she was going to have to trust that there wasn't anything there between them.

"Okay, any pointers on how best to handle Ben."

Zoe laughed, "I use the harsh approach with him, so just be honest with him. And if you're interested in getting laid, I'd recommend taking the initiative because he moves like molasses."

"So walking into his bedroom naked might get the point across?"

Zoe snorted, "Please tell me how that goes if you do it, because if he doesn't have a heart attack then he should be able to figure out what is supposed to happen next."

Ben came back inside with the platter of steaks and found Zoe and Alex snickering and speaking with conspiratorial looks. He knew he was being discussed by the numerous glances he caught through the window to make sure he wasn't coming in yet. He hoped they could get along, but maybe having the two of them bonding might not be such a good idea.

"So who's ready to eat?"

Both women turned and smiled.

Zoe cleaned up after dinner and sent Alex and Ben for a tour of the farm. She thought the alone time would be good for them, so they could find out if they had something to work with or not. Zoe wondered if pushing them together was such a good idea, but she had assured Alex she wasn't interested. Now she just needed to believe it for herself.

Alex was impressed with the updated barn, which Ben had turned into his own personal car lot. She knew he was a car guy, but she didn't know exactly how deep he was into it until she saw the numerous cars parked inside.

Ben grabbed Alex's hand, "Come with me, I've got something else to show you if you're up for a little hike."

"Are you trying to lure me off into the woods with you?"

Ben felt his face flushing, "I wouldn't say lure, but yes I want you to come into the woods with me. Winston will go along and make sure you're safe."

Alex laughed as she headed down the well-worn path with Winston running up ahead sniffing at all the bushes. She noticed it was getting quieter and more isolated as they headed further on the path. The path was getting less distinctive and Ben kept urging her along as the bushes and trees started closing in.

"Where is Winston?"

Ben chuckled and pulled Alex along, "He knows where we're headed, so knowing him he's already there and waiting."

"Is this going to be worth it, because I'm not feeling too comfortable right now?"

"Trust me, it is worth the walk. So this means you aren't used to being in the woods?"

Alex smiled grimly, "I grew up in the city, worked in the city, and plan to die in the city. Being all self-sufficient and isolated is not something that appeals to me."

Ben walked silently, hoping that the surprise might help change Alex's mind about country living.

"Okay we're almost there. I need you to close your eyes."

Alex stopped, "Wait a minute. The path ends at those bushes. Do you really have a surprise out here?"

Ben grabbed her hand, "Yes now close your eyes, I'll lead you to the surprise."

Alex let herself be led, enjoying the feel of Ben's hand with hers. "Full disclosure here, if this involves any kind of animal other than Winston, I'm really going to be pissed."

Ben laughed as he pushed aside the bushes and hanging vines, "Okay you can open your eyes."

Alex cracked her eyes to peek, fully expecting something bad. "Oh Ben, it's beautiful."

She walked forward and turned to take in everything. The pond was surrounded with plants and flowers on three sides, with a dock and beach area in the other. The last thing she saw was the picnic area off in the shade of some trees with the little cabin tucked back into the tree line.

Winston woke up from his nap on the dock and sprinted over to them.

"See I told you he'd be here waiting for us."

Alex turned in circles, trying to take in the totality of the area. "Did you do all of this?"

Ben shook his head, "No I had some ideas and plans for what to do with the pond. I always knew about the pond back here from when we were kids. Old man Deeter wouldn't let anybody come back here, but it was the unofficial hot spot for fishing and other extracurricular activities."

Alex smiled, "So you brought me back to your high school hook up spot?"

"No unfortunately no hooking up for me out here."

"Uh huh, I bet. Is that a tire swing over there?"

Ben looked over into the trees, "Yeah, it was there when I bought the place and I couldn't bring myself to get rid of it. It's my link to Old man Deeter."

Alex walked over and took Ben's hands, "I think it's a very romantic place."

Ben was going to respond, but she stopped his talking when Alex pulled his face down for a kiss. She ran her fingers through his short hair and flicked her tongue into his mouth, teasing him. Ben tried to maintain his poise, but felt himself going over the edge. He grabbed her hair with one hand and thrust his tongue into Alex's mouth while pulling her body tight against his with his other hand.

Alex ran her fingernails down Ben's chest, while trying not to whimper as she felt his manhood rigid against her stomach. She had meant to coax and tease Ben a little, but this was going to a four alarm fire quickly.

Ben came up for air, "Whoa, okay that was great, but I've got something else to show you."

Alex looked down at Ben's bulging crotch, "I know what I'm hoping to see."

Ben looked away and pulled himself away from Alex before he did something he would regret. "No the real reason I brought you here."

He took Alex's face and tilted it up into the group of oak trees at the far corner of the cabin.

"Is that a tree house?"

Ben nodded, "It is, but it's not like any tree house you've probably ever been in."

Ben took her hand and pulled her over to the trees where a lone rope dangled. Alex hadn't even noticed the rope as it looked like the various vines which ran throughout the forest. She had no idea the tree house was even up there, as it blended in perfectly with the canopy of trees.

A rope ladder dropped to the ground when Ben gave it a sharp pull.

"After you milady."

Alex grinned and pulled herself onto the ladder, climbing quickly up. "I guess this is one way to ensure some solitude."

Ben followed Alex up the ladder, forcing himself to not look up and enjoy the great view he would have of her climbing above his head.

"I always enjoyed the pond, and it just came to me one day to have the tree house built. The trees seemed to almost beg to have it completed."

Alex reached the landing area and pulled herself upright. She was on a small deck which wrapped around the enclosure. Alex could see she had climbed at least twenty or so feet off the ground. She really wanted to open the door and check out everything, but she forced herself to wait until Ben had hoisted himself onto the deck.

"You didn't have to wait for me."

Alex smiled and pulled Ben in for a quick kiss, "It didn't seem right to just go in without having you here to lead me on the tour. Whoa did this deck just move?"

Ben chuckled, "Yes it did, but it's designed to do that. The architect explained it's the best way to build something like this because the trees need to move, therefore the house must also shift."

Alex took a deep breath as Ben opened the door. The interior was completely modernized, but on a smaller scale than a traditional home. There was chair and couch in one corner, with a wooden ladder leading up to a second level. Alex noted there was a small refrigerator and grill in the other corner of the room.

"What's behind the closed door over there?"

"That would be a bathroom."

Alex stared at Ben intently, wondering if he was messing with her.

Ben could see the questions, "It really is. The pond is fed with a natural spring, so it wasn't that difficult to have the plumbers engineer access to water. I also had solar panels added, so it's fairly self-contained."

Alex walked around the room, turning to take in all of the views and nuances of the house. She'd never been in anything quite like this before.

"So what's up the ladder?"

Ben blushed, "It's a bedroom, but you don't have to check it out."

"Are you kidding?" Alex took off and started climbing the ladder.

Ben sat in the chair, hoping Alex knew he hadn't brought her out here to try and seduce her. He was wondering what was taking Alex so long when she hung her head upside down through the access hole.

"This is phenomenal. Do you ever spend the night here, because it has to be a spectacular sight with the skylights in the roof?"

Ben nodded, "I spend the night here about once a month. It's a nice place to just get away and chill out."

Alex smiled, "For somebody who chills out here, you look extremely uptight. Does it bother you to have me up here in your bedroom?"

"Something like that."

"Let me guess. This is the guaranteed for sure 'gonna get laid' deal closer."

Ben glanced up to see if Alex was serious and found her grinning down at him. "I don't think I've had a woman up here before."

"Zoe doesn't come out here?"

"She's come out to the cabin, but she thinks it beneath her to climb a rope ladder."

"Well it's her loss, this place is magnificent. Why don't you come up here and show me what these buttons do? I promise it will be safe."

Ben eased out of the chair as Alex pulled her head back up into the room. He started climbing slowly, hoping that the pressure building in his crotch would subside before he reached the top.

Any hope of Ben's pressure relief occurring ended when Ben reached the top and found Alex lying on his bed, staring out of the skylights. Her dark hair was fanned out on the pillow, and her shirt had ridden up giving Ben a glimpse of her tanned midriff.

Ben stood along the wall and pointed to the remote Alex held, "The upper buttons control the shades on the windows. The button in the middle can dim the lights. The toggle on the bottom is for opening the skylight."

Alex rolled onto her side and beckoned Ben over with her finger, "You look so nervous, I won't bite. Hard."

Ben eased over to the side of the bed and sat down. "I am a little nervous. I wanted to show this to you, but I wasn't picturing all of this."

"I hope you like what you see."

"That goes without saying, but I don't want to rush things or pressure you into anything."

Alex ran her fingernail down Ben's back, enjoying the feel of his muscles contracting. "I don't feel pressured, although these clothes are constricting me somewhat."

Ben turned to gauge her sincerity, and was astounded to find Alex had removed her shirt. Her white bra glowed in contrast to her dark skin. "Alex that might not be the best idea."

Alex smiled, "I think it's a great idea and I really would like to find out if tree houses are a good place for fooling around."

"We can't Alex, I really want to, but I don't have any protection."

"It's okay Ben, I'm on the pill."

Ben was going to offer some more weak protests and then Alex was pushing him down and climbing astride his waist. Her dark hair hung down, brushing his chest while her eyes sparkled like black gems. Ben couldn't argue because Alex had bent down and started nibbling on his earlobes, causing his mouth to stop working.

His hands did not and Ben ran his hands up Alex's torso until his hands reached the bottom of her bra. Ben felt Alex's body stiffen as she took a deep breath.

"I can stop," Ben managed to squeak out when he caught his breath. He wasn't sure if he could, because his body was desperate for Alex to be naked.

Alex pulled herself upright, straddling Ben's hips with his erect penis lying between her legs. Her hair hung down partially covering her bra and her dark eyes flashed.

"I really want to Ben, I'm just a little nervous. It's been a while since I've let myself go this far and I guess my body is not used to this yet."

Ben managed a chuckle, "Are you serious? I've though your body would be listed somewhere as a sexual weapon."

Alex's phone vibrated on the dresser and she glanced out of habit. It was from the crime lab, probably calling to confirm the preliminary results from the murder scene.

She focused back on Ben, who had unhooked her bra and was running his hands up and down her back, when the phone buzzed with a text message to call the lab. That was not normal and she struggled with what she should do.

"Why don't you check your phone, because wherever we were in this process, you just left."

Alex smiled and leaned over to grab the phone, allowing Ben's mouth access to her nipple, which he gently nipped at through her unhooked bra. Alex took a quick breath as she read the text instructing her to call the lab ASAP.

"I know this is not the best timing, but I need to make a phone call to find out what is going on, this isn't normal."

Ben really did not want to stop, but he also knew this wasn't going anywhere since she had slipped back into work mode. "It's fine, I'll just go on down to the pond so you can have some privacy."

Ben considered jumping into the pond to assist him with getting rid of the raging boner he had. The cold water in the pond would likely be more effective than an extended cold shower to bring his sexual desire back to reality. He opted to sit on the dock with his feet dangling in the water, throwing stones at the lily pads, while Winston sunned himself on the bank. He knew Alex had been on the phone for a while and could tell something was wrong when he saw her face when she climbed down the swing.

"I'm sorry Ben, but I've got to get back to the office. My easily solved case has just gotten more difficult."

Ben walked over and pushed Winston aside, who was vying for Alex's attention, "There's nothing to be sorry for, I understand you've got an on call job."

Alex looked at her feet, "I don't want you to think I was leading you on in there. I really wanted to – hell I still really want to get laid, but we might have to hold off for a bit until I get this under wraps."

Ben smiled and lifted her chin, "It wasn't the right time, its okay. We'll know when it's perfect."

Alex pounded the steering wheel when she finally got in her car. She hadn't planned to go that far yet with Ben, but the cabin and woods just made her forget about everything. Alex was more than ready to end her self-imposed sexual sabbatical, and she knew Ben was more than ready based on the feel of his erect penis between her thighs when she was straddling him. He handled the letdown well, but Alex knew he was not comfortable as they walked back out of the woods.

Zoe watched as Ben and Alex returned from the woods. They both looked flushed and Alex's hair was not as neat as when they had left the house. Maybe Ben finally stepped up and pushed the envelope a little bit out there in the woods. He seemed at home out there with the trees and nature.

Ben entered the kitchen and headed for his bedroom, not really wanting to have any interaction with Zoe, but she was waiting at his door.

"So is your lady friend staying for dinner?"

Ben looked at Zoe, noting she was watching him carefully, "No she had to get back to work. Something came up with her case and she had to leave."

Zoe stepped out of the way, "I didn't think she would go for the quick shag and goodbye routine."

"For your information there was no shagging, not that it's any of your business."

"Everything to do with you is my business remember. I am supposed to watch over you and make sure you are safe from others and yourself."

"I'm fine Zoe, I don't need a babysitter. It's not Jamaica anymore."

Zoe followed Ben as he headed for his bathroom, "You are correct, but someone still needs to look out for your best interests, because most of the time you do not."

Ben turned on the shower and turned to Zoe, "Thank you for your concern, but I'm fine. I just need a shower."

Zoe nodded and reached into the shower, adjusting the temperature, "Judging by the state of your 'affairs', I would think the temperature should be colder."

Ben was going to respond, but Zoe just walked out.

Alex stormed into the crime lab. She'd replayed the afternoon with Ben the entire ride into the station and had worked herself into a frenzy. She wanted answers and right now.

"What's going on Burroughs? I want you to know you have awful timing."

Jessica Burroughs lifted her magnifier and looked up at Alex, "Sorry to disturb you, but I think your instructions were to contact 'asap' if there was a problem."

Alex slumped into the chair, "I'm sorry. You interrupted a very intense moment."

Jessica smoothed her lab coat and sat in the adjacent chair, "Give me some dirt, I've been hearing about you hooking up with some hot guy."

"We aren't hooking up, thanks to your call. What have you got?"

"Fine. Your suspect did not commit suicide."

"What? I was there; it looked pretty open and shut to me."

Jessica nodded, "That's why the data comes to the underpaid backbone of the department. Based on the trajectory of the bullet wound and the blood spatter, your man couldn't have done this."

"So now you're saying I have a murderer as well as a sexual predator running around out there."

"If it's any consolation, the pictures you found are a match with the originals. It looks to me that your murderer might have been trying to frame someone to cover up being a predator."

Alex closed her eyes and rubbed her temples, "This means we are back at square one."

"Other than you now know the suspect is really smart and he knows you're looking for him."

"Thanks for the bright spot."

Jessica leaned back in her chair, "Now let's hear about your new man. The rumor mill around here has been working overtime about little Miss Ice finally finding herself a man."

"Little Miss Ice?"

Jessica smiled, "You didn't think I'd call you the Ice Bitch to your face did you?"

"Okay here's the dirt, but I need you to make sure you spread it to everyone and please embellish it as much as your imagination can handle. His name is Ben Princi, he's probably six foot five or so, ripped like a wrestler, and he's got more money than probably anyone in the county."

Jessica looked up from her iPad where she had been taking notes, "How am I supposed to embellish on that? Wait is he horribly scarred."

"Why don't you use your little devise and google him? Remember he's a famous author."

"Oh my, it's no wonder you came in with all that attitude. If I interrupted anything serious, please accept my apologies. Does he really look this good?"

Alex glimpsed at the screen, "Oh yeah and he's got great hands and lips."

"Wait you can't walk out without giving me more, that's just wrong."

Alex paused at the door, "Good talking to you Jess, I've got a predator to catch."

Jessica sat her iPad down and started typing. Usually she was last person to know any dirt about anyone, but this time she was going to lead the rumor mill.

* *

Ben sat in his shower with the water as cold as he could stand it before he finally felt he could walk again without his balls feeling like they were going to burst. He knew Zoe had boundary issues, but he didn't expect her to make comments about his penis.

"So are we feeling relieved?" Zoe asked with an arched brow while she snacked on cucumber slices.

Ben grabbed a few slices and sat down at the table, "I'm clean if that's what you mean?"

"Sure we'll go with that. While you were soaking your parts, Trevor called about an idea for promoting the company. I know you are going to hate it, but hear me out because it's actually pretty savvy."

Ben crunched the cucumbers and motioned for Zoe to go on.

"Trevor thinks we should audition a group of young unsigned artists and work elimination style, learning the business and writing songs."

"Sounds like what we are doing right now, what's the catch?"

Zoe took a deep breath, "He also wants to have a film crew document it all as a reality show for television. Trevor has already contacted a producer he knows and there is interest in the concept."

Ben continued chewing and stared out the window. He wanted nothing to do with the media, but he understood the need there was for publicity and what could come from this project.

"I think it's a great idea, but I don't want to be on the show. It's Trevor's thing, he loves parading around for the cameras anyway."

Zoe leaned back against the counter, "Evidently that cold shower worked on your brains as well as your balls."

Ben nearly choked, "Jesus Zoe, do you have any type of filter?"

"Why should I? I've discussed with you about having a baby. I've seen you at your worst when you were detoxing, so I think being anything less than blunt with you is unfair."

"I'm just not comfortable with discussing my private parts."

Zoe waved him off, "Whatever. The offer still stands though if you need to relieve the pressure, we could run upstairs for a quickie."

"No thanks Zoe, although the thought of relieving the pressure as you put it sounds so intimate."

"Oh I could give you intimacy if you wanted it, but I wasn't sure you could handle it," Zoe purred.

"Okay I'm done with this discussion. I'm going out to work on a car or something in the garage. Tell Trevor full speed ahead."

Zoe laughed as Ben headed for the door, "That's right darling run off to the garage, we wouldn't want to talk about intimacy and where that might lead."

* *

Gerald smiled when Alex stormed into the office, "Well look who's back."

"I never went anywhere, so how could I be back."

"Huh it took you thirty minutes to get to the crime lab for the news, which indicates to my detection skills that you were somewhere or with someone that required thirty minutes to finish."

Alex glared across her desk, "You're really pushing it. Don't we need to start this investigation over so we can look with fresh eyes?"

Gerald leaned back in his chair, "Guess you didn't get laid after all."

Grabbing the files, Alex stalked to the copier and started scanning some of the crime scene photos to her personal account. She could use this file to access the file even when she was at home, which was how she spent the majority of her evenings.

"Hey I'm sorry. I was just busting your balls," Gerald said quietly from his corner.

"It's fine, I'm just pissed because I got ahead of myself and thought we caught this sonofabitch."

"I know, but it was a little too neat, which always makes me nervous, but then again I'm a pessimist. So where are we headed now boss?"

Alex smiled at the little dig. "I think we need to look at the crime scene since we know it's a homicide now, because it has to be linked with the sex stuff."

Gerald returned her smile, "That's my girl, get back into the saddle."

"I think we need to look at why he was picked to be the scapegoat, and we definitely need to keep it out of the papers for right now that it was a homicide."

Gerald mulled this over, "Not a bad strategy. I'll check with his probation officer and see what I can find out about Robert Griffin the week before he died."

"I'll start trying to tie Griffin's storage unit to the pictures."

* *

He sent the text out as soon as he heard the rumors from the crime lab about the suicide now being investigated as a homicide. Hurting Junior's feelings were the last of his concerns at this point.

You screwed up, police know it wasn't a suicide. Fix the problem now!!

* *

Ben finished working on the sanding project and headed back into the house, hoping that Zoe was involved with something so he wouldn't have much interaction with her. She had inserted herself into this thing with Alex and seemed intent on making sure she stayed there.

Zoe was typing away on her laptop when Ben entered and he went straight to take another shower, this time for legit reasons. Ben hated when he was sweaty and covered with the fine particles which invariably ended up in his hair and on his skin when he sanded.

"Better now?" Zoe asked when Ben emerged from the bathroom.

Clenching his towel tighter around his waist, Ben headed for his closet, "Yes, I finished the project, so Chet should get off my case."

"I didn't mean the car. Did you get your frustrations all out of your system?"

Ben closed the closet door and dropped his towel to pull on his boxers, "Not going to drop it are you?"

"Why don't you just call her up and invite her back here for a quick shag? Trust me she needs it as much as you do."

Ben cracked the door open, "Maybe I'm trying for more than just that."

"I'm not saying you can't try for more, I'm just advocating for you two to diminish this sexual tension so you can work on the feelings stuff. Go for the black trunks instead of those boxers by the way."

"I'll handle things Zoe, thank you. Did you come in here for something other than just to hassle me?"

Zoe smiled as she curled against the oversized pillow on the bed, "It's my job to keep tabs on all aspects of your life. We've never had to worry about anything serious with a woman before, so this is new ground."

Ben pulled on the black trunks and some jeans, "So why are you so hell bent on getting involved in this part of my life."

"For one I'm your friend and trust me nobody needs a wingman like you do. The other is that I need to make sure you are not getting into the highs and lows of your possible bipolar condition."

Ben shot her a quick glance as he pulled on his t-shirt, and noticed she was smiling. "I'm not bipolar."

"I know, but it's so much fun to push your buttons. So when are you going to go to Nashville next to meet with Trevor?"

"Do we have anything scheduled coming up this weekend?"

Zoe gazed at her phone, "You are clear from Friday afternoon until Sunday evening, sounds like a good time to get you down there. Also you've got the barbeque with Alex on Monday."

"You aren't coming along?"

"Not this time, I've got plans. Also your other young lady, Ms. Collins called and left multiple messages for you to contact her. She sounded despondent, but remember what she is before you make that call."

"Maybe I won't call her back."

Zoe pulled herself off the bed, "Sure you will because the damsel in distress thing is something you have a hard time staying away from."

Ben finished cleaning up his towel and dirty clothes before following Zoe into the kitchen. "I can't see anything we need to discuss, especially considering she lied to me."

Zoe turned to smile at Ben and adjusted his rolled up sleeve "You talk a great game love, but ultimately you enjoy women and hate to see us upset. You make it your mission to fix things if we are."

Ben grabbed a water from the refrigerator and took a long swallow, trying to find a good rebuttal for Zoe. "It's true that I don't like to see women upset, but I don't try to always fix things to make them happy."

"Are you serious? What about Nicole? She was a certifiable lunatic and you kept going out with her because she would turn on the tears when she thought you were trying to end things."

"Zoe, I was trying to end things with her and it got complicated."

Zoe shook her head, "No it's not complicated. If there is a connection go for it, if not end it and move on. Everyone is supposed to be with someone, it's not a logic class, its chemistry."

"That sounds easy, but it gets messy when feelings are involved."

"God, you sound like a woman. Trevor would agree with me on this point and if you repeat it I will deny it. That is why I'm pushing you with Alex. There seems to be a connection, why beat around the bush about it, give it a whirl."

Ben thought about the conversation and wondered if it was true and maybe his person had been Monica, which would mean he was destined to be alone now. He couldn't deny that he felt something with Alex, but then there were times when she pulled back as quickly as she rushed forward.

"Stop it right now."

"What?"

Zoe put her hands on her hips, "I know that look. You're over there feeling sorry for yourself about Monica probably. My speech was to get your ass back out there, not have you shut down."

Ben waved her off and finished his water, "Relax I'm fine, just mulling over your theory and thinking maybe I had my shot."

"Whatever Ben. If you'd open your eyes and try to live a little, there are a number of women who have tried to have a relationship with you and you kept sabotaging things or shutting down."

"It's not that I did these things intentionally."

"I know you did it to protect yourself, just like you did when I found you in Jamaica. You thought if you stayed drunk all the time then there would be no pain. Didn't work so well now did it?"

"Thanks for the trip down memory lane, but I did have some relationships."

Zoe snorted, "Really. I remember a couple of bimbos you hooked up with for some companionship, but it was never serious because that might make you hurt again. Guess what loving someone is scary because you might get hurt, but it does have some great rewards too."

Ben smiled and gave Zoe a hug, "You're pretty smart for being a pain in the ass."

"And I intend to continue being a pain in your ass, because someone has to ask questions and push you or you'll just sit around and get old all by yourself."

****

Alex threw the files back onto her desk as she stood, before bending over to touch the floor. Her back was knotted up from sitting in one position all day, and she couldn't think about how wonderful Ben's hot tub would feel right now.

Neither she nor Gerald had come up with anything useful while reviewing the evidence. All the probation reports indicated that Griffin had been a model probationer, checking in as required and never having a dirty screen. He had also volunteered to try one of the county's new GPS ankle monitor system for two months and never violated his probation rules.

Gerald had gone home hours ago, claiming he needed to get some sleep at some point or he'd be of no use the rest of the week. Alex had ordered him to go home before that, but he insisted on staying past his usual quitting time. It wasn't often that Gerald put in extra hours anymore on cases. Alex knew he'd been looking into the retirement process and what he needed to get situated before he made his decision.

Alex debated calling Ben, but decided he'd probably had enough of her late night phone calls, and that was before this afternoon's botched hook up. Alex had been too damn close to just throwing caution to the wind and having a great afternoon of sweaty sex. It would have taken care of her needs, but it would have created a bigger mess on a different level. She also didn't want Ben seeing her as the needy girlfriend who couldn't take care of herself unless she was with her significant other. Alex never wanted to be in a relationship again where the intensity was so much that it became unbearable.

Walking out to her worn out Crown Vic, Alex noted something was on the hood of the car. As she got closer and realized what it was, Alex pulled her Glock from her shoulder harness and clicked off the safety. Someone had killed the cat and thrown it on her car, but Alex wasn't sure if the culprit was still around or not.

She moved quickly along the passenger side of the car, staying within the shadows of the building as much as possible, with her gun cocked and locked. Alex had been trained for this, but it always caused her adrenaline to surge when she actually pulled her weapon.

Satisfied that no one was around, Alex opened the trunk and pulled out a large evidence bag and worked the cat's rigored body in. She would take it down to the crime lab and leave a note to find out if there were any prints left on the car.

Now she was leaving the office an hour later than she intended, but Alex had devised a plan to get a great night's sleep. She called Ben and asked him to meet her at her house if he was available.

Being scared was just part of the problem for Alex. She'd decided that playing these games was not getting her anywhere about sorting out her feelings for Ben. Opting for a full steam ahead approach, Alex met Ben at the door with a smile and a "rock your world" kiss. She pulled him to the couch and they started kissing and exploring each other. Ben was receptive and even pushed the line by running his hands under Alex's shirt teasing her breasts with his thumbs as he worked his hands up and down her stomach.

"I thought you had me come over to talk about this afternoon," Ben whispered into Alex's hair.

Alex took a quick breath as Ben's thumbs gently grazed her nipples, "I was hoping to do a little more than talk, but I needed to make sure we were on the same page. I was hoping to get a great night's sleep and you might know how to get me there."

"I've got a couple of ideas, but first I need to use the restroom."

Alex went to the bedroom when Ben closed the bathroom door to proceed to stage two, which was to pull the comforter off her bed and remove her clothes. She'd gotten some good glimpses of Ben in the whirlpool and ran her hands all over his chest and shoulders, so she was interested in seeing the whole package unwrapped. What she didn't expect was for Ben to stop at the doorway of her bedroom. He looked at Alex as she dropped the sheet she had covering her naked body, "I've got an itch I need you to scratch."

Ben backed out of the bedroom as he pulled his shirt back on. His brain was screaming for his body to stop and turn around and go back into the room where Alex stood, naked and willing.

"What the hell is wrong with you?"

Ben turned to look at Alex as she stood in the doorway with the sheet wrapped around her body again with her eyes blazing. "I can't give you what you want Alex. I told myself I wouldn't just make this about sex."

"You're an idiot. I don't think this is just about sex, but I do know I was pretty interested in having sex and seeing if we were as compatible there as we seemed to be everywhere else. We're adults, its okay to have sex without being married."

Ben shook his head, "I don't want to get married, but I refuse to just be someone to meet your needs because you're horny."

"Are you freaking kidding me? Yeah I'm horny, but it wasn't the only reason I wanted to have sex. You know what, never mind. I didn't need all this shit before so I'll be fine without it now. You know your way out."

Ben turned and walked out without a word. He knew it was something he needed to deal with, but hearing Alex say she wanted to have sex to scratch her itch had rubbed him the wrong way.

Once the door latched as Ben closed it, Alex turned her head and began to sob. She'd messed up by thinking that maybe she had found a good guy who would think about her first and not just what he wanted. Her crying spell lasted longer than she intended and Alex straightened up her bedroom before heading into the office, where she could bury herself in paperwork to help forget about her aching heart.

Ben banged his hand off the steering wheel as he cruised the country roads. He'd been aimlessly driving around for the past two hours and his head was still a mess. It wasn't like he had never just had sex with a woman to scratch her itch or his own needs. This time he knew he had some kind of feelings for Alex and he didn't want it to just be about sex and it seemed to her that she was only interested in getting laid.

He felt caught in this vacuum of wanting to be with Alex and build something long standing there and then there was Zoe and her baby request. Maybe that was what had his head all messed up since

Zoe just wanted him to be a sperm donor. Thrown in amongst all of that was Samantha, doing her best to remind him about Courtney and the feelings he thought he'd suppressed or locked away. She'd lied to him to get close to him and question him, and now he realized part of her appeal had been the physical similarity she had with Courtney.

Ben realized the driving was not helping and he was just stalling from heading back to the house to answer questions from Zoe about his latest disaster of a date. Guys have ended or walked away from relationships before, but not usually when the woman is naked and ready to give herself. Ben knew that his timing was probably totally out of whack, but he didn't want to be another man who just used Alex for his own needs without there being a relationship.

He'd always held out for a relationship before he climbed into bed with anyone, except when he had been drunk in the Caribbean. Ben waited a long time, in hind sight too long to try and have a sexual relationship with Courtney. Monica made sure he knew it was okay to move to that level of their relationship in college. Since then it had been one night stands that centered around enough alcohol for Ben to not think about the consequences of just falling into bed with the current woman he was with.

Zoe had ended that practice when she arrived on the island and figured out what was going on. She either confronted the women outright or slept in the room with Ben to make sure no one was entering without her knowledge. Since then Ben had made stringent efforts to ensure that he didn't put himself into a precarious position or worse give the wrong impression to a woman. Now for the first time in a long time that he wanted to just have fling with no pressure and his conscience starts working on him and he walked out of Alex's bedroom.

Ben had numerous conversations with Trevor when they were in rehab about the trappings of being famous. Trevor admitted he'd never turned down any woman who wanted to go to bed with him, looks, size, ethnicity, or any other characteristic would be a rule out. Trevor made one of his first songs about Ben, calling it "the

Discerning Male". He found the lyrics quite humorous, but Ben didn't see the humor in the subject of the song ending up alone because he spent too much time sifting through the options.

Trevor also pointed out that meaningless sex was supposed to happen for famous people, it allowed the fans to feel like they were on the same level. Ben told him he was full of crap and that was just an excuse to make himself feel better about not having a relationship with who he was having sex with at the time. Trevor chuckled and informed him that sex was a relationship, it just fluctuated with how long it lasted based on how well you did it.

Zoe glanced up from her laptop when Ben slammed his car door. She intended to interrogate him when he entered, but decided that wasn't a good idea when she saw the look on his face. Ben headed straight for his bedroom and closed the door without speaking.

"Leave me alone Zoe," Ben said when the soft knock came later.

Zoe cracked the door and peeked to make sure he was clothed, "So do you want to talk about this or am I going to have to deal with this attitude for the rest of the week?"

Ben put down the book he was holding, "I don't want to talk about it, okay?"

"Some people consider talking about issues as therapeutic."

Ben smiled, "Said the counselor. It is a personal issue between me and Alex and it'll all work out."

Zoe looked him over, "Well you're too pissed to have had sex, so was it a question of performance anxiety?"

"Just go Zoe."

Zoe slid out of the chair and stood, "It happens, especially with guys near your age. It's normal."

"I didn't have a performance problem. Physically I was ready to go, but I'm not going to just be a tool so Alex can get her itch scratched."

Zoe sat back down, "You do know that it would benefit you to get your itch scratched as well. I don't know if you remember, but sex can be mutually satisfying."

Ben shot a glare.

Zoe continued, "Anyway, as I recall, sex is a great rush of chemicals in the body. Something that would be of great benefit to you and your stodginess."

"I don't want it to just be about sex. I thought there was something more going on there than just physical. I have had opportunities to just have the physical act."

"Don't I know it."

"Not funny Zoe. You know what I mean. I'm just trying to figure out if we've got something or if we are just wasting our time."

"Did you ever think that maybe this was one of Alex's steps to determine if there is something there or not? And news flash, there is something there dummy, because you are all worked up like this."

Ben flopped back onto his bed, "This is all a pain in the ass. I'd just like to have sort of normal relationship, without having to figure out the clues."

"I wasn't there, but Alex doesn't strike me as being terribly difficult to understand."

"No her meaning was very clear. I opened the door to her bedroom and she was naked."

Zoe shook her head, "God you are an idiot. Please tell me you did not just walk out."

13

Zoe handed Ben his phone, interrupting the flow he had been generating with the new riff Trevor had sent.

"It's Louisa at Joyland. She called you because your little friend is down there."

"Hey Louisa. Wait what do you mean I need … Okay, I'll be there in fifteen minutes."

Zoe stood in the doorway, waiting for an explanation.

"She said Samantha got there about an hour ago and she's really drunk. They won't let her drive and she's angry, started complaining about her ex-fiancée getting married and being stood up by a big shot author."

Zoe didn't try to hide the smile, "Well looks like you get to save the damsel in distress after all."

"Aren't you going to go with me?"

"No, this is your problem to deal with. I told you to firmly get rid of her, but you couldn't risk hurting someone's feelings, so now you get to reap what you've sown."

Ben closed his laptop and grabbed the keys for his Blazer. It was the biggest vehicle he owned and thought she could sleep in the back seat if necessary. Also the upholstery was not in great shape, so if she did get sick then it wouldn't be a problem to cleanup or replace.

Driving through town he wondered why Louisa had called him, other than Samantha didn't know anyone else from the area. Normally they would just call the sheriff and let him deal with whoever had overextended their stay. Evidently Louisa had felt sorry for Samantha and decided a trip in the county drunk tank wasn't worth it.

"Okay Louisa, where is she?" Ben announced, after parking his Blazer in the carry out parking spots next to the door.

Louisa pointed to the corner booth in the back, "I think she's asleep now, but she was yelling and cryin something fierce earlier. Said her fiancée had ditched her and now she didn't have a job or man. She was drinking margaritas like crazy, but I stopped her when she started stumbling around."

Ben handed Louisa a fifty dollar bill, "Thanks for looking out for her. I'll let her sleep it off at my house and we'll come get her car in the morning."

Louisa halfheartedly tried to return the bill, "I don't need this Ben, just look after her. She's all broke up about losing her job and then her man just up and leaves her. All she kept talking about was how she needed to find a great guy like you."

"Keep the money, consider it payment for leaving her car overnight and not having Billy tow it."

Louisa smiled and tucked the bill into her bra. She wiped the counters again while watching to see how things went between Ben and the pretty little girl. She'd always wondered why Ben remained single and that they made a cute couple.

Ben walked quietly into the corner where the booth was. Samantha was curled up, using a tablecloth for a blanket, snoring softly.

He was going to try and talk to her, but figured it might just be easier to just get her out to the Blazer without an incident. Since she was sleeping it was better to leave her that way. Ben gently scooped Samantha into his arms and she leaned into his chest wrapping her arms around his neck.

"I knew you'd come," Samantha slurred.

Ben carried her outside and opened the rear door, gently laying Samantha across the bench seat. He could hear her soft snores again before he even made it out of the city limits.

Zoe was waiting with the kitchen door open when Ben parked.

"Where is she?"

Ben opened the door and pointed to Samantha, still sleeping.

"Could you pull the covers back in the guest room? I'll bring her in and we'll let her sleep it off."

Zoe left the door propped open and went to prepare the extra bedroom. She thought Samantha looked like an oversized doll in Ben's arms as he carried her into the house.

"She smells like a liquor factory."

Ben smiled as he laid her down gently on the bed, "Yeah she either spilled some on her clothes or something, because I had to drive with the windows down because of the smell."

"Go bring me one of your t-shirts. She'd never fit in any of my pajamas, but one of your shirts should work to sleep in."

Ben walked off as Zoe started pulling off Samantha's boots. He threw the shirt on the bed as Zoe struggled with the buttons on Samantha's shirt.

"I need your help here. I thought I could do this easily since she was passed out, but its worse because of her being dead weight."

Ben held his hands up, "Wait a minute Zoe, I'm not helping you take off her clothes."

"Yes you are, because I'm not going to have this room smell like a brewery for the next month. It's not like you haven't seen a naked woman before, and it's not like this one is going to know."

"She'll know in the morning that someone undressed her, and I don't need that kind of problem."

Zoe finished with the buttons, "I'll talk to her. Now do me favor and reach around and lift her butt up some so I can pull these jeans off."

Ben tried to think about numerous other things than the sight of Samantha lying on the bed with only her matching black bra and panties. Her hair was twisted across her face and Ben unconsciously brushed it off to the side, noting how young she looked and that she could have been Courtney's younger sister.

"Okay Mr. Embarrassment, I can handle these last two pieces of clothing so you can maintain your dignity."

"Thanks Zoe, I'll see you in the morning. I appreciate your help with her."

14

Ben flinched when he felt the bed move.

"Dammit Winston, how did you get in here?"

Ben was reaching for the dog when his hand brushed against skin, "What are you doing in here?"

Samantha continued crawling along the bed towards Ben's pillow, "I woke up and was cold, and so when I figured out where I was I came over here."

"You shouldn't be in here. Let's get you back to the guest room and I'll get you some more blankets."

"I don't want to be alone. I want to stay here with you."

Ben pulled himself into a seated position and turned on the lamp, "Listen Samantha, you've had too much to drink and sleep is what you need right now."

Samantha sat on the edge of the bed with her knees folded under her torso, swimming in Ben's Rolling Stones t-shirt. "I don't want to be alone right now."

"Well let's go to the kitchen then and we can talk."

"Why can't we talk right here?"

"Because it's not appropriate. It's my bedroom and you are drunk."

Samantha fell back laughing, "The big writer is scared of little old me, and that's after you rescued me and took my clothes off."

Ben pulled the sheet tighter around his body, cognizant that he was naked underneath, "Listen I brought you here to sleep it off and Zoe took off your clothes, not me."

"But you are scared, I can see it in your eyes," she said as she started crawling towards the head of the bed.

"Stop Samantha. You need to leave right now."

Samantha surprised Ben by actually stopping, but it was only long enough for her to pull the t-shirt off and throw it in the corner. Ben tried to be polite and look away from her body, but it was difficult. The past few days with the sexual dance he'd been engaged in with Alex didn't help with the frustration he was feeling. That combined with his natural reaction to having a beautiful naked woman in his bed had rendered him rock hard.

"I just want to crawl in with you, I'm cold. What's wrong with me? Don't you want me?"

Ben knew logic was the wrong method to use, but he tried anyway, "Maybe taking off your shirt wasn't the smartest thing since you are cold."

Samantha didn't respond, intent only on trying to pull back the covers which Ben held onto tightly. "Come on Ben, I know you're naked under these covers. Keep me warm."

Ben intended to grab her arm to stop her from pulling the covers, but she twisted away and his hand brushed against her breast. Instantly he thought about Alex and the dance they'd been doing with whatever kind of relationship they had or didn't have.

Samantha smiled, "Come on Ben, I don't bite and you might enjoy yourself."

Ben intended to argue, but Samantha ended that by jumping onto his lap, straddling his hips and kissing him. Ben's resistance ended quickly and he ran his hands up and down Samantha's back, allowing his thumbs to gently glide along her small breasts.

"So are you going to take this cover off, because it feels to me like there is something under there I want," Samantha said playfully as she bit her bottom lip.

"We shouldn't do this Samantha. You're upset and drunk, two big reasons that this is not a good idea."

Samantha smiled and pulled the covers back and slid against Ben's body, "Maybe, but I know one really big reason why I should do this."

Ben was going to ask what her reason was, but she grabbed his penis and he knew. He knew it was wrong to be doing this, especially in her condition, but it was impossible for him to think clearly when Samantha slid on top of him and started easing him into her. She was moving slowly, getting wetter and pushing herself further and further down onto Ben until she was completely filled.

Samantha leaned back and Ben found his hands on her breasts, stroking and kneading them until her nipples ached for his mouth. She rocked herself back and forth, feeling the pressure building until she collapsed onto Ben's chest, biting into his shoulder to keep from screaming.

Ben picked her up and flipped Samantha onto the bed, marveling at how her lithe body looked so small in comparison to his muscular physique. Her eyes were open and she was smiling as she spread her legs, "Please Ben, I'm dying here. Finish it."

Ben woke to scratching at the door, and after glancing at the clock knew why. He'd slept in and Winston was demanding to go outside. He glanced down at Samantha who was lying with her head on his chest and one leg draped across legs.

Guilt came slamming down on him, castigating him for what he'd done last night. Samantha was an adult, but not nearly old enough to be making these types of decisions.

Ben eased out of the bed and picked up the t-shirt and tossed it next to Samantha. He needed to get some coffee and figure out how to handle this situation when she finally got up.

Winston sprinted to the door and sat patiently while Ben shuffled to let him outside. The coffee was already brewed and he noticed that Zoe was sitting outside on the porch eating fruit.

"Good Morning."

Zoe shaded her eyes as she looked up at Ben, "Yes it is and it's a better morning for some than others."

Ben slumped down in the chair and sipped his coffee, "I don't know what to say. I did not plan for this to happen."

"I'm pretty sure you just slept together, you didn't get married."

"It's not that easy Zoe. I tried, I really tried to get her out of my room last night and then it just happened."

Zoe continued typing on her laptop, "On the positive side, at least you know you didn't forget how to perform."

"I didn't think I'd forgotten how to perform, but you don't have any proof."

Zoe stopped typing and turned to gaze at Ben, "Well you have teeth marks on your shoulder and then there were the Oh God Ben, and other screams of passion. You might want to make sure there aren't people around before you get back into action."

Ben sipped his coffee, knowing his face was crimson. There was nothing he could say, because Samantha had been loud and enthusiastic.

"Uh time for me to go, looks like the sex kitten has arisen, and I am stressing kitten."

Ben turned to see Samantha pouring a cup of coffee. Zoe pointed her in the direction of the aspirin and headed off to her room.

"So this is really awkward," Samantha said as she sat with her back towards the sun and facing Ben.

Ben ran his hands through his hair, "We need to talk about last night."

"Listen I know the deal. We had sex and it was fantastic, but I was drunk and upset about Greg, not to mention being suspended from work because I wouldn't air my story."

"I don't need any of this turning up in the media please."

Samantha set down her coffee, "I would never do that. I knew we had a connection, but I wouldn't exploit that just because we had sex."

Ben noted that was twice she'd commented about them having sex. "I think you are a wonderful woman, but last night, it was a ..."

Samantha's eyes flashed, "A mistake is that what you were going to say? I don't just hop into bed with anyone and I don't think you do either, so let's not try to paint this as a mistake. Maybe bad timing, but definitely not a mistake from my vantage point."

"You're right; I was using the wrong word to describe last night, but my being horny was no reason to take advantage of you."

Samantha leaned back and winced, "Now as humbling as this is, could you please tell me where my clothes are and how can I get to my car."

Ben smiled, "Zoe washed everything and it's probably folded in the living room. I can take you to your car once you're ready to go."

Samantha stretched as she rose, "You are a great cure for a hangover, because I should feel like road kill after last night, but I feel pretty good considering."

Zoe watched as Samantha leaned over and gave Ben a quick peck on the lips before coming inside. She was glad about Ben finally giving in to his desires and not overthinking everything, but Samantha was not the best choice to relieve his urges. Then there was the whole relationship dance he was starting with Alex. Zoe knew she would have to keep a tighter rein on Ben for the foreseeable future or he'd be wallowing in his depression again.

"Thank you for washing my clothes. I'm really embarrassed about you having to take care of me like that."

Zoe smiled brightly, "I thought you'd be embarrassed for the lack of sleep I got last night because of you two."

Samantha almost choked on her coffee. "I'm sorry about that; things just got a little out of control."

"Uh huh. A word of advice. Don't mess with his head. He's already dealing with enough and the last thing he needs is someone trying to latch on."

Samantha set the mug down and faced Zoe, noting her brown eyes were not their usual friendly shade, "I can admit that I'm attracted to Ben, but I'm not looking to 'latch on' to anyone. I drank too much and wanted to forget about what a shit my ex-fiancée is and being suspended from my job, which ended up with me in Ben's bed. He didn't ask me, I pushed the bar so to speak."

Zoe didn't back down, "He hasn't had a serious relationship in almost three years and I won't have your little bedroom romp mess with him. He'll sit around all day now brooding about how he took advantage of poor little Samantha and feel guilty. A guy with his history of depression does not need that type of stressor."

"Point taken and I'll make sure that he understands it was more for my needs than his, but I have to admit he did enjoy himself."

"He probably did, but then most men enjoy themselves when they're horny and haven't hooked up recently."

Samantha grabbed her clothes and traipsed off towards the bathroom. She didn't want Zoe to have the satisfaction of seeing her cry. Waking up in Ben's bed had been a wonderful feeling, but she instantly knew she had probably pushed him into something he was not altogether comfortable with. And having Zoe throw it right into her face was not something she was ready to deal with yet.

Zoe finished her juice before heading outside to speak with Ben. She knew Samantha was on the verge of tears when she stormed off, trying to maintain an air of class carrying her clothes wearing Ben's ridiculous t-shirt which barely covered her ass.

"So somebody slept well last night?"

Ben noted the sarcasm and sipped his coffee before responding, "I know I made a huge mistake, so can we leave it at that?"

Zoe sat in the chair in front of Ben, pulling her robe tight, "Oh I'm not upset that you had sex. Trust me you needed to do that. I'm just a little disappointed that you pick a girl who's infatuated with you and a reporter."

"It's not something I planned. Things just got out of hand. I tried to reason with her and then the next thing I know ..."

"Seriously if you needed a roll in the hay, I believe I offered and there wouldn't be any of these potential aftershocks."

Ben sighed, "I'm sorry Zoe. I screwed up and I already talked with Samantha and she knows it was a case of bad timing."

"I doubt how much she really believes that, because I've seen the way she looks at you. Samantha is a very smart woman and is probably in there changing right now trying to figure out her next move to create a relationship out of this bad timing."

"What is this about Zoe? I expected some flak from you, but I also thought maybe you'd be impressed that I finally did something without thinking it all the way through."

Zoe turned her head to break the eye contact. She really didn't want to admit she was jealous, because Ben had not picked her.

"I just want you to be careful Ben, because you have put yourself in a very precarious position. You also might want to figure out what you're going to tell Alex."

Zoe went back inside before Ben could answer and he tried to finish his coffee. His taste for the coffee was gone, so he poured it over the banister of the deck.

He knew Zoe was going to be upset, especially after the conversation they'd had recently, but her behavior seemed more extreme than that. She'd been pushing him and cajoling him to get out and date for years, but this wasn't something she'd probably seen coming. He wasn't interested in a relationship, but Alex had made him think about it recently. He'd forgotten how much he'd missed the physical aspect of being with a woman, but that had changed recently with Alex. Now he had to figure out how to tell Alex about what had happened with Samantha

Ben waited on the porch until Samantha returned. He noticed that little had been said between Zoe and Samantha when she exited the bathroom. They were like two cats circling each other trying to figure out the pecking order. Ben knew he could have eased things by going inside, but chose the easier position for him by waiting outside.

"I'm ready to go."

Ben noticed Samantha had taken a few minutes to apply some light makeup and pulled her hair into a ponytail. "Let's get you back to your car then."

They rode along silently.

"Okay this is really weird and I didn't mean for it to be."

Ben took his eyes off the road briefly to take a quick glimpse, "Weird is one way to describe this."

"I mean us not talking. So what we had sex, it shouldn't ruin whatever relationship we were building. We're both adults and it shouldn't be a problem."

Ben continued staring straight ahead, "I'm not in the habit of having one night stands, unless I was drunk and then all bets were off. It isn't something I do, so that's why I'm having a difficult time figuring out which direction to go next with you."

"Well Zoe made it very clear to me that I'm not supposed to mess with your head, so you let me know what you figure out."

"I thought she might confront you, she never thinks I can make my own decisions."

Samantha twisted in her seat so she was facing Ben as he drove, "Are you sure there's nothing going on between you two? In my experience, women only go that far over board when they feel threatened or are in love with the guy."

Ben hesitated, thinking about his own questions he had earlier, "There's nothing going on between us romantically. I think it's a territory thing for her and she doesn't like anyone else in her space, male or female."

"Sounds good, but my opinion still stands. She's got some feelings for you beyond the professional."

* *

Gerald set the phone list down and looked over at Alex as she continued scrolling through the online files. "I thought you had a date with lover boy tonight?"

Alex flicked a look toward Gerald to see if he was actually asking or just busting her balls. "We needed to have a little space. Things were getting a little too intense, so I needed to slow Ben down."

"So that explains the attitude."

"I'm over here working, how is that having an attitude?"

Gerald leaned back and put his feet on his desk, "I know you're here working, but you're not being yourself, so something's wrong."

"I really don't want to talk about this with you."

"Okay fine."

Alex pushed the mouse away and rubbed her eyes, "I hate it when you do that shit?"

"What? I dropped it."

"Sure you want me to think you dropped it, but it's just your little way of getting me to talk. Fine, I told Ben he needed to move on, because I couldn't give him what he wanted. No sense in dragging things out."

"What did he want that's got you so pissed off?"

"Oh, he wasn't interested in just having sex, no he wants to have a full blown relationship. Claims he can't have one without the other."

Gerald struggled to contain his smile, "I can see why that would have you pissed off."

Alex glared, "I'm sure you think this is hilarious, but I'm not looking for anything like that. I was just fine before I met Ben, so I'll be just fine now that he's gone."

"No you weren't fine. You were a short tempered workaholic, who built a wall around herself to make sure no one got too close."

Alex prepared to fire back, but Gerald continued, "Maybe you need to realize that every guy out there is not like your ex, so it's possible that Ben might really want those things."

"You called him by his name."

"I just do that to yank your chain. Truth be told, I was hoping you might actually have some kind of relationship."

"I wanted to. I thought maybe we'd go out a few times, have some hot sweaty sex and go our separate ways."

Gerald shook his head, "That's not a relationship, and I'm impressed he told you what he wanted."

Alex lowered her eyes, remembering the look on Ben's face as she told him that she had an itch she needed scratched. This clearly was a trigger for Ben. He'd slowly backed away from her doorway, pulled his shirt back on and left without a word. Initially she had kicked herself for opening her mouth before he had a chance to climb into her bed, but later Alex realized Ben would likely have not made love to her without some form of commitment.

"Well it's finished so, let's get focused back in on this case," Alex said, trying to ignore the heaviness she felt in her chest.

"Okay boss, it's your life."

Yes it was her life and she'd let one man screw it up once, she'd be damned if it would happen again. Alex pushed Ben out of her thoughts and zeroed back in on the details from Gregory's arrest.

* *

Zoe placed Ben's cell phone back on the table. She knew he'd be pissed that she had looked in his contacts to get her number, but she'd worry about that later. Right now it was time to get things back on track, because Ben moping around the farm was worse than putting up with him being offended.

She answered on the fourth ring, "Hello?"

"Is this Alex?"

"Yes, who is this?"

"It's Zoe. We need to meet somewhere and talk."

Alex let out a long sigh, "If this is about Ben, then I don't think it's a good idea for us to meet."

"He doesn't know I'm calling you and we do need to discuss some things."

"I suppose you aren't going to take No for an answer."

Zoe chuckled, "Not in this lifetime."

"Meet me at Casa Lupita at say 1:30 tomorrow for lunch."

"Done."

15

Alex found Zoe already seated when she arrived, "Sorry I'm running late, it took me some time to get away from the office."

Zoe took a long drink of her water, "Has there been any progress in the investigation?"

"Nothing really. We thought we had the guy and it turns out somebody else was trying to set him up. It's back to square one."

The food arrived shortly thereafter and both women started eating.

"They told me you had the food already set up ahead of time, but I wasn't sure if that was true or not."

"I know the owners and eat here frequently, so they cut me slack with ordering ahead or making sure I have a private area."

Zoe looked around at the vacated area they were in, "I noticed that too. I wasn't sure if that meant you were going to shoot me or not and didn't want any witnesses."

Alex smiled, "Nothing like that, just wanted privacy. So what do you want Zoe?"

Zoe took a deep breath and focused on Alex's body language, which had noticeably tensed up after the initial chitchat was over. "Please relax, I just want to talk and I feel like I can be blunt with you. I know things between you and Ben didn't pan out, but I wasn't sure why."

"Why don't we leave it at we wanted different things and decided it was better to be apart."

Zoe bit into her food and thought about her comment, "No that's too easy. What did he do that caused this? He's been moping around for the past week and driving me nuts. All he does is mess with his cars and workout. I was hoping he'd be getting some workouts with you."

Alex paused in midbite, "If I can be frank, I wanted some of those workouts, but he was not just interested in that."

"Ah the relationship thing. I figured that might be the problem."

"It's not a problem, but I will not be bullied into some kind of permanency when I am not looking for that."

Zoe nodded, "I understand, but he's not wired that way. Well he wasn't and you've probably got something to do with that."

"I don't think I understand."

"Well a few days ago Samantha, the deceptive little bitch, got herself drunk and somehow she ended up at the farm. It seems at some point during the night she ended up in Ben's bedroom and they had a go."

Alex was stunned, "So he turns me down flat when I'm lying on my bed naked and he's nearly there and just walks away. But he'll give it to the little reporter."

"In fairness I think some of his general moodiness is about guilt, because he knows he shouldn't have been with Samantha. I think he ended up with her because she looks like his first true love Courtney, but most of it is you. He doesn't just want the sex, you've seen him, he could have sex anytime he wants. Ben's thing is he wants the relationship because he feels he is cursed to spend the rest of his life alone."

"Good I hope he does feel guilty. I was trying to be honest with him and he rejected me. I don't think I've ever felt as humiliated as when he turned and walked out without a word."

Zoe leaned forward, "Are you finished with him or do you want to work this out?"

"I don't know. I'll be damned if I'm going to get all revved up again and have him leave me like nothing."

"Listen I'll lay some ground work, but you have to figure out if being in a relationship with Ben is something you're interested in. If you aren't then walk away because he senses some connection with you."

Alex sighed and finished her drink, "I can't answer that right now. I've got too much to do with work and thinking about Ben just makes my head all fuzzy."

"Well don't wait around too long, because you've already got someone hoping to jump into the saddle with him."

"He can be with whomever he wants; I'm not some consolation prize."

Zoe was going to respond, but figured at this point it was best to just finish the meal. "You're right of course, no woman should be a consolation prize. Let's come up with a plan to get Ben back on track."

* *

Ben continued with the sanding project on his 55 Chevy Nomad. It had sat in the barn for years and now with all the other cars finished up he decided to jump into the arduous process. He knew Zoe was giving him his space right now, but there was no way to know how long it was going to last.

He'd been kicking himself ever since he woke up with Samantha in his bed. One night stands hadn't been his style since he got sober and he wasn't looking to return to that mode, but when Samantha climbed into bed with him, his resolve didn't last very long. Ben tried to reason with her, and then his body just took it from there. Samantha, who reminded him of Courtney, was naked and very willing and he had to admit the sex had been wonderful.

His problem was the following morning when he woke up with her snuggled into his chest. Ben loved the feel of her naked body against his and her blonde hair draped across chest and stomach, but his conscience was working overtime already. He knew he'd screwed up by leading Samantha on, who he knew had feelings for him and then the added stress of her ex-fiancée getting married. The sex was wonderful, but he knew it wasn't worth the pain he was about to cause Samantha when she woke up.

Ben was switching out the pad on his sander when he looked at the phone and noticed the fifteen missed calls. He scrolled through, noting almost half were from Samantha, and dialed the final caller.

"What's up Trevor?"

"Oh you big dog you! Why do I have to hear all the good news from Zoe? You nab a hot little twenty something and I can't hear about from the source?"

Ben leaned against the quarter panel, "I thought you were calling about work."

"I was, but Zoe gave me better news, said you haven't been doing shit because you're sulking about having a fling with some chick."

"I'm not sulking, I've been busy with other things."

"Let me guess, you're working on that metal pile of shit you call a classic car. You always do that when you're supposed to working on something else."

"I got the riffs you sent me, but I haven't been able to concentrate enough right now to get the lyrics following."

Trevor's laughter on the other end interrupted him, "That's cause you've got other stuff flowing. Seriously man it's about time you finally tapped into some of those women who throw themselves at you. If there's anybody that needed to get laid it was you."

"Are we done discussing my sex life? Maybe you can call Zoe up and talk to her about it."

"Don't get pissy with me. I'm sure you're feeling all guilty, but remember this. If she didn't want to have sex, she would have said no. Zoe said she practically threw herself at you."

Ben knew his logic was mostly on point, but he felt like he took advantage of Samantha, "Anyways I'll put in some time tonight and email something to you before morning."

"Okay, but if some other little twenty something throws herself at you ..."

Ben ended the call before Trevor could get his last little jab in. He knew he'd sequestered himself in the garage, because it gave him things to do and also because Zoe wouldn't come out there. He needed some time to process this whole situation without her knowing eyes watching.

He knew what needed to happen next and that he'd been avoiding it.

"Hi Samantha, we need to talk."

Zoe looked up when Ben walked in before dinner. She'd been acting like she was busy with reports, but was actually surfing the web and keeping an eye on the barn to see when Ben would try to sneak out.

"You're in here early today."

Ben gave her a brief smile, "You can spread the word. I'm done brooding, not sulking, brooding."

"Good to know. Please tell me you called Samantha because the girl is driving me nuts with her constant barrage of phone calls. I kept expecting to see her pull in the drive."

"We just finished talking and I think she knows where things stand. I appreciate you giving me space to work through this."

Zoe rolled her eyes, "It was sex Ben, not working on a doctorate."

"You know it was more than that for me and I appreciate your concern, even though filling Trevor in about the details was a little underhanded."

"I thought he might be able to pull you out of the funk, since his belief is women are like clothes, totally interchangeable."

Ben laughed as he peeled off his shirt and headed for his bedroom. He needed a shower and something to eat. The conversation with Samantha was needed and he felt like they could move forward without things being too awkward. She seemed to understand that there wasn't going to be a relationship and that what had happened, while great was a onetime occurrence. Ben knew if he didn't start getting back into the regular routine Zoe was going to start pushing more buttons to force him to move forward, and she didn't always believe in playing fair.

"Do you want me to grill something for dinner tonight?"

Zoe closed the book she was reading, "How about some chicken and I'll throw some vegetables together, and you can fill me in about your conversation with Samantha."

Ben paused at the freezer door, "Do you think maybe sometimes it might be good to have some boundaries?"

"Might work for you, but I'm going to find out anyway, so we should just throw it out there now."

Ben pulled out some chicken breasts, "Okay here's how the conversation went."

* *

"Hey Gerald, do you know how thoroughly the crime scene techs went over Gregory's house?"

Gerald flipped some pages down and scanned, "It looks like they focused on the crime scene and entryways, why?"

Alex turned her monitor around and pointed, "Because every time Gregory was arrested, he had stuff hidden in little hidey holes in the house somewhere. The stuff he thought was too important or in his case incriminatory to leave lying around. Do you want to go on a goose chase?"

"Might as well, because we have zip."

Alex walked to the car and was surprised when Gerald hopped in the passenger seat. "Been a while since you let me drive."

"Figured if you are concentrating on the road, I can ask questions."

Alex got quiet, "What kind of questions?"

"The kind Janice told me to ask you. Like what kind of a guy are you looking for?"

Alex drove silently, thinking the simple question over. "I don't have a type, but intelligent and honest are prime factors."

"So no physical requirements?"

"Well it's always a bonus if a guy is taller than you are, it allows for fancy heels, but other than that no."

Gerald reached into his pocket and looked at the notepad, "Are you looking for just good sex or a complete relationship?"

"Did you take notes? And no way did Janice have you ask me that."

"Answer to your questions is yes and yes she did, now answer please because she is going to grill me when I get home."

Alex checked all her mirrors and focused on the road, "I don't want to talk about this stuff anymore, and it doesn't matter."

Gerald flipped a couple pages, "Janice said to tell you suck it up, and answer the questions. Also I'm not supposed to let tears deter me."

"I'm not gonna cry," Alex replied, hoping the lump in her throat would pass so she made good on that statement. "I think I would like a full blown relationship, but it's a little scary for me so I just shoot for the easier ones."

"Do you think all men are like Robert?"

Alex shook her head slowly, "No, I know there are some good guys out there."

Gerald put his notepad away, "I don't know much about Ben, but he seemed to be okay and he showed something when he told you he wanted a relationship. Sounds like a good guy."

Alex wiped her cheek before the tear became obvious, "It's too late, so let's just focus on finding something in this house to help the case."

"It's never too late Alex, especially if he wants a relationship."

Alex exited the car without answering, focusing herself on the task ahead, which was to find something, anything which might lead her to the person responsible for this case. The job was what she always fell back on when things were too tough everywhere else. It provided the structure and purpose she needed, so she wasn't stuck with figuring out any relationship gamesmanship.

"I'll take the living room if you want the bedroom," Alex offered as she angled to the right under the crime scene tape.

Gerald didn't respond, just lumbered off into the back of the ranch home. He wanted to push Alex some more about the whole thing with Ben, but knew she needed some time to deal first. He knew relationships scared the hell out of her and Ben came flying in pretty fast not knowing that, which made it only worse. If Alex didn't get moving, maybe Gerald would take matters into his own hands and make a preemptive strike by seeking Ben out on his own. For Alex's own good.

Alex quickly examined the center of the small living room before pushing all of the furniture to the middle. She then crawled around the baseboard, checking to see if all of the trim was snugly attached to the wall. Her knees ached by the time she finished the perimeter of the room, and she'd gotten a splinter that refused to stop bleeding from a jagged piece of corner trim.

"I think we're clear in here Gerald, I found nothing of interest."

Gerald was lying on the floor, shining his flashlight under the sink and finding nothing of interest. "It looks pretty clean in here too. I can't believe a guy lived here, because this place is immaculate."

Alex wandered into the bathroom before Gerald could get up, "I was thinking the same thing. Either he's a clean freak, or somebody whitewashed the place before we got here."

"Wait a minute, what the ..."

Gerald pulled himself further under the vanity and pointed the flashlight into the crevice. "Can you find a pipe wrench or pliers? It looks like we've got an extra pipe down here."

Alex handed some pliers to Gerald, "Are you sure?"

"I just finished remodeling our bathroom last summer. Trust me I know more about plumbing than any detective should, and this pipe over here is not connected to anything."

Gerald strained with the end cap on the pipe until it broke loose, revealing a pipe stuffed with papers. He pulled the rubber banded roll of papers out and passed them to Alex, before pulling himself out from the cabinet. Alex had taken the papers to the kitchen table and was laying them out to photograph them.

"I'll call the crime scene techs back, so don't mess anything up."

Alex nodded at Gerald as he headed outside; knowing she'd already compromised the scene by unrolling the papers. She wanted her own documentation of the papers before the CSU unit confiscated everything and held onto it until they had everything documented. She knew the rules about handling evidence before the techs, but this case needed this kind of jump start.

Gerald returned and headed over to the kitchen sink and started removing things from underneath. "I figured if he used the fake pipe in the bathroom, then it's possible he might have under here as well."

Alex glanced briefly at the bottom half of Gerald's body as he wiggled further into the cabinet, before returning to her unofficial documentation of the evidence.

"This set up looks legit, so maybe it was just the bathroom."

"Regardless we're going to need to tear this place apart. One hiding spot makes me think he's got more."

Gerald smiled up at Alex, wiping some of the grime he'd gotten on his hands off, "That's my suspicious partner. And you'd better hurry up with the papers, they expected to be here within the next twenty minutes."

Alex continued snapping pictures with her phone and flipping the sheets over. She had expected to find porn, but there hadn't been one picture or DVD. It was all hand written bits and pieces, like a disjointed diary or memoir.

True to their estimate, CSU arrived a few minutes later and ushered the detectives out of the house. Alex informed the techs that she had transported the papers to the kitchen table and left them to be processed. She noted the skepticism in their eyes, but no one questioned her further.

"I assume you'll be forwarding those pictures to my computer?" Gerald asked as they sat in the car.

Alex was already scrolling through the pictures, trying to get a feel for what Gregory had been trying to capture. His rants were against the judicial system at times, noting that it used its power to stifle the needs of the common man, even if those needs were taking pictures of five year old boys.

"I'm going to check back with the techs since you are so talkative."

Alex barely noticed when Gerald left the car, because she was back reading Gregory ranting about the blackmail he was being forced to cooperate with or his probation was going to be revoked. He was ordered to rent a storage unit and pay for it with cash every month. This proved that the storage unit was his, but he had been paying for it under duress, which brought them back to the beginning again with no idea who was behind the sexual assaults.

Alex looked up as Gerald came huffing up to her window, "What did they find?"

"One of the techs went into the crawl space and found another fake pipe. It's loaded with porn. Pictures, flash drives and DVDs. They're going to call in another unit because there is so much stuff."

Alex handed her phone to Gerald, "Read this."

Gerald scanned the picture of the paper she had been reading, "Son of a bitch."

"That's what I thought too. When can we know what the porn is?"

"You don't think it's going to match the stuff we've got?"

Alex shook her head, "No I don't, but let's see if the techs will let us get a basic preliminary overview of what they uncovered."

Thirty minutes later they headed back to the car and planned the next step. The porn, while extensive, did not have one picture so far of any Hispanic girls, or any girls for that matter. The investigation was just beginning with a lot of data still left to sort through, but it was fairly evident that Gregory was not the perp for their sexual assaults.

"I'm going to call it a night and sleep for a few hours while I try to process this," Gerald stated as they sped back to the office.

Alex kept her eyes fixed to the road, trying to sift through the new information they had just gained. "I'll probably put in a little more time tonight."

"You might think about getting some sleep as well. No offense, but you're looking a little rough."

Alex glared at Gerald, "Thanks for noticing. Sorry I can't look like a million dollars all the time."

"Wasn't what I meant. I just thought it might help you if you got some sleep."

They drove on in silence, Gerald texting Janice to let her know he was coming home and Alex pouting about Gerald's comment. She knew she was tired, but sleep had become difficult recently because she kept thinking about Ben every time she tried to close her eyes. Alex had hoped a hot round of hide the salami would curb her body's needs so she could get back to doing the job. Ben had screwed all that up with his talk about having a serious relationship and not just a roll in the hay. And then to top it off he goes and allows little miss sorority girl jump into bed with him.

She'd never had a problem with finding a guy willing to scratch her itch, but the now the one she wanted wasn't interested in just having that. Who would have thought she'd ever find some guy who was everything any girl would want, but he wasn't interested in a casual relationship.

"I'll see you tomorrow around eight in the office okay. And I'm sorry about my comment," Gerald mumbled as he got out of the car and unlocked his.

"It's okay Gerald, I'm just bitchy because of this case."

"Sure that's it, probably has nothing to do with a certain guy."

"Good night Gerald."

* *

Ben lowered himself down into the hot tub, enjoying the feel of the jets pounding into his lower back. He'd really pushed himself with the weights earlier and his body was letting him know about it. Trevor sent some of his new riffs, but Ben hadn't been able to concentrate to make any good progress with lyrics. Lifting was always his best way to relax and clear his mind so he jumped back into his old lifting routine, and now his body was reminding him it had been a long time since he'd been that intense.

He leaned his head back and listened to the music softly playing in the living room. The last time he'd been in here was with Alex, and it was definitely not relaxing. She'd made it clear he could take her to bed if he wanted to, but he'd played things cool and kept his distance. Now Alex wanted nothing to do with him and he was back to sulking around with his cars and avoiding his friends.

His thoughts didn't even touch the situation with Samantha. He'd dealt with most if the guilt with what happened, but it still bothered him that after all this time his self-control was really that weak.

"Can I join you?" Zoe asked as she came onto the deck, followed by Winston at her heel.

"Sure, it feels pretty good."

Zoe dropped her robe, and Ben tried to avert his eyes from the miniscule orange bikini.

"Jesus Zoe, the suit barely covers anything."

Zoe slid down into the water and adjusted herself on the opposite side, "I prefer to sit in here naked, so consider yourself lucky I put anything on."

Ben shook his head, "It's always an adventure with you around here."

"I had an interesting conversation today."

"Do I even want to know with whom?"

Zoe smiled, letting the tension drag out. "I had a nice long conversation with Alex this afternoon. We talked about your hang-ups and if there is any hope for a relationship between you two."

"Are you serious? Can't you just leave things alone?"

"No because if I did that, then you'd mope around the rest of your life all by yourself. Even I could see there was a connection between the two of you, so I thought I'd help with matchmaking."

Ben laid his head back and groaned. He kept getting all these mixed messages from Zoe. She openly talked about having sex to make a baby, but then spent time trying to repair a relationship with a woman who intrigued Ben as much as she scared the hell out of him.

Zoe ran her foot up Ben's leg, "Talk to me."

"What do you want me to say Zoe? You don't listen anyways, so it's just easier to say nothing."

"What are going to do about Alex? We both know she's interested and so are you, so how are you going to get this repaired."

Ben glared at Zoe as she smiled, "There is nothing to repair. She made it clear she wants a roll in the hay and I'm not interested in just that."

"Don't I know it?"

"Not funny Zoe. Just drop it, I'll be fine."

"I don't know. I thought your attitude might improve after your little horizontal bop with Samantha, but you act like a monk who broke his vows."

"Good one Zoe. I shouldn't have taken advantage of Samantha, but that's cleared up, so can we change subjects?"

"Okay. I heard you lifting in the basement. Let me guess you are having troubles with coming up with lyrics for Trevor."

"Maybe I just wanted to work out, why does it have to mean something else?"

Zoe reached back and untied her top, "I doubt it's as simple as just working out. You lift to clear your head."

Ben noted her untying the top, "What are doing?"

"This top is killing my boobs, so I'm taking it off. Relax I'm not going to throw myself at you."

Ben focused his attention off into the shadows creeping along the deck as the sun continued to set. He knew Zoe was right, but he hated having her throw it right back at him.

"So if I stop lifting and starting sending Trevor some lyrics the interrogation will stop?"

Zoe tilted her head as if listening to a faint voice, "Probably not, but it would make some of your friends not so concerned."

"I'm pretty sure the only one being a worrywart is you."

"Wrong, you think Trevor isn't bright enough to pick on the halting pattern of returned song lyrics?"

Ben pondered this, "Doubtful, he's usually only concerned about the next party or finding the next budding superstar that he can mold."

Zoe sighed and leaned back, causing her breasts to nearly come out of the water. She noted Ben had his eyes fixed on a point far off near the barn, which probably meant he had caught a good glimpse. "Give Trevor some credit. He knows your patterns and has been hounding me to get you moving again and not moping like a teenager."

"I'm not moping. It's called processing and I think I'm coming around. I need to lift to help me concentrate and think, not avoid."

"We all thought maybe your dalliance with Blondie would have taken your mind off things and gotten you off the mat."

Ben took a deep breath, again realizing he was in here with someone who was trained to analyze things and had been with him for a long time. Zoe had seen Ben at his lowest point and helped bring him out, which meant she was an expert when it came to monitoring his patterns.

"I thought getting back into my routines would help focus me back with them music, it's just taking longer than I thought it would."

"Ah some honesty, that's good. Have you thought about calling Alex and seeing where things stood?"

Ben laid his head back and closed his eyes. He remembered the look of embarrassment on Alex's face as he walked out of her bedroom. Knowing that she wanted to have sex was one thing, but he refused to just be someone to scratch her itch.

"I'd say that boat has departed. Let's just say when I left her she was rather humiliated, which doesn't bode well for rekindling a relationship."

"Can I be candid with you?"

Ben almost choked, "Do you have any other way?"

Zoe gave Ben a look to show her disapproval, "I meant about something personal for me. I can understand what Alex is struggling with, because I've been dealing with men and/or women hitting on me for half of my life. It's very flattering at first, but it becomes a nuisance because you never know if someone is truly interested in you or just wants the trophy. So rather than being a trophy, it's easier to just have sex and move on. Sex is easy, but relationships take work and risk, something that probably scares Alex even more based on her failed marriage."

Ben stared into the dark for a long time. He'd never imagined things from that point of view, and his actions made him feel more like a heel than before. "Is that part of the baby plan, get the end result without all the messy stuff?"

"Some of it. I find it difficult to connect to men when I spend the majority of my time playing manager and keeping your head on straight."

Ben stared straight into Zoe's eyes, "That's bullshit Zoe, you're scared."

Zoe shrugged, "Probably. You amaze me sometimes with your ability to believe that love is out there. With everything that you've been through, you still believe in love."

"The alternative is just depressing, and you know I've been on that side of the mountain. I enjoy sex as much as anyone, but it's got to be in the right context. That's why I felt bad about what happened with me and Samantha. I tried to explain things, but she took off her clothes and then it just happened."

Zoe nodded, her amber eyes were misty, "I'm sure there was more to it than that, and it sure sounded … let's say enthusiastic."

"You were listening?"

"No, but when I went to check on Blondie and she wasn't in the bedroom, it wasn't too hard to follow the moans and groans to your room and figure out what was happening."

Ben felt his face flame, "I'm completely embarrassed."

Zoe shrugged, "You shouldn't be, sounded to me like you hadn't lost any skills from lack of practice. I would think Alex would have been quite pleased with a roll with you."

Ben noted her smirk, "Why do I get the feeling you have been talking with Alex a lot more than I have recently?"

"I won't confirm or deny, but I will tell you she is scared of getting involved and it not working out. She's pretty gun shy about being a relationship since her marriage was a catastrophe."

"How the hell can she know that if she doesn't even try?" Ben answered angrily.

"She's doing what is easiest. Having sex is generally a no brainer because it almost always ends well."

Ben glared as if Zoe was a co-conspirator.

"Trust me there have been sexual failures, but generally that happens with too much build up or too much pressure for more."

Zoe's comment hung in the air.

"So are you saying I might have some of the blame for this mess?"

Zoe turned her back before standing up and wrapped a towel around body to maintain the warmth, "Something else for you to ponder, but honestly it's a question you can't answer alone."

Alex glanced up from the monitor and saw Ben's face on her cell phone. She considered ignoring it, but figured it would better to just meet this head on.

"Hello."

Ben noted Alex was using her cop voice, stern and distant. "Hi Alex, I know you're probably busy with the investigation, but I wanted to apologize for my behavior and see if possibly you wanted to go out sometime to talk about things."

"I don't think that's such a good idea. I think you made things pretty clear to me already."

"I was wrong and someone helped me see the error of my ways."

Alex took a deep breath, "I assume this someone is a beautiful Jamaican."

"Yes, Zoe pointed out some faulty thinking I operate with, which makes everything black and white and that is not fair."

Ben knew Alex was still on the line because he could hear her breathing softly.

"You do know that she is in love with you right?"

"Zoe? No, we're just friends."

"Keep believing that, but mark my words. I'll be free tomorrow around noon for lunch. If something comes up I'll call you."

"Thank you Alex, I'll see you at your usual spot I assume."

"Yes, good night Ben."

Alex leaned back in her chair and ran her fingers through her hair, noting she was going to have to be back in the office in less than seven hours. This case was eating at her because she knew there was something she had missed or failed to see the importance of. She also knew having Ben swirling around the case was not helping her focus, as she kept finding herself thinking about going out with him or inviting him back to her house. Not conducive for solving a crime.

* *

He sent the text, expecting to get no response, but he needed his intentions to known.

Meet me tomorrow at 5 at the usual spot. Your plan has failed and the detectives have more info. Don't be late.

He was putting the phone away when it vibrated one time. Evidently he was expecting to get some type of correspondence. Opened the phone and squinted at the tiny words.

Will b there at 5. Need a solid plan.

He snapped the phone shut. This was not his problem and now he was going to be expected to sort everything out. Maybe he needed to just cut ties and sacrifice his dumb ass, which was a fairly viable option, even if it involved his son. His business partners would understand if anyone else was dealt with this way. Problem was that the detectives would keep digging once they realized there was no way Brooks was responsible for such an elaborate scheme.

Things to figure out before tomorrow.

16

Ben was out of the house before the sun had risen. He'd slept poorly with his mind racing the night before and even music hadn't helped to calm him. This upcoming date was even more nerve racking than the first one since he now had some history with Alex. He knew what he wanted to express, but Ben also knew if he went too fast or deep that Alex would distance herself.

He'd gotten into a good rhythm and his legs were feeling pretty good as he travelled deeper into the woods. Running had always been a solace for him when he needed to think or sort out plot lines when he was writing. Maybe this would jumpstart his block he had right now with coming up with lyrics. Trevor was being patient, but eventually he would start complaining to Zoe and she would come honing in with her razor sharp insight.

Ben slowed as he neared the house, allowing his body to cool down some before he headed inside. It had been a while since he had made the entire four mile lap around the property in less than forty minutes, but he was feeling pretty good and not as winded as he expected to be.

Zoe threw a towel at him as he entered the kitchen. "Looks like somebody couldn't sleep again."

"Sorry to have woken you," Ben apologized as he wiped the sweat from his face.

"It wasn't you," Zoe replied as she pointed to Winston sitting by the door. "He came to join me in bed when you left without him. So which of the world's problems did you solve today out there?"

"Just trying to get back in my routine."

Zoe poured two glasses of juice and handed him one. "Routine my butt. Usually you run to sort through things and you didn't sleep well."

Ben drained the juice and rinsed the glass, "Do you have cameras in my room?"

"No, but when you sleep well it sounds like a bear snoring in your room. No snoring, no peaceful sleep."

Ben was going to respond, but his phone interrupted first. "Hello Trevor."

"Huh, I thought maybe I'd dialed my partner, but clearly I got a wrong number since you answered. I still haven't gotten any lyrics back for two weeks' worth of work."

"I know Trevor, but it's been a little chaotic up here recently. I've had some trouble with focusing."

"Oh bullshit! You're up there moping around like a little girl because some chick isn't interested in happily ever after with you. I thought maybe you had moved on when you banged the little college girl."

Ben rolled his eyes, "She wasn't a college girl, she ..."

"I know she isn't a college girl, but she looked like she was like nineteen. Pretend like you are single and successful and it's okay to have a one night stand. Face it your other lady didn't want what you had to offer, so move on."

"Are you finished with the sermon?"

"Yes, but more importantly do you have anything for me"

"Not yet, but I should have something by this evening." Ben ended the call before Trevor could start back in again.

Zoe gave Ben a smirk, "Here's a thought. Why don't you use the slower songs and write something about heartache?"

Ben flipped her the bird as he walked to his bedroom. He'd already thought about doing that, but he wouldn't give Zoe the satisfaction of admitting it to her. He was nervous about the upcoming lunch with Alex and he needed to get his head straight without all the distractions.

* *

Alex arrived at the restaurant early this time. She'd pushed around paperwork and tried following up with Gregory's probation officer, but hadn't gotten anywhere. Alex wanted to put all of her frustration on the circles she seemed to be going in for this case, but the truth was this lunch scared her.

She wanted to make sure there weren't any unintended messages, so she purposefully dressed in her most casual outfit with a minimum of makeup. This was a final meeting to clear the air and move on, so maybe her partner would stop fretting about her. The only thing Alex couldn't control was her heart rate, which kicked up noticeably when she saw Ben walk in the front door.

Alex had to admit he was a hell of a specimen. His hair was still damp and looked almost black, but Alex knew it would lighten to a deep brown when fully dry. She smiled at his Deep Purple t-shirt, which looked like an antique and perfectly covered his upper body. Ben followed the hostess to the table, oblivious to the appreciative looks he got from the primarily female customers.

Ben leaned down, kissing Alex's cheek before sitting down and Alex found herself struggling to figure out the best way to get her thinking back on track. He smelled as good as he looked, and she remembered how well he knew how to use those lips.

"It's good to see you again," Alex said as she signaled to the waitress for another refill of her iced tea.

Ben smiled and took Alex's hand, "Yes it is. Thanks for taking the time to meet with me."

"What are we doing Ben? This didn't work, so let's just move on," Alex blurted quickly as she removed her hand from his.

"I needed to apologize first. I'm sorry about what happened, especially if I offended you or embarrassed you. It was my issue and I took things too far."

Alex lifted her eyes and stared at Ben, "If I recall it was me who took things too far."

"Maybe so, but I was expecting more from you than you were ready to give. I have realized I enjoy being with you very much and would like to have another chance to be with you."

"It's not that easy Ben. We want different things, so why are we wasting our time?"

Ben shook his head, "We weren't wasting time, because neither of us was doing anything other than existing anyway. We work and go through the motions without ever really connecting to anyone except our friends. Isolating ourselves to protect ourselves is not the answer."

"I can protect myself, I don't need that from anyone," Alex fired back.

Ben just smiled, "I know you are a very strong woman, but your heart is what I'm talking about. You can't deny there's something between us."

"Stop smiling and being all calm. Hell yes there's a connection between us, it's called hormones. Physically we are a great match, but you want the fairy tale."

"You're right I do, but I'm not going to push you as hard. I'll prove to you that I'm a good guy and I'm not going to hurt you like your ex."

Alex prepared to snap another snarky comment back, but stopped. She'd worked herself into a frenzy to make sure Ben understood that things weren't going to work, but now she just felt tired. His calm rational talk was not what she had expected or wanted. Alex wanted to fight, to hash things out and cuss and yell so it was perfectly clear that things were over.

Alex took a deep breath, "I don't have time for this right now. The case is reopened and I need all my attention being focused there."

"I understand, because there might be times when I've got deadlines to meet, which might interfere with our plans."

Alex felt her lips curve, "We don't have plans."

"We could if you weren't so stubborn."

"Fair enough, but we need some ground rules before this goes anywhere. I can't handle serious discussions about forever after, and I promise not to put you in compromising spots that make you uncomfortable."

Ben chuckled, "I think you might have misinterpreted my actions before. I very much wanted to make love with you, but I didn't want you to think I was only interested in just that."

Alex tilted her head, "Are you for real?"

"Sadly, yes I am."

* *

Brett Sandridge plopped into the chair and waited for the questions. He knew they would be coming after Gregory killed himself. Rumor around the courthouse was his notes were being dissected by everyone to determine if he missed anything while Gregory was on probation.

"So what have you got for me Sandridge?" Gerald Vilnew asked as he entered the room.

Brett knew Gerald from hanging around the courthouse, but had never crossed paths in person before. Vilnew had a reputation for being a hard ass in his youth, but seemed to have mellowed over the past couple of years being paired with Alex Milnero.

"Nothing that isn't already in my notes sir."

Gerald waved him off, "Save the sir shit. I've heard about you. Everybody says you're a good probation officer, so how did you miss this with Gregory?"

Brett leaned forward, "I didn't miss anything. He was the best probationer I've ever worked with. He did everything I asked and never got caught up in anything out there. He's the one guy I finally believed about turning his life around."

"Looks like you missed something. Are we going to find anything in all these notebooks we found?"

"I have no idea. I'm as curious as the rest of you, so if there is something, could you let me know before I hear via the rumor mill."

"I'll do what I can. If you think of anything that doesn't seem right, contact us okay?"

Brett stood and headed for the door, "You know I've been tossing this case around in my head since I heard about his suicide, and there isn't anything that gave me red flags. It's almost like he wrote the book on being the perfect probationer."

Gerald entered his notes in the database. Everything about this case was not what it seemed, because the more they dug the less they found. He called Alex's cell and left a message about the meeting, secretly happy that she didn't answer and interrupt her date.

* *

Robert Macias cruised by Alex's home for the second time, noting she had not taken the time to plant flowers or any other plants outside. He figured she was too busy trying to play policewoman to handle her regular duties. He'd stopped at the neighbor's but had gotten little information, other than she kept weird hours. His story about being a cousin from out of town seemed to cure their hesitancy to answer his questions.

He debated just going to the hotel until later, but he couldn't pass up the chance to let Alex know he was back. The single red rose was what he always left for Alex when they were married, to let her know he was thinking about her.

Alex listened to Gerald's message as she drove home. She'd considered answering his call at the restaurant, but opted to let him leave the message since he was so hell bent on her meeting with Ben. There wasn't much in the message, but she hadn't expected the probation officer to really have anything since he'd been snowed like everyone else.

She tapped her nails against the wheel as she drove. The discussion with Ben had gone much better than she could have imagined. It sounded like they were going to give things another shot, but with more parameters, which was something Ben needed to have so he knew where everything stood.

Alex pulled into her driveway and walked down to the mailbox, waving to her neighbor out working with her flowers. She was shuffling through the junk mail when she stopped at the front door when she spotted the single rose lying there. Immediately she turned and scanned the area, expecting to see Robert parked or standing nearby.

He'd started the tradition when they were dating, and what started as a romantic gesture had become anything but. Alex remembered the numerous times she had woken with a black eye because the laundry hadn't been folded correctly, or dinner was burnt, but there would sit a single blood red rose. It was his way of showing his affection, but Alex saw it as another way to try and control her.

Alex entered the house and did a quick inventory to make sure he had not been in her home. She had her hand on her revolver as she checked each room, and took a few cleansing breaths before she pulled out her cell phone.

"Hey Gerald, something has come up, can I stay with you and Janice tonight?"

* *

Ben backed his car into the barn and hopped out to greet Winston who had heard him coming down the lane. He grabbed the big dog and rubbed his ears as Winston whimpered with the raggedy shoe in his mouth.

Zoe was waiting on the porch as Ben walked towards the house. She appeared to be reading the paper, but Ben knew it was just a ploy to make sure he couldn't sneak into the house without talking to her.

"Interesting article?" Ben asked as he sat in the chair next to Zoe.

"It's just a prop. How did everything go?"

"You're shameless. Did you think maybe it's private and I wouldn't want to talk to you about it?"

Zoe pulled her hair behind her ears and nodded, "I considered that, but I really don't care. Did you tell Alex how you feel?"

"Yes I did and the conversation went very well. We are going to proceed with caution."

"Caution doesn't sound like much fun. Does Alex know you need to be pushed and prodded to get anywhere?"

Ben chuckled, "I'm sure you'll set her straight if you get the chance. I'm not supposed to push the relationship angle and she is not going to throw herself at me."

Zoe rolled her eyes. This relationship had a snowball's chance in hell of working with one person afraid of commitment and the other not willing to move forward without one. "You guys let me know how it all works out for you."

* *

"What the hell are you thinking making this meeting?"

He bit his tongue so he didn't say what he really thought about this situation. There had always been rules and the first was the easiest to remember, no pictures or videos ever. Follow that rule and there was never any evidence that needed to be suppressed or planted elsewhere.

"Shut up and listen. Your fuck up is the reason we are meeting, so listen. We have discussed this situation and Milnero is getting too close, so we need her to be distracted and get off this scent."

He leaned back in his chair and thought about the situation and how all of his attempts so far had backfired. "Do you have something specific in mind?"

"I've got a few ideas, but we need her personal bloodhound to be out of the picture for a while. When he is gone, make sure the evidence is gone from the basement."

"Jesus, you aren't going to kill Vilnew are you?"

"I'm not going to do anything, however this is what you are going to do."

* *

Angela Vilnew was crossing Broad Street with her grocery bags. She had wanted to get the last few items for her famous homemade chocolate cake before the weekend. Her attention was on the key fob and making sure she had unlocked the hatchback of her car before she got there and never saw the truck turn from the alley.

Witnesses later informed the police that the truck never seemed to slow down, even after the impact of Angela's body dented the bumper before flipping into the windshield and onto the asphalt. Others claimed they had heard the truck gun it's engine, but didn't know if was after the impact or prior.

The EMS units arrived within ten minutes of the accident and had Angela in the emergency room within twenty, which is why she was still alive when the visiting surgeon from Columbus was pulled out of his training and brought down for a look. He worked for seven hours and did everything he could, but admitted to his colleagues that it was out of his hands at this point.

Angela was placed in a medically induced coma to allow her swelling of the brain to reduce. The family was camped out in the waiting room and had prepared themselves for the worst, which was why only one person came to the operating room doors when the surgeon emerged.

"Mr. Vilnew?"

The large man tried to remain strong, but the tears were leaking, "Yes doctor."

"My name is Dr. Fording. Your daughter is in medically induced coma and will likely remain there for at least a week. She has multiple skull fractures, a broken femur, and multiple lacerations, so her body needs some time to heal. At that point we will need to see what steps to take then."

"What else can you tell me?"

Dr. Fording took Gerald's hand and squeezed, "She's young and strong, so that's in her favor. I can't make a prognosis at this point because we don't know what's going to happen with the swelling in her brain. In seven days I should have a better idea of what we are looking at."

Gerald looked the doctor in the eyes, "Is my baby going to die?"

Dr. Fording took a deep breath, hating this aspect of his profession. "I don't know. Your daughter appears to have at least three fractures to her skull, which is the worst of her injuries. I've done everything I can do at this point, but she might not recover. It's going to be touch and go for the next week. She will need your family's support right now, and prayer always helps."

Gerald released the doctor's hands and staggered back to the corner with his wife and delivered the news. He held her as she collapsed into his chest and sobbed. He'd been to numerous emergency rooms and questioned families, doctors, and patients, but never had he been summoned there for a family member.

Alex burst through the doors of the emergency room and saw Gerald and Janice holding each other. She could tell by the image that the report she had received was accurate and possibly worse than she had originally feared. Captain Kilpatrick had phoned her and told her to go to the emergency room, only saying that Angela had been in an accident.

Walking slowly, Alex tried to slow her breathing down and focused on Gerald as he stroked Janice's back as she continued sobbing. He looked up and locked eyes with Alex and they both started crying.

"How bad is it?"

Gerald wiped his nose, "It's bad. Sit down and we'll fill you in."

****

He continued driving as fast as possible until he reached the other side of town. There was no way Vilnew's daughter could have survived the impact, because she had barely registered the truck until he was almost on top of her.

Pulling the truck in and making sure the front end was sufficiently hidden was the next step, before he slipped out and walked away. If this went like he planned, then he was going to rid himself of two problems with one simple accident. Time to send the text.

It's done.

* *

Alex called Ben later and cancelled their date for the evening, explaining about the situation with Angela. He understood and offered to bring the family some food while they waited at the hospital. She declined, saying she would have to leave soon to get back to the office and start going through the material Gerald had been working on. He would be taking a leave of absence for the time being while he waited with Janice.

Family friends and fellow police officers stopped by for Gerald as the afternoon wore on and Alex slipped away. She didn't want to burden Gerald with the idea that she would have double duty trying to sort through the case, but it would be harder. They had a good working style which allowed both sifting through the material in their own way and getting all the pertinent information.

Gerald noted Alex's graceful departure and gave her a quick nod to acknowledge he understood what she was doing. He debated leaving to give himself something to do, but there was no way he could leave. His little girl was lying in the room with machines and monitors attached.

Alex lost her composure when she got inside her car and punched the dashboard before breaking into tears. She hated crying, and swore after all the crying she did while going through her divorce that it wouldn't happen again.

Gerald's desk looked like a bomb went off when Alex entered. He been going through the evidence logs and comparing it with his mental list of items from the two crime scenes. It was one of the gifts Alex took for granted, because he was like a walking computer in the field. Now his unorganized piles of data on his desk looked exactly like that, with no savant to unlock the mystery.

17

Ben woke the following morning to Zoe shaking his shoulder, "What do you want?"

Zoe arched her brow, "Lose the attitude, the state patrol is here to ask you some questions."

He slipped on some clothes and went into the kitchen where Zoe was busy brewing coffee and dazzling the officers as she glided around the kitchen in her silk nightgown and robe. "Here he is gentlemen. If you need anything, please let me know."

Her mega wattage smile faded when she turned away from the table and walked towards Ben.

"Good Morning Officers, is everything okay?"

The relaxed atmosphere Zoe had created ended immediately and police mentality took over. "Good morning Mr. Princi, I'm Officer Paxton and this is Officer Billingsley. Could you verify your whereabouts yesterday around 3 to 4 pm?"

Ben sat down and looked between the two officers. "I would have been here at the house, probably working in my barn or in the basement. Zoe was here with me."

The two officers looked at each other and Billingsley took the lead, "Do you own a black 1982 Chevy Blazer?"

Ben nodded, "I do, and it's at Chet's getting some work done."

This response led to another shared look.

"Listen, what is this about, because I'm starting to get a little freaked out?"

Paxton took over again, "What kind of work was being done?"

"I needed an upgraded exhaust system put on and Chet has a kid working there who could customize it the way I want, why?"

"We're pretty sure your vehicle was used in a hit and run yesterday and then returned to Chet's."

Ben sat down with a thud, "The police officer's daughter?"

"You know Sergeant Vilnew?"

"Not really. I know who he is, but I've never officially met him."

The officers gathered their hats and notepads as they headed for the door. "We'll have your vehicle in the crime lab for a bit before we can release it back to you. Could you come in and provide a fingerprint sample to help rule you out?"

Ben nodded, "I'll stop by in an hour or so. Do I need to have my attorney with me?"

Billingsley handled this question, "No, you couldn't have been here and in Blandale at the same time, so you aren't a suspect. You could bring your assistant along if you like."

The officer gave Ben a knowing look as he closed the door and followed his partner to the cruiser. They left with a wave and smile.

"Why does everyone assume because I live here that you get a pass to have sex with me?"

Ben looked over at Zoe, who he knew was eavesdropping in the other room, "Probably because you answer the door dressed like that."

Zoe looked down at her sleeping attire, "I'm totally covered."

"Covered yes, but every curve is quite visible, which makes you a walking fantasy."

"So do I get to tag along to the police station? I want to make sure my prints are eliminated also," Zoe said as she poured coffee into her mug with half and half.

"We're leaving in thirty minutes, so make sure you're ready. And try to dress to blend in."

Forty minutes later they climbed into Ben's Chevelle and headed into Blandale. Ben had shook his head when Zoe came downstairs in faded jeans tucked into black knee high boots with a bright fuchsia top.

"Blending in, huh?"

Zoe laughed as she buckled the seatbelt, "Never was my style."

Most male conversation stopped when Zoe entered the police station, as everyone wanted to catch a glimpse of the beautiful woman who the troopers surely informed them about. Zoe to her credit walked up to the counter as if nothing was out of the ordinary.

"Could we meet with Detective Milnero please?"

Ben shook his head and followed Zoe to the corner where they waited until Alex came to get them. He could tell Alex had had a rough night as there were dark smudges under her eyes and she'd been crying.

"Your girlfriend is not looking her usual stunning self."

Ben nodded, but rose to meet Alex. "Hey, we're here because they need finger prints from us. Is there someone specific we need to see? How are you doing?"

Alex smiled weakly, "I'm tired, but better than Gerald."

She'd heard the rumor mill around the precinct about the vehicle being one of Ben's. Alex also knew they wanted his fingerprints to compare with any lifted from the interior of his Blazer. What she didn't know was that Zoe was coming with him to the station and she was made up to the hilt.

Alex had already noted the men were hanging around the entrance just to catch a glimpse of her. She knew being tired was only part of her feeling bitchy towards Zoe; the rest was the underlying tension between them about Ben.

"Why don't we go to my office so we aren't under a microscope?" She left no option to decline as she walked off expecting them to follow.

Ben trudged along, wanting to say something, but not knowing what would be best. "I'm so sorry Alex. I feel awful that my truck was used in this incident. I hope you know I had nothing to do with this."

Alex ushered them into her office, "I know Ben. We know the Blazer was dropped off for repairs about three weeks ago and you have an alibi for last night." She spared a glance at Zoe, again inwardly cringing at how bitchy she sounded.

Zoe smiled, "Is there anything we can do to help your partner's family?"

"No, it's just a waiting game at this point. I'm sorry for my attitude. I'm exhausted and this case is dragging me down."

Ben flicked a look at Zoe and walked forward, "What can I do to help you?"

Alex smiled up at Ben and pulled him in tight for a hug. Ben ran his hands down her back gently as he felt her breath hitch. She pulled away with tears in her eyes.

"I appreciate the offer, but there isn't anything right now. I'll have you guys go down to the basement and ask for Jessica. She's the best tech down there and she'll get your fingerprints."

Zoe led the way out of the office and Ben lingered long enough to sneak a brief kiss on Alex's cheek.

The basement was a maze, but Zoe followed the signs directing them to the crime lab area. They peeked in the door when no one answered their knock and noticed the thin blond woman with pig tails listening to her iPod as she entered information into her laptop.

"Excuse me?" Ben said as he tapped the woman on her shoulder.

To her credit the woman casually removed her ear buds and turned slowly. "Well, well look who we have here. I'd wondered who had Alex all stirred up and I can see why. And you must be Zoe, heard about you too." They exchanged handshakes while Jessica explained the fingerprinting procedure. "I can see why the boys all were sprinting upstairs," she added as she eyed Zoe.

"It's a problem I deal with."

Jessica snorted, "I bet you just struggle honey. Must be hell for you having to walk amongst all us average people."

Zoe threw her head back and laughed, "I like you. Don't have much of filter do you?"

"Don't need one for this job, so why put in the effort. Okay Zoe the supermodel, let's get your right hand up on the screen."

Zoe sat in the chair and let Jessica maneuver her hand around as she glanced at her computer screen and frowned. Finally she seemed pleased with the image and shooed her out of the chair.

"Your turn tall dark and handsome," Jessica said as she led Ben over to the machine. "On a personal note, I don't have many friends, but Alex is one of them. So if you do anything to hurt her, I know many ways for you to die without leaving any trace."

Ben glared at Zoe as she chuckled in the corner. "I didn't think Alex was making anything known about our going out."

Jessica glanced over the screen, "Seriously you think she didn't let anybody know about you and her? You're a pretty smart guy, but you don't know shit about women."

"Amen sister," Zoe added from the corner.

"I mean you are a nice piece of arm candy, but don't think you can push my girl into anything. She's made of strong stuff and she won't be bullied."

Ben noticed the machine was turned off, so he removed his hand and headed for the door, "Nobody is trying to bully Alex."

Jessica shrugged her shoulders, "Being in a relationship with you might not be a bad thing, but you need to remember that Alex came out of a bad relationship, so she has a different reference point."

Zoe grabbed Ben's elbow and guided him out the office before he had a chance to open his mouth and make things even worse. "Let's go home."

****

Gerald stared at the numerous flower arrangements scattered around the room. He'd read some of the cards, but most of them he just handed to his wife. Gerald had always been a man of action, doing the job and doing it well. Now he felt as useless as the plants around the room, just sitting there trying to keep the atmosphere positive.

Angela's head was partially shaved where the surgeons had done their work. Gerald focused on the line between his daughter's hair and the smooth part of her scalp, willing her brain to stop swelling so she could recover. Janice sat by the bedside and held her hand, squeezing and murmuring prayers.

The most recent news from the investigation was that Angela had been hit by an unknown assailant, probably intentionally based on eyewitness accounts. State troopers had found the truck used in the hit and run after an anonymous tip directed them to Chet's Body shop. The owner of the truck, Benjamin Princi, Alex's lover boy, had dropped the truck off over three weeks ago and had already been cleared with his alibi.

Alex called to check in regularly and Gerald gruffly told her to do her job and stop calling. He knew Alex was concerned, but she was a crappy detective when her head wasn't in the game.

* *

Robert watched the activity surrounding the hospital room. He'd done some digging and found out that Alessandra's partner was at the hospital, tending to his daughter who had been involved in a hit skip accident. Robert surmised the easiest way to meet with Alessandra was to have her come to him and he knew eventually she would show up at the hospital.

Hanging out in the cafeteria proved to be the best source of information. Robert pretended to be a family friend and approached nearly every person in uniform, who were more than willing to discuss the tragedy involving Detective Vilnew's daughter. Being a lawyer allowed Robert to know how to talk around the officers which made them at ease with discussing the aspects of the unsolved case.

The one disturbing fact Robert had uncovered was numerous officers had been talking about Alex's boyfriend somehow being linked with the vehicle involved. He didn't know Alex had been involved with anyone seriously, and it didn't take long to get a name he could work with. Benjamin Princi.

Two hours later, Robert had as much information as he could gather off the internet regarding the former author who now wrote songs. There was also a mention of some substance abuse issues which had led him to rehab, resulting in his collaboration with junkie named Trevor Blaine.

Robert could feel his blood pressure spiking as he read the various articles. There were numerous pictures of Princi with a tall light skinned woman at various award shows. The woman was identified as his manager, Zoe Meloncourt. Robert felt the pictures showed a little too much familiarity between them to just be professional and now Princi was trying to move in on Alessandra. She needed to understand what type of man she was with and that Robert had changed and wanted her to come home.

Because he was concentrating on his laptop so much, Robert missed Alex enter the cafeteria, but she quickly got his attention when he heard her voice as she spoke with one of the officers. Robert noted she had let her hair grow and the long thick black hair looked good on her. She had also gained a little weight, which provided her with some curves that previously been missing.

She moved like a cat, gliding around the room, but taking in everything. Robert crouched down behind his laptop, certain that his beard and longer hair would conceal his presence. He tried to ignore the immediate erection he got as his mind replayed all the times he had seen Alessandra naked.

Alex paused at the checkout long enough to pay for a coffee before heading up to Angela's room. She needed a break from looking at the notes and pictures from the case. Gerald was pushing her hard to stay focused, but she knew at this point she was worthless to try and complete anything, so the visit to check on her friend was the next best option.

Janice smiled as Alex entered the room. "It's good to see you Alex. Gerald had no right to grouch at you the way he did."

173

"It's okay, he was right about me needing to stay involved with the case and not hanging out here with him. How is she doing?"

"No real change yet, but we're still early in this process. Gerald needed to get some air because he has zero patience and wants things to turn around quickly."

Alex nodded and stared at her friend. She looked like she was sleeping if all the tubes were removed. Alex wiped away a stray tear as she realized they had shaved the one side of her head for the surgery. Her long brown hair was gone and replaced with an ugly looking incision.

"Angela, its Alex. You rest for now, but I expect you have your skinny little ass out of this bed next week. We'll need to get some girl time in to get our nails and hair done," Alex whispered before stepping away.

Gerald had entered the room and seen Alex bent over talking softly into his daughter's ear. He didn't know what she was saying, but he could feel the power of her words as he watched Janice sob in the corner watching them.

Alex pulled Gerald into the hall with her as she exited, "So how are you holding up?"

"I'm fine," Gerald started before he stopped and leaned against the door frame.

Alex wrapped her arms around him and did her best to console her friend. Gerald laid his head on Alex's shoulder and sobbed. He had maintained his composure since the initial call, but the sight of his wife breaking down was too much.

"Okay, I'm done," Gerald said as he wiped his eyes and turned away from Alex. "I assume you're not down here to tell me you solved the case."

"Unfortunately no. I needed a break from the paperwork, so I wanted to check in here before I went home to get some sleep."

"Well now you've seen everything. Angela is resting in there while we worry. Go get some sleep and I'll text you if anything changes."

Alex grabbed Gerald's hands, "I just want you know I am so sorry and if there is anything I can do."

Gerald looked down at her, "Tell me your boyfriend had nothing to do with this."

"It was his truck, no doubt. Problem is that everybody in town knows Chet leaves the keys under the mat when he's got vehicles in his shop. Ben was nowhere near the truck when this happened."

"That's what I've heard, but I needed to hear it from you before I decided to go hunt him down myself."

Alex kissed Gerald on the cheek and headed to the elevator. She needed about ten hours of sleep and knew there was only about four on the menu.

Robert followed at a discreet distance. He had already circled her subdivision a few times, but this time he knew she would be there at her silly little home.

* *

He didn't even bother with the text this time. This situation was spiraling into a huge clusterfuck and he was damned if he was going down with the ship.

"At what point did you think this was going to be a good idea Junior?"

"Listen I was trying to give the police a good suspect and take out one of the lead detectives, so don't give me any shit about my thinking, Dad."

He wanted badly to throw the phone through the window. The level of disrespect was approaching a point of no return.

"You should remember your place and dial down your attitude."

Deep steadying breaths, "I'm sorry, but every time I try to fix this, something pops up outside of my control. Do you think I should point the investigation back towards Princi?"

"He has history, but he might be too much of a figure in the community to take the fall for this. Let me think it over tonight and we will talk tomorrow. In the meantime, do not do anything which will bring any attention to either case right now."

He ended the call before there was any chance for a response or rebuttal. He'd had enough of letting the underlings try to handle things, now it was time for the master to step forward and take the reins.

Brooks was still talking when he realized no one was on the other end. He had been dismissed like he had been his entire childhood. Nothing he ever thought or tried to do was good enough. He tossed the phone on the seat and fumed, running through the various scenarios he had sketched out. His vision briefly went to the back seat where the little girl lay, drugged and duct taped. Planting her on Princi's property would have been a good plan, but he had been ordered off the project, but there was no need to give up a gift.

* *

Alex barely took the time to lock her department issued Glock in the safe, before crashing on the bed. She wrapped her comforter around her and drifted off, too exhausted to do anything except kick off her shoes. Alex wanted the next four hours to go as slowly as possible so she could energize.

The sound of scraping wood was bouncing around in her head, and Alex sat up, blinking at her clock which showed she had only been asleep for twenty five minutes. She prepared to lay back down when the scraping started again, and Alex knew this wasn't some figment of her exhausted imagination. Someone was trying to break into her house.

Alex rolled off the bed and crawled over to her nightstand. She pulled her personal 9 millimeter out and worked her way towards the front of the house. It was quiet now, but Alex continued her progress.

She peeked around the corner and couldn't see anyone through the front window, but the front porch light was no longer on. It was something she did every night, but she couldn't remember if she had done it tonight before heading to her bedroom.

Alex crouched and shuffled to the door, making sure her torso stayed below the storm door window.

Twisting the knob quickly and thrusting the door inward, Alex stayed in her stance until she was positive that no one was there. She flipped the light switch up and down, but the light never came on.

Certain that no one was there, Alex went to the kitchen and got her flashlight while holding her pistol at her side. She turned every light on in the kitchen and then the living room as she returned to the front porch. Using the flashlight allowed Alex to see the smashed bulb on the sidewalk, but what disturbed her most was the single white rose lying on the mat.

Alex quickly slammed the door and locked it. Robert had been at her house and left this stupid memento from their time together. She had no proof, but there wasn't a doubt in her mind that he had been here and was following her.

Alex grabbed her cell phone and scrolled through the contacts. She took a deep breath before making the call.

"Gerald I hate to be a bother, but can I stay at your house again?"

****

Winston's barking woke Ben. He tried to figure out what the problem was because Winston rarely barked when he was in the basement with Ben. As he struggled to get his wits, it became clear as smoke wafted under the door. Ben blinked and struggled to listen for alarms blaring, but it was strangely silent.

Ben leaped out bed and pushed the armoire out of the way, revealing the door to the tunnel. He opened the door and forced Winston inside, closing the door before heading upstairs.

Flames were already spreading from the curtains to the furniture in the living room, and Ben could barely see the kitchen, which was completely ablaze. Covering his face, Ben shuffled towards the stairs and listened for Zoe. He could barely hear anything as the fire crackled and growled as it devoured more of the downstairs furniture.

Ben took time to wet a towel from the bathroom before running upstairs. The flames were rapidly moving to the staircase. It dawned on Ben that he had not heard a single smoke alarm.

"Zoe!!"

Ben heard nothing but crashing from the kitchen as dishes and bowls fell from the burned carcass of a cabinet.

Touching the door first, something Ben remembered vaguely from some safety class he had attended, it felt cool and Ben kicked the door in. Flames roared out at him and Ben dove to the floor.

Ben peeked inside and saw Zoe lying on the floor, not moving. Her bedroom was almost completely engulfed, including all of her furniture and the bed.

"Zoe!!"

When she failed to move or respond, Ben knew he had to get her out of the room before it collapsed. He tied the towel over his nose and mouth and plunged through the flames. Ben veered into the attached bathroom and tore the shower curtain from the rod.

Ben crawled to where he remembered Zoe lying, but the smoke was making it difficult to see anymore. The house was groaning and straining as it fought to resist the fire's onslaught.

Ben bumped into Zoe's arm as he crawled and he pulled her limp body to his. The heat was unbearable and Ben was struggling to get his breath.

An explosion downstairs interrupted the fire's relentless destruction as it sucked the oxygen from the room. The reprieve was short lived and the flames roared back in intensity as the outer wall collapsed, allowing the roof to start coming down.

Ben had shielded Zoe's body when the explosion happened, but he knew they had to go and quickly since the roof was collapsing. He took as deep a breath as possible and stood, picking Zoe up in his arms.

He stepped onto the landing and was amazed at the devastation. The entire lower floor was burning and all Ben could see was smoke and flames with little to use as a visual reference to figure out how to get to the basement. Ben leaned against the wall and went down the steps as fast as he could, noting that his feet were starting to get very hot on the tiles.

Ben weaved through the remnants of his living room and started down the stairs to the basement. The air down here was better and Ben pulled the towel off his face and gulped in breaths, fighting hard not to hyper ventilate.

He tried to check Zoe's pulse, but his fingers were shaking too badly, so Ben decided it was time to get into the tunnel and head for the barn. Ben opened the door and Winston greeted him.

"Go Winston, go to the barn."

Ben hunched his shoulders and shuffled as quickly as possible, making sure he didn't bump Zoe's head as he moved through the tunnel. Winston ran ahead, but stopped frequently to make sure he wasn't alone heading through the tunnel. Ben was certainly happy about not closing off the tunnel connecting the basement to the bomb shelter room in the corner of the workshop in the barn.

Old man Deeter said his father had told him the Russians were going to blow our country to smithereens and he wasn't going to go down that easily, so when the old barn burnt down in summer of 1957 it seemed like a sign to build a shelter. The design originally was just supposed to be the bomb shelter itself in the corner of the barn behind the two foot thick concrete walls, but Deeter decided to add the connecting six foot storm drain pipe tunnel to the basement of the house. Although it never served as a bomb shelter, the tunnel was a great way to sneak presents into and out of the house. And allowed Young man Deeter to sneak girls in during his high school years.

Ben had researched the house before buying it and there was nothing in the county's architectural paperwork which indicated Deeter had ever officially submitted the plans for approval. His lack of trust in the government made his secret tunnel an urban myth in the community.

By the time he reached the opening in the barn, Ben's lower back was screaming from shuffling down the tunnel with Zoe in his arms.

Winston was lapping from the underground spring which kept the trough in the barn filled at all times. Ben laid Zoe carefully on the worn couch he kept in barn and stretched his back.

Ben could see Zoe's chest was rising and falling so he relaxed some about her condition. He took a rag and wet it in the trough before wiping the soot from her face, and watched her pull away from the cold cloth and open her eyes.

"It's okay, we're safe."

Zoe's eyes blinked as she coughed, "What happened?"

Ben stepped out and grabbed a bottle of water from the adjacent room and opened it for her. "Drink this slowly."

Zoe tilted the bottled and drained half the bottle in one swallow, "I feel like I have gravel in my throat."

"You do kind of sound like Stevie Nicks," Ben smiled as he wiped the tears off his face.

Zoe looked around and realized she was in the barn, lying on the most disgusting piece of furniture Ben possessed, "Ben can you explain why I'm here and why you're crying."

The sound of sirens stopped Ben before he could attempt to explain. "We'll talk later, but let's get you upstairs so I can have some professionals check you out."

Four hours later, Ben stared at the smoldering remains of his house. The preliminary report was it was a complete loss. The final verdict would be in tomorrow when the fire marshal would have a chance to sift through things to determine a cause and be better able to gauge the severity of the damage. Paramedics had given them both a bill of clean health, minus some minor smoke inhalation, and a few first degree burns. An overnight stay at the hospital was suggested for precaution, but they graciously declined.

"Seriously Zoe, you can go to a hotel, I'm just going to stay in the cabin with Winston."

Zoe took Ben's hand, "I'll stay with you. You can't bottle all of this up and pretend it didn't happen."

"You've never wanted to even see the cabin, let alone stay there overnight."

"Special circumstances tonight, so deal with it."

Winston gloriously led the way as he sprinted up the path, knowing the destination. He was panting on the porch by the time Ben and Zoe arrived.

Ben let Zoe take a shower first while he drank water at the table. His adrenaline had faded an hour ago and he felt depleted, wanting nothing more than to sleep for the next twenty four hours. Ben realized as he finished his water that he would likely be on the couch since Zoe was there as well.

"I wanted to stay in there longer, but I wasn't sure how much hot water there was," Zoe said from the doorway as she roughed her hair with a towel.

"I don't know, I've never had a reason to have back to back showers here before."

"I wanted to say thank you. The paramedics said if it wasn't for you then I'd …"

Ben looked up as Zoe's voice trailed off, knowing exactly what she was thinking. "Actually Winston deserves some credit too, because his crazy barking was what woke me up."

Zoe touched Ben's shoulder as he walked by, "I don't know what I'd do without you, thank you anyway."

"I'll take the couch when I get out."

"You can share the bed, it's not a problem."

Ben smiled and headed for the bathroom, which was fogged up and smelling like Zoe's lotion, which one of the paramedics had loaned her upon her discharge. He wiped the mirror clean and stared at his grimy face. He'd nearly lost everything, his house and his best friend.

The water felt like heaven as Ben stood under the stream and let it run down his chest and back, when the tears started again. Someone had tried to burn his house down and nearly succeeded in killing both of them. He was leaning against the wall letting the stream loosen the lower back muscles he had strained earlier, when he felt cold air hit his back moments before Zoe's hands.

Ben turned to question why she was there and lost his ability to speak. Zoe had removed her robe and entered the shower.

"I don't think this is a good ide ..."

Zoe pushed Ben against the tile wall, pulling his head down to meet hers. Ben ran his hands down Zoe's back before settling onto her perfectly sculpted bottom. Ben's hands moved freely over Zoe's bottom while his tongue was busy melding with hers. A vibration of a purr from Zoe's throat made Ben come up for air.

"Did you say something?"

Ben knew he should stop this before it got further out of hand, but his brain and his mouth was having a hard time connecting. "I was saying something about a bad idea."

Zoe dropped her hand down and grasped his erection, "Somebody doesn't think this is a bad idea and neither do I. I could have died earlier and you saved me, so I'm not holding back anything anymore."

Any hope of protest ended as Zoe slowly started moving her hand towards the head. Ben leaned against the wall and stared at Zoe's glistening body as she stroked his penis. He knew she had a magnificent body, but seeing it nude was a completely different experience. Her mocha skin was set off only by her darkened nipples, which Ben trapped in his hands as he slowly caressed her.

"You need to stop, or this is going to be over way too quickly," Ben managed as Zoe's strokes had become more urgent.

Zoe stopped touching and dropped to her knees, taking Ben in her mouth with a brisk motion. Ben arched his back and thought his heart was going to explode as the blood rushed to his head.

Zoe stopped and looked up at Ben, "This first time needs to be quick, because I can't wait, but I expect you to take your time with me later."

Ben was going to discuss about the next time when Zoe stood on her tip toes and lined Ben with her fold, before lowering herself until Ben was completely sheathed. They didn't move for a few seconds before Zoe started shifting her hips and moving. Ben froze and then his body took over.

He lifted Zoe off the ground and she wrapped her legs around his waist as he pressed her against the wall. Ben could feel Zoe's fingernails raking across his shoulders as she bit into his shoulder as his rhythm increased to a fever pitch. He staggered out of the bathroom with Zoe wrapped around his waist before dropping her onto the bed. Zoe smiled slowly as Ben closed the door and lowered himself down into her open arms.

18

Ben cracked one eye to see Winston staring at him, imploring him to open the door so he could go to the bathroom. He staggered to the door and the dog flew by. The bedroom looked like a bomb had went off and Ben couldn't believe it was almost noon.

Wandering around the cabin, Ben finally found Zoe's note under the coffee pot.

> **Hope you slept well, I know I did. We will need to discuss last night later.**
>
> **Z**

Ben rubbed his face and tried to remember everything about last night. He certainly recalled the shower, but he wasn't certain if they made love two or three more times throughout the remainder of the night and early morning. All Ben was certain of was that he had not slept that soundly in a long time.

While drinking his coffee, Ben started to think about what actually happened last night. His house was a complete loss and if not for his dog, Ben and Zoe would both have been casualties. The lack of smoke alarms bothered Ben, because he knew they were not only hard wired into the house, but with a battery backup. During the entire trek through the burning husk of his house, Ben had never heard one alarm.

That was his biggest question of the night. At least until Zoe had walked into the shower, because the reason for that move was still unclear. He considered briefly at first that she was freaked out and was following through on her desire to get pregnant, but the subsequent passion was about more than procreation.

"Alright Winston, let's go see what kind of a mess we've got on our hands."

Ben walked up the path towards the smoldering remains of his house. Portions of the second floor remained attached to a fragment of the staircase, with thin tendrils of smoke still whisping from the rubble.

Ben noted there were two sheriff's cars and a couple of arson unit cars parked on the unaffected portion of his driveway. The fire department's pumper truck was positioned close to the house so they could douse any potential flare ups. Two men were off together having a discussion while three others were sifting through the rubble and entering items in their laptops.

"Mr. Princi, sorry about everything, could you come over here and provide some background?"

Ben eyed the man speaking to him. John Barrett had been the sheriff for Fleming county for almost twenty five years, and he looked as fit as he had when Ben remembered him. He had to be closing in on sixty, but he was still trim and kept his flattop as precise as ever. The only indication of age was that the flattop was white now instead of the deep brown of Ben's youth.

"Sheriff Barrett, what can I do for you?"

"Sorry we have to meet under these circumstances. Seems like the only time I ever have interaction with you its bad news."

Ben released his handshake, knowing he was referring to his trip to the house to inform Ben and his mother that his father had been killed in the factory. The sight of the sheriff's car had been traumatic for years after that visit.

"I figured there would be a lot of questions today and I've got some too if you don't mind."

Sheriff Barrett motioned with his hand towards the other man waiting patiently, "This is Chief Inspector Burroughs. He's the top arson investigator in the area and his people are doing their thing right now."

"Mr. Princi, it appears from all preliminary data that the fire started in the kitchen and foyer areas. Both contained residue of an accelerant, which caused the fire to spread quickly. I don't know the exact composition of the accelerant yet, but I should have the information within a few days."

Ben slumped against the fender of the cruiser, "Are you saying this fire was deliberately set?"

"That's why I'm here Mr. Princi. I need to ask you some more questions, because this could have been, hell should have been a double homicide scene. Have you had any problems with anyone recently?"

"No, no I've just been writing songs and working on my cars. I need to go find Zoe, she needs to know about this."

Sheriff Barrett grabbed Ben's arm to prevent him from walking off, "I already spoke with Ms. Meloncourt earlier, and she said to tell you she went to Maggie's. I just have a couple more questions."

Ben ran his fingers through his hair, "Okay, what else?"

"What exactly is your relationship with Ms. Meloncourt?"

"What the hell does this have to do with the fire?"

The sheriff looked at his boots, "I'm just trying to get feel for what happened and you two were the only people in the home. She didn't have much to offer, other than you've recently had a couple of romantic entanglements is how she worded it."

Ben looked over at his barn, vaguely remembering the journey through the tunnel that saved his and Zoe's life. It was that escape from death which had led to them falling into bed together last night, but it wasn't anything more deep seated than that. He couldn't see anyone trying to kill them for an imagined relationship.

"She is my manager, and she makes sure that I stay clean and sober."

The sheriff wrote short notes in his pocket notebook, but didn't act as if he believed everything he was being told. He made no disguise about the line of crap he was being shoveled. There was something going on between Princi and Meloncourt, and it was that odd relationship was probably at the root of this arson.

"If there is nothing else Sheriff, I'm sure I need to meet with my insurance agent."

Ben walked off before he could be stopped this time, heading to the barn. Winston was curled up on his blanket inside the door and he thumped his tail as Ben stormed inside. Ben rubbed his neck; silently reminding himself to make sure Winston got a bone for his quick thinking last night.

****

"Hey did you hear about your boyfriend's house burning down last night?"

Alex pushed herself away from her desk and looked at the desk phone blinking to indicate numerous messages. "What are you talking about Gerald? I've been here almost all night and nobody called me about anything."

"Well turn on a television, because the news was just on and they are reporting that the home of famed novelist, Benjamin Princi was destroyed overnight. No causalities reported."

Alex snatched the remote and turned on the television, switching over to the local Dayton news report. A petite blonde was providing the basic information, while the cameraman was scanning the area, showing the smoking remains and various officials roaming around. Alex did recognize that this was the same blonde she'd seen crying leaving Ben's house last week, which meant it was the Samantha person Zoe had told her about. Alex tried to see if there was any sign of Ben, and realized Gerald was still talking to her on the cell phone.

"What?"

Gerald took a deep breath before continuing, "I said instead of working yourself into a frenzy, maybe you should go check it out."

Alex slipped into her chair, "I'll try to call him first then maybe I'll stop out and see what's going on. Sorry I snapped at you."

"No problem, I've been dealing with you for a while now."

Alex smiled and ended the call. There was no answer on either Ben's or Zoe's cell phones, which could mean a number of things, so a trip out to his house was the next order of business.

She closed up her files and logged off the computer before stopping by the restroom to check her hair and makeup. The long night and early morning had done nothing to help with her looks, so she pulled the hair into a ponytail and walked out.

Robert watched from across the street in the McDonald's parking lot. He knew Alex had been in the office since early this morning, and was just waiting for a chance to meet with her to talk. Knowing she was spooked now, he understood is best option was to try and meet with her in a public spot where she would be more receptive.

His plan was ruined as Alex stormed out of the office and jogged to her car. Robert reminisced about how many times he'd watched Alex move like that when they were married.

* *

Ben parked on the street and walked to the house, trying not to get nostalgic about his high school days at this house. Maggie opened the door as he walked towards the house.

"Where's the hero?"

Ben smiled, "I left Winston at the barn. He seems pretty worn out by all the commotion."

Maggie welcomed Ben from the top step with a full hug and kiss on the cheek, "Thank God you are safe. Zoe was filling me in about everything that she remembered."

Ben averted his gaze, hoping Zoe was not sharing everything she remembered from last night. "No sense making a big fuss, we're okay."

Zoe met them in foyer as they entered the house, "My hero. I've contacted our cell phone provider and they will have new phones for us later this afternoon. I also need to get a new laptop."

Ben watched Zoe tick off the items with her finger, noting that she was not really making eye contact with him. "Sounds like you've got things rolling already. Has the insurance company called yet?"

"I called them when I got over here. They will send out an agent to talk with either you or I, probably better if it was me since I know what items we will need to have replaced."

Zoe looked up and caught Ben's gaze, knowing he was unsure about how this morning was going to play out after last night's activities. She had originally gone to check on Ben in the shower when she heard him sobbing, but it all changed when she opened the door. Seeing him there and knowing what he had done to save her was all it took to cross the line.

She'd only intended to show her gratitude and feeling alive, but it became so much more. Ben had been cautious at first, but then let his guard down and relaxed. Zoe knew they were two people celebrating being alive, but she also knew Ben's guilt would be back in force this morning about what happened.

Maggie pulled Ben into the kitchen, interrupting the awkward moment. "Sit down and eat something. I want to hear everything from the beginning, because Zoe's version was shorter than yours."

Ben started talking about the evening and watched as Zoe hovered around the kitchen. She got out drinks and plates for sandwiches, which had been delivered from the Red Cross earlier in the day. Ben knew Zoe was listening intently to the story while appearing to go about her usual duties.

"How did this happen?" Maggie asked as she grabbed Ben's wrist to look at his bandaged hand.

"I'm not really sure. I think it was either from Zoe's door knob or grabbing the stair rail by accident. The EMT said it is a minor burn, just needs some ointment and to be covered so it doesn't get infected."

Zoe blinked back her tears as she turned towards the sink, "Well lunch is served. I think it's time for your number one fan to give her report."

They watched Samantha report live from Ben's property while they ate silently. Ben tried a few times to catch Zoe's eye, but she seemed fixated on the news report.

"I guess it's a good thing that our cell phones didn't make it or we'd have a million calls, which reminds me I need to call Trevor."

Zoe laid a hand on Ben's arm, "I called him when I got here to let him know we are okay. I also called Alex and told her where to find us."

Tires squealing outside let them know that Alex had likely arrived. Ben met her at the door and introduced Maggie, who greeted Alex coolly.

"I just heard about the fire. I've been so wrapped up in the case that I didn't even know."

Ben brought Alex into the kitchen and sat her down. Maggie gave her a drink and offered some sandwiches.

"It's been pretty weird this morning with answering all the questions from the sheriff and the arson investigator."

Alex stopped in mid bite, "Are you saying this was arson?"

Zoe jumped in at this point when she sat down, "It seems to everybody that the fire was deliberately set. If it wouldn't have been for Winston and Ben, I don't know if I would have got out."

Alex looked up at Ben and noted his red face, clearly uncomfortable with the praise. She'd already noticed his hand was bandaged and he seemed embarrassed with all the fuss going on.

"It was really nothing."

"Whatever, you came upstairs into my room and carried me all the way through the burning house to the barn. There was no way I was going to get out on my own," Zoe continued.

Alex noted Zoe was looking directly at Ben and the look seemed to be conveying much more than her words, as Ben broke eye contact and looked at the floor. There seemed to be an air of tension in the room.

Maggie broke the spell, "So Alex, how do you know Ben and Zoe?"

"Well I ran into Ben at the office and we have gone out a few times and through that I met Zoe."

Maggie seemed to weigh this out, knowing that this was only part of the story. She'd not gotten much from her sources around the town about the young detective, but everyone seemed to know who she was.

"So, when do we need to get to town for our new phones?"

Zoe gathered her things and walked with Maggie, "Maggie already planned to take me, so you guys spend some time together and we'll talk later."

Alex watched the women leave, and the tension in the room didn't seem to dissipate. "That was odd, even for Zoe's standards. Is there something I'm not catching?"

Ben took a long drink of water. Since last night he couldn't seem to get enough to drink. "I don't know. Things have been really amplified since the fire and it spooked Zoe about how close she came to dying."

Alex walked over and hugged Ben, trying not to notice his initial stiffness at her contact, "Are you really okay? I can tell you've got some burns that were taken care of, but is there anything else?"

"They said I have some minor smoke inhalation, but nothing that shouldn't clear itself up over time. I'm just a little shook up over the fact that someone set this fire and how bad it could have turned out."

"I'm just glad you're safe. Let me know if you need some place to stay."

Ben looked at Alex and wondered what the offer meant. She was clearly concerned, but he didn't know if she was just being polite or suggesting the relationship move forward.

"I'll probably just stay at the cabin, so I'm close by while the insurance people come to do their thing."

Alex smiled and stepped back, "Okay, but the offer stands and let Zoe know she's welcome to my spare bedroom since I know how she feels about the cabin."

Ben looked away as his face reddened, remembering how Zoe had overcome her previous feelings about the cabin. She hadn't complained about anything while she was there, only offering herself to Ben repeatedly. Of course he had done little to discourage what happened.

"Careful what you ask for, she might take you up on that offer and then she'll try to take over," Ben answered with a smile that didn't reach his eyes.

Alex pulled Ben down for a quick kiss and headed for the door, "I'm sorry I have to run off, but I just wanted to make sure you were really okay."

Ben watched Alex walk to her car. He'd wanted to start something with her and it had backfired, and now he got the feeling she was trying to reengage something. The timing sucked because he had just made love with his best friend.

Maggie drove for a while before she started with the questioning. "Okay what was that all about back there?"

Zoe adjusted her sunglasses and focused on the scenery, "I just thought Ben should have some alone time with Alex."

"I got that, but there seemed to be something going on between you two. If I didn't know better I'd call it a lovers tiff."

Zoe swung her gaze over, "Really Maggie, you've been trying to play matchmaker for us for years and it isn't going to happen."

"If you say so, but I don't think the marks you have on your jaw line came from the fire. If my memory serves me correct that happens when someone, typically of the male persuasion hasn't shaved recently and you get razor burn."

Zoe didn't answer at first. She thought getting out of the cabin with Ben would help with making the memories of the previous night fade. Zoe knew the razor burns were there and she vividly recalled how Ben put them there, not to mention the ones on her inner thighs.

"Before I go any further we have to have a pact."

Maggie eyed Zoe suspiciously before agreeing.

Zoe took a deep breath, "What I'm about to tell you stays right here between us, at no time can you say anything to Ben. And most importantly is that I can't have you try to push things along."

"I don't like the terms, but it sounds like a hell of a story, so I agree."

Zoe turned towards the window and started talking.

Ben punched in the numbers after Zoe dropped off his cell phone at the barn. He wanted to talk to her, but Zoe claimed she needed to get back into town with Maggie before the computer company closed for the night.

"Hey Trevor, this is my new phone number, so call me back when you get a chance."

Ben barely put the phone down when it began to vibrate, "That was quick."

"I didn't recognize the number, so I had to make sure it wasn't some honey I'd ditched trying to track me down."

"Oh what a life you have to lead."

Trevor chuckled, "You're saying that to me. I saw on the internet that you single handedly saved yourself, your dog, and carried our unconscious manager to safety."

"Slight exaggeration, because Winston saved himself," Ben replied quietly.

"Don't want to talk about it?"

"Not really, it was a very eventful evening and I've got a lot to take care of, but I wanted you to know we're okay."

"I know buddy. Zoe called me as soon as she picked up the new phones and she didn't want to talk about it either."

"Trevor, I lost every everything I was working on, so it will be awhile before I get some stuff going again."

"Don't sweat it, it wasn't like you were giving much to work with anyway. Hey before I go. What band did Randy Rhodes leave to join Ozzy?"

Ben was preparing to answer before he realized Trevor was gone. A playful jab followed by a rock trivia question, which was Trevor's way of saying everything was okay. He never wanted to let on that he worried about anyone except himself.

"Quiet Riot," Ben answered to the empty barn.

He found some of his old clothes in the storage containers and took out some of the acceptable things to transport to the cabin. Neighbors had dropped off some casseroles and desserts, so he wasn't going to starve anytime soon. Ben had hoped Zoe might return at some point so they could discuss what had happened last night, but he gave up hope when it got dark.

19

Ben was bathed in sweat when he hit the floor wrapped in his sheet. He'd been running through the fire and he couldn't find Zoe. Winston leaned over the edge of the bed and whined at Ben, clearly wanting to know what he was doing on the floor.

The sun was just coming up, so Ben figured it would be fruitless to attempt to go back to sleep. He staggered to the kitchen and got the coffee pot going, hoping the caffeine would help erase the residue of the nightmare.

Ben grabbed his new phone when he realized it had a light blinking on the screen. It indicated he had a new text message and after a few minutes Ben figured out how to access the message.

Figure you are at the cabin, didn't think it would b a good idea for me to b there as well. Staying w Maggie.

Ben didn't recognize the number, but knew it was Zoe. She was trying to avoid him so they wouldn't have to discuss what exactly happened the other night and what it meant for the future.

****

Alex picked up her cell before the first ring ended, "What's going on? Is there a problem?"

"No Alex, I'm calling you with good news. Angela is improving and they may try to ease her out of the coma later this afternoon. I also wanted to see if you had found anything out about Ben's fire.

Alex filled Gerald in with what she knew, which was precious little. They knew it was clearly an arson case and that it started with two separate ignition points, but had no other clues as of this time. She's bribed one of the arson investigators with a pizza and a 6 pack of coke to get that information.

"Why are you so interested in the fire? I thought you didn't like Ben."

Gerald scoffed, "It's got nothing to do with liking him. I respect the hell out of him for even attempting to engage in a relationship with you."

Alex wiped the tears out of her eyes, as she recognized her partner's sarcasm returning now that his daughter seemed to be out of the woods. "I suppose that was meant to be a compliment. I've missed you too."

"Okay enough of this sentimental crap. I called because it seems a little too coincidental that something has happened to both of us outside of work."

Alex leaned back in her chair, "You know I didn't think of it like that, but I guess it's true."

"Well I've had nothing but time on my hands while we sat her with Janice and it kind of struck me as convenient that both detectives on the case are distracted. It could be nothing but bad luck, but both things were premeditated, so …"

"We must be getting close and someone is getting nervous," Alex finished. "Something that bothers me about this premise is that means someone is watching us very closely." Gerald sighed, "Or someone is already very close to this investigation. It would be likely someone would know about my daughter, but your relationship or whatever you call it with Ben is fairly new and under the radar."

Alex ended the call and promised to stop by tonight for a face to face meeting. She needed to review the case, starting from the beginning and to pay attention to anyone who might have been on the fringe that might have accessed any of the data from the investigation.

* *

They met at their usual spot where it wouldn't attract much attention.

"Please tell me that you had nothing to do with the fire. I specifically told you to leave it alone . . ."

"Me? I thought that was something you did to cover things up."

He wanted to choke him for the interruption, but that would have created a scene which couldn't be explained. "I wouldn't go and do something I told you not to do. Clearly somebody is inserting themselves into this situation, so it might be best for us to just fade to the background right now. I need to see if any of our people are trying to give us some unwanted assistance. Let the arson investigators and detectives follow the evidence, since it won't lead to us."

He watched the younger man closely to make sure he wasn't being deceived. Clearly this arson had been a total shock for him, although he seemed to enjoy that it had happened to Princi.

"Okay so the plan is to lay low, and that means under the radar's radar."

* *

Ben finished with the insurance adjuster and returned to the cabin. The insurance company was going to submit their paperwork and hoped to have the sign off for the architects to submit some plans for the rebuild quickly. He'd hoped that Zoe would handle this aspect of the claim, but the adjuster said it had to be Ben because it was his policy and property.

"Hey have you finished with the adjuster?"

"Yes, I'm done and signed everything."

Zoe took a deep breath, "So about the other night, I assume you want to sit down and talk about it."

"I think we need to talk about it don't you?"

"I didn't think you'd just pretend like it didn't happen, so how about if we meet for dinner at Maggie's?"

Ben sat down, "Please tell me that you have not talked with her about this."

"I didn't intend to, but she kind of knew that you'd rung my bell so to speak, so yes she knows."

"Is she going to be involved in this conversation?"

"No she is leaving for the evening, said we needed to have this conversation without her influence."

Ben arrived as Maggie was walking out to her car. He tried for nonchalant, but knew his face was bright red.

Maggie grabbed his hands, "Now don't you go over thinking this Benjamin. We all know there is chemistry between you two, so this was inevitable."

"I thought you weren't getting involved?"

Maggie kissed his cheek, "Trust me, this is my not getting involved. Remember to use your feelings and not to analyze everything."

Zoe was curled up on the couch, tapping frantically on her laptop. Ben walked into the kitchen first to get something to drink and take his mind of the thoughts swirling in his head.

"You might as well stop stalling and get in here."

Ben entered the room and took the other end of the couch. "This is the first time I've felt this nervous around you since you arrived in Jamaica, and at least I was drinking then."

"You need to relax Ben and not make a big deal about what happened. We had sex and I don't want to get married."

Ben recoiled, knowing she was throwing his relationship issues out there. She had set the laptop down between them, making a division on the couch so Ben knew there was a definitive separation.

"I didn't think you did, but shouldn't we talk about what happened?"

Zoe took a deep breath, "What do you want me to say Ben? I almost died and I was happy you saved my life. I didn't intend to have sex with you, but when I heard you crying in the shower, I just went in."

"Why have you been avoiding me since then if it was just some meaningless sex?"

"Because I know you and your whole relationship trumping everything else mentality, so I wanted you to have some time to clear your head and realize it for what it was. We're friends and business associates, but adding couple to that mix is not something we 're ready for."

Ben looked out the window, "But it wasn't that long ago that you were asking me to father a child with you."

"Touché'. Maybe you were right about that being a potentially catastrophic mistake."

Ben stood up and stalked to the door, "You're full of shit Zoe. There's more going on than just you being happy to be alive. You know how to find me if you need to really talk about this."

Zoe flinched as the front door slammed and wiped the tears from her cheek.

* *

Alex rubbed the bridge of her nose to ease the discomfort in her eyes. She'd been scrolling through screens of log notes covering Gregory's criminal past. He'd started as a juvenile and continued right into adulthood, which was documented in a precise, logic based database.

"Alex, why don't you go get some sleep?"

Gerald gave her a look, letting her know he was pulling rank and that arguments weren't going to work. He'd immersed himself back in the investigation once the experts assured him that Angela was out of the woods and there was little chance of a setback.

"It's that bad?"

"You look pretty rough, so why don't you go soak in your tub and then get about eight hours of sleep. I will see you tomorrow, but not before 10."

Alex wanted to debate, but the thought of soaking in the tub was too much of a lure. "Okay, but I'm going to take this file to read while I'm soaking."

"Whatever makes you feel better, but don't get any pages wet."

The file lay on the bathroom counter as Alex reclined in the tub. She'd refreshed the hot water once and knew it was about time to get out, but wanted the last ten minutes in the fragrant water. Her mind was racing, knowing there was enough information in the paperwork with Gregory to lead her to the actual person responsible, but not finding that key to unlock everything.

Her phone was within reach and she had seen the lights indicating calls coming in, but Alex made a silent vow not to answer anything at least until her bath was finished. She did bend the rule to at least listen to the voicemails, since she could choose to respond or not.

Most of the calls were of minimal importance, but there was one from her mother and one from Ben that caught her attention. Family trumped possible romance, so Alex hit the redial button.

"Sorry Mama, I was resting and didn't get your voicemail until a few minutes ago."

"It's fine dear, I did some checking down here and you were right. Robert has taken a leave of absence from his firm. I spoke with the secretary and tried to insist that I would only work with him and she told me off the record that he had abruptly left town a few days ago and no one knew when he planned to return."

Alex let out the breath she'd been holding. It wasn't just her imagination that she been feeling monitored. And the rose at the door was his way of letting her know that he was around.

"Alessandra, are you okay? Do we need to contact anyone?"

"It's going to be fine mama. Remember I'm are not in Texas anymore. Up here, my friends will help me and make sure he does not violate the restraining order."

They talked for a few more minutes about work and the plans they were making for a visit at the end of the summer.

Alex ended the phone call, before checking the alarm system and double checking her deadbolt. She was preparing to make the next phone call when the doorbell rang, causing her to drop the phone and press against the interior wall. It couldn't be a coincidence that someone was at her door at this time of night and Bobby was potentially roaming around the area.

Ben waited patiently, wondering if he had stopped by too late. He'd heard something from inside, but Alex had yet to answer the door.

Alex opened the door quickly with her pistol at her side, "Oh it's you Ben. Come inside."

Ben stepped inside as Alex engaged all the locks. "So is there a reason you are answering the door in a robe with your pistol?"

"Let's talk in the kitchen."

Ben walked into the kitchen and sat down, while Alex stowed her pistol back in her work bag. "If this is a bad time, let me know and I'll shove off."

Alex ran her fingers through her wet hair before taking a seat, "It's not you, just some shit from my past. I was getting ready to call you back when you rang the bell."

"I just needed to talk with someone, and I thought you might be able to help me work through this. A disclaimer up front is if this is too much, then just shut me down and I'll stop."

"Deal. Let me have it."

Ben started talking and pacing as he tried to explain everything that had happened over the past few days. Alex knew he was stressed about the arson, but she had no idea about the Zoe situation. It explained about how uncomfortable he'd been with her the day before.

"So am I out of line here?"

"I don't know what to say Ben, this is a lot of stuff. I can say I didn't expect a good portion of what you shared."

Ben sat back down and grabbed Alex's hands, "See and all this doesn't even encompass that I've got these feelings for you and whether we've got something or not."

Alex pulled her hands from Ben, "Listen right now is probably not the best time for me to be giving you any advice, especially since you're having sex with your manager or handler or whoever the hell Zoe is."

"I didn't want to hide this from you, because I knew it would just become a bigger problem."

"Well I don't want there to be a bigger problem, so maybe you should just go back to your cabin or play house with Zoe wherever she is staying." Ben watched the tears roll down Alex's face as she yelled at him. He expected there to be some emotion, but hadn't anticipated that Alex would get this angry. He thought laying everything out would be best, but the door slamming at his back was a final sign he had misjudged things.

"I need you to be quiet and listen for a minute. I'm not sure what to do and you're probably the wrong person to ask, but I need some advice."

Trevor leaned back in his chair, knowing it was not like Ben to talk to him this way, so something major was going on. "Alright I'll save my questions until the end."

Ben rambled for nearly fifteen minutes, trying his best to get the facts in order. He didn't want to add too much speculation into the mix, but felt the surrounding things might help.

"So what do I do now?"

Trevor had expected to hear something out of the norm, but nothing would have prepared him for all this. "First off I'm glad to hear that you are becoming more social, but seriously dude. You're banging our manager. This is not going to end well."

Ben ran his fingers through his hair, "Could we not focus on the sex with Zoe?"

"How can I not? You mess this relationship up and it's going to affect my financial future. God, of all the people you could have screwed. Have you never heard the saying about not shitting where you eat?"

"Okay this was a mistake to talk with you about this. I need to know about the future with Zoe and what to do."

"Knowing Zoe, since she's three steps ahead of us, she already knows you are freaking out. Maybe act like it was nothing and go about business as usual."

"I can't act like it was an oops. We had sex four times that night."

"See now I don't have any sympathy for you because that is just bragging."

Ben ended the call after swearing Trevor to secrecy and he could not even talk with Zoe about it if she called. He decided Trevor was probably right in that getting back into a routine was probably the best way for him to deal with this. Moving past this was going to take time, but Ben didn't know how else to get past it all.

* *

"Hey Alex, did you notice that every note that was in Gregory's file from his probation officer was nothing but glowing?"

Alex looked up from the monitor and pushed her glasses up into her hair, "Yeah we noted that from before."

"Well Miss Smarty-pants, did you compare them with the previous probation notes? No comparison, because he was not following any of his rules in his previous probation stints."

"So either he really did turn his life around in his prison the last time or ..."

Gerald finished her statement, "The probation officer was putting in fake notes to cover something up."

Alex scrolled back a few websites, "Wait, I've already looked at his personnel records. He was identified as one of the best probation officers the county has ever used, which is why he took the promotion in Darke County."

"That may be, but something is not adding up here and we need to find out what it is. I think this is the key to getting out heads wrapped around this case."

Gerald's words hit the mark and neither had a response. Alex continued surfing through the online records, while Gerald handled the paper files. It was his slower, old school approach which finally gave them a starting point.

"I've got something I want you to read."

Alex looked up from her screen, "Give me a case number and I'll pull it up."

Gerald shook his head, "No come read this report. I don't want anyone knowing that you are pulling files up on your computer."

Alex grabbed the file and started skimming through the details, "Oh shit Gerald this is bad."

"That's what I thought too, so we need to get a plan in place before we proceed."

* *

Ben threw the extra burger on top of Winston's dog food. He'd tried to eat some of the stuff he had grilled, but it wasn't happening. His thoughts kept going back to the shower and bedroom in the cabin. Ben was pretty sure he still smelled Zoe in the bathroom when he finished his shower.

Winston grabbed the burger and trotted off to the bedroom to savor his treasure.

"I see you're still spoiling him."

Ben turned to see Zoe standing in the doorway, "Well I didn't want to waste the food, so it seemed like a good option. Come on in, you don't need an invitation."

Zoe set her bag and laptop on the table and settled into the chair across from Ben, "So we haven't talked for a couple of days. Are we okay? Because it might make our working together weird if I can't talk to you."

"It's probably going to depend on what we need to talk about, since you made it clear certain topics are off limits."

"I'm here as your manager. You haven't submitted anything to Trevor for weeks, and boredom for him is just one step away from him relapsing. Maybe you could come up with something about a hook up."

Ben shot her a glare.

"Too soon huh? Thought maybe a little levity in the situation would help get you out of this funk."

Ben stood and started pacing around the small kitchen, because it was easier than staring into Zoe's eyes. "I know you deal with things by compartmentalizing, but take it from someone who thought he was a master at it. It will bite you in the ass."

"Can I be blunt?"

Ben motioned for her continue, bracing himself for what he was pretty sure was coming.

"I can deal with the fact we made love and it was pretty freaking spectacular, but I'm not ready for your head games about us having a more serious relationship based on that. If, and it's a big if. If we move towards having a more romantic relationship, there will be no doubt in your mind what's happening."

Ben exhaled and sat back down.

"Let me guess, you were expecting something harsher."

Ben nodded, "Figured I'd hear something about you not turning into a drunk because you couldn't deal, like I did."

Zoe covered his hands, "I wouldn't throw your addiction in your face, but I need you to get your head straight. You have an appointment tomorrow at 10am with Blondie at the barn."

"Why did you schedule something with Samantha?"

"The newsies are dying to speak with you about the arson, and I think we can spin things with her because of how she feels about you."

"So you want me to meet with Samantha and manipulate her because she has crush on me."

Zoe tilted her head, "It sounds bad, but yes that is what I want you to do. Notice I didn't schedule the meeting here, where Blondie might try some unorthodox reporter tactics to distract you."

Ben winced at the jab, "Okay I can handle it."

Zoe gathered her bag and headed for the door, "I'll be staying with Maggie again, but I've got my phone if you need something."

"You don't have to go, I could stay out here on the couch."

Zoe smiled, "Yes I do need to go Ben, no sense tempting fate."

It took Ben a long time to fall asleep, with his mind swirling around Zoe and the upcoming interview with Samantha. Mixed in was whatever he had going with Alex, or if there was anything and if his escapade with Zoe had jeopardized that.

* *

Gerald followed Alex home to make sure no one was tailing her. She'd confided in him about the rose she found at the door and that she was pretty sure her ex-husband was around somewhere. He knew she was serious since there was little that bothered her, but her reluctance to go home was a clear sign he'd gotten in her head.

Alex waved as Gerald drove on past, signaling to him that she was okay and there was no need for the babysitting duty. There was no one else in the department she would confide with about how Robert had given her a dose of the creeps. She'd tried to close that chapter of her life, but he seemed intent about inserting himself back into her, whether she wanted it or not.

The case was moving along and Alex wanted to soak in her tub and think. She'd always enjoyed the process of sipping her wine and mulling over the facts of the case, which often led her to know which direction to take a case. Gerald had scoffed at her bathtub theories, but he admitted the results seemed to back up her premise.

Alex reset the alarms, checked all the locks and headed for her bathroom. This was one of the few times when Alex actually wished she had someone in the home with her, either another person or at least a large dog with snarling teeth. Being alone was one of her favorite things, but Robert was starting to chip away at that now by leaving his little hints that he was near and she knew he was probably watching as well.

The bath had done little to help Alex sort out the complexities of the case, but she did feel somewhat revitalized. She also knew it was time to return the call she'd been avoiding all day, and maybe put some closure on this awkward dance she'd been engaging in.

"Hey Ben, how are you holding up?"

Ben stretched out on the couch and stared into the dark of the woods, "I guess I'm doing okay. Tired of answering questions and speculating about the value of things that were lost in the fire."

"I can't imagine losing everything. Did you have pictures and things in the house?"

"No, thankfully Zoe had stored all of the original pictures and major documents in a safety deposit box in town. I thought it was silly at the time, but now she's looking like a genius again. How is the case going?"

Alex leaned back into her chair, "We've made some headway, but now we have to figure out if we have enough actual proof to solve it. I was hoping my bath would help jump start my brain to locate the proof I know we're overlooking."

"I take it by your tone that was not the case."

"No it really didn't help. I've got this other thing on my brain and it keeps distracting me."

"Anything I can help with or is it super-secret police stuff?"

Alex smiled, "Not police stuff, I just have this feeling that my ex-husband is lurking around, creating enough ripples that it messes with how I function."

Ben sat up, "What does he look like?"

"I don't know anymore. He used to have dark hair with dark eyes, goatee and average build. He's probably 6 feet tall. Why?"

"The last time I stopped by to see you at your house, I passed a guy parked down the street, who I thought seemed out of place. He acted like he was on a stake out, but he could have been watching your house with his mirrors."

Ben had her attention now and Alex moved to the kitchen for a paper and pen. "Okay tell me why you felt that way."

"Well most of it was just gut feeling, like why would someone park right there. He was like between two houses, not like he was waiting for someone to come out. Also he just acted like he was trying to be casual, which looked funny."

"Ben, tell me you got the license plate."

"I didn't, but I can tell you he was in a 2010 black 300 Chrysler. I can't remember if it was the SE package or not."

Alex smiled as she wrote down the information, "Of course you would know the car. Any description of the driver?"

Ben closed his eyes and tried to rewind the drive. He'd been focused on talking with Alex, so the other things were mostly on his periphery. "I can't tell you height since he was sitting in the car, but he had short dark hair with dark eyes. No goatee."

"That's great Ben. I can get this circulated around and hopefully he will be one less thing I have to worry about. This has been really helpful."

"Is there anything else I can do to help?"

Alex paused, wondering if Ben was again just being nice, or if he meant something more by the innocent statement. "This is weird, especially after our conversation the other day, but I don't feel comfortable staying here by myself and I don't want to bother Gerald again. Could you come over and spend the night? And bring Winston please."

"I can be there in twenty minutes, just let me pack a few things, I've got an interview in the morning."

Alex hung up and started gathering some pillows and a blanket for the couch. She figured if Ben saw this then he would not feel pressured into sleeping with her. If he initiated things and that was where they ended up, well then it would Ben's decision and not something she manipulated him into.

20

Ben woke as Alex's phone began to chirp. He'd arrived at her house about fifteen minutes after he ended the phone call. Winston beat him to the door and Ben entered, catching a glimpse of the pillows and blanket on the couch. Clearly Alex wanted to make sure that Ben understood the ground rules upon arrival. Ben sat at the table while they chitchatted about various things until Alex headed for her bedroom. He intended to sleep on the couch and help Alex feel safe in her house, but the next thing Ben knew he had her in his arms and his fingers wrapped in her hair.

"Is it morning already?"

Ben looked over at Alex as she struggled to lift her face off her pillow. Her dark hair was covering her head, face and a good portion of the pillow. "Yes it is and I would assume that your alarm means you have something planned."

Alex turned her head and peeked at Ben. He was perched up on one elbow and gazing down at her with what could only be described as total adoration as his finger lazily traced the tattoo on her lower back. "Please stop looking at me like that. I have a pretty good idea that I'm a train wreck right now and you've got this look on your face."

"What? I think you're beautiful. You sleep a little unconventionally, but other than that ..."

Alex rolled out of bed, wrapping the sheet around her torso as she went, leaving Ben lying in the bed completely naked, "Good God, my hair's a rat's nest and I've probably got eye gunk. And would you tell Mr. Man there that we don't have time for any early morning shenanigans."

Ben laughed, "I think you're probably aware that I have little control over whether I have an erection or not. It mostly depends on the stimulation."

Alex staggered to the bathroom, trying not to notice her bra was on the dresser and her panties were on the other side of the room, "Well I've got to get to work, so no stimulation happening."

Ben chuckled as Alex shut the door and turned on her shower, "I can make breakfast."

Alex took as long a shower as she dared and peeked into the bedroom, but Ben was gone and the smell of food cooking was wafting in from the kitchen. She was preparing to chastise Ben for cooking her breakfast until she walked out and found him standing at her stove in his boxer shorts, flipping eggs.

Alex took a deep cleansing breath to remind herself that she didn't need this magnificent type of distraction right now, "Thank you, but you really didn't need to."

Ben handed her a plate of scrambled eggs and toast, "I needed to eat, so you get some too. The coffee is almost finished. Sorry it's not more, but you really need to stock your refrigerator."

Alex wanted to shoot back a smart comment, but doing that to a half dressed man who just went to the effort wasn't worth it. "I'll try to remember to keep more items on hand when you come over, but I don't think this is going to be an ongoing situation."

Ben smiled and sat down, "I wasn't trying to imply it was, just commenting that you need some more actual food in your refrigerator."

Alex sipped her coffee, purposely focusing on her plate of food, rather than the broad chested man sitting across from her. She knew it would easy to just take his hand and head back to the bedroom, but that might be a mistake for both of them.

"Well I appreciate you coming over last night, but I want you to know I did not plan on us ending up in bed together."

Ben smiled and his eyes burned green, "I did, but I didn't think it would be after having sex. I really just planned on sleeping with you so you felt safe."

Alex turned away from Ben and placed her dishes in the dishwasher, "Well I'm going to finish getting ready for work. You're welcome to stay and clean up if you want."

"That's okay, I need to head back to the smoldering ruins before my interview this morning. Hey I've been dying to know what the tattoo is about."

Alex stopped, "It's the phoenix rising from the ashes, got it after my divorce was finalized. Please tell me that you aren't meeting with your little cheerleader."

Ben laughed as he finished slipping on his jeans and shoes, "Yes the interview is with Samantha, but Zoe set it up not me. Trust me, the last thing I want to do is be interviewed by her."

Alex watched Ben close the door behind his dog. She'd wanted to make a snarky comment about making sure he kept his clothes on this time when being interviewed, but thought it might come off bitchy. Instead she chose to focus on the pleasant feeling she had this morning waking up next to Ben, not a bad way at all to start a day.

****

Robert was seething by the time Ben drove past his SUV. He figured he'd need to switch vehicles about every three days to make sure that nobody started making complaints about familiar cars being on the street. What Robert hadn't figured on was Alessandra playing house with this Benjamin Princi.

He'd spent considerable hours and money digging into the background of Mr. Princi, which had revealed numerous nuggets. Princi had a substance abuse problem, with some questionable interactions with law enforcement over the past decade. All of these could be used if needed, but right now Robert needed his attention in other areas except his ex-wife.

Robert assumed the fire he set to Ben's house would have created a number of headaches, all of which could, and should have occupied him for days. Instead he found Princi pulling into Alessandra's driveway at nearly midnight, and based on his directional microphone they hadn't spent the night talking. His first instinct when while listening to Alessandra's moans was to drive the SUV into the bedroom and hopefully kill them both, but Robert had learned to dial back his initial anger. Patience always provided him with a better method of retribution, so Robert knew it would just be a matter of time before something better presented itself. He'd bide his time and find a way to punish both of them, before he started in with Alessandra's reeducation process.

* *

Ben finished his shower and pulled on some shorts with a t-shirt. The weather was starting to heat up, so the days of wearing jeans were coming to an end. Ben wanted to be casual and not send any type of unintentional message to Samantha.

Ninety minutes later they'd finished with the interview and Samantha had directed her photographer to get a number of shots of the remainder of the staircase. She'd asked all the obvious questions and still wanted to speak with the arson investigator, but he'd stalled her off with the actual arson report.

"So how are you really doing?" Samantha asked casually as she pulled off her heels and slipped on her flats. She'd needed the heels to not make the difference in their heights so obvious on camera.

Ben leaned back in the chair, "Probably as good as possible given the circumstances."

"I didn't notice Zoe around today, that doesn't seem normal. Usually you two are both in the vicinity of each other."

"Well she's taking care of things at a friend's house because she doesn't like the cabin." Although for one spectacular night she had moved beyond her feelings about the cabin Ben thought.

Samantha glanced at Ben over her oversized sunglasses, "I've heard about the cabin in the woods, do I get a tour?"

"Uh, I don't think that's something I'm willing to share with viewers."

"It could be off the record. Just a quick tour between friends," Samantha said softly, with the emphasis on friends.

"I really don't think it's a good idea for the two of us to be there."

Samantha chuckled, "What are you afraid I'll throw myself at you? You made it pretty clear that there isn't going to be a second lapse in your judgment."

Ben sighed, "See this is why I didn't think this was a good idea. You're trying to use the fact that we had sex to get inside information."

"We made love, and yes I'm trying to manipulate you right now, but not for the reason you think. I think there is more to the story of how you got Zoe out of that fire."

Ben looked over at Samantha as she perched on the edge of the fence. Her natural beauty fooled most people who looked at her, because underneath that innocent, sweet façade was the teeth of a tiger.

"Okay, I'll give you the tour and tell you about the rescue, but details of the rescue need to remain off the record." Samantha pouted, but agreed to the terms. She didn't like having to use their lovemaking as a trump card, but she knew it was the best way to get Ben to come around to her way of thinking.

"Can I get a few still shots of the cabin?"

"No pictures."

Samantha smiled, "Well poop."

****

Gerald watched Alex as she settled into her desk. Moving the files from last night onto the extra chair and logging onto her computer. She was dressed as usual, but Gerald noticed she seemed to be more relaxed and not as hyped up as she had been.

"Why are you watching me like my mother used to?"

Gerald scoffed, "Shit knowing you, your mother probably needed to keep close tabs on you."

"She did, you don't. I'm a big girl and I'm fine."

"Did you get a good night's sleep?"

Alex thought briefly about Ben's eyes as he locked onto hers as he was positioned above her just before thrusting … "Yes, yes I did actually."

Gerald noted the color on her cheeks and thought about commenting, but realized she actually did need some privacy. "Well good. Hey I need to take a longer lunch hour today, Angela is coming home and I want to make sure I'm there to help."

"That's great, is there anything you need me to do?"

"No we've got it, but you need to get our little plan into place so we're ready."

Alex gave Gerald a look, indicating she was already ahead of the game. She'd stopped on the way to work to pick up a few printouts from some of the county cars. It was the only way to get the information they wanted, without tipping off anyone, by casting a really wide net to catch one fish.

* *

The harvesting of the young Hispanic girls had been going on for years, which meant a number of advance tripwires were in place in case someone accidentally got too close. By accessing the travel logs for one county car, Alex had inadvertently popped a trigger. This immediately, thanks to the speed of computer systems, sent an email to a number account.

When he received the notification that there was an unread email on the secret account, he knew things could be spiraling out of control. In all the years he'd been involved, no one had stumbled this close to the truth of what was really going on in central Ohio. The practice, which ultimately started as drunken whim to see if it was possible to snatch a girl and get away with it, had turned into a profitable human trafficking operation. He didn't want to shut the operation down, as his profits were going to take a hit, but the thought of prison was unacceptable.

He knew once the phone call was made that everything he'd cultivated for the past two decades was going to cease. History was great, but within a month someone else would take over the lapse in coverage in this portion of the state and the human trafficking operation would be right back in place again.

Locking the door, he pulled out the burner phone and sat in his chair. He knew there would be no answer to the call, but a message was expected.

"Ortiz, I've got to shut down. The detectives up here have stumbled too close for comfort, so I'll be closing shop. Send my order next month to Hattery in Dayton, I assume he'll take over the operation."

And with that he was finished.

* *

Ben walked Samantha back to her car after the tour of the cabin. He held on to her cell phone, because he knew she couldn't resist the opportunity to click a few quick shots while they were talking. Samantha didn't seem to mind the inconvenience and was pleased when he gave her a glimpse of the tunnel that had led from the house to the barn.

"So I can't put anything in my report about how you saved Zoe?"

Ben shook his head as he returned the cell phone, "That was the deal. I don't want it all over the news about Zoe. Her parents would freak out if they knew how close things had been."

Samantha stepped up and looked into Ben's eyes, "But you're a hero. She would have died if you hadn't carried her out of the fire."

"See that's what I'm talking about. You're trying to sensationalize this into some kind of ratings thing, but I'll give you this. If you can convince Zoe that it's okay to talk about, then I'll be quiet."

Samantha grinned and gave Ben a quick hug, "No problem, because she already told me I could use whatever you gave me however I wanted."

Ben stood there stunned, because he knew he'd just been played. He was feeling pretty good until Samantha pulled up to show him that she had a second cell phone, which meant she had likely recorded everything and taken pictures with the phone he hadn't confiscated. Samantha was laughing as she sped off while Ben leaned against the fence.

"Did you really give Samantha permission to use anything I said during the interview?"

"Well hello to you too Benjamin. Yes I did because I figured the good publicity would maybe help with finding some clues about the arson. You didn't do anything stupid and you kept your clothes on right?"

Ben laughed, "Now you've got jokes. Yes it went okay, but I think she took some pictures of the cabin and the tunnel."

Zoe sighed, "I'm using Blondie to promote you. Stop being so damn secretive."

"I didn't want your parents to worry."

"No worries, I already informed them about everything and they are very thankful that you saved me."

Ben looked up at the clouds, "You don't mean 'everything', everything do you?"

Zoe's laughter filled the air. "No if they knew you were shagging me, then mum would expect a proper wedding."

Ben ended the call after assuring Zoe that he would make sure to run all the follow up interviews she expected to receive through her first. Manipulating the media had become a trademark of Zoe's leadership style for Ben. She rarely missed a chance to use a platform where they would be seen in a positive light.

Ben was feeding Winston when his phone started going off. He didn't answer any of the numbers he didn't recognize and his voicemail was filling up fast. At last Alex's number popped on the screen and he took her call.

"Hello Alex?"

"So are you like a superhero now? I kept expecting to see a picture of you with a cape."

Ben smiled, "I didn't even watch it. How bad was it?"

Alex leaned back in the chair and propped her feet on the desk, "Well if Blondie got all her facts right, then you are probably a hero since you saved Zoe from certain death."

"What is with you and Zoe calling her Blondie? Her name is Samantha."

"I call her Blondie because she's everything I wanted to be when I was younger. She's blonde, petite, and has that perfect little smile. It's no wonder you fell for her charms."

Ben felt the blush rising on his cheeks, "I wouldn't say I fell for her charms, it was a moment of weakness."

"You might need to talk with her, because it's obvious she's got a serious thing for you. It didn't come across as a very objective piece, just that the man of her dreams had saved a damsel in distress."

"Boy I hope you are exaggerating, because Zoe will not be pleased to be portrayed as a damsel in distress."

Alex chuckled, "Well she showed a number of old photos of the two of you. I must say, I never realized what a good looking couple you made, which makes for great television. I'm sure your phone has been going off."

"Yes, it has and Zoe can deal with this, because I never wanted to do the interview in the first place. How are things going with the case? Any closer to getting it wrapped up?"

"Closer yes, but it's still like trying to solve a cold case with minimal evidence. It'll be another long night."

Ben noticed she paused before the last statement, "Not to be forward, but did you need somebody to make sure you felt safe? I could recommend someone."

Alex smiled, "You could huh? I'll let you know later, it's going to depend on how things play out this afternoon. I will call later."

217

Ben was going to respond before he realized she'd already ended the call. He tried to ignore the desire to push Alex and try to get her to agree to spend the night together. Last night was more than he expected, but Ben knew it was something he could easily get used to. Rather than dwell on that, Ben decided it was time to deal with all the messages and keep himself occupied.

Alex burst into the office without knocking and sat down.

Kirkpatrick looked up from his paperwork with little change in his demeanor, almost as if Alex's intrusion was a scheduled meeting. "How can I help you Detective, since clearly it's an emergency."

"I'm not sure how to proceed with our investigation."

"Please elaborate."

Alex leaned forward and laid out the scenario and all the potential pitfalls. She figured it was better to include him into the loop, before he found out where they were snooping from the rumor mill.

The captain leaned back in his chair and closed his eyes. "Do I need to alert the union or anything about the groups you are looking at?"

"Ethically you probably should, but practically I don't see how we can properly complete this case with everyone having a heads up. Surprise is going to be our key."

"I don't like having you and Gerald combing through the records of our employees. This thing could blow up and I'll be sitting here with shit all over me."

Alex dialed back her temper, which was surging, "With all due respect sir, if we don't solve this and one of your people is the culprit, then you'll be sitting in a bigger pile of shit."

Kirkpatrick spun his chair around so he could look outside where the sunshine made everything look good, as opposed to the things he dealt with on a daily basis. "Fine, do what you need to do, but I want immediate notification before you two proceed with any warrants or arrests."

Alex nodded, knowing this concession was almost a given due to the nature of the investigation, "I understand sir, and we will be as discreet as possible."

Kirkpatrick waved her off, "Get the hell out of here and solve this case."

Alex rushed back to her desk and text Gerald, letting him know they had been cleared to proceed. The timing of this sting was going to be the key, and Alex knew it would be fifty-fifty if it was going to work.

Alex was hurrying to get out of the parking lot when she spotted the note tucked under her wiper.

Careful you slut, because the path you choose could be your last.

Alex left the note and rushed back into the building, heading straight to the IT department. She wasn't sure who would leave this note, but she prayed they were dumb enough to get caught on surveillance.

"I'm sorry Detective, it just shows a guy with a hoodie going up to your car. I've tried to enhance everything I can, but there is no clear view."

Alex focused on the person approaching her car, trying to determine if she recognized the gait, or any other mannerisms. "It's okay Randall, I was just hoping for a break."

"I wish the TV shows would stop showing how the computer guys can enhance and digitize a microscopic piece of evidence to solve the case. It isn't reality or how the surveillance cameras are designed to operate."

"I understand Randall. I was thinking maybe we'd finally rattled someone's cage enough for them to make a mistake."

Alex called down to have the crime tech people take the note and to lift prints. She assumed it would be pointless, because the video looked like the perp had been wearing gloves, but it was better than doing nothing. She also put in a request for a new car to drive, since clearly someone knew exactly which vehicle was hers.

"Hey Jessica, call me when you get some results please. I'll owe you one."

Jessica gave her a nod as she watched Alex swagger over to the motor pool to choose her next Crown Victoria to drive.

* *

"So did you get a chance to run through the latest lyrics I emailed?"

"Yes I did, and I must say you seem to have gotten your head straightened out, because they were actually pretty good."

Ben smiled as he watched the latest recap of his interview with Samantha, "I told you it would just be a matter of time before I started cranking out some stuff again."

"Hey Zoe sent me a copy of that interview you did with the little blonde. She said you actually tapped that. I'm impressed, she's cute and young."

Ben sighed, "Let's just mark that up to me not thinking things through long enough."

"I'd say from what I saw, kudos to you. She looks like she'd be a little spitfire in the sack, which clearly is something you needed."

"Goodbye Trevor."

Ben deleted the interview from his DVR. He wanted to see if Alex had been exaggerating, but even he could tell that Samantha was not being objective. It was a wonder the station allowed the segment to be broadcast.

Ben had met with the architects this morning to discuss what he wanted to do with the property once it was cleared by the arson investigators. He'd debated leveling the remainder of the house and not rebuilding, but that never carried much weight. His attorneys had suggested some other options which might be more advantageous for tax purposes. In the end Ben decided to have three of the firm's architects draw up some new plans for him to look at and compare.

Zoe had not called Ben for the past two days and while not unusual, it was noticeable with everything going on at the house.

"So how long am I going to get the silent treatment?"

Zoe laughed, "Believe when I say the silent treatment would be a preferred method of having me deal with my anger. I just needed to sort some things out."

"Do I get to know how it plays out? Or is that just a need to know basis?"

"Well here is what I've decided. We will remain friends, but without the special benefits part. I will be moving into a condo in town until the house is finished, at which time I will return to my role of mistress of the house."

Ben hesitated, not quite sure if all this was serious or for show. "Is there any part of this that I get to decide and how do you even know I'm going to rebuild?"

"For one, the architects won't do anything without consulting me first. Secondly it's just easier if you go along with my plans and then it will all work out."

"What about all of the sexual tension that will be between us?"

Zoe sighed, "Let's face it. I would think the tension is gone. You were a wonderful lover, and I know I'm spectacular, so we should just leave it at that before we continue and mess things up."

"Well since we're back to business, Trevor called and said he approves of the lyrics I sent yesterday."

"I know Benjamin, who do you think directed him to call you? Maybe our little roll in the hay was worth it to snap you out of your funk."

Ben had already thought maybe his recent carnal adventures might have got his brain refocused on work. Whatever it was, the creative juices were flowing and he seemed to be in a rhythm. He was already trying to formulate some things around being lovers and friends.

"Since you've got everything under control, is there anything I need to accomplish for you?"

"Yes I do have some requests. One I want some submissions every morning by 10am in my inbox. The other is that you need to come see me at least twice per week to go over various things. I will text if I need you more than that."

"Daily submissions? I don't do so well with that type of pressure."

"I think I've relieved whatever pressures you might have had, so submit something every day. I know you keep a file of what you consider unacceptable material, use that if needed."

"The work stuff is under control, are you okay? I don't think I've had this much time away from you since I was in rehab."

Zoe nodded as she stared at the ceiling. This was diciest part of her plan, giving Ben enough freedom to realize he did want to be with her. "Somehow I managed before, so I'll do it again. Remember every morning by ten."

* *

Alex handed her service weapon to Gerald and pulled her hair into a ponytail, "I'm giving her ten minutes. If I don't get anything, then I'll be back."

"Remember she is going to be skeptical, so hint around about the trafficking. If she starts fading off, remind her about her thirteen year old daughter who's staying with her mother while she's locked up."

"And you're sure she was part of this pipeline."

Gerald shrugged, "We never got her picked up for anything but possession charges, but I've had a number of other people say she was always willing to do whatever to get her drugs and she started really young."

Thirty-five minutes later, Alex crawled back into the car. The interview didn't really provide much in the way of facts, but it did provide some more fringe details. Connie didn't know any names, but she had heard of Diablo Gringo, who she figured was a myth. Other than that, she claimed to not know any of the men she had worked for, but did supply a few other names of former coworkers. One of whom rang a bell was a Danielle Murdock, who Alex had busted a number of times and was now out and clean.

Connie made her call as soon as Alex had left the building. "I told her what you wanted and I dropped the hint about her little friend, so I'm begging you to keep your end of the deal. Leave my daughter alone."

She never knew who was on the phone, but she knew exactly what they wanted when the picture of her daughter was lying under her plate at breakfast. It was cooperate or her daughter would pay the price. The picture was accompanied with a note explaining not to mention any of the pimps, only girls who had been in the stable, especially Danielle.

Alex called Gerald on her way to the restaurant, "Hey I need to take a lunch and it might run long depending on what I find out."

"This better be legit and not some lame excuse to catch a nooner."

Alex laughed as she ended the call. Jumping into bed was the furthest thing from what she was going to have to do, but Dani might have some information to allow her to get closer to the source.

Danielle had a lengthy arrest record before Alex ever moved to the area. She'd started in high school with minor offenses and graduated into the adult system when she got hooked on heroin. The growing heroin addiction led her into a number of solicitation charges. Alex linked her with various AOD programs after each arrest, but it wasn't until the third time that Dani actually worked the program and got off the heroin.

Dani smiled when Alex walked in the door, "Hey long time no see. Where is your good looking date?"

Alex didn't return the smile, "Can you tell your manager I need you for about thirty minutes? I've got some things we need to talk about."

They walked outside and sat at the lone picnic table which was in the shade. Dani had already lit a cigarette on the way out the door.

"I swear I've been clean. You can check with my PO."

Alex motioned for her to take a seat, "I know you're clean Dani. I need you to tell me about the crew you ran with when you were using. Who was running the show? I need anything that you can remember."

"Really Alex, I hate talking about the old days. It brings back a lot of stuff I'm not very proud of."

Alex put her hand on Dani's, "I know and I wouldn't ask if I had anywhere else to turn."

"Okay, sit down. It's going to take some time."

Alex left twenty minutes later with some more knowledge of the workings of the stable Dani had been in, but little information on who was pulling the strings. There were big gaps, which Dani attributed to being high when she was turning tricks. She turned in most of her money to the crew leader, who in turn supplied her with her fix of black tar heaven. Alex knew she was embarrassed about discussing the sordid details of her past, but Dani provided as much as she could.

Alex gave Dani a hug, thanked her for the information and left to meet with Gerald.

Dani finished her second cigarette before heading back to work. She knew everyone was probably gossiping about what the detective wanted to talk with her about. She crushed the out the butt and walked back inside, oblivious that the whole conversation was being observed.

* *

Zoe finished going through all of her emails and sending out the prerequisite responses. Most of the correspondence was confirmation of dates and appointments for the upcoming summer season of acts. Some of the songs that Trevor and Ben had put out were generating interest from some of the bigger artists in Nashville. Those were the easier responses, because her parents were still emailing multiple times a day to check and make sure she was doing okay.

She'd called and spoke with them and also sent pictures via text to prove she had not minimized anything. They had seen Samantha's report on the internet, which brought a whole new round of questions when they realized Zoe had been unconscious and Ben had carried her to safety. Zoe assured them that it was just the reporter embellishing the situation for ratings.

Zoe ordered carry out before going onto the balcony. She'd discussed with Maggie about staying there longer, but ultimately decided it would be better to have some distance. Maggie was providing a number of strategies to bring Ben back into a more meaningful relationship, but Zoe felt time would serve her best. She wanted Ben to know he could do whatever he wanted and he wasn't obligated to be with her just because they had sex.

Just thinking about the night they spent together made Zoe's stomach tighten. She'd considered the prospect of having sex with Ben to get pregnant, but Zoe never expected the heat that was generated. There never was a plan about having sex, it just happened when she arrived at his cabin.

Zoe needed to be with Ben that night after she was given a clean bill of health. She took it as sign to stop waiting around and show Ben how she truly felt. Her original intention was to just spend time with him and talk through all the layers of feelings she had for him, but that changed when she heard him in the shower. At that point she knew exactly how to convey what she felt.

Sipping her wine, Zoe tingled remembering the numerous times they made love throughout the night. Ben made her feel like she was the greatest prize a man could have, as he kissed and touched her all over. It wasn't until the following morning when Zoe woke up that she realized the mess she had created. She knew Ben's conscience would be working overtime and convincing him what had happened was a bad thing and he needed to coddle her. She decided then that some distance would be the best way to deal with everything. Zoe made the decision if Ben truly wanted a relationship, time would bring them together.

The doorbell rang, bringing Zoe out of her thoughts, and signaling that her Chinese had arrived. She set aside the wine and thoughts of Ben before answering the door.

Samantha smiled as she handed the takeout food bag to Zoe, "May I come in?"

"You aren't like those vampires that can only come in when invited are you?" Zoe replied with a sneer.

"Nothing like that. I'd like to do a follow-up interview with you since I've gotten so much airtime with the interview with Ben."

Zoe set the bag on the table and motioned for Samantha to sit, "I don't think so. I set up your interview with Ben and made sure he cooperated with you, which is more than enough."

"I'm not dumb you know. I know you are just using this interview to make sure Ben gets some positive exposure, which in turn benefits his company which most likely benefits you."

"Goodness you figured that out all by yourself. I was manipulating the media long before you came along."

Samantha glared at Zoe. She'd came here with intention of getting the interview and possibly networking some with Zoe which could help career down the road far more than the interview would. The last thing she needed was to get into a cat fight with Zoe.

"What is your problem with me? I've tried to be professional with you and all I get in return is sarcasm or hostility."

Zoe finished placing her meal on plates. Takeout food or not, she was not eating out of a box or a bag.

"My problem with you is that you used my friend's good nature, your lack of restraint, and maneuvered yourself into his bedroom. That is my problem. I'd warned Ben about you, but he thought you were harmless."

"So that's it. You're jealous. I always knew there had to be more between you two than just a business relationship."

"Get with the program Blondie. My business is protecting Ben from bad relationships, it has nothing to do with jealousy. Don't think I haven't noticed your little ploys. Getting your hair lightened and styled to look similar to Courtney is just desperate."

Samantha closed her mouth before retaliating. She was prepared to defend herself, but it was all true and Zoe had laid her plan out in plain sight.

"I know you don't believe me, but I would very much like to have a relationship with Ben. However he's made it clear that isn't going to happen, so you can relax."

Zoe motioned for her to go on.

"I didn't exactly throw myself at Ben during the interview, but I made it clear that I was his for the taking if he wanted."

"Let me guess, he politely made it clear that wasn't going to happen."

Samantha slumped in her seat, "I felt like such a fool, but Ben spun it around to make me feel it was his fault."

Zoe pushed a plate in front of Samantha before sitting down with her own, "Let's talk off the record."

21

The phone rang, jarring Alex from her dream.

"Yeah."

"Alex, you need to meet me at the emergency room."

Gerald's voice was deadly serious, and Alex assumed the worst. "Is it Angela?"

Gerald hesitated, wondering if his partner could hold it together long enough to get to the hospital in one piece. "It's Dani and she's in pretty bad shape."

Alex was grabbing clothes while Gerald gave her the bare minimum of facts. She knew it would take at least ten minutes to get across town.

Alex stared in the observation window as her friend lay there. Her pretty blond hair was partially shaved and streaked with blood from the head wound that had required fifteen stitches to close. The surgeon had also informed Alex about the one hundred and fifty stitches that were used to close up her mid-section.

"Did I bring this on her Gerald?"

Gerald leaned against the wall and sipped his coffee, "Somebody is trying to get your attention and it just seems to coincide with your meeting this afternoon and now we're here."

Alex blinked back the tears, "Jesus Gerald did you see what he did to her? She was raped, beaten and then carved like a piece of meat. This is personal now and I'm going to nail this son of a bitch if it's the last thing I do."

* *

Once he started receiving the reports from the hospital, it was inevitable that things were spiraling and there would likely be only one conclusion. He'd warned him about laying low and not bringing more attention to this case, but this was over the top. How the hell did Brooks expect the detectives to leave it alone when he assaulted their friend?

He typed the message.

Meet me at 6am at the dump site

The phone buzzed inside his jacket draped over the chair. Brooks knew protocol demanded he answer within two minutes of receiving any correspondence on this secure phone. Untangling himself from her body caused her to moan and roll over, cursing the interruption of her sleep.

Brooks smacked her bare ass before she could cover up, "Don't hide that away, I'll be coming back for seconds once I finish responding to this."

"You already had seconds, and I need a few hours of uninterrupted sleep before I have to get to work."

He chuckled as Jessica curled into a ball as he stepped into the hallway and read the text message. Besides being cryptic, the rules dictated that they never meet at the dump site, so having an early morning meeting there was way out of the box. Something bad must have happened.

Will be there, did something happen?

Of all the responses Brooks could have used for a reply and he decided to play dumb. It was bad enough that he was barely following orders, but now Brooks wanted to play games.

I would say something happened, but then you probably know all about it.

229

The last thing Brooks wanted to do was play this word game with his father, when he could be climbing back into Jessica's bed and trying to wear that nice ass of hers out. He'd stood down just like he was supposed to, even though a preemptive strike would have likely been a better alternative.

Don't know what you are talking about Dad. I was off tonight and I've been banging Jessica like a drum most of it.

Leaning back in his chair, he propped his feet on the edge of the trash can. If Brooks was telling the truth then there was no way he was responsible for the assault on Alex's snitch. That would mean there was someone else out there with a very similar agenda. An agenda which could create many more problems than anyone could imagine.

Disregard the first text – meet me in the morning at the office after you are done playing the drum.

* *

Ben got to the hospital as quickly as he could after Zoe called him about the assault. He didn't really know the girl, but he knew Alex would be there and need someone.

"How bad is she?"

Alex looked up from the magazine sitting in her lap. She'd been sitting here most of the night and gotten past most of her crying spells, but the sight of Ben standing there brought it all back and she rose to bury her face in his chest.

Ben stroked her back and waited until she could talk. He noticed her partner was down the hallway watching them.

"Sorry about that. It's been a hell of a night."

"Zoe called to tell me and I came over a quickly as possible."

Alex sat down and pulled Ben into the adjacent chair, "Gerald called me about 2am when he heard. Dani is in bad shape. She was raped and stabbed multiple times. The doctors aren't sure if she has any permanent brain damage. If she pulls through the next twenty four hours they think she will have a chance."

"Does anyone know why this happened?"

Alex took a deep breath and wiped a few stray tears away from her eyes, "I think it's because I was asking some questions about her past yesterday. It happened less than twelve hours after I met with her."

"That's your proof?"

"That's part of it and then whoever did this carved WHORE into her stomach. It took over a hundred stitches to close it up and she'll be scarred forever. I was asking her about the trafficking group she was linked with back when she was using."

Ben listened as Alex told him about how she came to know Danielle, and her struggle with gaining her sobriety. She'd been arrested multiple times as a teen and into her twenties for possession and solicitation charges. Alex used her experience with the sex trafficking females when she worked in Texas to break through Danielle's shell and get her started towards her path of staying clean. Dani had just celebrated her second year of sobriety a few months ago and they had gone on a shopping trip to Chicago for a weekend.

Alex was smiling talking about the waiters they had flirted with shamelessly, with her being a cop and the other being a recovered junkie. "Go tell Gerald he can stop monitoring me from down the hall, would you? He's like an over protective father."

Ben walked down the hall, knowing Alex had sent him away to get herself together before her partner returned. He knew who Gerald Vilnew was, but had never actually spoken to the man before.

"Mr. Vilnew, Alex said you should come down and join us."

Gerald looked down at Ben's outstretched hand before giving a quick shake, "Looks like you got her mind off feeling guilty, so good job. And it's Gerald or I'll be forced to call you Mr. Princi, and that isn't going to happen."

Ben tried to stop the smile.

"Something funny?"

"No sir, it's just that Alex described you as an overprotective father and that's what it felt like."

Gerald shook his head and smiled back, "It's probably true, and sometimes it feels like I have to try and rein her in like my other daughters. An FYI for you though, don't believe her tough girl image, because she tries extremely hard to convince everyone else and herself that nothing gets inside her armor."

"I've gotten a sense that she wants to keep some distance between us."

"That's self-preservation. Her ex was a son of a bitch, who messed with her head, so now she doesn't know what to do with you when she starts feeling something."

Ben looked back down the hallway and Alex was just returning from the restroom. Her face looked freshly washed and her hair was wet from where she had run her fingers through it. "I'll keep that in mind."

"You do that, because if you hurt her then I'll be forced to retaliate."

Ben never got a chance to respond as Gerald shouldered his way past and pulled Alex into an awkward one arm hug, "Let's get you out of here so you can get a shower, you look like shit."

Alex laughed and punched him lightly on the shoulder, "We need to get back to the office and get to work. I've got a sadistic s.o.b. who is going to wish he'd never messed with me."

"I'll have the hospital call you if there are any changes with Dani's condition," Ben replied as he headed down to the nurses' station.

"We're cops; don't you think we get notified?"

Ben waved them off, "You may be cops, but I donated a pile of money to the new wing here, so I get a few perks."

Alex turned and jogged down the hallway to catch Ben, "Thank you for stopping by."

She gave him a quick kiss and caught back up with Gerald who was scowling at the door, "We're cops, not some horny teenagers."

"Quit complaining, let's go see what's going on at the office."

"So you thought I was responsible for what happened to Milnero's informant?"

Normally he wouldn't allow the attitude which accompanied the question, but this did show some actual intelligence. This organization had thrived for years because he kept his eye on the big picture, but his son was proving to be a slave to his impulsive behaviors.

"Yes I did and based on your track record it was a logical assumption. But clearly you were otherwise engaged, so now we have someone else messing around with the fringes of our situation. Either way we need to figure out who else is involved before the detectives do, because then we can spin things and hopefully take the heat off us."

"This is what I like to hear. We are actually going to be proactive and do something rather than these shadow games."

"Remember son, these shadow games have worked for years until you failed to follow the rules. Now lose the attitude and get out there and find whoever is messing with Milnero."

* *

Robert lay on his bed in the truck stop hotel. He'd paid cash for a semi-private room, which meant it was the closest to the stairway. He was soaking his hands in a bucket of ice water. The previous night's activities had worn him out more than he expected. Following the waitress to her rundown apartment was easy and then he slipped in when he heard the shower running. Robert was waiting outside the bathroom door when she came out. His first punch stunned her and she never had a chance to recover before he was on her.

Robert sat at the edge of the room. He'd been waiting for the girl to regain consciousness for the past thirty minutes. If he knew back when he was married to Alessandra that violence was such a turn on, he'd have started smacking her around. Every time he hit Dani, he could feel his erection grow and the need to finish things with her.

He'd held Dani down as he raped her and timed his climax with when she had lost consciousness with his hands around her throat. The feeling of power, knowing he was holding her life in his hands literally as he drove himself in and out of her body. She'd begged and pleaded, offering to do anything to just have him stop hitting her. Robert took enough time to allow Dani to give him oral sex, before he held her down and entered her from behind.

The plan in his head was just to beat Alex's friend up, but it all got out of control. All he could see was Alex leaving her house the other morning with the satisfied glow of having had sex. The big guy left soon after that and Robert remembered the anger build and crest. After the first punch, Robert went into a rage, kicking and punching until the girl was a bloody mess. He raped her the first time as he held the knife against her throat.

It was the discovery of the knife which gave him the idea to leave Alex a message. The girl was barely conscious when he started carving into her stomach, and he had a difficult time holding her still to finish the word. By the time he was finished they were both covered in blood, and he expected that the girl would most likely die before receiving treatment.

The news report caught his attention when it focused on the unnamed victim of an apparent attack, who was recovering at Blandale Memorial Hospital. The reporter emphasized that anyone with any knowledge should come forward to assist the police. Robert smiled despite the throbbing in his fingers and wrist, because it was doubtful that anyone would be able to provide any type of credible tip.

22

Ben parked his truck and called to make sure he knew the right number.

"Hey there Zoe," Ben said as he entered her condo, not knowing if he should give her a hug or not.

Zoe sorted this out by pulling him in for a hug and quick kiss on the cheek, "Hello Benjamin. It has been a few days, how are you holding up out there?"

"Pretty well actually. I sent some lyrics to Trevor this morning."

They rehashed some business stuff and Zoe gave a quick tour of the condo. It was clear there was still some ongoing tension in the room.

Ben sat at the table, "So this really awkward. I haven't felt like this since high school."

Zoe snorted, "What are you talking about, you never had to have a normal conversation with someone you had sex with in high school."

"Well there is that."

"I got a preliminary sketch of the house from the architect and I think it looks pretty good."

Ben was nodding, "I glanced at it, but it looked like most of what we wanted. Feel free to make whatever changes you want."

"Don't worry I will. Now let's talk about how things are going with Alex."

"I thought you were taking a break from meddling in my love life."

Zoe smiled, "Not in this lifetime and Maggie is pressuring me to get more info about Alex, so there are now two of us trying to push you along."

* *

Robert watched through the binoculars. He'd followed Ben over to the condo, so now he knew where his manager was staying. The condo had a fairly secure system which required a keycard or to be buzzed in by the doorman inside the main lobby. Breaking in was going to be nearly impossible, so the next best thing was to find out more about Ben Princi and the people in his life who would make him vulnerable.

They seemed more like a couple than business partners, but Robert hardly blamed Princi for that. When your manager looked like Zoe Meloncourt, then it was understandable that the line between personal and professional would be blurred. He enjoyed the view through her patio door which provided him with an unobstructed view of her long legs.

* *

"Hold on a second while I answer this call, it's from the lobby."

Ben heard Zoe asking some clarifying questions, but he wasn't paying attention until she returned with a look in her eyes.

"What is it?"

Zoe grabbed his hands and pulled him to his feet, "I need you to play along. We're going to stand by the patio door and give me a long hug. While you do this try to get a good look at the man in the green Taurus in the parking lot."

Ben followed along, "What is this all about?"

Zoe turned to face Ben and pulled him into her embrace, "Security noticed a guy out there watching this side of the building with binoculars. See if you can recognize him."

Ben rested his chin on Zoe's shoulder and focused through her hair on the car. He could make out someone in the car, but no specifics. "I can't make out much."

"You are getting your eyes checked. Alright let's change this up a little."

Ben was going to ask what the plan was, but Zoe spun him around and pinned him against the patio door before moving in for a kiss. While kissing, she peered over his shoulder and got as many details as she could."

Ben caught his breath as Zoe ended the kiss and wiped the lipstick off the corner of his mouth. "That's one way to get information."

"Relax loverboy, I got most of the license plate number and a decent description of the creep. A small price to pay for one little kiss."

Ben was going to ask more questions, but Zoe silenced him with her finger as she connected with the front desk.

"Yes, this is Ms. Zoe. Please send my regards to Frank for his attention to detail and making sure I feel safe. I've text the info I got to his phone, so now you can contact the authorities."

"You do have a way with turning on the charm when you like. I don't think James Bond's accent is that accentuated."

"Men are so easily swayed with a sweet word."

Robert was so focused on watching Princi and his manager making out, that he almost missed the security guard peering at him from inside. He wasn't sure if he had made any phone calls, but it was time to get out of the corner parking area.

He noticed two unmarked vehicles come sliding down the side streets, along with a county sheriff car pulling into the parking area. Somehow they had spotted him watching the room and he'd nearly been snared. He would need to be more careful as this proceeded because they were clearly on guard now.

* *

"Hey did you hear about the stalker they almost cornered outside of Princi's manager's condo?"

Alex looked up from the printout, which was giving her nothing except a headache, "I didn't even know Zoe had a condo. Did they catch him, or at least get a good description?"

Gerald walked over with the printed out sheet, "Oh they have an excellent description. Remind you of anyone?"

Alex scanned the features and compiled the face quickly in her mind, "Son of a bitch."

"My thoughts exactly. I think you need to give Ben a heads up, so he's aware of who he's up against."

"Hey Ben, its Alex. I need to meet with you and Zoe."

"So why would your ex-husband be stalking me?"

Alex stared at Zoe as she sat perched on the love seat, which was the only furniture out of the sight line from the patio doors. "I think it's another attempt for him to mess with my head. He could have found you by following Ben."

Ben stepped away from the patio doors and walked back into the living area, "Is Zoe in danger from him?"

"Anyone who is close to me is probably in danger, especially you Ben. He is jealous and has a temper, which could make him very unpredictable."

"So he might have followed Ben over here, rather than following me."

Alex slumped in the chair, "I don't know. He's called me recently and then there have been a number of instances where I think someone has been trying to break into my house, so clearly I think he's had some kind of breakdown. Bobby was always a little crazy, but this is off the charts even for him."

"Are there any leads where he's staying right now? Zoe got most of the license plate."

Alex shook her head, "We know it's a rental car from one of the major agencies in Dayton. Other than that, he used a fake id with a fake credit card, neither of which has been used to get a room."

Ben watched Zoe as she curled her legs under her torso. He'd seen her in a number of contexts, but he'd never seen her scared until now. "Is Zoe safe to be here by herself?"

"Probably, because these condos actually have a pretty good security system, but I have an idea to run by you."

Zoe glanced back, "I really don't think I can handle being bait."

Alex smiled, "It's nothing like that. We're thinking about using my house as bait for him and I thought maybe I could stay here with you. That way you have somebody with you and I can have a place where I don't feel Bobby's presence."

Zoe looked over at Ben, "You okay with your girlfriend and your manager shacking up?"

Ben caught Alex's red face as she turned away, "I think it sounds like a good idea to keep both of you safe. I should be fine, because it's doubtful he knows about my cabin."

"Still you need to keep an eye out for him. If there is anyone who's most at danger it's you. He was always jealous and impulsive, a bad combination."

Ben noted the sadness in her eyes and how she was likely rewinding some past incidents.

"I will get the extra bedroom ready for you and make sure the office knows you will be staying here for a few days."

"Thanks again Zoe, I just need a place to crash. You're helping me by allowing me to concentrate on this case and not have to be worrying about Bobby."

Zoe glanced at the phone and took the call out on the balcony. Alex had been crashed on the couch for the past hour. She was talking about the complexities of enforcing an out of state restraining order and then just stopped talking as she slumped over. Zoe had thrown a comforter across her and continued working on her laptop.

"I didn't know you had company," Samantha said as she looked at Alex's prone body.

"She's just staying for a few days while they sort out some of her personal issues."

Samantha moved closer and got a good look at Zoe's couch mate. "Hey that's Detective Milnero. I've been trying to get an interview with her for weeks."

Zoe pulled Samantha out onto the patio. The last thing she wanted was for Alex's location to be broadcast on the nightly news. Zoe waved to the plainclothes cops sitting in the sedan at the edge of the lot.

"So why are you here Samantha?"

Samantha slumped into the chaise lounge, "I don't really know. I guess I came here to have someone to talk with who I know is going to be honest with me."

"I'm not going to talk to you about Ben."

Samantha looked down and blinked back tears, "I don't know what to do. I can't get him out of my head. I know I should move on. I know there are guys interested in me, but I keep hoping Ben is going to come around."

Zoe sat down and stared at Samantha, "Come around to what? He made it pretty clear that whatever happened between the two of you was a onetime thing. Remember what you had, but know that someone else has his heart."

"Sounds like you're talking from experience."

"Are we off the record?"

"Of course."

Zoe sighed and stared out into the night. "Like you I had one night with Ben. It wasn't planned, and it was wonderful. The problem is that the next morning I knew it wouldn't work because I might have his body, but his heart belonged to someone else."

"So you're just giving up? You?"

Zoe chuckled softly, "The looks don't matter, it's a chemical thing. And I can't make Ben have the reaction."

"Well shit if you can't do it, who can?"

Zoe didn't answer as she continued to stare.

Alex slammed the shot glass back onto the table. They'd been trading shots for the past hour as well as stories. She'd never had any close female friends before, mainly because she assumed there was some underlying jealousy.

Samantha stared at the glass and hoped she could do one more. She knew she was at a disadvantage since she was smaller, but she wasn't going to use that as an excuse.

"So do the guys in the force ask you out all the time?"

Alex leaned back in her chair, "It's always an issue when I start somewhere new, but eventually they back off."

"You aren't a lesbian are you?"

"No nothing like that. I just don't want a relationship."

Zoe snorted and licked her lips after downing her shot, "Or you're scared."

Alex was getting ready to argue when Samantha started crying. She put her head down on the table and sobbed.

"What's her deal?"

Zoe smiled, "Our sweet little friend here is heartbroken."

"You can't let a man have this kind of power over you. If he's not interested, then tell him 'Fuck You' and move on."

Samantha looked up, "But Ben's the best guy I've ever been around."

Alex shot a look at Zoe who was laughing, "Are we talking about our Ben?"

Samantha only nodded.

Alex took another shot before replying. "Well Mr. Princi thinks he's quite a catch. It's my understanding that you've already had a roll in the hay, so you got the best part."

Samantha looked at Zoe, "She's the chemical thing isn't she?"

Zoe nodded before looking away.

"What chemical thing?"

"Never mind. You've got him hooked and don't know what to do with him."

Alex glared at Zoe, who stared back. "Have you been talking to her about me?"

"No Alex, but she just put it together about it's not who shares his bed, but who has his heart."

Alex lined up the shot glasses and poured. "Well since we've all had the pleasure of being bunk buddies with Ben, let's talk."

23

Alex cracked her eye open as the sunlight streamed in. Her head wasn't throbbing too badly, but she figured her drinking partners would not have fared as well. She noticed her shirt was on the couch with her jeans and vaguely remembered taking them off as she explained that she got hot when she drank.

Alex almost tripped over Samantha in the bathroom, as she lay curled up by the toilet with a bath towel covering her. Stepping over her, Alex started the shower and wrapped her hair up with a towel before getting in.

Samantha vaguely realized she was on a bathroom floor and there was a naked woman in the shower. Her first attempt at getting up only resulted in her reaching a sitting position, where she tried to get her bearings. It had been a long time since she had that much to drink, much less on an empty stomach.

"Hey Blondie, you're gonna have to move because I'm getting out and you are in the way."

Samantha gave up on walking and crawled out of the bathroom and into the living area. She could see one of Zoe's legs sticking off her bed, so it must have been Alex in the shower. They both seemed to hold their alcohol much better than Samantha did.

Alex left the bathroom wrapped in a large robe, "Anybody want me to fix anything for breakfast?"

Samantha groaned as Zoe kicked her door shut.

Ben knocked on the door and waited before Zoe finally opened. He'd never seen Zoe look like this, as her hair was tangled and her skin actually looked almost yellow. "Are you okay? What happened?"

"It was a rough girl's night last night okay, and can you talk a little softer?"

Ben followed Zoe to the table where she began nursing a disgusting looking green concoction. "Do I even want to know what's in there?"

Zoe shook her head, "You don't, but it will have me back on my feet in a few hours."

"So where is Alex?"

"She left about an hour ago I think. I'm pretty sure she doesn't have a liver or it's pickled, because she acted like nothing was wrong."

"Were you drinking tequila with her?"

"Yes, why?"

Ben smiled, "She told me she has been drinking tequila since she was sixteen, so I'm sure you were never going to keep up."

Samantha staggered into the kitchen, "What is all the racket?"

She stopped immediately when she realized Ben was sitting at the table with Zoe. Her initial inventory of things didn't provide a good picture. Her hair was matted and her mouth felt like she had eaten a dog turd.

Ben pulled out a chair for Samantha, "Looks like it was one hell of a party."

"Ugh, now I know why I quit doing this in college. And stop smiling, this is not funny."

Zoe slid the drink in front of Samantha, "It's awful, but I promise you will feel better. And don't ask what's in it, just drink."

Samantha swallowed some of the substance with a grimace, "Why is he here?"

"I am here because I'm supposed to have a meeting with my manager, but I'm not so sure I trust her decision making abilities right now."

Zoe shot Ben a look, "I should have used some discretion last night, but it was a very enlightening evening."

Samantha almost choked on the drink and pushed it away, "You can say that again."

"Anything I need to be aware of?"

Samantha and Zoe looked at each other. "No, we all shared more than we probably should have and there's no need to increase our level of embarrassment."

"I agree, so since your appointment is not happening, maybe you can leave so we can get ourselves back among the living."

Ben pushed himself away from the table and headed for the door, "So call me later Zoe when you can function and we can talk about some work. I'm going to go have a big juicy cheeseburger with fries."

Zoe closed the door in his face as Samantha rushed to the sink before she got sick on the floor.

Ben stared at Zoe as she sat down across the table from him. She was wearing large sunglasses, but other than that she showed no signs of the rough night before. "So I assume we're feeling much improved?"

"A bit of a headache, but altogether not bad. Much better than Blondie. She was staggering to her car when I left."

"I must say I was a bit surprised to find Samantha there. You two seem to be rather close."

Zoe tilted her head, "Better to keep her close and under my watch than lurking around trying to sweet talk you into public relation nightmares."

"I told you, we talked and she knows whatever relationship we have it's strictly professional."

Zoe took a long drink of water, "Let's just say that she may have told you that, but she is still hoping to snag her man."

"She did not say that."

"Okay not in that many words, but it's clear she's in love with you or at least infatuated with you. On the other hand we've got your girlfriend, who is freaked out by her feelings for you and wants to keep you at arm's length."

"I didn't realize I was the topic of conversation."

Zoe leaned forward and removed her sunglasses, her brown eyes were their usual beautiful color but surrounded by a sea of red. "When three women, who all have slept with you start drinking, guess what? We compare notes."

"You told them we slept together."

Zoe put the glasses back on, "No, but I didn't have to, they figured it out.

"Why did you three think drinking all night was a good idea?"

"It wasn't planned, but looking back I think Alex was fishing for some stuff from us about you. She has good instincts and knew we could fill in some gaps. Oh and I might have mentioned about the whole pregnancy thing."

Ben started rubbing his head, "Seriously Zoe, I thought that was between us and I thought it was no longer an issue."

"It just kind of happened after a number of shots and I think I might have made fun of you about your initial reaction."

"My next interaction with Alex ought to be fun."

"Speaking of her. She did tell us something that I'm going to share, but you need to keep a lid on it."

"Go ahead."

"When I was talking about my desire to get pregnant, Alex made a little comment about not being able to have children. She considered it a blessing because of her ex-husband, but I think it's weighing on her now with this thing she has with you."

"Ah shit."

* *

Alex finished her third bottle of water as she continued to flush her system. She was tired, but overall feeling pretty good this morning, but she knew the key for her was to hydrate. The evening had not been planned, but it had been informative.

The shots had helped with loosening everyone's tongues, so it wasn't long before the subject that linked the three women came up.

It was totally obvious that Samantha was completely smitten with Ben. She was quite open about her decision to take advantage of being in Ben's house when she got drunk over her ex-fiancée hooking up with her roommate. She knew Ben would come rescue her, but by taking her to his house was a sign that she should take advantage of.

The bigger surprise was what Alex learned from Zoe. She admitted she had spoken with Ben about having a baby with him, and he almost flipped out. This was well before the fire, so his shock must have dissipated when Zoe climbed into the shower with him after the fire. Alex wanted to be jealous, but she knew they had been in the lull of their relationship dance.

Alex had never been in a conversation with other women where they had all slept with the same guy. It was a consensus that Ben had a phenomenal body and nobody admitted to being unsatisfied, but there seemed to be different agendas going with why they crawled into bed with him. She knew the physical part was great, but getting wrapped up in the whole relationship part terrified her. Samantha had kept making comments about Alex having Ben's heart and not wanting it.

She'd never done anything to capture Ben's heart, hell she'd went out of her way to make sure he didn't want to be with her. Alex could tell he was resisting his natural instincts to try and further the relationship. Ben was doing his best to not box her in, but she was not pleased about the sex discussion. Jealousy was never an emotion Alex had ever dealt with.

Alex wanted to focus on the case, but she couldn't keep her head from drifting back to the conversations last night. Zoe's confession about wanting to have a baby was surprising, but more surprising was the hurt Alex felt when she admitted she couldn't carry a baby to term due to her damaged fallopian tubes. Children had never been on her radar, but Ben was the type of guy who wanted the entire package of wife and children. Something she could never deliver.

"What's your deal?" Gerald asked as he entered the office, noting the line of empty water bottles.

Alex looked up from the file she was holding, "I need to hydrate, it was a long night."

"So your new roommate was foolish enough to try and drink with you?"

"Not really. We had a surprise visitor and an innocent girls evening turned into a college drinking game."

"Good to see you still haven't lost your touch."

Alex smiled and threw the folder on the desk, "Can I ask you a serious question, without you reading anything into it?"

Gerald plopped into his chair, "Well that certainly ties my hands, but go ahead."

"We both know I'm a train wreck when it comes to relationships. What do you think Ben is trying to accomplish with pursuing me? And more importantly is he going to be disappointed?"

Gerald steepled his hands as he thought about his answer, knowing it was much more important than Alex's cavalier attitude made it appear.

"Good God is the answer that hard to think of?"

Gerald walked over and perched on the corner of Alex's desk, "Despite what you try to convince yourself, you are a beautiful desirable woman. Any man, not just Ben would be thrilled to have someone like you. I think it's possible that Ben might be able to see beyond the porcupine exterior you show the world. I have a feeling Ben could have his choice of women, so it's doubtful that he would be disappointed."

"I feel like I'm in a competition for Ben and I have never felt like that. He's got this twenty year old throwing herself at him and don't get me started about his manager."

Gerald arched his eyebrow, "She would be the extremely attractive light skinned lady."

Alex glared back.

"Clearly there is something you have that they don't, or he would have latched onto them sooner."

"I guess. This is all too complicated for me to deal with right now, so let's just get on with the file work."

* *

"I think I know who we're dealing with."

"I haven't got all day. Who do you think it is and more importantly why?"

Brooks was beginning to hate the condescending tone that accompanied every conversation. If it wasn't for their history, he'd stage his own little coup to make sure he didn't have to answer to anyone ever again and everyone would know was running the show. Instead of a small operation in Ohio, they could branch out into the larger more metropolitan areas.

"I think its Milnero's ex-husband. They have been circulating a bunch of enhanced photos around the office. Supposedly he left Texas a week ago and nobody knows where he is."

"Nice theory, but why?"

"My sources in Texas say he can't stand the thought of his ex-wife having any kind of positive future, and that got further ramped up when he found out she's seeing Princi."

"Sounds plausible. Why don't you make sure we find him before the other authorities? Maybe we can come to some type of agreement, you know with similar adversaries."

* *

Ben headed back to the farm after his meeting with Zoe. He needed to have some down time before he talked with Alex, especially after he learned about their conversation. The crews had started with the foundation work for the house, so he figured he'd be able to kill some time supervising them.

He watched for approximately forty five minutes before Ben was bored with watching the men walk around and tie the rebar in what would be his basement floor. The down time did little to take his mind off what Zoe had dropped on him.

The drinking evening had made it appear that Ben was somehow playing all three women against each other. He'd admitted to Samantha that he should have stopped things before they led to them having sex, but he had not. They had talked since then and Ben thought she understood about the type of relationship they were going to have from here on out. Based on Zoe's account, Samantha was still hoping that Ben was going to come around and be her personal knight in shining armor.

The unspoken and biggest fear for Ben was exactly what Alex was thinking about all of this. He'd tried his best to not push and give her space, but he looked like a wild dog that was out to have sex with anyone who wanted. Zoe had made it clear that their one night was a onetime thing, not a mistake, but not the beginning of anything serious.

Ben speculatedwhat was going on in Alex's mind. There were times when he could sense she wanted to connect, but Alex would step back anytime Ben made any sort of inquiry about her past. Other than conversations about her mother, Ben knew very little about Alex and how she ended up with what everyone acknowledged was a world class asshole. Ben assumed her aversion to these conversations was her own way of protecting herself, even though Ben just wanted to find out how someone as self-assured as Alex ended up with an abusive husband.

Ben wondered how Alex found it easier to be intimate but keep Ben at arm's length whenever discussions of future or past came up. She seemed to live solely for the day and wanted no commitments beyond this twenty four hour period.

The car pulling up the drive brought Ben out of his daydream. He'd left a message with Sheriff Barrett's office to get some type of an update on the arson investigation, but he hadn't expected a face to face meeting.

"Good afternoon Sheriff."

"Mr. Princi. I see they have started with the foundation for the house."

Ben shielded his eyes from the sun and motioned for the sheriff to follow him to the garage. "I thought I wanted to supervise, but since I'm clueless about what they are doing it seems pointless. They could be doing everything wrong and I'd never know."

"I understand. Listen there really isn't a lot of progress being made on your case. They have determined that the fire was started in the upper bedroom and the kitchen. The investigators think approximately four or five glass containers were tossed inside to start the fire. Outside of that, we have very little in the way of leads or suspects."

Ben handed the sheriff a bottle of water, "Well I can't say I'm surprised, but I appreciate you coming out and delivering the news personally."

"No problem. I was out on patrol on this side of the county anyway. Thank you for the water."

Ben watched Sheriff Barrett walk back to his cruiser.

Looking around the garage, Ben knew he needed to get back into some type of routine to get his mind back. Someone was willing to risk killing both Zoe and him and he wasn't clear who that might be. It could be Alex's ex-husband, but it would be doubtful that he would have figured out where he lived.

"I figure we need to have dinner to sort out everything that happened last night and whatever questions you might have. Call me."

Alex listened to the message a second time, trying to determine if Ben sounded anxious or embarrassed about having three women talk about him. She decided he sounded like he usually did, like someone without a care in the world.

"So what's loverboy got to say for himself?"

Alex tossed her phone on the desk, "You're not calling him by his name again."

Gerald snorted, "Shoot I ought to be calling him superman for juggling the three of you. He clearly has a big set of nuts."

"He wants to have dinner and sort things out. Is that male speak for something else?"

"I'd say it's going to be his opportunity to explain the knowledge he clearly knows you have now."

The light bulb clicked for Alex, "He talked to Zoe. Of course she'd be the one who would spill her guts. She just wanted a quick romp in the sack as payment for him saving her life."

"And she would be the ..."

"Yes Gerald, she's the gorgeous one with the body of a playmate. She also wants to have his baby, but with no strings attached."

"Well if she is looking for a sperm donor, I'm sure Janice would understand."

Alex turned quickly to find Gerald smiling at her.

"Go to dinner with him. You know your curiosity is going to eat you up anyway."

Ben got to the restaurant and took a few minutes to get his head straight before he went in. He'd spotted the Crown Vic close to the door, so he knew Alex was inside already. The dinner idea seemed good earlier today, but he was having second thoughts now that it was time.

Alex pushed her cell phone aside when Ben walked up. She'd primed herself to remain aloof and let him know how much she didn't care, but it all went away when he walked up and smiled.

"So do we order before we jump into things, or do you want to hash it out first?"

Alex took a deep breath and motioned for Ben to sit. "I just want to state for the record that you are a shit. I've never had to compare notes with other women before and I don't like it."

"But I ..."

"Wait Ben. It's my own fault because I kept you at a distance because I'm scared, so I'm also mad at myself."

Ben smiled and took Alex's hands, "I know Alex, and I'm sorry if I pressured you. I can honestly say I never intended for anything to happen with Zoe or Samantha."

"I believe you, but it would help if you chose to have sex with some unattractive girls. Scratch that, I don't want you having sex with anyone else."

"And that means?"

Alex squeezed his hands, "It means I'm willing to try and work out whatever it is we have."

"That sounds great, can we order now because I'm starved."

"I don't know if Zoe said anything to you or not, but I need to confess something which might impact if we go forward."

"We don't need to do this right now if you don't want."

"No it's okay. I found out about six years ago that I cannot have any children due to complication with my fallopian tubes, so if being a father is important to you then you need to move on. Hell it sounds like you've already had an offer."

Ben felt his face heat up, "Zoe and her big mouth. I haven't thought about being a father for a long time. I didn't even know Monica was pregnant until the coroner informed me, so fatherhood wasn't a quest. As far as Zoe, I think that's an issue she has."

Alex chuckled, "Her reenactment of your conversation was pretty funny. Did you really look sick?"

"Probably because it was something that I never expected to hear from her."

"I could see you being freaked out, but I do agree with her that you two would make some good looking children."

"Does it matter that I'm not interested?"

"Yes and it means a lot to me that you are still interested in me when it would easy for you to play house with Zoe."

"We are friends and although I crossed a line with her, it won't happen again."

The dinner progressed from there with little mention of the girls evening from that point on. Ben could see the cool edge Alex arrived with start to fade as they laughed and planned for future times to get together.

* *

He answered the phone on the second ring.

"This had better be good."

Gripping the phone as tightly as possible, he responded as calmly as he could manage. "I put out the word on our network about our person of interest. One of the truckers thinks he saw a guy matching the description going into the back room at the truck stop on St. Rt. 127."

"Good work. I wouldn't have thought to spread the word in our network. I assume you're headed over there to keep an eye on the room."

"I'm parked outside right now. I'll keep you posted if I see him. Do you want me to bring him in the conventional method or any means necessary?"

"If you see him, get his ass over here anyway you see fit."

That was the answer he was hoping for, as he checked the charge on his Taser. His plan was to take out of a few birds with this stone.

* *

Ben collapsed into his bed after finishing with the emails. He'd approved the majority of the architectural designs and they were hoping to get moving forward with the foundation work, so they could be inside for the winter finishing up. Trevor was encouraged with the latest batch of lyrics Ben had sent, but as usual he wanted more. This was a problem because Trevor did little except play his guitar and record everything. Ben was trying to have some sort of life outside of working.

Winston jumped on the bed and sprawled next to Ben.

"Hey buddy. Looks like you might have your new house by next spring if the weather cooperates."

Winston responded by wriggling on his back to relieve whatever itch he was currently feeling.

Ben picked the phone up.

"What's up Zoe?"

"I wanted to congratulate you for completing the paperwork for the firm so they can get started with the house. I assumed that you'd drag your feet or just procrastinate since you despise change."

"Glad I could surprise you."

"How did your dinner with Alex go?"

Ben rolled onto his back and smiled at the ceiling, "That's private, but it went better than I expected."

"I'm glad. For the record, I do like Alex. She's self-assured enough to deal with all your crap and not let you fall into your old stodginess."

"I'm not stodgy."

Zoe chuckled, "Yes you were, but it's becoming less of an issue recently and I attribute it to Alex. I hope Alex finding out about our encounter did not present a big problem."

"Of course it's a problem. You can't have sex with your manager, who you live with and looks like you without it being a problem. Alex is willing to move forward and not hold my past dalliances against me."

"So I'm a dalliance. That's a new one for me. I've got to admit I'm used to being the prize or trophy, I'll have to see how I feel about that."

Ben laughed, "I'm sure you will. I'll see you tomorrow at 11."

"Good night Ben, get some rest after your very productive day."

24

Zoe was lying on the patio with a miniscule bikini struggling to cover all of the vital areas. Ben purposely sat so his view wasn't directly aimed at her body.

"This may sound like an insensitive question, but I'll ask anyway. Why are you lying out in the sun trying to get darker?"

Zoe propped her herself up and squinted at Ben through her sunglasses, "I'm biracial, so I'm trying to get a couple shades darker for the awards ceremony tomorrow evening. My coral dress is really going to pop when I put it on."

Ben was going to debate, but realized it was an accurate statement. The coral would absolutely play off her dark skin, which would be in direct contrast to the other pale or airbrush tanned women.

"I am still going with you to the awards show, correct?"

"Of course. Alex said she wouldn't be able to get away for the evening."

Zoe swung her legs to the side and struggled to keep her top covering everything, "Great, now I'm not even the first choice."

* *

Robert watched with dismay from the parking lot adjacent to the hotel. The undercover cars were really dismal, which made picking them out easier, but it prevented him from getting close enough. He was fairly sure that Alex was staying with Princi's dark skinned manager. She was the only person staying at the apartment complex that Robert knew had a connection with Alex.

He'd snapped a few photos of the various combinations of surveillance in the lot, but it was still too tight to allow him access to the lobby. The police had been cruising around the truck stop, but he made sure to leave before they started asking any questions.

The passenger door opened and the gun was in his face before Robert even had time to react.

"Keep both hands on the steering wheel and listen."

"What do you ..."

The rabbit punch to his kidney brought tears to his eyes.

"Shut the fuck up and listen Robert. Yeah I know who you are and we have some common problems that we need to eliminate. I think our upcoming partnership is going to be very productive for both of us."

Robert blinked away the tears and stared into the dark eyes of his passenger, "Why would I want to help you?"

"Let's just say that I'll deliver someone you want and in return you'll take care of a problem for me. I'm about the best friend you've got in the whole world right now. You keep hovering around making things worse, so we should merge forces."

Robert smiled, "Why don't we go somewhere less obvious to discuss this plan?"

The cabin Robert arrived at provided him with everything he wanted and kept him out of the glare of the police search. The key was under the rug, just like it was described. His new partner assured him that he would receive a text message when they figured out exactly where Alex was going to be.

His job was to dig through the background information on Ben Princi and figure out where would be the best place to set him up.

* *

Ben finished off his water and wiped the sweat off his face. The free time he'd gained by being at the cabin alone had made it easier to get back into a more intensive workout regimen. He'd really picked up his running schedule and was eating better since there was little junk food to be had.

He'd talked with both Alex and Zoe earlier and neither wanted to get together because of various work issues. Ben thought they each were avoiding any extra contact with him after their revealing discussion the previous evening. Zoe was unusually cool, with little banter or jokes about anything. Ben forgot how much he enjoyed the easiness with her.

Alex said she was wrapped up with the intricacies of the case and how they had a plan to lure a person of interest in their investigation to come forward. To Ben it sounded like a chess game where it came down to moving the right pawn to lure the queen out into the open.

Alex put her cell phone away and held her friend's hand. She'd been here for the past hour, trying to get some straight answers from the doctors. The only assurance she'd received was that Dani's vitals had stabilized, which was a great sign she was going to pull through. Alex was not sure as she stared at the various tubes and beeping machines.

Gerald had dropped her off prior to him going to Angela's latest round of physical therapy. He hated seeing his little girl in pain, but he went every appointment to give her the support she needed. The TBI examinations seemed to indicated there should be no long term brain functioning problems, but right now Angela struggled with her balance. He knew his little girl was depending on him being strong for her during this period.

As he watched Angela concentrate on making sure her next steps were in line, it finally clicked for Gerald. He finished his coffee and spoke briefly with the therapist before slipping out to find Alex.

He found Alex down near the nurse's station as she attempted to get more information about her friend. She was in mid-sentence as he pulled her off into the lobby area.

"What's the rush Gerald? Is everything okay?"

Gerald motioned around, "This is the problem. It hit me down with Angela, somebody is messing with us by distracting us."

"That's kind of stretch don't you think?"

"I won't speak for you, but I know my head has been half out of the game ever since Angela got hit. What better way to slow down an investigation than by having the lead detectives not using all of their energy and motivation."

Alex turned around and looked towards Dani's room. "What kind of sick freak would hurt innocent people just to keep us off balance?"

"The same kind that gets their jollies with little girls, but that's only one aspect. The other is how to know which people would impact us the most."

"So we're back to looking at some of our own people again. I keep thinking this case can't get any worse."

Gerald pulled Alex down the hall, "I don't like it either, but only law enforcement can easily find our families and our informant information."

"Now it's pissing me off that somebody hurt them because we were getting too close. Do we go to Kirkpatrick, or is it better to stick together?"

"Right now the only person I trust is you, so this stays between us. We'll fill Kirk in later if we need to, but it's best if we just keep it close to the vest."

"Okay, I'm going back to the condo with Zoe and get some sleep. Tomorrow we need to start looking at things through a different lens and maybe we should send out some red herrings to see who bites."

"I like the sound of being proactive. I feel like we've been behind the eight ball since we got this case."

Alex took a long route around to Zoe's condo to make sure she wasn't being followed before parking in her reserved spot by the door. The doorman had the door open by the time she hit the steps.

"Good Evening Detective."

Alex flashed him a smile, "Now Ralph I've told you to call me Alex."

Ralph's face blushed all the way into his white hair, "I just don't think Ethel would approve of me calling a young woman by her first name."

Alex blew him a kiss as she walked to the elevators, "You're a gem Ralph and Ethel knows it."

Zoe finished the last of her yoga poses as she heard the door locks. She'd gotten a lot completed today without having to worry about Ben or the relationship dilemmas going on. Alex set her bag on the counter and pulled out a water from the refrigerator.

"Do you need one?"

Zoe caught the bottle and drained half of it. "Thanks."

Alex pointed with her bottle, "Good to see that you can sweat and not look perfect all the time."

"I work hard to stay in shape, and I have to work extra hard this week. There's an award show in Nashville and my dress is custom fit, so I can't slip up."

"So that explains the gorgeous dress I saw hanging in the closet. What is your date wearing?"

Zoe snorted as she wiped the sweat off her neck, "I'll fight him tooth and nail to wear some new jeans and a nice dress shirt, but at least it won't be a t-shirt."

"How'd you ever convince Ben to go to these shows?"

"He balked at first, but realized that it's a ton of free publicity, even if we don't win anything. His business sense was strong enough to override his fear of the fans."

Alex plugged her cell phone in to charge, "I notice there are a lot of pictures of the two of you on the internet at these shows. Do you get a new dress every time?"

"What can I say, I'm a girly girl. I not only get a new dress, but the matching shoes as well. It's a business expense. Nashville tends to promote us in the shows because I'm one of the few women of color in the audience, it makes them look progressive."

Alex shook her head, "You certainly know how to market yourself, how is it you have stayed single? I mean come on. You are a walking magazine cover, and as much as it pains me, you're actually pretty down to earth."

Zoe shrugged, "My plan was for me to be married with two kids by now, but I never seemed to find the right guy. I seem to attract men who just want me to be the next notch in their belt."

"Well for the record, I still hate you for being able to look like you do with minimal makeup or effort."

"Duly noted."

Robert glanced through the list of possibilities he had compiled for meeting his end of the bargain. He'd already ascertained that Princi was no longer residing with the mulatto. The county tax records indicated that Princi had at least eleven buildings he owned, so it wasn't going to be easy to figure out which one was where he had holed up.

He knew using the mulatto for bait would bring Princi out, but that would only be a last ditch effort. Robert wasn't sure what the fixation was for Princi, but having him out of the picture would be beneficial for him with Alex. He'd kept tabs on his ex-wife and she had only had a few casual dates prior to linking up with Princi. There was a connection there that he needed to make sure was smothered.

Robert pored over the online records from the county and first noticed the discrepancy. The amount of square footage Ben had at his house and barns was not adding up, which meant he had some other type of building somewhere on his main property. He'd contact his new partner and let him do some leg work while he was out tomorrow. If the footage added up like the thought it would, then it would be a piece of cake to set him up.

25

Ben woke with a start at the banging at his door. He noticed that Winston was nowhere to be found, so he pulled on some shorts and shuffled to the door.

"Why are you pounding on my door?"

Samantha walked in and handed Ben a cup of coffee. She tried to focus on the tidy little cabin and not Ben's barely dressed body, or his sleep mussed hair.

"Well I got the final report from the arson investigator and I wanted to get your comment about it."

Ben sat on the couch and took a long pull on the coffee, "You couldn't call me for a comment? Because it's the same, no comment."

Samantha plopped onto the couch, "Come on Ben. Like it or not you are in the news. You can't hold a grudge against me just because we had sex."

"The sex has nothing to do with it; I'm holding a grudge because you snookered me in the last interview about the cabin. And here you are."

"Okay I was somewhat deceptive during our last interview, but it made great television. Like it or not you are a celebrity around here. Also Zoe told you to cooperate with me."

Ben squinted across the coffee cup, "I don't care that you and Zoe are BFF's or whatever. Interview her."

Samantha pouted as she got up, making sure Ben got a good glimpse of her cleavage as she stood. If he wanted to be childish, then she'd just talk to Zoe and make inferences to how Ben was really feeling about the arson.

"Fine Ben, I'm leaving."

Ben opened the door, "Have a great day and thanks for the coffee."

Alex watched as Samantha stomped back up the path from the cabin. She'd arrived just as Samantha started down the path, so she thought she'd see how it played out. Judging by the look on her face, things hadn't gone as she had planned.

"Fancy seeing you here."

Samantha glared, "Good luck with him, he's certainly in a mood this morning, but I'm sure you'll get a better response than I did."

Alex walked down the path, marveling at how Ben had hidden the cabin from nearly everyone because of how well it blended into the woods. She knocked on the door.

The door flew open and Ben stepped out, "Dammit Sam, I ..."

Alex smiled and batted her lashes, enjoying the confused look on Ben's face. "You were saying."

"I thought you were someone else, but never mind. Come on in."

Alex walked in, taking a good long look at Ben in his boxers. If she had more time, she could think of a number of ways to peel off his boxers.

"Sorry I need to throw on some clothes."

"Don't worry about me, I've interviewed suspects in much less than boxers and they don't look nearly as good."

"I'm a suspect?"

Alex smiled, "No you're not. The point is you don't need to get dressed on my account since you clearly didn't for our reporter friend."

Ben sipped on the coffee, "She wasn't very happy with me because I refused to give her a comment. I think she's using the bonding she's had with Zoe to get an exclusive."

"I'm pretty sure what she would like to exclusively have and it's got zero to do with a story," Alex said with a knowing smile.

"You know if I cared, I'd be filing a sexual harassment suit against the police department."

"Great, it would be a new twist on my reputation. But I did come out for a reason other than the view. I was wondering if there was some type of job you could find for Dani when she gets out of the hospital."

"I'll check with Zoe and see what we can do. I thought she was still in a coma."

Alex nodded and blinked back the tears, "She is, but the doctors are controlling it and plan to slowly bring her out of it within the next couple of days. I wanted to have some positive news to give her when I start asking all the unpleasant questions about who assaulted her."

"I'm glad you thought of me, but we both know Zoe is the one who could make this happen, not me."

"I know, but you've met Dani and I planned to exploit that fact."

* *

"So let me get this right. You want me to plant this folder of pictures in Benjamin Princi's house."

He took deep breaths to maintain his composure from dealing with this condescending asshole. "I don't care if it's his house, his garage, or his mailbox. I just want it planted somewhere in his possession."

Robert moved over to the table and flipped through the pictures, making sure he did not snag the rubber gloves. "Can I ask why you've got such a hard on for Princi? You could just kill him, but this is a pretty impressive smear campaign."

"It doesn't matter what my issues with Princi are. You should stay focused on two things. One we've given you a way to get off the radar and the other is Princi is wearing your ex-wife out from what I hear."

Robert tried to drown out the voice in the back of his head which chimed right in about Alex hooking up with the author. He'd found other outlets for his anger, but it kept growing as he replayed seeing Alex leave her home after Ben spent the night.

"What do I do after I plant this stuff?"

"Send me a text at this number and then we'll handle everything."

"Once this happens I'll be getting some alone time with my wife, right?"

"You take care of your end of the bargain and we'll make sure you have all the quality time you need."

Robert smiled as he closed the folder, knowing his hands would be healed up enough to inflict some serious education upon his ex-wife. She'd realize the error of her ways and start making amends.

* *

Alex looked from the computer screen to Gerald. It seemed too simple to actually have any type of effect.

"I don't know. You think posting fake emails to Kirkpatrick is going to get these guys to come forward?"

Gerald turned the screen back around, "It will work if we put in enough information to indicate we know exactly who we're looking at."

Alex was still skeptical, it seemed too easy. "You're sure they are monitoring the computers."

"No, but they have to have some kind of early warning system for when we are moving forward, so it's a safe bet it's the computers."

The flagged email copied itself and routed into the secure off site server. Working with child pornographers had provided them with the ultimate system for creating their own false network which searched for key words. Any combination of key words would lead to the email being duplicated and moved, which gave them at least a 24 hour window of early response time.

This email indicated that Vilnew and Milnero were getting entirely too close. They had an informant that they would be meeting with later this evening to discuss what they knew about the human trafficking problem in Ohio. Supposedly this informant was from Dayton, which created yet another ripple of concern.

He left the brief message

"I need you to monitor the station tonight around 8pm, the dynamic duo are meeting with a snitch. If you recognize the snitch, eliminate him."

* *

Gerald adjusted the extra surveillance cameras he brought from his home. They were positioned around the parking area to provide a better view of the entire lot, so they could have the entire picture instead of a partial. The officers had figured out long ago where to park to allow access to the building without proof they were at the office. This had allowed a number of affairs to occur between coworkers without the surveillance to provide proof.

"That is great right there Gerald," Alex's voice crackled over the radio.

They'd convinced the office it was an experiment to figure out how to catch who was skateboarding during the evening hours at the fire department parking lot next door. It was just a quick turn for Gerald to actually position the camera to get overlapping views of the back doors to the Halls of Justice.

Alex was setting up the remote DVR system to record everything in the parking lot. They had decided since they were unsure about who was accessing the system, it was better to just go with a separate system.

"Are you sure your guy can pull this off?"

Gerald shrugged, "I think so. He's been performing in the local theatre for years, so I expect him to give an Academy Award winning posing as our snitch."

"Do you think he's in any real danger?"

"I don't think so since whoever will be watching will not recognize him. It would be more of a problem if it was someone they knew could give us some dirt."

"Okay, well let's get the rest of this plan in place so we're ready."

* *

"I don't know about this plan. It feels like a set up."

There was no response and he wondered if the radio communication devise had malfunctioned. He watched from the adjacent tree line, using his sniper scope, but his gut kept screaming this was wrong.

"I said this ..."

"My hearing is fine, can you shut the hell up and do your job. This is more about what we can learn from them than anything else. My plan is they show their cards and then we can proceed, but I need you to maintain your composure."

Dismissed again, just like when he was first starting out. When this storm blew over, he was going to make his bid to start a new pipeline, without the old hierarchy. He'd be the one making the decisions and to hell with the others.

"Hold on, I've got some movement by the back entrance. Milnero is propping the door open with a wedge. She never came out, but it looked like she was checking to see if anyone was in the back parking lot."

"I still haven't seen any sign of anyone coming from up the street, but it seems like they are planning for someone to slip in the back without the cameras catching them in the lobby. I've got the scrambler going so any attempts they are making to record any of this is a waste of their time."

* *

"I don't think this is going to work."

Ben sighed as he leaned back in the chair. He'd been arguing with Trevor for almost an hour on Skype about the lyrics. They'd made some real progress with the latest batch of lyrics Ben had sent last week, but Trevor was hung up on one song and wanted to debate every piece.

"Do whatever you want Trevor. You know what's going on down there. If it sounds better to have the guy sing the song about his true love rather than an object of lust, then go for it."

"Seriously dude, why don't you fight for your creative license? I can make it work either way, but I want to know what you feel."

"So this is just a test. Why don't you have it done both ways and then see which one you like. And if you're feeling really wild, why don't you have a girl sing it about some guy she's lusting after."

"See that's what I want to hear, some thinking outside your tight little box. I'd think since you discovered having sex is okay that maybe your overall attitude would improve."

Ben chuckled as he flipped Trevor the bird, "Are we finished yet?"

"I guess so. Zoe told me to mess with you some and get your head out of this relationship funk you've been in. I heard there was a pretty impressive girl party where you were the main topic of conversation."

"Again we're venturing into topics that I don't want to discuss."

"I would have loved to be there watching the three chicks you've been banging compare notes. It's a wonder any of them still talk to you, but I guess Zoe has to and then the little reporter thinks you're Adonis."

"Alright then Trevor I'll talk to you next week."

Ben ended the feed as Trevor was making a joke about how they might come up with a time share plan for Ben. He realized the conversation had helped him laugh some, which wasn't something that happened often anymore.

Winston dropped the slimy tennis ball at Ben's feet. He'd been enjoying all the extra individual attention Ben had been giving him lately, so in his world it was always play time.

Ben threw the ball as far as he could out the open front door with Winston running his fastest trying to catch it in the air. He was getting a great rhythm going with his exercise and writing.

He hadn't mentioned anything to anyone, especially Zoe, that he had started formulating a short story. Ben knew it might not amount to anything, but he could feel the characters tugging at his thoughts throughout the day, which used to be a great sign there was a story wanting to be told. To accommodate this, Ben worked in a few hours of writing after he finished with his exercise.

Since Ben assumed he'd lost whatever gift he'd had for writing after Monica died, he wasn't getting too excited about the prospect of finishing the story. He couldn't deny the bliss he felt by sitting down and losing himself in his make believe world while hard rock pounded from the speakers.

Ben first felt the idea for the story of three friends searching for an old teacher after finding a cryptic note in an old yearbook when he received the box from the fire department with his old yearbooks. He'd flipped through the fire damaged books, reliving some of the best and worst times of his life through the pictures and hand written notes from friends. It was actually Courtney's note which pushed the story as she encouraged Ben to embrace his gifts and find his way.

Ben quickly closed the laptop and slid it under his couch when he heard Zoe's voice as she spoke with Winston.

"At least someone is glad to see me," Zoe said as she set her bag on the table and grabbed a bottle of water.

"What's that supposed to mean?"

"Well since we've had to alter our living arrangement, it is like pulling teeth to get you to stop for a visit."

"We talk nearly every day on the phone and I know you have your spies checking in on me."

Zoe smiled, "Such a harsh way to put things, but I suppose it's true. By all accounts you are doing very well here in your little cabin. I just needed to see your face and make sure for myself."

Ben stood and did a quick twirl, "Look mom, I'm doing fine."

"Sarcasm is such an overrated attribute. It does appear you have been exercising and eating well. Maybe you don't need me doting over you anymore."

Ben sat back down and smiled, "You know the plan is to share the house when it's finished, so don't get too comfortable in your swanky condo."

"I was going to tell you the same thing about not getting too comfortable with being alone, but we should discuss some other things. Samantha said you were rude to her when she came for a comment."

"I think I was very upfront with her about my feelings and how she manipulated me the last time we had a session."

Zoe arched her eyebrow, "She mentioned you threw your sexual encounter up in her face."

"Actually she brought it up first, and I just let her know that didn't give her license to stop by."

"So while we're on the subject of sexual encounters, how are things coming with Alex? She seems to be overly involved with her case right now."

Ben pulled his hand free and walked to the window, "I don't know where things are with Alex, it seems to fluctuate with the day. I decided I'd just get myself back on track doing the things I enjoy. I've been exercising and working on the cars, and I bet Trevor hasn't been bugging you about my lack of production."

"No in fact he called to say you've really been cranking out some good stuff. I just wanted to make sure you aren't out here alone brooding and ..."

"And what Zoe, sneaking in some booze to take the edge off?"

Zoe shrugged, "I can't say it hasn't crossed my mind, but after seeing you I can tell you really are doing well."

Zoe walked over and gave Ben a kiss on the cheek before leaving. Any fears she had were gone. Ben seemed to be coming right back and not wallowing in all the drama that seemed to find him.

* *

Robert made the call as soon as he saw Zoe drive back down the driveway. He'd been studying the various online court documents and knew there had to be something he was missing, and now he knew what it was. Princi had a little cabin tucked back on his property that few people seemed to know about.

Robert had assumed they counted the barn as more than one structure due to the modifications that had been done, but clearly the extra building was to the south of the house. All the aerial views had had shown nothing except the barn, house and a large pond, which was likely near the cabin. Robert had watched the news report on Princi after the fire and he had assumed the cabin that was being referred to was somewhere else in town, not right on his main property.

"Listen I know where Princi is staying, and I'm pretty sure he will be alone, so setting him up shouldn't be a problem."

Robert pocketed the phone after finishing his message and walked back over to the truck he'd purchased. His truck blended in well with the other older model trucks which were scattered around the site as workers were clamoring over each other to complete various projects on the rebuilding of the house. He'd figured that eventually following Princi's half breed bitch was going to pay off and now he'd hit the jackpot. Soon Benjamin Princi was going to have his life turned on its head.

* *

"Am I interrupting?"

Alex looked up from the monitors and smiled, "No, we're trying to figure out what we did wrong with our surveillance cameras."

Gerald pointed to the screen, "I really don't know what the deal is. I know it was hooked up correctly and you confirmed you had a good view."

Ben glanced at the screens and couldn't make out anything; it looked like a perfectly snowy screen. "Would a scrambling device do something like that?"

"Hell I don't know, maybe you can ask your nerd buddy in the crime lab." Gerald responded.

Alex motioned for Ben to have a seat as she dialed Jessica's cell phone, "Call me when you get a chance, got a tech question for you."

"So if I'm interrupting, I can just come back later."

Gerald placed his hand on Ben's shoulder to prevent him from standing, "Relax big boy, I need to get some fresh air and she could use the break."

Alex smiled, "Subtlety is not his forte. What brings you here today?"

"I just haven't had much of a chance to connect with you recently and I had to go see Chet, so I thought I'd swing by and see if I can take you out for lunch."

"Glad to see you're thinking about me, but I'm not sure I can afford to get away. We thought we had a plan in place and it's really not progressing. Somehow we're always one step behind."

Ben smiled as Alex ran her fingers through her hair and stretched, "I'll let you get back to work then."

Ben was walking by when Alex grabbed his hand and pulled him over. She snuggled in close to his chest, "I wish I could go, but I've got to get this figured out."

"I understand."

"I don't think you do. I think about you and feel your hands on me," Alex whispered as she pulled Ben's head down and kissed him lightly, teasing his tongue briefly with hers.

Ben pulled her in tight and ravaged her mouth as he ran his hands down her sides. "Just don't forget about me."

Alex took a deep breath as she gathered herself, "No chance of that. I'll call you later today and maybe we can find some time to spend together."

Ben smiled as we walked out of the building. He hadn't gotten a date, but he knew he was in her head, which was just as good.

Jessica knocked on the door and walked in. She noted that Alex was fixing her lipstick, but her lips looked different.

"Were you just doing something here that most of us only fantasize about?"

Alex turned and smiled, "If you mean kissing an extremely hot guy, then yes I'm guilty."

Jessica plopped into the visitor chair, "Okay business first and then dirty details."

Jessica confirmed that there were scrambling devices which could disrupt video signals as well as auditory, and she felt certain the snowy images were a result of such a device.

"Now let's get to the dirt. Was it a certain tall handsome writer?"

Alex blushed, thinking about his large hands running down her body. "Yes Ben was just in here and I had to turn down a lunch date, but I did get some dessert."

"Without being too graphic and making me hate you forever, is he as yummy as the package indicates?"

"I hate to brag, but oh yeah. He's got this incredible body and he seems to make his hands and lips go in three directions at once, which makes me melt."

Jessica pouted, "Its official, I hate you. It's not fair that you just stumbled into this relationship with Mr. Wonderful. I've been working my ass off to try and get Brooks to move along, but he's content to keep sampling the milk."

"I told you before that you might need to cut off the sex if you want him to commit."

"I know, but he really does the sex well. He might not be ideal for me, but he sure knows his way around the bed."

Alex smiled and twirled a strand of her hair, "There has to be more than sex Jessica, trust me on this one."

"No offense, but I don't have your natural attributes to help in my cause. You've been on your sexual sabbatical by choice, because we know men have been throwing themselves at you for years."

Alex was going to argue and deny the charge, but realized Jessica was probably right. "You are a smart beautiful girl Jess, you don't have to lower your standards for anyone."

Jessica smiled, "I am smart as hell, but I'll never turn heads like you do. I am going to take your advice and play hard to get and see if that gets Brooks to come in line."

Alex was giving Jessica a hug when Gerald returned.

"Great, I just missed girl bonding time."

Jessica laughed and gave Gerald a quick hug, "There's some love for you too, you big teddy bear."

"Surprised to see you here still. I figured you and loverboy would be going to lunch."

"Well I told him we're too busy for your information, so let's get back to work. Jessica confirmed that a scrambling device is capable of creating the snowy picture. My question is who would think to use one and also have access to one?"

* *

Ben parked his truck at Chet's and walked into the open garage area.

"Shit boy can't you read the sign."

Ben glanced at the Employees only sign and laughed, "I read just fine Chet. I wanted to know if you need any help or if you've found anything of interest for me."

Chet snorted as he stood up from the engine he'd been bent over, "Now why would I need someone with your limited abilities in my garage?"

They wandered over to the computer at his desk. Chet typed in his code and pulled up the picture of the half-finished Nomad station wagon.

"Owner wants ten grand, but I think you can talk him down. He claims he's stuck and his wife is nagging him to get rid of it. I thought a nice money pit like this would be right up your alley."

Ben looked at the various pictures of the car, wondering what had caused the owner to stop with the restoration project. He knew usually the reason was monetary, but the love seemed to always make the money worth the cost. Initially he thought this project would be a nice addition to his current Nomad project,so it made sense to work on something similar.

"Does the ten grand mean all the parts come along with it?"

"When I talked to him the other day he made it seem like it was the whole kit and caboodle."

Ben looked at the pictures once again, trying to determine if he was just bored or if he really wanted this project. Typically he used the vehicle restoration to keep his mind off other more pressing things.

"Call him back and let him know we'll take it."

Chet squinted at the screen, "Ain't we gonna talk him down some? It's not worth ten."

"I know, but it is to him so pay it."

Ben walked over to paint shop and peeked through the window to see the Superbird sitting there. It had been painted and was drying.

"Wow Chet, she looks beautiful. I wondered how that gloss black would look, but it was the right choice."

Chet smiled before spitting tobacco juice into his ever present cup, "I do good work, but she really did come together well. I was afraid the all blacked out look would be too much, but she looks bad as hell."

"Gee Chet, that's almost a compliment."

"Don't let it go to your head. If it wasn't for my unique abilities your color choice would have looked wrong. And I got the damn extras you wanted added."

Ben shook his head. He was still complaining about adding power steering and a cd player. "Thanks Chet, I'll make it worth your while when we tally up the damage."

"Darn right you will. Hey how come you haven't been bringing the fine looking woman of yours around anymore?"

"How many times have I explained to you that Zoe is not my woman? She works for me and that's it."

Chet narrowed his eyes, "So she lives with you and works for you, but there's nothing going on?"

Ben knew there was no way to explain that one night something did go on. "It's a work relationship, that's all."

"You're a damn fool."

"So I've been told before."

* *

Robert found the yellow legal envelope on the counter when he returned to the cabin. The note said to stash it at Princi's property and then call in an anonymous tip. This was the final part of his agreement with his partners and they were then going to deliver Alex to him for some reeducation classes.

His curiosity got the better of him and Robert opened the envelope to see the contents. The massive quantity of pictures was impressive, as were the variety of victims. Clearly his partners were trying to pin the tornado porn case on Ben Princi, but it made little sense why they were going after him.

Robert slipped the envelope back into a worn book bag and threw it in his truck and headed over to the construction site. He spotted a couple of obvious hiding spots along the edge of the pole barn, which would make sense because everything would have burnt in the fire. The key for him was to get the bag dropped off without any of the other workers going to investigate what it was.

Because he was getting back around five, some of the guys had stopped working for the day, which made slipping over to the pole barn no challenge. Princi had left the door opened so the workers could use his bathroom and refrigerator if they needed, which made going inside was even easier.

Robert checked the refrigerator like he was getting something to drink, but actually was looking for a cubby hole to stash the envelope. An older tool chest covered with dust looked to be a perfect spot to slip the envelope inside, and Robert quickly transferred the goods into the bottom drawer.

Ben got the text from the company as he drove. He'd wired the garage with the best surveillance equipment he could afford after the fire. It was originally a request from the insurance company to help prevent someone from burning the garage down as well, since there were zero suspects. Ben wrote the checks and never paid much attention until he started getting phone calls regularly from the monitoring company because someone was noticing something showing up on the various systems.

The systems were initiated by movement and started recording whenever there was any movement within twenty yards of the barn. Usually it was a raccoon or even a deer wandering too close to the proximity of the barn, but lately it had been the never ending stream of workers entering the barn to use the restroom or finding a place to get out of the sun.

Ben called in to check in and see what had tripped the system this time and was informed that it looked like someone had slipped a package inside of one of his toolboxes. There weren't any clear views of the person's face, but they could verify it was a man.

Armed with the knowledge from the company, Ben slipped into the garage from the rear entrance and walked over to his toolboxes. His first instincts told him to call Alex and get her expert opinion, but he was curious about what had been left. The bottom door was not closed tight and Ben immediately saw the edge of the yellow envelope. Slipping it under his shirt, Ben walked out the back of his barn and headed for the cabin.

An hour later, Ben paced in his cabin trying to figure out what he'd just stumbled on. There was no doubt the massive collection of pictures was meant to implicate Ben into the investigation, but he couldn't figure out why. It was evident he couldn't handle this himself and he also couldn't use his relationship with Alex and risk dragging her into the middle of this mess.

Ben made the call and luckily avoided getting voicemail.

****

The sheriff department and state highway patrol arrived later that evening. They consolidated their efforts after the anonymous tip came in. There were discussions about bringing in the CBI agents, but the underlying organizational rivalry prevented that from happening. It was going to be a huge public relations coup by having this solved by the local agency instead of the hotshot outsiders sent in by the governor.

There was going to be some backlash when the news got out that Blandale's resident celebrity was at the center of this sex scandal. Spinning that was going to take some skill, but it should evident that some with the resources of Benjamin Princi would be able to effectively hide his nefarious exploits.

They attempted to serve the warrant, but none of the officers could locate Mr. Princi. The door to the barn was not locked, so the warrant was taped to the window and the search commenced. Crime scene techs started at one corner and moved methodically through the building, recording and documenting as they went.

They did not uncover any of the items reported in the anonymous report, but did uncover an extensive surveillance system. The warrant did not cover the surveillance system, so for the time being there was nothing more to be done.

While the search was being executed at Ben's barn, he was with Zoe at her condo staying in constant contact with the surveillance company as they recorded the search. Ben had filled in Zoe about his discovery and subsequent phone call. Despite her arguments, Ben had decided his plan would have a better chance of success if they limited the number of people in the circle.

"Do you think we should get some legal representation to cover ourselves?"

Ben looked up from the laptop screen, "Eventually, but for right now I don't need a lawyer sticking his nose in the middle of this."

Zoe frowned, "You do realize that you are not law enforcement. You should let them handle this."

"They are handling it and I'm bothered by the fact that someone tried to implicate me in this and then called in an anonymous tip. We'll see how this plan plays out."

"So how is this going to play out with Alex?"

Ben had tried not to think about Alex. He hoped she would understand about why he chose not to involve her in this, because if it backfired she could get caught in the crossfire. "I'll deal with Alex."

"Uh huh, let me know how that works out for you."

Ben focused back on the screen, watching as the toolboxes were being fingerprinted and moved systematically into the center of the room. It seemed that the call had specifically told the location of the items. He'd racked his brain to come up with who he knew who hated him enough to set him up for this level of a fall.

"Still can't think of anyone who would go these lengths?"

Ben shook his head, "No I can't. I've resisted forming relationships with people for so long that it makes it easy to scroll down them and see who I could have crossed."

Zoe held up a long manicured finger, "If Samantha wasn't completely besotted over you, I'd nominate her for going over the edge and setting his up."

"It was never that intense between the two of us."

"Maybe on your part, but she's got this infatuation of you wrapped in love, which can be a scary thing in some women."

Ben looked up, "Speaking from experience Zoe?"

Zoe chuckled, "I'm sure I had some intense puppy love escapades when I was like twelve, but I learned pretty quickly that it was a game."

"That's awfully young to get hardened to love."

Zoe smiled as she gazed out the window, "See there is a difference we have. You've spent most of your adult life looking to find the great love of your life. You desire that exclusive, all consuming relationship. I, on the other hand, realized pretty quickly that I was just another trophy for some man. Once I figured that out then the game was easier, it gave me power because I determined who I would be a trophy for and who I would not."

"So love never enters into the equation?"

"I don't think love is in the cards for me."

Ben leaned back in his chair, "I know you give me crap for my quest for relationships, but I don't know what I'd do if I thought the relationship was never out there for me."

"Even when it falls apart and you fall into depression?"

"Well yeah that sucks, but I wouldn't trade it. I had fairly normal relationships with both Monica and Courtney and they didn't work out. I'm way outside my box with Alex and I don't know if it's going to work or not, but I'm trying. I'm not even going to speculate on what happened between us."

Zoe smiled slowly, "We'll call it a lapse in judgment. I was scared about coming that close to dying and I wanted to thank you. And well we know one thing led to another."

Ben's face burned, remembering their night together. "You can say that again, but I am trying to sort all this out. I'm trying my best not push and just let things happen. It's easier said than done for me."

"Just an observation from the outside, but keeping this information from Alex is not going to make things better. She will see that as a deliberate act of deception."

"Yeah I agree, but I still think its best."

"Okay big boy, but it's your future."

* *

Robert was leaning back on the chair on the porch when the cruiser skidded to a stop in the gravel. His initial instinct was to bolt for the front door until he saw his new friend climb out. Judging by the scowl on his face Robert knew it wasn't a social call.

"What's wrong?"

Brooks threw his hat on the table and ran his fingers through his sweaty hair, "I'll tell you what's wrong. You can't even complete a simple job. All you had to do was ..."

"What are you talking about? I planted the envelope and called in the tip. I even made sure it went to the non-emergency number so it would get routed to the county department and not the CBI."

"Well I just left Princi's property and they haven't found a damn thing, other than a really sophisticated surveillance system. A system which likely has your face on it somewhere."

Robert took a deep breath, "Listen it's doubtful they have a picture of me, because I had my hood up the entire time I was in the barn, but there's something else that bothers me."

"What's that?"

"I left that envelope in the tool box, so if it's not there then where the hell did it go? Somebody is playing a game with us."

Brooks smiled, "You must have a mouse in your pocket boy, because this game is with you. I got nothing to do with this and I could haul your ass in right now and look like a hero."

"I don't think so, because you know I'm not stupid, so I would have some sort of proof to cover my ass."

"I figured you would, but trust me if I decided to take you in, you'd never make it there because I'd shoot you for trying to escape."

Robert didn't respond as Brooks snatched his hat and stomped back to his cruiser. Clearly his partnership wasn't on nearly as stable ground as he thought, so it might be time for more extreme measures. Something a little more up close and personal.

26

Ben was back at his cabin when he received the text. He knew some communication would happen, but it was the waiting he had been struggling with. The instructions were concise and to the point.

Have the envelope at your cabin tomorrow at 8pm. No cops or one of your friends gets hurt.

Ben read it twice and made the phone call.

"I just got the message. Its tomorrow night at 8pm at my cabin, so we need to be discreet if he's watching my place. And he threatened my friends if I contacted the police."

27

"Good boy Mr. Princi, I'm glad to see you can follow instructions."

Ben watched carefully as the man crept into the living room, leading with the pistol. He'd never had much experience around guns, but it appeared to Ben that this man seemed fairly competent and comfortable with the gun in his hand.

"I'm here and I haven't talked with anyone. What do you want?"

Robert chuckled, "There are a number of things I want, but we're going to start with dealing with you. It's going to become very apparent in the near future that you are not the person everyone thought, so we'll start there. I need you to sit in this chair."

Ben sat in the chair and placed his hands behind it as he was instructed. The duct tape wrapped tightly around his wrists and the frame of the chair, which put an enormous amount of pressure on Ben's shoulders.

Satisfied that the duct tape was going to hold Ben, Robert put the gun down and removed the mask. "See I really didn't have an issue with you until I found out you were screwing around with my wife."

Ben knew his plan was in serious trouble once Robert removed his mask. By exposing himself it meant he wasn't worried about being identified in the future. The only thing he could think to do was start talking and hope the stalling would be enough.

"I'd apologize, but it's my understanding that Alex is divorced. And happily by her account."

Robert's smile never wavered as he approached and he punched Ben straight in the left eye. He'd aimed for Ben's nose, but he moved at the last second. "Probably not the best advice to piss off the person who directly effects your future and if you have one."

Ben leaned back and tried to blink the blood out of his eye, "I never did well with advice."

Robert grabbed Ben's hair and pulled his head back, "Now for the last time, where is the package I left for the authorities?"

"I don't know ..."

Ben didn't get to finish the statement before Robert's fist slammed into his eye again. The pain was exquisite as black dots bounced around in his vision as his left eye reduced to a sliver.

"You know what. Maybe I need to go pay a visit to your little half breed friend. I'm sure you can take some pain, but I'm sure your tongue will loosen up if you're watching me carve up her pretty little face. Where is my package?"

Ben leaned forward and watched the blood pool on his hardwood flooring. His face was hurting and his shoulders were throbbing. "In my garage is a cement block which comes out. The package is behind the block."

Robert smiled as he wiped his bloody knuckles on a dishtowel, "See that wasn't so hard. Now I'll just tip off the authorities and be on my way. You've made this much more difficult than it needed to be."

"I still don't see Alex coming back to you."

Robert nodded, "I agree, but I don't want her back anymore since she has been whoring around. I will give her an education about why she should never have left me though."

Ben hoped the microphones were picking everything up and Gerald was getting everything he needed. There had been no names mentioned, but there should be enough evidence to at least lock Robert up for a while.

Robert finished stuffing the dishtowel into the bottle he pulled from his pocket. "I've gotten a better feel for how these work since my first time. If I'd used a thinner bottle, then I wouldn't have to be dealing with you now since the first fire would have removed you from the equation."

Ben strained against the duct tape, but it failed to budge. He'd flexed as much as possible when Robert wrapped his wrists, but it had done little good. "So good to know who to have my insurance company send the bills for the new house to."

"Stall all you want Ben, it's time for me to go and for you to burn."

The lit dishtowel smoked on the counter as Robert walked out the front door. He'd completed the text message as he walked out the cabin, so the police would know where to find the incriminating materials. If he'd have been looking up he might have spotted Gerald Vilnew walking down the path with his service weapon drawn.

"Freeze Robert Macias! Hands where I can see them!"

Robert slowly raised his hands and dropped the cell phone to the ground. He expected the police to show up, but it shouldn't have been this soon or this person. Somehow Ben had set him up and Vilnew was here to clean up the mess.

"Officer, I just text some important information to the authorities about Benjamin Princi. He confessed some things and is ..."

Robert didn't finish the statement as he sensed someone coming from behind and turned to catch the full brunt of Ben's punch to his nose. The pain was instantaneous as the bones crunched and blood exploded from his nose as it was crushed.

Ben had got to his feet as Robert left the cabin and slammed himself into the corner of the refrigerator. The wooden chairs Gerald had purchased earlier were much flimsier than the original chairs and Ben shattered the chair with one blow. The make shift Molotov cocktail was doused and Ben ripped the duct tape and a substantial amount of arm hair off before coming outside to find Robert with his hands in the air. He knew it was wrong, but the admission about starting the fire and Zoe almost dying was too much and he needed to extract his blood payment.

"Back off Ben, he's had enough," Gerald said as he moved in and handcuffed Robert while he writhed in pain in the grass.

"Did you hear everything? He admitted to starting the fire and he threatened Zoe."

"Yes I not only heard it all, but got it recorded. You better get that eye looked at, it's swelling fast."

Ben stalked back to the cabin, knowing what Gerald was saying was right, but he wanted to inflict more punishment. He'd contacted Gerald as soon as he got the message about the proposed meeting, knowing that Alex needed to be kept out of the loop. Gerald came up with the surveillance plan and possible contingencies that might have crept up.

The flashing red and blue lights bounced around the living room as the backup team moved in for Robert. They'd set the bait and he'd bought it hook line and sinker, so now it was time to explain to Alex why they done this without her. She'd been spending most of her time at the hospital since Dani had come out of her coma. Dani had identified Robert as the man who had abducted her from the restaurant and physically assaulted her.

Alex knew something was going on when she spotted Gerald coming down the hallway at the hospital. She'd been there for a few hours and helped Dani with the start of her physical therapy. Besides being her friend, Alex felt more responsible due to her ex-husband being the reason Dani was targeted.

"What's going on? You look like there's a problem."

Gerald grabbed Alex's arm and pulled her into the cafeteria for a seat. "I wanted to be the one to tell you we arrested Robert tonight."

"That's great, now we can relax. What?"

"Don't ask questions yet, just listen. We set Robert up at Ben's cabin. Ben will be here pretty soon and he looks a little rough, but he got the information we needed and Robert admitted to starting the fire at Ben's house."

"You did this without me? What the hell Gerald, I thought we were partners."

Gerald nodded, "We are and sometimes partners have to protect each other and you needed to be out the loop on this one because of your personal involvement."

Alex paced around the cafeteria, mulling over everything that she'd been thinking after Dani identified Robert as her assailant. "Okay I understand the protective stance. How is Ben?"

Gerald shrugged, "He won't win any beauty pageants right now, but his eye should be fine."

"Jesus Gerald what did you let him do?"

"He agreed to have everything recorded and wanted to try and bait Robert into making his admissions. Part of the baiting process meant taking a couple of punches." Gerald was going to explain some more, but spotted Ben moving down the hallway with his eye covered with an ice bag.

Alex saw Ben and ran to meet him, "I just talked to Gerald you big dummy. Let me see your eye."

Ben removed the ice bag and smiled when Alex winced, "It's okay, because I got to break the son of bitch's nose for burning down my house."

Alex smiled back and pulled Ben into Dani's room to give her the good news that Robert was now in custody. Ben tried not to grimace when he saw Dani lying in the hospital bed. Her blond hair was mostly shaved off and the bruises were still visible along her face and jaw line. He could also make out the wires where her jaw had been wired shut to allow the jaw to heal properly. It did make him feel a little better when she tried to smile when Alex informed her about Robert getting his nose broken prior to being arrested.

They left when Dani fell asleep and wandered down to the cafeteria. They hadn't spoken about the evening, but Ben knew Alex was running the brief amounts of information she had accumulated through her head.

"Do you need to get some meds or anything? That looks like it really hurts."

Ben shook his head and smiled, "My eye is thumping like a son of a bitch, but being a recovering addict means you can't get any of the good pain meds."

"Well let's get some coffee, because I've got a few questions."

287

"I thought you might, but I need to tell you something first. Robert was trying to frame me with an envelope of pictures like the ones from your case."

Alex stopped walking and grabbed Ben's arm, "Are you telling me that Gerald knew this and still didn't pull me in? I understand about keeping me out of the loop due to Robert being involved, but dammit that was my case."

Ben directed Alex to a table and started talking, filling in the blanks as best he could and answering her questions.

Forty minutes later, Alex finished with her questions and got another cup of coffee. She'd been through the gamut of emotions as she sat with Ben. He'd patiently told her the story and provided the clarifying answers, but Alex was still hurt she had been left out of the loop.

Ben watched Alex with his good eye as she took her time filling her cup with fresh coffee. He knew there was a battle going on in her mind as she processed everything that Ben had dumped on her. Ben tried to block out the thumping in his head, which was increasing in intensity as his left eye continued to swell completely closed.

"Okay let's get you out of here since it's been a long evening for you."

Ben smiled as he stood and took Alex's hands, "I'm sorry that I didn't come to you about this, but I thought it would be a problem with Robert being involved."

Alex pulled his head down and gently kissed his cheek, "Thank you for not getting yourself seriously hurt, but Gerald and I are going to have a talk about how partners are supposed to interact."

Ben chuckled as they walked out holding hands, "Be gentle on him, he struggled about his role in this."

28

Robert smiled as they pulled off to the side of the road. He'd endured the trip to the emergency room while handcuffed to the gurney. The gauze that was shoved up his nose had been excruciating, but it had stopped the blood flow and the doctor said it was the easiest way to marginally set his nose for the time being. The doctor had explained that eventually he would likely need some reconstructive surgery along with minor plastic surgery to get his nose back close to normal.

He was considering this option when he saw his favorite deputy walk into the room. They made brief eye contact before the doctor was handed some paperwork and signatures were obtained. Robert assumed was going to be taken to the jail for his intake and then processed into the holding tank until the morning for his arraignment.

Robert never said a word as he walked to the waiting cruiser before being placed in the back and belted in. He barely noticed the pain in his face as he watched the hospital grow smaller.

"Thanks I owe you one for getting me out of there."

Brooks pointed at the small camera on the dashboard, "Shut the hell up until we get to the jail."

Robert grasped the meaning of everything being recorded by Brook's gestures and the scowl on his face. He leaned back and got as comfortable as possible with his hands and feet cuffed.

The cruiser screeching to a stop on the berm rousted Robert from the twilight sleep the pain meds had allowed him to drift off into. He watched as Brooks pulled open the door, motioning for Robert to scoot out.

Robert shuffled his torso as best he could and Brooks grabbed him by the arm. Hauling him out of the back seat and onto his feet. Robert watched Brooks reach for his serve weapon and motioned for Robert to start running. This was when he began to understand this might not be as much a plan to free him as it was to close up a loose end.

Robert smiled and stood his ground, "I'm not going to run Brooks. Do you think I haven't put provisions in place to have everything I know turned over to the media if something happens to me?"

"Either you start running right fucking now, or I'm going to shoot you where you stand."

Robert was weighing this threat when Brooks pulled the trigger and Robert dropped to his knees. "Have you lost your mind? You just shot me."

Brooks stared at the bloodstain growing above Robert's left knee. He'd managed to disable the dashboard camera and now this was his chance to ensure that Robert didn't make it into the system where he could cut a deal to offer up his accomplices.

Robert writhed on the ground as the pain in his knee overrode the pain meds he had in his system and the ache in his face. He'd tried to bluff about the information and knew now he'd miscalculated by not having a contingency plan in place prior to going after Princi. He'd forgotten his main rule with the court; always keep something back just in case, and now it was going to cost him.

Brooks smiled as Robert tried to fold himself into a ball and protect himself. The next two shots were head shots and Robert Macias felt no more pain. Brooks peeled the crime scene gloves off and tossed the gun into the wooded area. CSI would find the gun and find the appropriate finger prints on the gun, so now he just needed to finish his final part of the plan.

29

Ben woke to the pounding in his head. He momentarily forgot about his eye and couldn't understand why he was half blind. Sitting up brought all the memories of last night back, and Ben struggled to keep the contents of his stomach under control.

Staggering out of the bedroom, Ben found Zoe drinking coffee as she maneuvered on her ever-present laptop.

"Well good morning Rocky."

Ben tried not to smile, knowing it would hurt. "I didn't know we had an appointment today."

Zoe poured a cup of coffee and set it in front of Ben, "We don't, but I thought I should check on my little fighter. I must say if that hurts as much as it appears then you might need some pain medication."

Ben grimaced as he swallowed the coffee, "I'll just take some Tylenol. How did you find me and then get into my room?"

"Come on Ben, do you really have to ask that? I called Alex and she told me where she dropped you off and then I just sweet talked the desk clerk for a key. He believes I am giving you the ultimate wake up call."

Ben shook his head and finished the coffee. He knew returning to his cabin last night wasn't an option since the crime scene people were likely still combing over everything. The city was picking up the tab for his hotel room and Alex made it clear she couldn't stay or there would be more questions. Ben acted put out, but he doubted that he could have performed even if she had stayed.

Zoe turned her laptop so Ben could read the headlines as her phone chirped with a new text message. "Looks like you can add crime fighter to your list of accomplishments."

Ben scanned the article and realized the state was keeping a tight lid on the sting and how a civilian had assisted them. They admitted that someone close to the case had assisted them with the apprehension of wanted fugitive, Robert Macias, but they were not releasing any more information at this time. A press conference was being scheduled for later this afternoon to provide more facts.

Zoe stopped reading the text message, "You need to call Alex, and she has something you need to know."

Alex answered as soon as Ben called and started talking. Ben asked a couple of questions, but mostly just listened. Zoe watched Ben's facial expressions and could tell whatever she was saying, it was not good news.

Ben ended the call and slid his phone across the counter, "It seems Robert escaped last night while being transferred from the hospital to the county lockup. The deputy had stopped due to Robert acting like he was having trouble breathing. When he assisted he was struck from behind and when he woke up, Robert was gone."

Zoe watched Ben as she snacked on crackers. He'd gotten quiet and walked into the bedroom, so she knew he was working through whatever scenarios he had bouncing around in his head. She'd wanted to come by and provide comfort for him after the events of last night. His face was a mess and she knew he was in pain, but there was no complaining.

Ben returned to the kitchen with his phone, "Is it okay if I stay with you for a few days until this sorts out? I can't go back to the cabin, and I'm not comfortable with you being there alone in your condo since Macias knows where you live."

"Have you thought to run this by Alex?"

"Why would I? She knows we shared the house and I need you to be safe."

Zoe shook her head slowly, "Trust me this is something you need to discuss with her first. Things changed when we had sex, and it would seem callous for you to make this decision without her being aware."

Ben stared at Zoe. He'd pushed the sex out of his mind, but it probably hadn't left Alex's, so Zoe was probably right. He grabbed his phone and headed back into the bedroom.

* *

Alex ended the call and refreshed her monitor. She appreciated that Ben had discussed with her about his idea of staying with Zoe for the next few days until Robert was recaptured, but she kept having images of the two of them making love in the cabin. Ben swore there was nothing there, but Alex had a hard time believing any male would be able to resist sharing a home with Zoe.

"So am I still getting the silent treatment, or are we okay?"

Alex gave Gerald her best dirty look, but smiled when he slumped into his chair. She'd frozen him out all morning after keeping the undercover operation from her, but the news of Robert's escape had given her more perspective.

"I'm getting better, but just know that I expect to be kept in the loop from this point on."

Gerald held his hands up, "Okay, let's go catch this son of a bitch before he does something else. I interviewed the deputy, but he doesn't have much more to offer. He's being suspended during the investigation, but he admits he broke protocol by checking on the prisoner."

Alex listened, but her mind was on how her ex-husband had sunk so low as to assault Dani and Ben. Now he was on the loose again and clearly had some type of accomplice to help him. She knew he likely had some mental health issues, but this was completely out the character she knew for him.

"Is Ben finding somewhere else to stay? He really shouldn't think about going anywhere near the cabin until Robert is back in custody."

Alex smiled, "Yeah he's in good hands. He'll stay with Zoe for a few days."

Gerald noted her smile, but recognized the tone, "I take it he was smart enough to talk with you about that first."

"Yes he did, but I'm pretty sure Zoe was the smart one who pushed him to call me about it. Can we talk about where to start looking for Robert?"

Gerald recognized the not so subtle nudge to stop talking about her personal life. He'd made a judgment call with Kirkpatrick's approval to keep Alex out of the initial sting, but now they were back at square one and searching for answers.

"Okay why don't we keep searching the surrounding roads and hope we get lucky. Also I had the photos we recovered from Ben's taken down to the lab to determine if they are from the same batch. They will also blow the pictures up to see if there is any new evidence that might show up."

"Good to see you've gotten back in the saddle."

* *

JB answered every question that was directed his way. He knew they were having two people ask questions to keep him off balance and hopefully screw up. He stuck with his story and he didn't need to play up the throbbing headache he had from getting hit with the flashlight.

He had been found where he parked the cruiser to rendezvous. JB told him to make it look real and he was paying the price now for the mild concussion he had suffered from the blow. He gave the location for where to find Robert's body and the gun, in case they needed to guide the search along.

JB grimaced and took a drink of water as he watched Milnero and Vilnew appear at the back of the room. They hadn't asked any questions, but they were whispering to the nurses and pointing toward the medical charts.

Alex watched as John Brooks Barrett answered the questions. He clearly had the signs of being jumped, judging by the bruised area on the back of his neck. It had already been confirmed that he had been struck by an object such as a metal flashlight. She'd already looked at his record with the county and he was a steady, if unspectacular employee. Alex was pretty sure he was also the deputy that Jessica was involved with.

"I'm about ready to go if you are," Gerald announced as he headed toward the door.

Alex watched a few more moments before leaving. She got the feeling he was lying about something, but it wasn't anything obvious and she couldn't put her finger on it.

Gerald came to get Alex after getting the call. "Come on they think they found Robert's body out on Old Rangeline Rd. A farmer spotted a body in the ditch and CSI is out there now."

It was an hour later that Alex confirmed that the body they had recovered was her ex-husband Robert Macias. He'd been shot in the left knee and there were two bullet wounds to his temple which were likely the kill shots. Alex had braced herself for the identification, but it still stung when she saw Robert's body lying covered in the ditch. Despite all the shit he'd put her through, it was the few good moments that kept popping into Alex's head.

* *

Zoe sat down in the lounger and placed the drink on the stand, "So have you heard from Alex?"

"No, I tried calling, but it went straight to voicemail. I figure she'll call me when she gets a chance."

Ben had been sitting on the patio for the past few hours, trying to read and responding to emails. His attempts to stay busy were not working and he became increasingly focused on his silent phone. Zoe had checked on him a few times, but knew it was best just to let him brood and get it out of his system.

"Well I did speak with Samantha and she confirmed that Robert Macias is dead, but it's an open case as to who shot him."

Ben looked over at Zoe as she stared at the adjacent buildings, "I guess that would be what is keeping Alex occupied. I'm sure it's difficult for her to be involved with the case, especially when the deceased is her ex-husband."

"Samantha confirmed off the record that Alex admitted to her this is a difficult case for her and Samantha also added she looked like shit."

Ben was going to respond when he heard the door beep as it opened and Alex walked in. Her dark hair was pulled back into a ponytail, allowing her dark eyes to show the pain of the past few days.

Zoe grabbed her drink and headed inside, pausing briefly to say a few words and give Alex a hug. She knew Ben needed some time with Alex and it would be best if she was not around.

Ben slid his chair around so he was facing the lounge chair when Alex slumped into it. He grabbed her hand and just held it as she laid her head back and closed her eyes.

"I don't know if I've ever had to do anything like that before. I did okay identifying his body, but I fell apart like a rookie when I had to call his mother and confirm her son was dead."

"I'm sorry Alex, I know this had to be rough for you."

Alex bolted upright and her eyes flashed, "It shouldn't be. The son of a bitch raped and beat one of my friends, and then tried to set you up before burning your cabin. I should be ecstatic that he's dead, but it just seems wrong when a mother is sobbing because the little boy she remembers is gone."

Ben pulled her into his arms as Alex cried. He just held her as she cried, waiting until her breathing had eased and it was evident that she had regained some of her composure.

"It took some courage to call Robert's mother, but it probably meant something to her that you would be the one who would step up to make the call."

Alex smiled as she wiped the tears off her cheeks, "I always got along with Marcia. I think she knew that Robert had his flaws and that was why I had to leave. We still exchanged emails occasionally to just keep in touch and she was friendly with my mother."

Ben listened, but didn't offer much in the way of opinion. He never really knew Robert, but he couldn't say he felt bad that he was dead. There was an extensive list of crimes he'd committed since coming to Blandale, and the majority revolved around Alex's circle of friends, which Ben felt was inexcusable.

"You've been awfully quiet and let me vent, what are you thinking?"

Ben took a deep breath, "My thoughts are probably not relevant right now."

Alex looked over at Ben's black eye, going to yellow on the edges and the scabbed over cut on his lip, "After what you've been through as a result of Robert's actions, I'd say you are warranted to have your say."

"I'm finding it hard to find much empathy for the guy. I know being shot is tough, but he put himself in that situation with some of the choices he was making. I can't say I feel bad about anything that happened to him."

Alex pulled her hands away from Ben and leaned back in the lounge and stared off into the sky. She'd expected Ben to have a strong reaction to Robert's murder, but this was a cold response she didn't see coming.

"I'm not asking you excuse his actions, but a man was murdered."

Ben could tell from her tone that he'd misjudged about how much of his anger to share. He knew her head was mixed up with the man she used to know and his saintly mother, but Ben didn't have that perspective and frankly he didn't care.

"I think it's best if I just hold my tongue before I make things even worse."

Alex knew intellectually she was being unreasonable, but the sight of her ex-husband lying in the ditch with bullet holes in his head was still fresh. She'd wanted him punished for his crimes, but being gunned down in cold blood was beneath everyone.

"I wanted to stop back here to get my things so I can get back to my house. I thought we should touch base as well."

Ben stared at his feet as Alex rose and walked to the patio door, "I'm not going to apologize for being glad he's gone after everything he did and attempted to do."

Alex knew his head was back at the hospital seeing Dani's battered face and the fear he'd had when he realized his house was burning and Zoe was still there. Alex didn't fault him for this.

"I wasn't asking you to, but I needed you to understand my part of it all."

Zoe watched Alex leave twenty minutes later, while also noting that Ben had not left the patio or offered to help. "So is there trouble in paradise or is it just you being stubborn?"

Ben shot a warning look, but Zoe pressed on.

"As someone who knows you intimately well, maybe this is one you should just suck up your pride and go apologize now for."

"I'm not apologizing for that s o b being shot and killed. If you hang around with criminal characters, guess what bad shit happens."

Zoe grabbed Ben's hand, "I understand your need for retribution after everything you've endured, but this is about Alex. She is most likely feeling torn by her own feelings of betrayal and revenge, but tempered with whatever happy memories she has of him. Personally I have a big problem with him for burning down your house, but it's not just about me."

"Well thanks for making me feel like a shit."

"Glad I can be of service, but you need to fix things with Alex so you can get out of here."

30

Alex flipped the photos over into stacks, separated by content. Most of the pictures were of only the women, but there had been a few which included what appeared to be a male in the edges. There were a couple which seemed to be shot into a mirror, but there wasn't anything definitive which provided any sort of material to work with at creating a workable drawing.

She was turning an enhanced photo which seemed to depict a girl performing fellatio on a white male. The male had taken the picture from his perspective looking down at the girl as she worked. These new photos provided more material to work with, but it hadn't allowed for any more progress. If anything it gave more credence to how elusive the perp was being and comfortable enough to taunt the police with providing more pictures.

Alex was throwing the photo down when Jessica opened the door after knocking. "Hey girl, do you want to go grab some lunch?"

"I really need to keep going through these pictures. Maybe you could pick me up something at the deli."

Jessica was walking out when the edge of the photo caught her eye.

"What is that a picture to?"

Alex flicked a glance at where Jessica was pointing, "It's with everything else we have gotten about the case for the past six weeks. You really didn't think I had time for anything else did you?"

Jessica gently pulled the photo out from under the folder it was under so she could see the entire picture. Her attention was not drawn to young Hispanic girl lying on the floor, but rather the edge of the frame.

"Where did you get this picture? Please tell me this is a mistake."

Alex looked at her friend, who'd gone an alarming shade of pale. "Jessica are you okay? Why don't you sit down in the chair over ..."

Jessica didn't hear the rest as she ran out of the office before she threw up. She made it to the bathroom barely before hurling everything she had eaten this morning.

Alex found Jessica slumped on the floor with a pile of paper towels, "Jesus, are you alright? You scared the shit out of me back there."

"I'm sorry, but I had to get out of there. That picture you had, it made me think of some things."

Alex sat down on the floor next to friend and leaned her head down onto her shoulder. "It's okay Jessica, you don't have to talk about anything. I wasn't thinking about the pictures triggering anything for someone coming into the office."

Jessica shook her head, "No it wasn't anything like that. I recognized something in the picture that might help you, but I'm not sure."

"What did you see Jess?"

"I think the edge of the picture I looked at was a tattoo I've seen before. It caught my eye when I walked by."

"Wait a minute. I thought you were having trouble with the naked little girl in the photo. What do you mean that might be an identifiable tattoo?"

"I didn't say identifiable, I said I think I've seen it before."

Alex ran back down the hall and grabbed the photo before returning. "I don't see a tattoo here, can you point it out to me?"

Jessica glanced at the photo, this time seeing the naked girl on the floor, covered in blood. She took a deep breath and focused on the top half of the photo and told herself it was just work. "On the right side is what looks like a black smear."

"Yeah, we assumed it was a distortion of the camera or some kind of reflection."

"I don't think so, I'm pretty sure it's a collection of Chinese characters on the inside of a thigh."

Alex turned the picture and tried to visualize the black splotch as characters. "How can you know that Jess?" She whispered.

Jessica turned with tears in her eyes, "I think that's the same tattoo JB has on the inside of his thigh. He got it when he was in the army and I tease him about not knowing what it really says."

Alex pulled the photo back and tried to get a better view which might make the view more clear. It still looked like a black blemish near the edge of the picture, but now Alex could kind of see that it might look like a tattoo if you knew it was there. She wasn't sure if it was enough to get a warrant or convince Kirkpatrick that it was anything other than a smudge.

"Jess, are you absolutely sure about this? If I proceed with this, it changes everything for him."

Jessica looked up at Alex with tears in her eyes, "I want to be wrong, but it fits with other things. Embarrassing things I know."

Alex hesitated, not wanting to push her friend, but knowing she had to. "I need to know Jess. I'll do everything in my power to keep your name out of it."

"I know, but everyone knows we've been going out so most of this information is only things I would know, unless he's been cheating with other women here at the office."

Alex sat silently, knowing how embarrassing this was for her friend. She wouldn't want to discuss any of her sexual activities with anyone else, and it was only harder when factoring in that the information would be spread all over the department once the rumor mill started running.

"JB, he had like appetites for certain things. He would want to do things that I wasn't really willing to try. He'd try to make a joke out of it, like suggesting we film me giving him a blowjob. I told him no way would that happen and then he tried to play it off that he was just kidding, but I could tell it was something he really wanted."

"Is there more than that Jess?"

Jessica looked up at the ceiling and nodded, "Yeah there's more and it makes more sense now. He used to always want me to you know shave down there. I tried to make jokes about how it made me feel like a little girl with no hair down there, but it really turned him on when I was freshly shaved or waxed. God, how did I not see that there was something seriously wrong with that? He also seemed to be only interested in him getting off, but I thought that was just him being a guy."

Alex was nodding along as she ran her hand down Jessica's back, remembering what it was like to feel humiliated and also that it was expected in the relationship. Robert had convinced her to a number of things that normally she would never have ever considered.

"He also tried to hint that maybe we should bring another woman in with us. I told him that I wasn't okay with that and it would feel weird. Again I played it off as some male fantasy about two women at once or the lesbian thing."

"Jess I need to go talk with Kirkpatrick about this stuff and try to get a warrant to at least look at JB's file to see if the tattoo is shown there. I'll do everything I can to keep this under wraps."

Jessica wiped at her tears with the back of her hand, "I know Alex, do your job. I'll be okay. I just need a few minutes to get myself composed before I head back to the lab."

31

Gerald knocked on the door, while peering through the side window. Warrant in hand, he hammered the door this time and motioned for Alex and the CSI technicians to join him on the porch.

"It didn't feel like anyone was here, but I think we should be careful before we go in. I read his army discharge dossier and he had some brief experience with demolitions."

Alex nodded at Gerald and brought up the lead technician, who pulled the oversized suitcase behind him. "Please tell me you have one of those mini camera devices in that rolling filing cabinet of yours."

Bryant smiled, "Sure do boss. I haven't got to use it yet in the field, but we've run simulations with it in the office. I'll run the cable under the threshold and see if there is any type of device attached to the door."

Alex stood with Gerald as Sgt Bryant set up the machine and snaked the cable under the door. He gave the all clear signal within ten minutes. Gerald had the extra officers use the battering ram to blast the door open.

Alex went in first, sweeping her gun to the left towards the open living room as Gerald covered her right going into the dining room. Both were mildly surprised at how pristine the house seemed. Jessica had warned Alex that JB was a slob and they rarely went to his house because she couldn't deal with all the squalor that he lived with.

"Didn't Jessica say his house was a pigsty?"

"Yes she did, which makes me think of two things. One he lied to her to make sure she didn't come over too often, or he knew we were coming and had the place sterilized."

Gerald nodded, "Just so you know I think the sink smells like bleach or some other cleaning agent."

"Dammit, let's get the crew in here so we can start this process," Alex said as she motioned for the crew to get inside and start inventorying the contents of the house.

Three hours later, Alex and Gerald were outside on the porch, looking over some of the documented items from the home. The only laptop found was nearly new and had only the basic programming on it, which screamed recent purchase. There were also only a handful of Playboy magazines that had been discovered. Gerald tossed the evidence bag with the magazines down and stalked off.

Alex was going to go after him when she heard the neighbor coughing in an obvious attempt to get her attention.

"Can I help you with something Ms.?"

"It's Mrs. Darrow, but please call me Jenni. Everybody does. I couldn't help but notice all of the activity over there today and I wondered why I never saw any of your people in the basement."

Alex turned quickly, "What are you talking about? The blueprints we pulled don't show anything about a basement."

Jenni came down off her porch and motioned for Alex to follow her to the rear of the house. "There see that blacked out window? I can see it from my kitchen window, but it's more obvious when he's got the light on in there."

Alex knelt down and looked at the blacked out window, which was designed to look like part of the tarred block wall. "Thank you Jenni, you've been a big help."

Alex ran down the street and grabbed Gerald, who was brooding while chomping on his cigar. "Come on I think we're about the get lucky.

They found the trapdoor in the floor boards under the armoire in the spare bedroom. It turned out to be a partial basement under only the back half of the house, but it held some of the materials that had been sought.

"Okay we've got enough stuff now to convince me we've got the right person. Now how do we locate this son of a bitch?"

Gerald shrugged, "I have no idea, but we're going to need to talk with his father, because you know this is going to blow this town apart."

Alex nodded. Kirkpatrick had called in a favor to get the warrant with total discretion so the sheriff wasn't alerted to the fact they were about to investigate his son. This investigation was under the radar, but it wasn't going to remain there for long.

Pulling out her phone, Alex took a deep breath. "I'll do it Gerald. I know you have a relationship with John, so he can rant at me if he needs to."

Twenty minutes later, Alex hung up her phone and ran her fingers through her hair. "That was pretty rough."

"He didn't take it well?"

"No it was the detached way he kept asking questions and asking for clarification. He seemed to shut off his feelings about five minutes into the conversation and then wanted to know the parameters of how he could assist."

Gerald nodded, "That sounds like John. He was always a cool customer, but it got worse when his wife, JB's mother, passed away. John just shut himself down. They call him the Terminator behind his back because he seems so machine like, but he knows and thinks of it as a good thing."

"He did suggest we check out the family cabin by Wayne State Park. That was the only place he could think that JB might run to if he thought he was in trouble."

"I think we need to get the SWAT involved if we're heading up into the woods. I've been to the cabin and it's almost a fortress on a hill, so he'll know we're coming for him."

****

Brooks watched from down the street with the binoculars. He'd been sitting most of the day in the cleaning service van and watching his house. Judge Sanchez had notified his father as soon as Kirkpatrick left with the signed warrant and Brooks was out of his house within the hour. He was feeling fairly confident until he spotted Milnero talking with his nosey ass neighbor and they started pointing at the blacked out window. How had that old bat figured out about his basement?

Sipping on his water and chewing the jerky, Brooks weighed out his options. He had some money stashed in case he needed to cut ties and run, but he wasn't as solvent as he needed to be. The backup plan was to disappear with the fake passport and wait in Brazil for word from his father. Brooks hadn't been able to do it, and instead of having a six hour head start he was sitting watching his house be torn apart.

Fuckers, he thought as the boxes were carried out to the van. He had moved most of the products, but he had run out of time and now they had it. Once the computer geeks got their hands on the laptops he was cooked, because the encrypted menu would eventually show the bones to the organization. The last thing he wanted to do now was call and listen to another lecture about his failings, but his father needed to know the fallout.

"Why are you calling me?"

"Listen it's a burner phone. They found some of the laptops in the basement, so you may need to execute your own burn notice. It will take them some time to get through the encryption, but they will get through."

"How do you know this? You're supposed to be on a plane out of the country."

Brooks didn't answer right away, "I'm watching them from down the street. I couldn't just leave without knowing and I wasn't sure if you would actually take care of me."

"Listen get off this phone and go to the farm. Do not go to the cabin. I told Milnero about the cabin, so that's where they are likely headed next. I'll be there within the hour and we can come up with an appropriate exit strategy that you can follow."

Brooks set the phone down and climbed into the front seat. This wasn't the first time he'd wondered about what the exit strategy would look like and if it even involved him walking away in one piece. He'd watched his father over the years do whatever it took to keep the business thriving, whether that meant something as simple as covering up evidence or leads, or as complex as having someone killed and the body hidden.

Driving to the farm was going to be enough time for Brooks to set up a plan to make sure he actually could walk away.

****

After throwing the phone back into his desk, Sheriff John Barrett leaned back into his chair. He'd been seeing all the signs over the past few months that his only son was going to have to be eliminated before he took everyone down with him. John had ignored the suggestions and comments from others previously when it came to Junior, and now he had no one to blame but himself.

The others were worried JB's rash behaviors, not to mention his disregard for sampling the merchandise, would ultimately lead to him being caught and then giving up everyone to save his own hide. John argued his son's point of view, but secretly held the same concerns, which meant Junior would need to be eliminated to protect the interests of the group.

John sighed as he pulled the clean pistol from the bottom of his filing cabinet. The gun had never been fired and there would be no way to trace it, which for this job was going to be essential. He tucked the pistol in his waistband under his windbreaker and left the messages with his secretary. He was going to have to kill his own child, something he never envisioned. His son had always been rebellious, even fighting against being called Junior or acknowledgement of his father. He always went by Brooks, anything that distanced himself from the man he clearly despised.

* *

Ben pulled his car off to the side of the road, fully expecting the cruiser to go blowing by. Instead the car stopped behind him with bright lights filling the mirrors and Ben wondered what was going on. He'd glanced at his speedometer briefly when he first heard the siren and saw he was two miles under the speed limit. Maybe he had a tail light out or something.

"Can you step out of the vehicle please?"

Ben looked up as the light shined into his face, "Is there a problem officer? I need to get my registration from the glove box."

"No need for that, you've got a tail light out that I want to show you."

Ben leaned away from the light and opened the door. He momentarily thought about grabbing his phone off the passenger seat, but dismissed that due to the no nonsense approach the officer was using.

Ben glanced back as he stood, recognizing who had pulled him over, "How's it going Brooks?"

"Fine Princi. We haven't run into each other since you moved back to the Deeter place."

Ben walked slowly, wondering why Brooks was talking to him like they were old friends. In high school they went to rival schools and Brooks was ejected from a game for sucker punching Ben during a scramble for a loose ball. This seemed to stem from Ben starting to date Brooks' ex-girlfriend, Courtney Daniels. Clearly there were no warm cuddly feelings from the past to discuss, and now he acted like they should go out for a beer together.

"I thought maybe that was the problem since I knew I wasn't …," Ben stopped talking, turning his head as his peripheral vision picked up something coming.

He never finished the statement as Brooks drove the steel flashlight into Ben's temple. He'd been aiming for the back of his neck, but Ben twisted at the last second. Ben's head bounced off the bumper as he went down, and Brooks smiled as he watched the blood pool under Ben's head while he moaned on the asphalt. Movies never got it right because no one could handle more than one direct shot to the head and keep functioning, let alone continue with a five minute fight sequence.

Brooks gave a quick glance before pulling Ben to the rear of his cruiser and lifting, pushing, rolling him into the seat. This had been an impromptu decision when he saw Ben drive by, but Brooks figured if this was the end game then he might as well close up all of his loose ends. Thanks to dear old dad's self-preservation instincts, Brooks estimated he had at least a two hour window to wrap things up and get the hell out of the county before he headed for Canada. This was his exit strategy, and he was the only one who knew about it.

Ben tried to calm his stomach as the waves of nausea continued. He'd tried to sit up in the back seat, but with his hands cuffed it made that nearly impossible. The wound on his head had stopped bleeding, but Ben assumed he'd sustained some level of a concussion based on the overall effects his body was experiencing. Ben didn't know exactly what was going on, but if Brooks was going this far then it wasn't headed to a good ending.

He tried to review what he knew and it didn't take long to circle back to Brooks being the transporting officer who let Robert Macias escape. Ben knew Alex was trying to get some further interview time with Brooks to better understand the timeline, but maybe this was the whole thing imploding now.

Brooks backed the cruiser on the backside of the barn, leaving enough room to open the door and haul Ben out. Killing Ben now would be his preference, but he needed to prepare for his father's arrival and subsequent escape plan. So he hauled Ben out of the backseat and gave him a moment as he fell to the ground.

"Get up Princi, and don't try anything heroic. I don't want to have to kill you now."

Ben rolled onto his side and slowly shifted himself onto his knees before shakily standing. "Gee Brooks, I always knew you were a whack job, but this is a little out there even for you."

Brooks motioned with his Glock and Ben shuffled towards the barn. "I hope you maintain your sense of humor Princi, because when I'm done with dad, we're going to spend a little quality time finding out how much pain you can handle before you beg me to finish you."

Ben was going to make a smart comment, but Brooks' punch to his left kidney dropped him to one knee and stole his breath. Brooks rolled Ben over to the gate for the horse stall and quickly snapped another handcuff onto the railing, ensuring Ben wasn't going anywhere.

"Well gotta go get ready," Brooks announced as he tore a swatch of duct tape and placed it over Ben's mouth. "If things had gone as I hoped, I'd have loved to have spent some time with your women. Be nice to compare Alex and Zoe to see who's better in the sack."

Ben was straining against the cuffs as Brooks closed the door and walked toward the house.

Ben could hear the argument start soon after the engine of the other vehicle stopped. He made out Sheriff John Barrett's voice as he yelled for his son. There were threats about not following the plan and still being here. Brooks was arguing back about his father not really trying to help him, just looking to find a way to get rid of him.

"For God's sake JB, put the gun down. I came here to help you."

Brooks maintained his rigid stance. "I need some answers before I leave, since I assume there isn't a return trip in my future."

"What do you want JB?"

"My name is Brooks, I've told you that for years and yet you still do what you want. I need to know what happened to Mom."

His father shook his head sadly, "After all this time, it still comes back to her. Your mother died in a car crash when a drunk driver went left of center. They were both dead when we arrived."

Brooks blinked back the tears, "And you had nothing to do with the crash or the cover-up?"

"You aren't listening, there was no cover-up. It was an accident."

"Tell me about Suzanna Princi."

Ben stopped moving as he heard his mother's name mentioned. "What are you talking about JB? I haven't spoken about her in over fifteen years."

Brooks smiled, "I really don't have time for your games Dad, so answer the question or I could just shoot you"

There was silence for a short period of time, but for Ben it seemed like an eternity. What the hell was Brooks talking about his mother and Sheriff Barrett. Ben knew they had gone to school together, but assumed that was the extent of their relationship.

"Trying to figure out an angle Dad? This might be a really good time to just tell me the truth. Let's pretend that I know more than you probably think I do about your relationship with her."

"What do you want me to say JB? I talked to Suzanne a few times after your mother died. She was a widow and you needed a mother around."

Brooks smirked, "I'm not talking about that. I'm talking about the affair you had with her when Mom was pregnant with me. I need to know if that son of a bitch Princi is my bastard half-brother."

Ben listened intently. He couldn't hear anything and he needed these answers as much as Brooks. If it was true, it explained why Brooks hated him as much as he did. Ben replayed conversations he'd had with his mother when she talked about the rocky relationship she had with his father. Ben knew there were problems, but he never suspected she'd had an affair, but then that wouldn't be something to freely admit to.

"Listen Brooks. Your mother and I were going through a rough patch and I knew Suzanne from high school. We talked or commiserated whatever you want to call it about our respective relationship problems. There was alcohol involved and one thing led to another."

"I knew you were a cold hearted bastard, but to do that to Mom when she was pregnant, what an asshole."

"Despite what you think you know, your mother was not the princess you want to make her out to be."

311

"You might want to be real careful Dad right now, because I've got a number of reasons to just put a bullet in you."

John sighed wearily, "I doubt it's going to matter much anyway. You are likely not going to get out of the country at this point, so what's one more body. Stop blowing smoke and just shoot me already."

"Not yet. I need to know the truth, because you won't see me again after today."

"Here's the truth then. I had sex with Suzanne and I wondered for a number of years that maybe Ben was my son due to the timing of his birth. I asked her a few times, but she refused to answer. I tried talking to her more frequently after your mother died, because it made sense for us to be a family, especially if Ben was my son."

"Well that way you'd have a son you were proud of at least."

John shook his head sadly, "He's not my son JB. I had a DNA packet completed years ago and Ben is not my son, so your rage is misplaced."

"Probably disappointed you didn't it?"

"A little. I've got admit you've been a huge disappointment. I expected you to take over the empire when I retired, but you are still controlled by your urges and lack the sensibility to run an organization like this. So if we're finished here, I'm going into the house to get some things, it would be best for everyone if you were gone before I returned."

Ben hung his head. He wasn't out there, but the drama might have well been played out right next to him. He'd learned some major news about his mother's past, but at least he knew the truth. As long as John was telling the truth then his father was truly his father.

The gun shot was startling in the silence, and Ben wondered who shot whom. The answer was provided soon when Brooks walked back into the barn without a word and climbed to the second floor with a scoped rifle.

* *

"Why are we stopping out here? We need to get going to the cabin," Alex squawked as they pulled off the road onto the lane leading to the farm.

Gerald put his phone away, "I've got a bad feeling that John might be misleading us. I just got done talking to Jennifer, John's secretary and she said he left the office about five minutes after you spoke with him. This tells me that he's trying to do something to help his son, even though you asked him to stay out of the mix. And remember, somebody else knocked JB out when Robert escaped and I always say look at family first."

"Do we need to get some backup out here?"

"I don't know. I want to believe John, but my gut tells me we need to check this out first. Let's just go take a quick look around and then we'll head to the cabin."

They both pulled their weapons and moved forward, slipping from tree to tree as they headed up the lane. Gerald made the call for back up when he saw the cruiser was parked in the driveway, which meant that John had called his son to warn him. Alex made eye contact with Gerald and motioned for him to cover her as she sprinted for the parked vehicle.

Alex never got the chance to take off, because Gerald came running towards her before she heard the shot. Gerald collapsed and rolled against the tree. He was bleeding heavily from his left hip and Alex crawled over to cover him, praying reinforcements were headed there quickly.

"You need to drop your weapon Milnero or I'll put the next bullet into his head."

Alex continued applying pressure on the wound as she tried to locate the voice and where it was coming from. "You might as well come out, this place is going to swarming with cops in a few minutes."

"Might be true, but we're not finished yet. Last warning, because after I kill your partner, I'm going to start in on your boyfriend."

Alex adjusted her hands, trying not to think about the amount of blood on the ground and soaking into her clothes. The bullet struck a few inches from Gerald's head and Alex stood with her hands in the air.

"Drop your piece and walk forward until I tell you otherwise."

Alex stumbled forward, waiting for the kill shot she knew was coming. It was then that she saw the open second story barn window with the rifle barrel jutting out of it. From that vantage point, she could see that she and Gerald had been sitting ducks as they had moved up the lane.

"Far enough Milnero. Sit down and put your hands on your head."

Alex sat Indian style and crossed her hands on her head. She listened intently as she heard steps, a few muffled curses, and then John Brooks Barrett walking out of the barn, nudging Ben along with the rifle. Ben stumbled along, his face a bloody mess as it appeared he had been struck near his scalp. His arms were cuffed behind his back and he was not moving very well at all.

"We know about everything JB, so don't make it worse. It doesn't have to go any further."

Brooks smiled through the greasepaint he had applied, "Huh, you sound like dad and he was planning to kill me. Going to prison for five or six life sentences is not an option, so I'm going to take my chances."

Ben stumbled and fell to the ground near Alex. She wanted to lower her hands and check his wounds, but knew it would be a fatal mistake for both of them. Ben lay face down in the dirt and Alex risked a brief glance noting he was still breathing.

"I had bigger plans for all this, but my timeframe got jumbled up when you figured everything out. I'm going to shoot you and then I'm going to shoot Princi. By the time this crime scene gets sorted out, I'll be in Mexico."

"What the hell is your problem with Ben?" Alex asked as she stole a glance at Ben, swearing that Ben gave her a brief bloody grin.

"You can discuss it with him in the afterworld. He and I have a history and you unfortunately have proven to be a pain in the ass,"

Brooks announced as he pulled the pistol from his waistband and aimed at Alex.

When Brooks pulled the pistol from his waistband, Ben rocked onto his left side and pistoned out his right leg as hard as he could. His size 14 shoe connected directly with Brook's left knee, causing his shot to veer wildly off base as his ligaments and patella were savagely torn. Brooks dropped to the ground trying desperately to grab his now useless left leg.

Alex had seen Ben rock and launched herself at Brooks when he dropped to the ground. She stomped on his wrist, making sure Brooks dropped the pistol and followed this up with a solid kick to Brooks' temple. Brooks was writhing on the ground when Alex heard the first sirens and she glanced over to see Ben smiling up at her, his teeth stained with blood.

"Sorry I waited until the last minute to be a hero, but I thought we'd only get one chance at this."

Alex maintained the pistol on Brooks, "Are you alright?"

"I probably need a few stitches. I don't know what he hit me with, but I think it's just a minor head wound."

"Okay, I need to cover him until there is some more backup."

Thirty minutes later the farm was swarming with law enforcement. Gerald had been airlifted to Dayton Memorial Hospital and was listed in critical condition with the gunshot wound to his hip. Alex had sat with Ben as the EMT had cleaned up his wound, closing it with a tube of superglue. The questions were coming in and Alex was at the center of all of it.

John Brooks Jr's father, John Barrett, sheriff of Fleming County, was found shot in the back in the entryway to the house. It appeared that JB had been waiting for his father and shot him in the back when he arrived. Ben filled in some of the blanks that the other investigators were finding.

Ben had been going to Chet's to pick up his car when he was pulled over for a broken taillight. Ben recognized JB and they were talking alongside the road when JB distracted him and when Ben turned his head he was knocked unconscious with a sap. He had woke up in a barn with his arms bound, but he could hear JB arguing with his father outside somewhere. They were talking about jeopardizing some business by him not following the plan. Ben wasn't about to disclose the information about his mother at this point.

"Detective, you're gonna need to come see this."

Alex walked away from Ben and headed back into the barn, where the crime scene unit had set up there temporary laboratory. There was a section of the wooden floor which had been pulled up to reveal steps heading into an underground room. Alex could tell the room was the heart of the business because it held the computers and what appeared to the bookkeeping aspect.

"Please tell me this is the evidence we've been looking for."

Sgt. Walker, who headed the CSU, brought Alex over to the desk and showed her the laptop they had been working on. "It's still preliminary, but this laptop seems to show a menu of girls for a human trafficking organization. It's going to take some time so we don't miss anything or accidentally trip any built in viruses, but it looks like you've solved your crime and uncovered a human trafficking operation that I think has been flourishing for at least twenty years."

Alex slumped into the nearest chair. She'd set out with this case hoping to find a sexual predator and it had led her into her own profession. Now it was becoming apparent that the law enforcement community was running this illegal operation.

"Was Sheriff Barrett part of this?"

"He had to be, and there are indications in some of the notations we've found in the files that there are other high ranking officials involved in the business. We're going to call in the FBI to have them sort through all of this, because I'm afraid of how deep this might go."

Alex smiled and rose to her feet, "Thank you Sergeant. I'll leave this all in your capable hands. I've got to go check on my partner."

Alex found Ben still seated near the ambulance with a bandage covering his superglued wound, "Are you cleared to leave? I've got to go check on Gerald."

Ben rose to his feet, "I'm fine, just waiting to find someone to catch a ride with. Let's go."

As they left the crime scene and avoided the growing news presence, Alex began to relax.

"So what was JB's issue with you?"

Ben shrugged, "We knew each other in high school because of playing basketball for rival schools."

"I can't see him harboring the hate he seemed to have for you coming from a basketball tiff."

"Well it might have had to do with Courtney breaking up with him and then starting to see me."

Alex gave a quick glance, "That's a long time to hold onto a grudge, even if it was for a girl."

"I agree, but clearly we weren't dealing with the most stable of individuals."

They finally left the hospital after midnight. The nurses were bending the rules as much as possible due to the number of law enforcement who kept filing in to check on the status of Gerald. Alex stayed in the lobby and answered questions most of the night, periodically checking in with Janice to see how he was doing. The doctors were not providing much in the way of a prognosis, other than to say his condition had stabilized.

Ben watched Alex as she handled the various people asking about the investigation, and marveled at how adept she seemed to be with tailoring her responses based on the person. The FBI was building a strong case against the Barretts and was looking to spread the investigation with some more well placed warrants. A nearby marsh was being dredged after JB mentioned a body dump. At this point, the remains of six bodies had been removed with the fear that it was only the tip of the iceberg. Alex was not interested in joining the next phase of this case, because she just wanted to make sure Gerald was going to recover.

Reporters were constantly trying to speak with Alex, but they were kept at bay by the other professionals. Samantha spotted Ben and walked over to sit with him.

"I've got no comment."

Samantha smiled, "Yeah I know, everybody is sticking with the company line. I just thought I'd check and see if you are really okay. I've seen you look better."

Ben looked to make sure she didn't have her pad or phone anywhere nearby, "I'm fine, just some superficial injuries."

"This is all off the record. Actually there is no record until tomorrow when the FBI will be holding a press conference. I thought I might be able to speak with Alex, but they are guarding her like a state's witness."

Ben could see the tone of the question and that she was waiting to see if he would confirm or deny that statement, "Samantha, just wait until tomorrow, it will be worth it."

"Can't blame a girl for trying," she announced as she rose, "I would like to talk to you sometime."

Ben gave her a quick look.

"I swear, it is not news related. I'll call you in a few days when things settle down because I hope to be extremely busy."

Ben watched her walk back over to the gaggle of reporters and saw Zoe slip in the side door from the nurse's station.

"How did you get in through that way?"

Zoe smiled, "I talked to the head nurse downstairs and told her about not being able to check on my boyfriend who was upstairs. She wanted to know if you were the good looking hunk with the facial injuries and I told her it was so."

"You are shameless."

"No it took some doing, I even had to force a few tears to show my distress. Now let me look at you and see for myself how you are really doing."

Zoe grabbed Ben's chin and turned his head to the left and right to get a full vantage of his injuries, "I really don't know why everyone is making such a fuss over you. It looks like you had a mild bike crash."

Ben chuckled, "Thanks for the concern and I could have told you it was no big deal."

"I know I could have called, but sometimes you minimize things when it pertains to you, so I wanted to see for myself. I'm sure most of the problem is the nurses just want to provide some one on one care for the resident stud."

Alex walked over and gave Zoe a hug when she stood, "Thanks for coming. Did you bring me some clothes to change into?"

Ben snickered, "Came to check on me, huh?"

"It's not all about you Ben, Alex needed some assistance and I am the person for this job. I left the garment bag with the nurse and she said you could change in their restroom. I'll run interference with all the nurses so they don't try to throw themselves at poor Ben."

Alex smiled and gave Ben a kiss on the cheek, "I need to freshen up so I can make a statement to the vultures outside."

****

Two hours later, Alex returned from the extended question and answer period she had been forced into with the FBI's lead investigator, Miles Harlow, who continually praised Alex's role in uncovering this conspiracy. There were a number of rumors which were squashed, including that the governor of Ohio was being implicated in the cover-up of the sex trafficking ring which ran through his state. Alex also confirmed that her partner, Gerald Vilnew was still in critical condition, but it looked like he was going to make it.

Ben watched most of the news conference in the waiting room with Zoe, before slipping outside to watch from the side. Alex was exhausted from the adrenaline rush and inevitable crash, but she handled herself with professionalism as she deftly answered questions without giving too much information about the ongoing investigation and where it could potentially reach.

Alex smiled as she walked away from the glare of the television cameras, "Hey there handsome, what do you think about going back to my place and get some sleep?"

"Is that code for anything?"

"I appreciate your enthusiasm, but I need a long soak in my tub and then about twelve hours of sleep before I can even think about any of your carnal desires."

Ben chuckled as he walked Alex out the rear of the hospital to his Superbird, which Chet had delivered earlier in the day.

"So it looks like you got your latest lady all cleaned up."

Ben smiled as he closed her door and admired the gleaming black paint job, "Oh yeah she's all ready to make her debut. Now let's get the hell out of here and get some rest."

32

Three hours later, Ben was scrambling around to find his phone.

"Are you sure about the results? Okay, well can I call you tomorrow sometime so we can meet to discuss things?"

By this time Alex was sitting up, holding the sheet around her covering her chest. She'd noted that Ben's tone had changed from the beginning of the conversation to his now detached manner.

Alex knew it was bad when Ben ended the phone call and sat on the bed.

"Just tell me Ben, I already know it's bad. Did something happen to Gerald?"

Ben took a deep breath, knowing this was about to drastically alter their relationship, "No it wasn't about Gerald. That was Samantha and she was calling to tell me that she's pregnant."

ACKNOWLEDGEMENTS

Writing is not done in a vacuum and anyone who puts pen to paper - or in this case finger to keyboard understands this

Mackenzie – thanks for the nudge
Lessie – proofer extraordinaire and sounding board for ideas
Zach, Alexis, and Sydney – three fantastic kids
Joan – Where to start. You're love and support means more than you can know. And you were right (as usual) I can write when I'm content

Whirlwind is the second novel for S Whitten Snider, who is a social worker in Columbus, Ohio. In his spare time not writing or working, time is spent rving with Joan and their golden retriever, Reggie

About the Author

Whirlwind is the second novel for S Whitten Snider, who is a social worker in Columbus, Ohio. In his spare time not writing or working, time is spent with Joan and their golden retriever, Reggie.

Printed in the United States
By Bookmasters